"I know I am deathless. No doubt I have died my-self ten thousand times before. I laugh at what you call dissolution, and I know the amplitude of time." — Walt Whitman

To all the ones who remember:
Love is the only compass of truth.   -
Toni Barca

Toni Barca

RECALL
Anima & Animus Series
Book 1

A WORD FROM THE AUTHOR

As I write this, Gaza is under siege. The West
Bank has fallen beneath greedy hands. Congo
and other countries are right now under
the onslaught of greed whilst ignoring the
debauchery of raping and killing of women
and children. There was a time when Y2K had
people panicking stocking guns, water, and
food for the apocalypse. Nothing much has
changed, as 2012 brought us another promise
of the world ending, yet presidents came and
went as we continued to progress as a people...
as multi-dimensional light beings.

In over 3,600 years we have not changed
much aside from the small rectangular
communication tool you take for granted,
called the cell phone which now has made
every human a potential boots-on-the-ground
journalist. Maybe this is what will change us as
humans, transform us to abhor war, genocide
above all! To see every angle of these atrocities
with our own eyes recorded by people like
you and me. Maybe it is the darkest before the
dawn. I believe in the basic goodness of people.

Power, human sacrifice to gain wealth are
still used by the powers that be... there are
no words to explain greed and excuse it

with violence. As humans we have seen the impossible atrocities of slavery, the genocide and subjugation of American Indians, the rise of the Third Reich and the Holocaust, the Japanese internment camps right here on American soil, the genocide in Rwanda. The brutal truth of racism hidden beneath the agenda of a toxic patriarchal father-knows-best attitude again shakes our world. The attacks that Israel has fended off and the revenge that takes over sense, over mindfulness and empathy to the triggers that bring about repercussion has the world currently holding its breath.

I am very aware of the human hearts' great capacity for love and empathy, but I am also very aware of how easy many humans choose to shut down and cement their hearts closed. Fear of being hurt is never an acceptable excuse to shut ourselves down from our humanity, and our capacity to love is the most precious gift we offer ourselves. I have witnessed magic within our human race: forgiveness of impossible acts so brutal that many of us could not forgive. Yet some souls rose above the chaotic voice of the false ego to offer forgiveness in order to seek refuge within the arms of peace. And so it is with our past lives, we will repeat mistakes and egoic-based illusions from one past life to another. Radical self-acceptance and recapitulation, self-forgiveness and repair is the only way out of the perpetual conveyor belt of repeating toxic loops. Our current bloodlines were chosen for a reason for they most likely reverberate unhealed past lives. Our past bloodlines quite often hold the key to what was left undone so when your soul downloads a particulate memory trust that within these images are answers to help you in your current life. Our angst of being awake and aware of the vibrational injustice can cause such impotent rage and grief that often the choice is to escape one's current incarnation. More is being asked of us. For we still don't understand the amount of power we hold with our will to create better.

Throughout this life, I have been fascinated by reincarnation. I first recall choosing my parents when I was three years old. By the time I was eight years old, I had a very focused view of the beyond and I trusted in the unseen. Light beings visited me, though I would not call them light beings until decades passed and my understanding of guides began to expend. At thirteen years old, I was a lone wolf and never quite fit in with others my age. I would take nude moon bath somehow understanding the frequency of the full moon upon my skin could somehow feed me with a different energy, in the way I sought sunbathing. I suffered from insomnia and would often stay up till 3 – 5am in the morning, tucked snuggly beneath my blankets. My little radio pressed against my ear lest I wake anyone in the household voraciously listening to a random AM radio station interview retired pilots and other whistle blowers about area 51 and UFOS.

Many truths can barely be accepted by the 3D brain AKA the monkey mind. 3D logic cannot be trusted as absolute truth since 3D logic is often based on the current norms of a society that has limited view of what is true and what is possible. Intuitively understanding that more had to be understood about the nature of reality and the limitation of these 3D brains, I was driven to read to seek knowledge that was not part of my public & private school education.

I began reading books on Atlantis, Lemuria, the Akashic Library, ancient history, third eye opening, Dolphin Babies, Tibet, the CIA and the KGB using remote viewing to spy on each other. Starseeds incarnations on other planets, the purpose of reincarnation and I explored how past life traumas impacted our current incarnations which we often dragged back from one life to the next. My fascination for the unseen, the veils that parted us from infinite knowledge became my passion! Within a few months of meeting my Twin, at the tender age of 18 years old, I began to teach myself divination via the use of tarot cards.

We are finally learning how the 19th Century Egyptologist, anthropologist, and historians contrived, subjugated, hid, denied, and destroyed ancient truths that brought a darkness to an age that should have been more enlightened. But here we are. The Divine Feminine is rising from the ashes as is the Divine Masculine. We are learning about Mary Magdalena and Jeshua. Every year more light is being exposed to those who wish to see.

There is nothing romantic or wonderful about the past life I am sharing with you, but it explains to me why I have shunned power within myself and why power in others frightened me for multiple incarnations. I had seen power used with greed and violence. Not much has changed since I lived as this Queen Bakor. I know my purpose now. Thus, I will never again look over my shoulder wondering why I exist. I know this path, for I have chosen it. What matters now isn't what I was, but what I have become because of these incarnations. Bakor has taught me how a woman can love two men and get so confused by it that she loses her grip on reality. Bakor taught me that she could only navigate what she was equipped to understand, and Kat taught me the power of forgiving the unforgivable.

There are no right answers, and nothing overrides your own past life experiences. Thus what you are about to read is just one humble scroll upon the wide expense of the Akashic records which may or may not resonate for you.

Recall was originally birthed in 2012, published by a small publishing house that soon de-funked due to the overwhelming task of competing with the big publishing houses. Now, I am re-releasing this book as a creative non-fiction. Why? Because I will take my own advice and stop dimming my light to make others comfortable. In fact, I have taken a sledgehammer to that dimmer switch and it is no longer operational for it only offers one setting... BRIGHT as FUCK!

This is a story that burned bright during a barbaric time. Many of the experiences you will read were downloaded over a period of months.

When I finished writing the book, I decided
that no one would believe these experiences.
After all, I had seen how Carlos Castaneda's
books and Lynn Andrews books on shamanic
experiences had been debunked as fiction
and so I decided to publish Recall as a work
of fiction. This book demanded to be birthed.
Howled to be birthed
!
I have been many both masculine and
feminine. I have loved my own gender and
opposite genders. Our souls are in truth,
androgynous, but some of us prefer one
costume over another. I have embodied
many egoic illusions under the banner of
bloodlines. I have loved and I have hated
with equal measure. I have walked in light. I
have walked in darkness. I have experienced
all religions… both recalled and those long
forgotten. I have been a loving husband and a
barbarian rapist. I have been a loving wife and
I have been a high priestess who used power
to destroy the innocent. I have been good
and kind. I have loved and I have lost. I have
been homesick: the kind of homesickness that
sometimes grabs the heart and squeezes the
very breath out of me. This feeling has never
left my soul.

We all want to go back home. We'll accomplish
the goal of going back home; none of us are
exempt from that success. What matters is
simple: what you do while you are here. What
will you learn, release, forgive, heal, and teach?
So understand this one truth when you heal,
I heal, and when I heal, you heal. That alone
is enough to understand how we are all so
connected.

I hope that within the pages of this book,
something begins to stir in your own soul to
bring forth a past life you need to make peace
with.

Sending you much love on your journey.
Namaste, Toni Barca
November 3, 2023
Northern California

This book is dedicated to:

Barron. My muse. My heart. My beautiful sun. Thank you for being such a light in the world.

To my beloved Twinflame, A.G. You are my beautiful Starseed nomad. Thank you for all the journeys we have experienced together. YOU are my heart beat and my breath. You are the taste of water. I am as I am; you showed me that this was enough to be worthy of love. Je t'aime.

To my Soulmate, N.A.B. Thank you for our son, our love that created him and your belief in me throughout my many dark night of the soul. You showed me humility, patience, and peace. I will always love you.

And to my Maman, Jacqueline. There aren't words to express my gratitude. In the end, we found the space to healing generational trauma. The journeys continues.

To George VoorGalos whose generousity, love and passion helped birth this book. I could never have done it without you. You are my jeweled angel.

Prologue
The Fertile Crescent 3,500 B.C.E

Thirty sunrises had brought forth the image of a god, tall as the cedars that grow in the forest of Besh'Hadem. This warrior's face was shielded from view. He wore a Ram's headdress, and clenched between his hands was a sword which he raised towards the heavens, his head thrown back releasing a howl that rose like smoke from the bowels of his being. There was always blood, blood upon his chest and hands, dripping upon his bare thighs onto the floor.

I always awoke with the sound of his cries echoing within the walls of my mind, and would abruptly sit up shivering and sweat drenched, the bottoms of my feet trembled as if I had been running. I would lie awake for hours before Malek rose.

It was that very vision that brought me before the Oracle. She lived in one of the many caves that overlooked our green valley.

I sat upon my heels and felt ill in my being, and my belly trembled like a hundred butterflies were trapped within. I had not spoken of the dream to Malek, nor had I told him that I sought her this day. For I felt that to speak the words to him would unleash the dream from within me into the bright sunlight of our world.

So when she uttered the following words, "You are not from this world." I was baffled.

"Who is?" I had answered softly. For who could tell from whence our souls came? Had we been created by the great mothers, Isis and Ishtar, or had we come from the stars, as my brother had often told me? She ignored my answer and allowed the silence to hang between us, like a winged spirit that hovered above us for what seemed like an eternity of breaths.

Two torches hung on either side of the cave; their flames moved and swayed as a cool wind blew in from the opening. It cast brittle shadows upon her ancient face, her hallow cheekbones jagged beneath the circles of her obsidian eyes, as if devoid of a soul. Her hair was alive, eternally youthful, swimming about her hips, undulating rich and fertile as the land she came from, it shone blue black without a streak of white. So it was her face, ah, yes, her weathered face, which had taken the toll of our tale as a people. Wrinkle by wrinkle had sunk their story until she was no more than a skeletal visage overlaid by white skin, mapped by very fine, little blue veins. She had been my mother's oracle, and her mother before her; no one knew how old she was. Though her ugliness made me shiver with revulsion, I needed to know what my dreams meant.

We were a kingdom abundantly blessed by our beloved Goddess Ishtar, mother to all of us. We were the people of the Fertile Crescent, and that meant that we were a prosperous people.

I nodded for her to continue.

Her voice was low, yet un-ravaged by time, and as clear as my own.

"One day your great hanging gardens will be remembered beyond this time. Men of a faraway future will fly in strange chariots, and yet they will speak of your gardens with great admiration...but your name will be lost." She paused, never once looking at me.

I stared at her, my eyes wide with question.

"Explain yourself, woman!"

"They will remember your gardens, but my dear and noble queen, you will be forgotten; you will be as inconsequential as the dust beneath your feet."

I was not here for trite prognostication. I had sought her in order to get this man out of my dreams! I wanted the howling madness of his cry out of my head. What did I care if my gardens were remembered? I wanted to ensure my kingdom's safety.

She rose abruptly and disappeared to the innermost womb of the cave, returning with a small goatskin bag. She poured the contents upon the small carpet that lay between us, and the bones of a fetus that had been sacrificed for such prophesies spilled out.

The carpet was a small weave that barely covered my knees and shins if I were to prostate myself upon it to beg Ishtar my most recent desire. It was blood red and the threads of an indigo sky crossed to interweave with the original color of the animal's tan hue. The whole of it was a barbaric design of skulls and patterns of bygone symbols that I did not understand.

I sat back upon my heels, lifting the linen tunic up to my thighs so as not to tear it, my bare knees pressed upon the hard ground. The hood of my dark red cloak fell away to reveal my face; my dark hair was rich with the red highlights from the henna I used upon it, and swirled about my pale shoulders and small breasts. My nipples hardened from the cold and by fear.

I looked down upon myself, but I could not find pleasure in my beauty nor at my newly acquired possessions, one a tunic of the finest linen imaginable, as thin as a spider's silk; it was a pale lilac with a hundred pleats. It had traveled from Egypt with many other riches such as the gold girdle set with smooth round stones of purple fires that sat low upon my hips rounded by the births of my children.

"...And one day you will recall us," she continued, "a thousand lifetimes from now. You will return to us. Tearing back the veils of time, it will be your Malek, your king who will guide you back."

My face tightened, my neck hurt. I leaned forward, my eyes intent on disrobing the truth.

"Tell of the vision? What is our future?" I implored.

She did not look at me but picked up the bones once again and shook them between white hands, bony, blue veined, and paper thin with wrinkles. She threw them upon the carpet and leaned deeply into them, as if sniffing them with her nose.

"Speak truth, you will not be harmed," I said impatiently, my heart pounding so hard that it pained me to breathe.

"A conqueror is coming." She paused. My hands knotted into themselves, and then I held them still, fingers squeezing each other until I felt the pain of my grip.

"My queen," she whispered, "I cannot say more... I dare not!"

"Truth!" I was relentless. She tore her gaze away from the bones, and locked eyes with mine.

"You will perish!"

I felt my breath escape like a goatskin wine bag pierced by a sword, and now sighing out the message of death. A tear fell from my eye to stream down my left cheek.

"What can we do?" I was now supplicant in my tone.

She stared at the fallen bones and then shook her head.

"This is the fate of this dynasty; nothing can be done. Your bodies will die in this life, but your souls are immortal, and you will go on. Do not fear my queen; this is but a passage from one reality to the next." She leaned towards me and was about to touch my hand in comfort when she realized she was forbidden to touch royalty. To do so meant death. I leaned towards her, and held her hand in mine, twining my fingers with hers as I had done with my own mother, and for that brief moment I felt comforted.

"My children?" I asked. Her eyes filled with tears or so I thought, or perhaps the light of the torches lit her eyes with a glimmer I had not seen before. Finally, she answered, "I cannot say."

I could not push her; I was afraid to.

I tossed a purse filled with coins upon the ground. It lay between us. I threw my hood over my hair. I stood up and stared down at the bones for a long time, and then walked away. Nothing more needed to be said.

At the mouth of the cave stood my slave, a tall Nubian. He had been waiting and was holding in his large hand the elaborate decorated leather bridle that looped simply over my gray mare's nose and jaw. He was holding a torch, which blinded me for but a moment until my eyes adjusted to the sinking light of the sun. I rubbed my mare's soft, downy mouth, adoring the warmth and scent of her. She licked the palm of my hand in greeting. I lifted my tunic and nodded to my slave to hoist me upon her back. Wrapping my thighs across her middle, I dug my knees into her, and she moved forward. The winds had risen since my arrival. I imagined they were howling of a conqueror coming, of a doom waiting to descend. I shivered.

"My queen?" he whispered. I shielded my face from his prying eyes. I kicked the sides of my mare and we trotted down into my beloved valley, towards the city and gardens I so loved. The sky's dark pink and purple streaks had vanished replaced by an indigo stillness lit by bright stars, and a full moon had risen to claim her royal right to rule the night. Below, my beloved city was aglow with torches and lanterns; in fact, the whole city glowed. This cannot be, I thought; this glimmering jewel cannot be doomed. Yet deep in my heart, I knew the truth of it. Then quite suddenly, it occurred to me that I had not asked her from which world I came. What had she meant?

I shrugged, shaking the feeling of fear out of my being and replacing it with hope. I forced a small smile which lightened my heart. I would see her again soon enough, and then I could ask her. For now, I was alive. The whole city was alive, and peace was a blanket the setting sun had deposited upon our land.

1

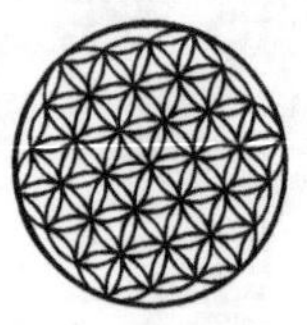

Pasadena
September 8, 1997

I read somewhere that Lilith was Adam's first wife. God created them instantaneously which made them equal in every respect. They were said to be created in God's image. Lilith was a spirited and sensual creature. She wanted to fuck Adam and ride him to the Promised Land, so to speak. Adam refused, shocked by her wantonness, revolted by her desire to straddle his erection and take his power. How dare she!

He was furious. I can imagine her derisive laugh. He wanted her submissive and grateful. He wanted her on her hands and knees with her ass in the air waiting to be rammed. A battle of wills erupted. Adam lost.

Lilith stormed out of the Garden of Eden to seek other amusements. She stumbled upon an orgy and partied her ass off! Meanwhile, Adam was in a rage. He whined to God that Lilith was disobedient. He pleaded for a new companion. So God made Eve from Adam's rib.

Eve understood her place.

Well-fed from her Bacchanalian escapades, Lilith returned. She found that she'd been replaced, and all hell broke loose!

There are countless versions of Lilith's tale. What I know for a fact is that she appears again and again in many different texts. We see her in the Kabbalah, the epic of Gilgamesh; The Sumerians speak of her; she appears in the Dead Sea Scrolls, in classic Greek tales. Some argue that she appears in the Bible; some say she is the serpent who tempts Eve with the forbidden fruit. Eventually, she would morph into the great mother, Ishtar, the beloved Mesopotamian goddess of fertility.

But before judging the tales as false, think about it. Women have always been marginalized. My mother once told me that the Catholic Church didn't recognize women as having souls until the 17th Century. Try wrapping your head around that one. Later, I read somewhere that the soulless women concept originated from the infamous Council of Nicea in 325 A.C.E., when bishops from all over got together to put the scrolls together that make up the Bible.

As they were talking about cutting this gospel and adding that one, the subject of women came up. Put a bunch of men in a room and women always come up in conversation. This time the hot debate was whether we had souls or not. Now, it got pretty volatile, and so they decided to vote on it.

So when the bishops counted the vote that was pro-female having souls, that camp won by just one vote. One fucking vote. Just one! Imagine our lives had it gone the other way. Yeah, it could have been even worse. Makes you wonder, doesn't it? Supposedly the Catholic Church says that it's an unfounded rumor, but weren't they the same group that took out the bit about any references to reincarnation? Yeah, the same bad-ass bishops!

Some say that never happened at the Council of Nicea, but instead claim that the aforementioned happened in France in Mâcon, Burgundy in 585 A.C. E. with another set of bishops who launched a very similar discussion and voted. The way the rumor spread was that a scholar by the name of Valentius Acidaliu, short on cash, took the rumor from the Mâcon meeting and wrote a little pamphlet meant to illicit titters among the well-heeled and raise some quick cash by selling the idea that women could not have a soul based on some linguistic translation of "Homo" which did not include female in its context and that, my friends, confirmed that we didn't have souls. The good news is, it backfired and there were many who refuted this with a ferocity that basically destroyed Valentius.

Sadly, a handful of pamphlets survived and were reproduced in France. In the end, does it really matter if this was a rumor started damn near 1700 years ago? I mean, as it stands, there is no doubt that the patriarchal society of its day thought of females as subhuman Grade B souls, if souls at all. But then the Catholic Church states that all creatures have some kind of soul. Is that how they saw us back then, as creatures?

Look, this kind of shit doesn't faze me anymore. There's been too much of it. It wasn't until 1972 that a woman in the U.S. got her first credit card. Ergo, we have been a sex that has been shit on from the day Lilith told God to fuck off! Anger issues? A rabid feminist, me? Believing in reincarnation as I do, I know that I have been men many times before, and the irony is this; I may have been one of the bishops at one of those infamous councils that voted against women. Life is that funny!

But where was I? Ah, yes. I have another memory that comes up quite often lately. I'm not sure why? Maybe I feel guilty.

I'm 18, and it's 1982. I'm dancing wildly with this blond boy about my age. We're at the Waterloo Club in Nassau, in the Bahamas. The video screens are streaming images from MTV; right now it's streaming David Bowie. He's singing Wild is the Wind, and I'm grinding my hips against the rigid length of the boy's erection straining against his jeans. We're both soaked with sweat having danced for hours. It's a slow dance of hunger. I'm not sure what I want. Attention? Love? No! Not here. Love doesn't exist here. It comes down to plain science; we are simply two forces that are magnetically pulled towards each other by nothing more than... his lust and my desire for power. That's what's makes me wet. I know he's caught my scent. Pussy and perfume. I see his nostrils flare wide to inhale me. I see his eyes blaze and then his lids lower to savor that moment. Perhaps he can taste me. He doesn't want to let go.

My nipples are hard points that occasionally graze his chest. He moans. I push my hips against his and place my hands behind the back of his neck. His damp hair falls over my fingers and his eyes are languorous and bright with light. I catch his mouth, capturing his tongue. This dance is slow. Dangerous in what it promises him. Promises I'll never keep. What I want is his desire. I want nothing else from him. I don't even know his name. I'll never know his name or he mine. There's a sort of symmetry to that truth. I feel safe buried in that truth and perhaps that's why I am so free with him. Why I am so shameless.

I let him go. I push away from his body. He

moves towards me grabbing my waist pulling me back against his length and pushing his hips against mine. Gridding his cock against my moist sex, I respond with an ease that sends a chill across my skin. He grabs a breast and lowers his mouth to capture a hard nipple through the bra and T-shirt and I let him suckle me. Shadowed by ambient strobe lights and dark corners, I know some of the dancers are watching us, and still I let him devour me. He's starving. I push myself further into his mouth and he bites me. That act sends a lightning bolt between my thighs. I move away from him as my hips undulate against the side of his hips, and I graze one index finger across the head of his cock outlined so beautifully against his jeans. If I'm not careful, I know he'll come. So I'm careful.

My pussy moans, hungry to be filled. What feeds me is the way his face falls apart like he's taken a hit from a bong and every muscle in his face is just melting into euphoria. We slow dance cocooned within that song, as if we were the only two people left in the world. As if time is holding its breath. We writhe against each other with a freedom I'll never replicate with another, but right now I don't know that because I'm in the moment and that means that we belong together.

I cannot pin down when it all began,

but somewhere along the road to my sexual awakening I'd captured the nuances and the very intricate games of sexual dominion over another. It was my weapon of mass destruction which I abused unmercifully. I was Marquis de Sade's devout student, in that I used sadomasochism in a purely psychological manner. I was the whore of Babylon, Lilith incarnate, or so I imagined. Frankly, what I was doing with the boy at that moment would have had me stoned, drowned, hanged, or burned a hundred years ago. Women then were not allowed to be wanton. Yet here I was. I lived in a part of the world that allowed my brash desire to unleash the long tendrils of sexual power over another. I was free, while women in other countries would have most definitely suffered the aforementioned fates and more: veiled, beaten, circumcised, raped, and killed at the will of men. Yet, I lived, and I was free!

Even now, as I write this, I see the images of Nicolas Poussin's The Rape of the Sabine Women, and Giovanni da Bologna's sculpture of one of the Sabine woman's screams immortalized in marble as she is carried off. I see the ancient chastity belts, the eight million women burned at the stake, the message clear as day that to be a woman is to be wicked. Even the Bhagavad-Gita speaks of women being less than men. The copy I last read even said that we were less than cattle. Perhaps they've edited that since the '80s, I'm not sure. It's one of the reasons I never joined Krishna.

Perhaps, on some deep level, I've always carried the images within the subconscious catacombs of my soul's memory of every life I had ever lived. I can graze my fingertips upon the stacked skulls and bones of those past lives, and I am shaken by the veiled images of those lives, my lives.

I cannot say when I realized that I carried an anger that was as strong as my sadness. I just know that I was shackled to them both for what seemed an eternity. I am haunted by past lives that I cannot recall. But I know as sure as taking my next breath that the answers I've sought all of my life lie in the events of those past lives.

For now, I am dancing. Hips undulating and my untamed red hair hangs wet from sweat and curls around my neck and shoulders. My white T-shirt clings to my body as do my white jeans, leaving little to the imagination. There's something about this song, the way David Bowie sings it. At that moment, I wished I believed in love. Wished it was real. So I control the one thing I can, the boy's cock, and I stroke it as if petting it to submission. It's his response that turns me on. I feel his cock pulse against my touch, and I imagine my lips wrapped around it. We grab each other, press hard against each other. Lips and tongue caught in a dance that is so primordial that I feel whole, innocent, and wicked all at once. Caught in a fire that envelopes me and this boy within a circle of... I can't describe it, but strangely, it's just plain fucking beautiful!

I disengage from his body, and I dance with an abandon that make many stop and stare. I have him, the boy, in the palm of my hand. And then inexplicably, I step away.

I remember how I just walked, leaving him standing on that dance floor without a word.

I wonder about that moment. What if I'd stayed?

But at that instant, and perhaps because it was getting to be more than I needed it to be, I decided it was time to go.

"Can I get your number?" he pleaded.

I shook my head and joined my friends at the entrance of the club. He was right beside me and grabbed my upper arm and swung me around. His face inches from mine, the lust in his eyes slowly succumbing to confusion.

"I love you!" His voice tinged with despair, his blue eyes bright with pain.

I laughed in his face, his declaration insulting to my very core. My back faced him, ignoring him as if he was nothing more than the arched doorway that framed him. I heard his labored breathing. For the briefest of seconds I felt pity for him. I remembered the feel of his mouth. The way he held me. I shuddered. But again, hate rose to destroy all that was soft inside of me.

Did he think I would fuck him just because?

We, meaning my three friends and me, began our walk back to the hotel. It was two a.m. and the unlit streets were dark, so we walked by the light of the moon and stars, jostling each other, trying to make each other trip, laughing loudly.

My friend leaned into my ear, "He's right behind us."

I stopped abruptly, swung on my heels and faced him, "What do you want?"

"I want to see you again. I've never felt this way before."

"Get the fuck out of here!" I snarled. I walked purposely towards him and stood my ground, matching his imploring gaze with my contempt. I hated him for begging. I didn't wonder at his declaration of love. Did he think that this thing we'd done was an act of love? I hated him for it! I wanted him to disappear from my sight. I was disgusted at myself. I'd allowed myself to forget everything. Had thrown all constraints out the window, and I had allowed him to make out with me for hours, and now, I could not bear the sight of him.

His eyes filled with tears of shame and somehow I felt healed by his grief. As if I had accomplished something of note. "Get the fuck out of my life! I never want to see you again!"

He fell away and disappeared behind the shadows of dark, unlit, dirt roads. I now wonder what happened to him. Did I wound him to the core of his heart, or has he forgotten me? Did I make him hate women? Or was I just the bitch that teased him?

Before long, we'd made it to our hotel. I was grateful to fall head first into the stupor that was alcohol spiked with good Bahamian grass. I passed out.

I'm not sure why I'm telling you this. What's the point to this story? That I was a bad ass? That I was angry? Yes, that's part of it. I guess I have a better understanding of my sexual acting out. I'd carried this strange weight for so long. I'd forgotten what peace was.

Inner peace was my holy grail, and I sought it like a heroin addict, and yet it remained elusive for the better part of my young life.

It's funny how memories crowd you all at once. How the mind brings forth memories that bang against your heart. Today is the day my father was killed. He was driving from Paris to Switzerland. They say that he may have fallen asleep at the wheel. I imagine his little silver 1960 Alpha Romeo weaving on the road and launching off a cliff. I never got to say goodbye to him. I speak to him every day; I miss him so much that it still hurts. Sometimes I wish . . . forget it, it's too weird.

My younger brother was away at college when he died. My mother was all I had for an adult influence, and we didn't get along. She hated me for my wildness, and I hated her for her hypocrisy. It seemed that I hated everyone back then. There was no way I could live with her. So I left New York City and decided that San Francisco would be cheaper. I didn't have any secretarial skills; I couldn't type; I couldn't dress the part; I just didn't have the money to buy business clothes; I couldn't play the game. What that meant is that I was unemployable in that very formidable world that was the financial district. It never occurred to me to get a job as a waitress or at a department store. Rent had to be paid, so I quickly got a job as a topless dancer at the O'Farrell Theater and continued to torture men with my body.

Then one day, out of the fucking blue, I met Daniel. I was sitting at a backgammon table sipping on rum and Coke at a bar on Polk

Street called The Rose & Thistle, one of the few straight bars in San Francisco. Suddenly, I saw this tall, broad-shouldered dude playing pool with some other guys. I couldn't see his face. I caught myself trying to catch a glimpse, which annoyed me to no end. There was something familiar in the way he carried himself. He wore a gray T-shirt tucked into 501 jeans and beat-up chocolate cowboy boots, and somehow I found his nonchalance riveting. The way he pulled back his long, light brown hair into a ponytail, the way the gray material pulled tight across his back, the way he walked around the pool table and bent down to find the perfect vantage point to make his move. The way his large muscular arms bunched and lengthened as he centered himself upon the edge of the table finding that right angle to gently pull back so very gently making that impossible shot with one stroke. Even from where I sat, I heard it. The connecting click of contact, the ball rolling into the side pocket. The groans of his companions interjected with rough laughter. He was on a roll, and he stood up, facing me, staring directly at me. His lips broke into a wide grin upon the kind of chiseled face that makes women wet their panties. Fuck him! I didn't take my eyes off him; I couldn't. It felt as if the room was suddenly emptied by the vortex of his impenetrable eyes and I was falling.

His large square jaw was supported by a strong neck that sat upon the broadest shoulders and chest I'd ever seen. His stomach was flat, heavily muscled, and swept into a surprisingly small waist; his 501 jeans hung low upon his lean hips. His thighs were muscular and his legs long. There was no mistaking he was well hung, as his jeans enhanced that fact.

Shit! I looked up and realized he'd watched me the whole time I'd been checking him out. He raised one dark eyebrow and nodded his head. His large eyes were bordered by dark and very thick lashes, but I could not see their color. He handed the pool stick to one of his buddies and grabbed his beer off the side of the pool table. He was coming my way.

I threw him an icy stare meant to warn him off. He kept striding in that slow relaxed swagger that rolled like waves crashing within my belly. I abruptly stood up and grabbed some quarters and moved away from my table leaving my drink behind and made for the jukebox. I was trying to concentrate on choosing a song but found it hard when I saw him sit opposite my chair. Waiting.

I choose a song by Sade, "Smooth Operator". I figured why not scare him back to his little friends.

I turned around and caught him. The S.O.B had been staring at my ass.

He shrugged and threw me a wink. I stood there for a minute trying to decide what I should do. I could leave right now. Instead, I returned to my seat, sat across from him, and took a sip of my drink.

"You don't waste time do you?" I challenged him.

He leaned back a slow smile broke open like the sun that appears after a rainstorm. I stared into his eyes and saw that they were green, light green like new grass. Fuck!

"You play?" He nodded towards the backgammon board.

"Sure." I muttered.

"You know you remind of Sade with a dash of Ava Gardner," he said admiringly. "Do you honestly think I'm going to listen to this kind of ..." I'd risen and was about to leave when he grabbed my wrist, pulling me back down.

" Shhhh..." He whispered soothingly. "Not your hair. Your face, you have that sexy, exotic thing going on."

I shot him a scathing look and pointedly glanced at my wrist.

He let go, and I sat back down. We stared at each other for a full minute.

"My mother says that Ava Gardner is vulgar."

I was sullen but captivated by him.

"Your mother, eh?" He breathed. He threw me a wide grin. Fuck me! I wanted him.

I pulled on a curl that hung down my back. I twirled it around my finger and realized that I was wearing my peacock earrings. Suddenly, I looked down at myself in self-disgust. I was dressed in a very short black leather skirt, black leather Maud Frizon pumps, and a tight black Henley T-shirt which was missing two buttons. Right now, I was hyper aware of how low it dipped and hyper aware that I hadn't bothered wearing a bra. I wish I had dressed up.

"Sade, eh?" I managed to utter.

"Yeah," he breathed, his voice low and gravely. His eyes heavy lidded as if he'd just come. "But better, red hair, red lips." His eyes flared bright with a fire that warmed me from the inside out. I wasn't sure I liked his power over me. I wasn't sure what I should think, or say, or do. He broke eye contact and began placing the pieces on the board. My pride actually wanted to walk out of that bar and never look back. But a strange hand held me still. I was glued to my chair.

He waved over the little waitress sporting a purple Mohawk and torn fishnets over a pink tutu.

He flicked his wrist over his bottle of beer

and my drink.

"Two more," he ordered.

I was mesmerized by him as he apparently was by me. He was all that was rough and male. All that was beautiful and sexy in a man. He had that look about him, a pirate, transported from the 18th Century into the 20th Century. I wanted to toss the table aside, kneel before him, and unbutton those jeans and watch his cock release itself into my mouth. That image was so powerful that I shifted in my chair, my pussy wet. I licked my lips. The fantasy of what he would be like filled my mouth with possibilities. I caught him staring at my mouth, but it was the little waitress bringing our drinks that broke the spell. I saw him reluctantly drag his eyes away.

He handed her a twenty. She giggled unable to contain her own inner turmoil. It was then I realized that I was not the only female he affected in this way. I was caught off guard by the jealousy that rose within me, for it was a foreign feeling.

"Keep the change." He mumbled to her. I saw that he was annoyed by her fawning and wanted her gone, and seeing that brought a slight smile to curve my lips.

His brow furrowed, his long brown hair falling over it and grazing his eyes. He was now placing my white pieces on the board.

I was fucked! I doubted I would be able to concentrate on the game. And then the funniest thing happened. I'd been so distracted by him that I hadn't noticed that the music had stopped and that someone had dropped some quarters in the jukebox and now David Bowie's "Wild is the Wind" was playing. Even at that moment I realized that a part of me was ending.

He looked up expectantly at me. The pieces placed perfectly on the board and ready to launch me into a life-changing course. It was my move.

"Shall we?" His voice was low and deep. My nipples hardened at the sound. Oh, this is really bad, I thought.

"I'm going to kick your ass!" I promised him.

He threw me a wink and laughed wickedly, sending a shudder across my skin.

He picked up the cup and tossed his black dice into it, shaking it all the while staring into my eyes. I looked away and was arrested by the size of his hands. Huge, long fingered hands that held that cup with an elegance that made my mouth water at the thought of his hands cupping my breasts.

He threw the dice across the table; they rolled towards me and presented us with a double six. I didn't bother placing my dice in the cup, but instead rolled them between my hands and threw them on the table and they rolled. Fate was playing favorites, and she handed me a six and a one. He leaned forward; he was impossible to ignore. I nodded for him to go.

I was unprepared by the full impact of his chiseled features, but at least now I could stare at him unmolested by his penetrating gaze. He was busy moving the pieces of his checkers across the board. He had a big jaw; his chin sported a slight cleft which until this moment I'd never known was my weakness. His mouth was thin and yet was sensually curved in a smile. His long nose was straight. High cheekbones gave him an elegance that was a surprising contrast to his rough maleness. I sat back a little stunned for he looked like my favorite self-portrait painting of the famous 19th Century painter Gustave Courbet, which he'd painted of himself when he was young. He's staring at us with wild eyes pulling his long hair back from his forehead; it's a very irreverent self-portrait hence why it's my favorite, and here he was, flesh and blood but with green eyes instead of brown.

He looked up. I hadn't noticed that he had finished moving his pieces. It was the eloquence of his large, almond-shaped eyes that detained me. He was tearing me open and staring deep down into me and asking me all sorts of questions with those eyes of his. That was his power over me. He could communicate in a way that made me comfortable with my discomfort. It was a strange dichotomy of whirling emotions that made me feel good in my skin. And for the first time in forever, I felt that things were going to be okay, and then of course, there was that feeling, this pulsing hunger that rang loud between my thighs. It felt as though we had left off from a conversation long ago interrupted.

We ended up playing for hours; we sat across from each other communicating all the desires, all the love, all that had been forgotten from past lives within a strange circle of silence. He didn't talk; he didn't have to. His gorgeous green eyes did all the talking. Anyway, it's how we fell in love. You could say he saved me from hating.

***

It's been twelve years since that first meeting, and it's been hell wrapped in the incandescent light of that strange idea we call love. But what is love, really? How do you really know what love is? Truth be told, we were both confused by it. Struck down by it. Enslaved by it. Is that what love brings a person down to? We refused to marry each other, and yet we lived as a married couple. It was from that vantage point that I began to realize one sure thing that marriages are fraught with challenges that cannot be understood, until the tender hooks have dug so deep as to disable any escape. In other words, marriages are campaigns fought for a deeper understanding. They can be sieges that last years, or battles that last a few hours, but at the end of those long challenging roads, the truth of marriages is that they are a way to work out the most challenging karmas. Say what you will, but I have yet to meet a married couple that does not struggle to stay married, no matter how bright the prospects, it's just too emotional, too big to believe that one person, one partner can give you all that you may need.

Besides that, add to it that if past life connections are sought to gain a deeper understanding of your partner, you may find that your husband, in this life, was your father in a past life, or a jilted lover, or a brother, sister, or child.

In those twelve years, we've never been apart. We live in Pasadena, now and though I miss San Francisco, this is our home. We're not "legally' married, but we've lived with each other this long, so we're common law. Our friends and family never could figure out what kept us together; it is, at best, a co-dependent relationship. Whenever I begin to pack my bag and am ready to walk, my heart twists into a painful fist that sits upon my solar plexus like a stone.

It was the unanimous opinion that we needed to either marry or split up. When I was ready to make that commitment, Daniel would shy away. When he was ready to move forward, I would balk at the idea. It was as if something kept us together and pulled us apart.

Daniel and I began to explore our connection to each other. Why was it so deep and yet so riddled with negative energy?

In one life, we were, in fact brothers, and as you might imagine, this knowledge impacted our sex life. It was a hell of a thing to recall that as brothers, we had fought in battles together, loved each other as brothers, and failed each other. I don't want to explore that life with you now, perhaps at some later date. Suffice it to say, that in this recall, I began to understand that everyone I met was not just a chance meeting but an opportunity to reconnect, to clarify, perhaps even to make amends.

In the past life I shared with Daniel, we both began to understand why he was so very protective of me in this life. He did not want to lose his little brother again.

Any marriage begins with deep friendship, or hot passions, at which point, the flame either leaps into a more committed scenario, or abruptly ends. Regardless, all relationships offer us a deeper meaning. If we would but silence the outside world and listen to our souls, we could hear the truth of our relationship struggles. This belief system is by no means exclusive to marriages, instead it ripples out. I will say this, that I do believe that we incarnate to become better people.

As for the attainment of Nirvana, it is an idea that neither troubles me nor is my ultimate desire. I am not willing, nor ready to attain Nirvana, also known as everlasting heaven, as many of us are not willing to do. And though that idea may very well shock you, the truth is this: I love living lives, I love every aspect of them, and when I recall my past lives, I relish the feelings that return to me like old friends. I even get homesick for ancient places now excavation sites. I am an eternal reincarnationist, if there's even such a term. I want to return again, and again, until I have sought, and experienced every aspect that life is.

That truth may frighten you, especially when one realizes that more lives are fraught with peril and grief than with ease and joy, but there is something about vanquishing and learning from even the worst aspects of lives that makes me realize that even at the worst hours, the darkest days, there is always light. It is that light that makes all souls reach out with hope. Call it God, or the Universal Mind, or the Great Father, or the Great Mother, whatever term moves you. I say it is light imbued with love.

So even when we are lost in the middle of a raging sea, even when the waves seem impossible to conquer, even unto our deaths, piercing through all the chaos is the eternal lighthouse that stands unwavering, stoic in the storm, lighting our way home. Yes, when I am home, I find bliss, but then I have the need to enter a new body, to touch skin, to love, to desire.

I know, I know, I should refrain from all these things, but I cannot. If I could, I would have long ago attained Nirvana, as you would have too, by the way. But here we are, fellow travelers enjoying the journey. Can you admit to that?

As esoteric as my words may sound, I will tell you that my relationship with Daniel was neither blessed with wealth, nor filled with ease. We fought each other for power; in fact, we fought every day, about money, about our future, about the smallest infractions. Our very deep spiritual understanding of what we had been to each other was our constant link. What other partner would understand such things as karma and past lives shared? Not many. So I felt lucky that with Daniel there was no convincing him of what I knew was truth, but only to go deeper.

Yet at times, more often than not I hated him. Then out of nowhere, he would make me laugh so well that it filled my soul with love. The very idea of leaving him brought me a deep sadness that I could never shake. We were co-dependent, tied at the hip like Siamese twins, unable to say good-bye and yet unable to live together with any sense of peace. We were caught in a tangled mass of heavy ropes coiled with hate, passion, and love. I could not understand what had kept us together for twelve years. The overprotective quality of my being his little brother in another life explained in some small part this tie but not all of it, not to my satisfaction. I was waiting for a sign that would release us from each other, but it never came, and I had resigned myself to the fact that perhaps it was my karma to work things out with Daniel for the entirety of my life, our lives. Perhaps if I did the work, our relationship would heal? I dreamed of affairs, and yet when faced with a possibility, I could not engage. My feet rooted to the spot that was this 'marriage' to Daniel. I felt doomed and at times I felt lucky that Daniel loved me so completely.

Many would say that I was waging a war with my self-esteem and not karma, but I would say that they could not understand the strong energy that bound us together. Those who witnessed our relationship at close range were confused and resigned by what could only be described as a force of nature in its very being. It made no sense, and yet it continued to whirl, full of life. But as the years began to stack, the chinks began to show, and the whirling was slowing. I was beginning to blink my eyes so that I could see beyond the four walls of my relationship with Daniel.

My unanswered prayers began to echo out into space, and they bounced back to earth with an answer that came to me in the only way that would make any sense to one such as me.

It was a past life that would visit me when I least expected it, when I had neither sought nor desired it. It would come unheeded and take me forcibly down the halls of the Akashic records. A messenger would descend upon me armed with an Akashic scroll in hand, and place it into my keeping to unravel. This would be a messenger I would never meet, whose voice I would never hear, whose eyes I would never look into, and whose touch I never would feel. He would use a new technology, and through that conduit, he would begin a dialogue that would take place over a period of weeks.

At the end of the day, it would all make sense. After all, I was not trained in astral projection, having only experienced this in my flying dreams when I had been a child when there was no sense of limitations. So how else could this man speak to me but through this new technology?

It was 1997 and everyone, and I mean everyone who used computers for their business, whether they were a mom-and-pop business or a huge banking system, was scrambling to roll out the new Y2K systems. IT companies were making money hand over fist, hurling themselves into that mosh pit of frenzied, apocalyptic energy for the conversions to roll out. There were talks that once Y2K hit, whole systems reliant on computers would freeze, that entire infrastructures would collapse, and if that happened, mass chaos would ensue. Many people began to prepare for the "Big Y2K Crash" by hording cash, guns, food, and water.

The flip side was the complacency of how retail businesses looked at the Internet with skeptical eyes. They were reticent to set up a website presence. They reminded me of those advertisers in the 1950s who had a wait and see attitude over how the television would play out.

Amazon.com was the lone kid on the Internet block. Victoria Secrets' PR people had decided to wait and see whether the Internet was going to go bust or not, and Tiffany & Co., had voiced the same caution. It seemed that the only visionaries were the pornographers.

IPOs were making kids millionaires overnight, and money ran like water.

I was an account manager, cold-calling clients to sell them our consulting services. We had contracted with more than twenty networking companies. The idea was to offer clients the opportunity to receive three to four proposals at no cost. From these quotes they were sure to choose one of our guys; nine times out of ten, we would get the deal.

I was always toggling between faxing, emailing my clients, and surfing the net. I was blown away by this technology! This all felt as if I was venturing into unknown territory like those early mavericks who'd ventured into the Wild West.

I'd already experienced my first cyber stalker, flirted wildly with a cybersex dude and had done my share of playing at being someone I was not with a couple of guys. Those forays did not last, ending as I soon grew bored.

In other words, by the time I received an instant message which blinked a small screen, I had been around the WWW block a couple times. I was by no means a web virgin. The message asked if I knew the sender to accept. The sender's name was Malek. I copied and pasted his name and his bio popped up with the following information:

Malek's Profile:
Sex: Male
Hometown: Paris, France.
Status: Married
Languages: English, French, Italian,
and Farsi-

So I clicked to accept, and when the message opened it revealed words I did not expect.

"Do you believe in reincarnation?"

The question stunned me. I sat quite still, feeling goose bumps ripple across my arm. What was I afraid of? I chided myself, after all he was married, and besides what harm could there be to answer? Anyway, the question had whetted my appetite for what I thought would be a short, passionate chat about a very favorite subject. Why not launch into it while I multitasked? What fun.

So I did, I answered.

"Oui!"

"You speak French?" he typed back in French.

"Yes, but I express myself much better in English," I replied in French.

"D'accord."

"So do you believe in reincarnation?"

"Why do you ask?"

"Well, your name fascinates me."

"How so?"

"How did you come about to choose bacchor as your email?"

"Long story short, I loved it because in Latin, it means to run wild and rebel."

"If I told you that I knew you in a past life would you believe me?"

I felt another chill run across my skin; I shivered.

I typed "?" and hit send.

After what seemed like a drawn-out pause, I saw my instant message screen blinking that Malek is typing. I sat still, and inhaled very deliberately.

"Close your eyes and tell me what do you see?"

I was about to shut down the instant message screen. What kind of nut is he? What kind of nut am I to respond? But a voice whispered inside of me, calmed me; I knew that there was truth here. I was afraid; I felt gullible, vulnerable and reticent to continue with this conversation, and yet I could not stop. I did not want to stop. I began the walk down a dark corridor. I trembled, and yet I needed to pursue this to the very end.

"Are your eyes closed?"

"Oui," I typed.

I sat back, closed my eyes. Within seconds an image appeared bright and still.

I saw a woman standing by the edge of a large cave, her long dark brown hair fluttering about her, her cape flying out behind her caught by a stiff wind. Framing her silhouette was a dark gray sky with thundering clouds, and lightning shot across the sky. She turned to face a man, and when I saw her heart-shaped face, I knew that this woman was me. She had large golden eyes, a long aquiline nose, and a large, sensuous mouth. She spoke in words I could not understand. The man she faced was tall, regal in his stance. He had hair as black as his obsidian eyes, a black beard that was long, and oiled. Within his large eyes I saw his love for me. He brought her, or rather me, to his chest and held her, and within that moment I felt this man's embrace, as if I had somehow flown down to fill her body with my soul. I felt his breath upon my forehead. I felt the warmth of his very life. My eyes flew open and grazed the computer screen.

"What do you see?" he typed.

I typed the very minimum of what I had just witnessed, leaving out any descriptions of myself or of the man. I only shared what I had experienced but not what I looked like in that life. I must have held my breath so long that I felt a wave of dizziness throw me off. I took a long breath in, held the sweetness of the air into my lungs and exhaled.

I imagined that he was sitting forward reading my words. And then he typed every detail I had left out.

"You are my most beautiful queen, my great love and my lady, Bakor. You are small, like a gazelle, lithe and long of limbs. You have very large eyes, like almond pools of gold; your dark lashes lower as you shyly slip your hand beneath my robe to stroke my chest. Your skin is pale moonlight, and your lips are the blush pink of a lotus flower. I am your king, your Malek. I am tall with the blackest of hair and beard, black like the feathers of a raven. I regard you with love, for we are one and thus equal in my eyes."

How could this be happening? How could he know what I had seen? And then the thought flashed like a telegraph, yes, he's been your husband, your king, that was then, this is now, relax. But then my ego cloaked in fear tripped forward. Why was this happening? And yet, the image of my life then leapt out of my subconscious mind into my conscious mind; it was beckoning me to close my eyes, and to look and see, in order to understand. I refused, shaking my head, and still the image pierced me. I could see us moving in that past, touching each other in that life, speaking words long forgotten in tongues no longer spoken, but I knew that we spoke of love, of the sky's wild beauty, of our people, and of the moment we were sharing. I recalled everything as if I was in an open-eyed meditation that I could not shake off had I wanted to. The truth was simple: I longed to go back, to go home, and so I did. Malek would become my conduit.

That night I lay by Daniel's side, away from his big body, feeling the heat of his life. I was afraid of what had begun, and yet I could not think of stopping. The following morning I rose early, coffee in hand, logging in to another piece of the puzzle. Malek was there waiting for me.

"Did you dream of us?" he asked.

I had not, and said so.

"Did you?" I asked.

"Yes! It was good to see you again, to feel you against me, to touch your lips."

"I do not have any memory," I sent him, sad that this was true.

"Close your eyes my lovely Bakor, and it will all come back to you."

So I did, and to my surprise, it unraveled before my inner vision, frozen images that began to move with life.

It all came back...

MESOPOTAMIA

That night, Malek held me in his arms. I could not stop shuddering.

"What troubles you my love?"

I began to weep, burying my face within the curve of his shoulder. "Tell me my sweetest Bakor, tell me the cause of your tears, and I shall slay the one who has so offended you."

Finally, much later, when the moon had reached its zenith and a morning star heralded the coming day, I whispered the crone's oracle.

He laughed. His chest rumbling like a sea cave, I buried my ear upon his left breast listening to the reassuring pounding of his strong heart. Feeling a cool morning breeze ruffle us with such a start, I drew furs around us and wrapped my legs around his, enjoying the prickling feel of his hairy calves.

"My love, my dearest heart, we will not be conquered, I assure you of that, my sweet." His long elegant finger grazed my jaw line, caressing my ear. I gazed into his large black eyes, searching for comfort. I leaned into him brushing my cheek bone against his lean cheek, enjoying the bristle of his beard, long and jet black against his pale skin. I wanted to believe him so badly. He threw the furs aside, straddling me. He was like a god to me, a god from the ancient past sung alive by our bards. His broad shoulders and lean, white body was covered with jet black hair that tapered to a perfect V down to his flat stomach, softening to surround his manhood now erect with his desire. "My beautiful queen," he murmured as he parted my thighs with his knee. I felt my vulva now moist and warm, part lips to welcome him home. He entered me with a swiftness that arched my back and left me breathless. My small breasts rose against his chest, my nipples dusky pink brushed against the soft hairs that covered his chest, which brought me great pleasure. His large, elegant hands cupped my flanks, holding me thus, and with every thrust, I matched him, rolling my hips like the wild sea, pushing against him with all my might desperate to allow him deeper still. His black eyes bore into my soul, his mouth capturing mine. I felt tears spring out, my very spirit moved by the link we shared.

"My golden-eyed gazelle," he cried out as his thrusts deepened, his hands grasping me, until I was sure to bruise. I tore my eyes away from his and looked down upon our hips rolling in rhythm, tied as one flesh. His pale whiteness, a contrast to my pale golden hue, sent a thrill down my spine. I felt that familiar shivering ripple ride through me like the end of a summer wind that rips the leaves off a tree preparing itself for winter, growing in speed until I felt my vulva explode into him, and my king, my love, met me halfway. We sunk into a waterfall of bliss that left us sliding back onto earth upon shaky legs. I fell asleep.

***

When I awoke, it was Ama, my most precious slave, who stood by our bed waiting.

"I have drawn your bath my Queen."

Not far from the bed stood a large basin that could easily fit three tall warriors. Made to my specifications, it was forged from bronze and shone bright and clean; the inside was inlaid with lapis lazuli tiles as small as my thumbnail.

Dark, red rose petals floated upon the surface of warm water.

"My children?" I asked sinking into the tub with a graceful sigh.

"They are eager to see you."

"Allow them in!"

Ama clapped her hands and within minutes, my three children stood before me. My eldest, Amytis, was my daughter of fourteen summers. She was a real beauty, and she had taken after me and my mother. She possessed the same large almond eyes with that strange golden color, rimmed by jet black eyelashes. She favored her father's face which was narrower than mine, and she had inherited Malek's narrow, long aquiline nose, and narrow mouth, but she was no less my beauty.

My son Damion, was nine, and stood as tall as any twelve-year-old boy. He had inherited the tall well-bred bones of my brothers. His close-cropped curly hair was a soft light brown, and his hairline met like a point of a helmet upon the middle of his head, as if forged by the kiss of a goddess who must have favored him. He had my large almond eyes, but they were green flecked with chips of gold, with long, thick black lashes any maiden would have jealously claimed to own. They rimmed the windows of his very good soul. He was too beautiful for a boy, and already my ladies doted upon him with too much freedom for my own taste; still he was assured his innocence for at least two more summers.

And then, there was my youngest, seven-year-old Cycrus, whose red hair was a puzzlement to us all, as no one could recall red hair on either side of our families. Nevertheless his face was the replicate of his father's, same long narrow face, large black eyes, pale skin, and elegant limbs. He was melancholy and preferred his own company. He often favored lying flat on his back staring up at the changing sky for hours. He was fascinated by what made us, men and women, and what brought about illness, so he was often seen following the court physicians. He was fascinated by what made up our world; he even pestered my gardeners with questions about what made a plant look as it did, and why did it grow dormant when it did, and why some plants bore fruits and some flowers, and why some plants healed, while others poisoned. Unlike my eldest son or daughter, he avoided hawking or riding at all costs. Though he did occasionally join us for our swimming games, all in all, he preferred the solitude of silence. Now he, I thought to myself, comes from another world.

As impossible a task as it may seem, I loved them all the same, but with the differences warranted by the diverse personalities my children presented me. They were unique, and I loved them for their own uniqueness. I guarded myself against any favoritism, something my own family had not done when I had been a child.

Malek shared my way of loving them. He could not pick a favorite any more than I could, and he could not understand why such an idea had been so foreign to his parents.

"My children!" I exclaimed, and they ran to me, kneeling about the bath, my daughter leaning in to hug me, my son Damion kissed my forehead, and Cycrus, waited his turn. I raised my arms to him, and he forgetting, that now he was seven winters, and could no longer share my bath as he had once done when he was quite small, ran straight into the tub, landing upon my arms with a violent thump which threw the water about everyone, nearly emptying the bath. I was not angered but laughed, as did they all.

That night, we dined upon roasted goat stuffed with figs and drizzled with date syrup. Flat bread brought me great pleasure from the warm smell of barley and wheat as it came hot and pliable. I loved to dip it into the gravy juice of the roasted animal; this was my favorite meal besides the melons and cucumbers grown in a section of my beloved garden. As we ate, a sweet tale of the kings and queens before us sang out in songs, accompanied by harps and flutes. Lights died out and were lit again as our children were sent to bed.

Malek, my sweet king, made a point that they should never part our side before he held them each in his arms to tell them how much love he carried in his heart for each of them, and tonight was no different.

"Are they not beautiful?" he said watching

them walk to their quarters.

"They are perfect!" I answered, "Perfect…"

Malek turned to me. His face took on a solemn look; he leaned towards me, his face so close to mine that his hot breath grazed my left cheek. His long index fingers caressed the line of my jaw, laying two fingers upon my lips. I had closed my eyes, enjoying this simple moment between us. Then his voice, deeper than usual, hushed with troubled tones, jerked me to sit up straight, to lock eyes with my love, afraid to hear the words that would tumble out. My mouth dry, and then he asked "Is your mind at ease, my love?" I laughed without mirth, a laugh that was filled with the wings of despair, the poison of fear. The peace I had felt within my heart had disappeared upon hearing the tone of his voice, like a rock thrown into the middle of a still pond. I was shaken. I stared into Malek's eyes, searching for an answer, afraid to ask him what this was all about.

"I have made sure that nothing but good tidings will reach your delicate ears." He leaned forth to kiss my earlobe. I was puzzled, and then a dawning erupted across my skin raising the small hairs on the back of my neck. Malek clapped his hands. The captain of the guards appeared, bearing a large tray. Upon it was dark purple linen, which my King drew aside as if revealing the most precious of gifts. It was the severed head of the old crone who had warned me at the caves. Her obsidian eyes were half shut, her long black hair caught the light off the lamps and glowed jet blue, and her tongue spilled out from between a half opened mouth, wet spittle upon her chin. I screamed in horror.

"Malek, what have you done?" I cried hot tears running down my cheek, my heart pounding so hard in my chest I was sure I would slip into a black world of mists to hear the voices of my ancestors.

"I did it to protect you, my love! For you! Because, you are my most precious, my most ... My most beloved!"

"My king, how could you have done this? You killed our Oracle, and we have no other! We are doomed! Doomed!" I felt my heart break. I fell to my knees cradling into myself, shielding my vision with my hands fearful to view the crone's face. I had promised her safety. I had brought her to this and brought us to ruin. It was beginning; fate's door had swung open, kicked by my king, and there was no turning back.

"Oh, Malek what have you done!"

***

I awoke with the sun warming my cheeks.

The rays fell across the granite floor and bounced off my large oval copper reflector. The soft curtains floated away from the large portals that overlooked my gardens. The slaves, having risen before the dawning of the sun, had removed the heavy weaved curtains that at night were strung up to protect us from malevolent spirits. Upon waking we were blessed by the gods as they awoke to find us waking with them. It was a good day for riding and hawking and I said so to Malek who offered me a wide grin of pleasure.

"The children?" he asked.

"No matter," I answered. "They will come; we'll coax them with promises of honey and dates, crushed with nuts, stuffed within apples baked in an open fire by the river."

"Yes," he nodded with laughter. "They will come with little else to tempt them."

Upon hearing the news our children leapt with joy, all except my little red-headed jewel, my little boy who disliked the sticky quality the honey offered but loved to roast apples in the open fire, not for the eating of them but for the joy he received from watching the skin of the apples wither and soften. He was glad to give his slave this bounty, and so he was pleased to join us.

He was my sweet boy, whose red hair was

a sure sign from the gods that he was anointed by their good will. He was so unlike my two eldest that I quite often worried about him and thus my copper boy joined me whenever possible, especially when I visited the caves, or rode to the pools to swim beneath the wide lotus leaves. Water was his home. He would slip out of his cloth and leathers, and slippery like a fish, dunk head first into the cool pools. He was fascinated by the tiny plants and creatures that populated this green world. His red hair floated about his face, his eyes wide open with wonder, and whenever something floated before his vision, he would send me one of his rare smiles. For a handful of heartbeats, life was silent and suspended into a cool silence. It was our lungs that protested for air, only the need to breathe that broke our exploration and forced us to rise. We inhaled deeply and sunk back into that other world.

We never tired of our underwater explorations. He loved the soft manner in which the water lifted him off his feet and floated him upon his back with little effort. He adored the lotus flowers that floated like lazy girls, he said.

We always lay by the river bank and dried in the sun, looking up at the sky watching the clouds roll past. He noticed how shadows fell across us and how chilly we would get when the clouds seemed to stand still above us and then a brisk wind would push them away, to allow the sun's rays to warm us. He spoke in such beauty about the world that surrounded him that I was sure he would grow up to become a great poet or philosopher, for he examined life so closely and with such detail and with the kind of deep sensitivity that would sometimes drive him mad with rage or grief. During those times we would give him a drink based with a strong dose of little white flowers with yellow hearts, and mix that with other herbs that seem to calm him and help him sleep. Sometimes nothing soothed his fevered soul and only long visits by the water pools appeased the demons within him, and he would return to me, my little copper-headed boy.

I was so very young then, so full of life, so hungry to feel all that life offered. I rose as early as the sun, afraid to miss a moment.

I loved riding my mare hard and fast across the terrain beneath a dark blue sky filled with the white perfection of palaces that I hoped to visit when it was my time to cross over. At this moment, I was alive and felt my heart cry out with gladness for the hot blood that ran with passion at being alive! So alive that my body was lifted by the power of this moment. I cracked my whip urging my dogs onward. They barked in response and gathered sinewy muscles beneath the taunt sheath of tan fur. They unleashed power as they leapt with ease, making headway. I followed close behind, my mare tossing her head. I felt a shadow fall across me, and I gazed towards the sun and saw the silhouette of her wings, spread wide caught in a breeze; she was Isis incarnate. She was patient, watching for any prey. And when my hawk spotted a hare or other worthwhile prey she swooped down with a great cry; the dogs knew, and they ran baying after her. My mare leapt over ravines to reach her side. I steadied my mare and approached carefully. She stood above her kill, waiting like a priestess, patient with hooded eyes, unafraid of my dogs barking wildly and my whip cracking above them commanding them to stop and to stay back.

I swung from my mare and ran towards the prey. A dead rabbit of no real consequence, but it was the pursuit and not the game I was after. My slave took the dead thing and threw it into a leather bag that slung over his shoulder, his ebony skin shinning bright with sweat.

I held my fist out and my hawk stepped upon it. I swung my eyes towards a sky transformed again and filled with large, clouds moving like ships across the bluest sea. I felt a rush course through my body. I wanted to throw my mouth open and let the wings of desire leap out into space and howl. I needed Malek between my thighs. I handed my hawk over to my slave, a tall Nubian my brother had sent me from Egypt as my wedding gift. She jumped off my fist onto his. I swung upon my mare and rode hard to the palace. I needed Malek; I needed his manhood to destroy all my desires—

I arrived quicker than imaginable and cried out for my king, walking with purpose, my footsteps silent upon the large slabs of smooth marble. I strode throughout the palace, the tall columns like gods standing as still as soldiers, the sun high in the sky spilled through the wide expanse of this place so that it glimmered bright. Slaves ran about their business, and my Nubian was close behind me.

The hawk still on his fist, he would not allow me out of his sight unless Malek was present. "Where is my king?" I shouted. A soldier stood by the entrance of the throne rooms answered my command.

"He is with his scribe, my lady."

I moved up towards the stone steps that led to our chambers. The children were out at study with their tutors, and so besides our lords and ladies, we were alone. I found him at the terrace of his battle room. He was sitting on a stone step that led to the top tier, to our private chambers that overlooked more terraces of hanging plants, swaying date trees, and fountains that tinkled with water. He was looking over a tablet, and dictating to his scribe who sat a few feet from him carving a message into the moist clay, a missive that would travel to another land, or perhaps capture records of events or such things. I cared not; I was hungry. He looked up and recognized the heat in my golden eyes. He abruptly stood up and grabbed my arm.

"Get out!" he ordered.

The scribe, poor man, was trying to gather the tablet.

"Leave it!" Malek roared.

And with that, we stood alone. I was breathless, shaking for him. His long elegant hand caressed my cheek, and he gazed into my eyes with a hunger that matched mine. "You are my goddess, my moonlight, my very breath," he whispered I caught the scent of his breath freshened by the mint leaves he often chewed. I stood on my toes and turned my face burying my mouth upon his shoulder, nipping at him and kissing his chest. I was pulling back his robe, admiring the elegant length of his body dappled with shiny black hair. He grabbed me and lifted me up; I swung my legs around his waist, and he carried me to our large bed. Falling on pillows of linen, and weaved tapestry, and I lay upon a blanket of white animal fur. He drove himself into me and I arched against him, my breasts pressing against his chest as he swung in and out. I cried out.

He tasted my voice with his lips and tongue, nibbling at my lower lip and still he did not stop riding me until I was buried deep within the pillows, arms flung above my head feeling fulfilled by our shared passions. It was time for sleep.

Later, tangled within Malek's embrace, the dream slithered between my breasts and woke me to the truth. I was breathless with fear, and found solace on the terrace hearing the sounds of exotic birds, of waterfalls, of scented things, and for a time I found respite from my nightmares. I wondered when fate and death would appear to demand their day.

3

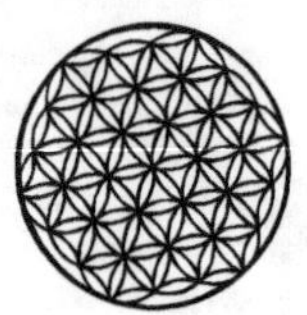

PASADENA
SEPTEMBER 12, 1997

I slammed down the phone and sat back in my chair. I just could not, for the life of me, get these big retail houses to believe that the Internet was alive and well and would flourish. It was like talking to a wall. I had just hung up with the Madison Avenue PR person for Victoria's Secret.

Hootie and the Blowfish had just done a video stream of their concert sponsored by MSN or some other Internet provider. But there it was, video stream. I had been telling Victoria's Secret to do a video stream of their fashion shows. They saw no need, but I told them that it would bring a huge audience of both men and women. Not to mention, a site presence that sold their products would reach people worldwide. Their answer was that they did not ship outside of the USA.

I was floored, apoplectic really. How could moi, with no college education, living an in attic apartment with my boyfriend of twelve years, see what they could not?

Bob, my boss, was on the phone asking me how my day was going. I was lucky; I had nailed a job where I could work from home. I mean, what could be better? Well, more deals which would equate to more money, but hey, life was good.

I told him about my calls with Tiffany and Co. and Victoria's Secret.

"Forget web pages, our techs want to concentrate on the Y2K conversions. That's where the money is anyway; go for that." I knew that he was right, and I wanted to hit my commission this month. Hell! What was I thinking? I wanted to hit it every month.

Daniel popped his head in as I hung up. "How's it going? Want some coffee?" It was eight in the morning. I had been up faxing and calling the east coast since sixty-thirty that morning. I needed coffee and a shower bad. I opted for both.

I padded barefoot on the old gray wall-to-wall carpet and made my way to our little kitchenette, which was the size of most people's closets. It had three large windows overlooking an old avocado tree whose branches lay upon the slanted roof. The counter took one side of the kitchen, a sink and small counter space. The opposite side was our old Cadillac fridge circa 1950's and the little stove that squatted so tiny and docile by the fridge. Daniel had to bend his head sideways to cook since the roof slanted close to any who stood over five-foot-five, which I was. It was an absurd and completely charming kitchen with large black-and-white tile floor. It was a wonderful warm and inviting kitchen where I could see the sun set, and if I stood on my tip toes I could see the Sizzler's parking lot. Instead, I would sit on a small, square table that I had placed against the corner, turning it into a reading nook. I was lucky to have such a space. I poured coffee into my sixteen- ounce mug and walked back to the bathroom. I was greeted with black-and-white floors, and a big bathtub with a see-through flamingo shower curtain. It was just a matter of drinking the coffee with my body tilted away from the shower spray; it's how I drank my hair of the dog after a particularly bad alcohol fest. Daniel came in to shave. He had showered earlier.

"I have to collect the rents and make a deposit at B of A, wanna' come?"

I was nursing my coffee, letting the water hit my back. To get a cut in our rent, we had accepted the position of being apartment managers. That's all we got, a forty percent cut in our rent.

Okay, granted that was good, especially since we only had a handful of tenants. We lived in the old Victorian home that had been cut into four apartments. Opposite our attic apartment was our Japanese student, who was always out. Her cat would come through our window to steal food from our counter, and the only thing that stopped his escapades was our cream Persian cat, Alexander the Great Pleiades Neptune, Alex for short. He kept guard and did not take kindly to thieves. He especially hated her cat.

Still, since she was never home, we had no issues. Her rent was always on time. Below her lived our resident pot head, and opposite him was our chef. He was a sexy beast who juggled two girls; one was tall and had long brown hair that grazed her hips and then there was the mod girl, with the short pixy blonde haircut. She, I liked. The brunette, however, was a bitch. Had she known that the chef, let's call him Eric, had a thing for exotic girls, and what I mean by that is that Eric had a thing for me, which I have to admit was not unwelcome, the brunette would have been mad as hell! As it stood, she thought she was his only one. Though I had a mass of waist-length unruly red hair, I was exotic. From my black father, I had inherited the strong jaw line, the broad shoulders, the full sensuous mouth, and wild curly hair. From my French mother, I had inherited the high cheekbones, the aquiline nose, the red cast to my hair, the large high breasts, and muscular legs. From both, I had inherited large, almond-eyes rimmed with very dark lashes and dark, high-arched brows. Some would say I was beautiful, others sexy, others striking. I was not a conventional type; I was a hodge-podge of races from both sides of the pond that converged into. . . well, me.

"I have so much work to do. I better stay put; I've got to hit my numbers. We need the money."

"Speaking of which," he paused, and then drew back the shower curtain leveling his green eyes upon me. I wrapped my arm around my breasts. I felt naked and at this moment that was not a good feeling.

I felt myself tense, something serious was coming.

"I'm going to have you write me a check into my account."

I wanted to explode. We had just done that two days ago.

"Why?" I wanted to howl.

"The phone company wanted a hundred dollars or else they were going to shut us down."

"And you didn't tell me?" I was so angry! I could feel myself shaking inside.

"You do realize that the bank could shut my account down, or yours, for that matter?"

"We have no choice; we have five bucks, no gas, and a bag of pasta. Besides coffee and sugar that's it until Monday." He paused and folded his arms across his massive chest.

"What do you want me to do?" He shrugged with a nonchalance that made me want start screaming but I held back.

"Fuck!" I mumbled trying to hold on. I closed the shower curtain trying to hide my rage behind the clear plastic sheet. I felt my eyes blur with tears.

He leaned towards me, "Come on, don't be like this."

I ripped the shower curtain back and stared straight into his eyes.

"Fuck you! Fuck this! Fuck you, just get out!" I shouted.

Today was Friday. I had until Monday before I got paid. I was dying here. I got out of the shower and placed my coffee mug on the side of the sink. I wrapped my long hair in a towel and stared at my nude form with critical eyes. I was forty pounds overweight. Between the wine and beer and the bread I preferred over meat, it was no surprise. For me, heaven was a bottle of French red wine, a crusty hunk of warm bread and a slab of sweet unsalted butter. I was never happier than eating that in front of a good BBC show, forgetting all my woes watching some kind of Masterpiece Theater presentation. I took the towel off my head and rubbed and squeezed the last drops of the water still dripping from my ends. My hair was fast curling around my waist and shoulders. We were experiencing an unusual hot spell in Pasadena. The air conditioner was on full blast. I tied the towel around my body and marched like a soldier to our bedroom.

I pulled out my checkbook and made the check out to Daniel W. McCabe for one hundred dollars. His face was tense, but nevertheless, he took the check. I was so angry. He'd stopped working a few months back. His plan had been to buy cars at auction, refurbish them, and sell them for profit. I was quickly losing patience. I was holding the fort down, and quite frankly I was sinking. We needed the second income. There was no going around that fact. I was tired, the kind of tired that comes with the dawning of depression rather than physical exertion.

Daniel tried to grab me within the big folds of his arms, but I pushed him away with one hand, a tight grip on my coffee mug, which he took from my hand and quickly deposited on top of the TV set. My towel was falling, and he ripped it off me, grabbing one of my breasts, rubbing the nipple between his thumb and forefinger. He laughed and growled like a bear. I was too stressed to join in this mischief. I was hungry to make goal. Later, I would realize that any distraction would have been acceptable, just not from Daniel.

"Just go!" I barked. I saw the hurt in his large green eyes. He was such a tall, big handsome dude, not much for elegance and subtlety. He was all that was magnetic and sexy, a large chunk of light brown hair fell over his brow, and I felt myself melt. I turned away.

He left, slamming the door behind him, obviously pouting like an angry child whose favorite toy had been taken. I don't like you either, I thought to myself.

I quickly dressed, bra, panties, black leggings and a large T-shirt cut into pieces by my own hand, the large neckline falling off my shoulders, a la "Flashdance".

I was logging on to my PC when I saw an immediate message blinking for my attention. It was Malek, and suddenly the time I would not make for Daniel, I gave to Malek.

"Good morning. Did you have any dreams you'd like to share with me?"

I sat there closing my eyes, and thoughts twisting like sheets in the wind rippled through me and spun my mind to the sounds of voices and blurred colors. I was a mess! I was trying to bring about any recall that was coherent... and then the images came, I began to tremble. I typed, please give me some time. I need...

I broke off.

4

THE CONQUEROR
3,500 BCE

The moon rose and fixed itself upon the sky like a spirit that watched over us. It was turning a golden orange, a dark orange, and I was unable to sleep. Malek had long drifted off after our battle of love. He was exhausted. Tomorrow, I would be led to the temple of Ishtar, where it was my duty to take coins from any man and have sex with him. Every woman from our land had done so. It was said that if a woman was ugly, she may have spent years sitting on the steps waiting for the coins to release her from her duty. Though I was queen, I was no less bound by my duty, and so it was that I sat on my terrace, watching the sky move and sway with the changing hour. I was spellbound by the lush beauty of my gardens, down and down the plants rose from obscure porticos, and large clay pots, all manner of flower, and fruit bearing plants, and large palms. All was green and rich with perfumes of orange blossoms and roses. I must say that I rose from my divan with the sun, and met the saddened gaze of my king.

"I will think of something," Malek assured me.

"I am not afraid my love." Malek had been the only man I had ever lain with. The idea of another touching me frightened me and enraged him.

Malek had planned to come to me in full costume, as a warrior, perhaps as a beggar; it mattered not. The truth was that my beauty was celebrated and men from all corners were traveling to see me and perhaps to be the one who would place their offering between my thighs.

My beautiful tub of copper inlaid with lapis lazuli was brought in. I bathed in a warm bath scented with rose oil, and then I was made to stand, legs apart over a pot of burning myrrh whose tendrils of smoke rose insolently and caressed my thighs and curled about my freshly plucked mound.

I was made new, a vestal virgin in honor of the great mother, Ishtar. None of it made much sense to me, but it was said to please all the gods. My maid had even whispered that perhaps a god would descend from the skies and offer me gold coins for the chance to taste me for one night.

It all seemed impossible to back away from, for this ceremony would assure the continuous abundance of our fertile valleys, and though my bloodline harked back to Egyptian Pharaohs, I was now their queen and bound by their customs, their laws. So I prayed to both Ishtar and Isis.

Part of me was filled with the beating wings of fear. The strain was so heavy that I was sure to burst open, as the Nile opens wide to flood the nearby valleys. These feelings showed a violent change that would bring its own kind of pain, and this alone bore down on me like a stone upon my chest. I could not breathe and was made to smell the bitter aroma of a solution made from deer horns and hooves, the dark, bitter smell brought me back.

The day was bright and high and the procession of married women who walked to the temple of Ishtar was plenty, and most were farmers. I was one of twelve women from the court and by no means was I the most beautiful of all the offerings, but I can say I was the most desired.

Malek carried me to my transformation in his chariot led by four gray horses of equal stature and gait. Still, I was jostled by the rough roads and sudden jarring stops.

The sounds of drums coupled with harps, and lutes banged as the procession moved forward. Large, round leaves protected me from the sun, the heat, and the rising dust. Bulls decorated with flowers and scented with spices walked before us and their powerful hooves kicked up dust.

One bull that was milky white and bigger than the rest had been bred to all the cows and now was ready to be sacrificed to the gods. The beast led the walk to our deaths, physical for the beasts, spiritual for others. I knew that today everything was going to change, and that there was nothing Malek could do to stop it. It was his duty to bear sons from many wives, but ever since we had first coupled, he had only lain with me. That too would change, had to change, and the thought brought tears to my eyes.

I gazed down at my body, barely covered by the softest spun linen, like a cobweb that exposed all of my womanhood, with no mistake that I was unmarked by scars or deformations of any kind. I needed to have this trial be done with as soon as the gods would permit; I hoped that Ishtar would favor me with a good man. I only desired to honor my king, my children, and my people.

We moved past the pair of griffins Bull guarded the gates to the temple, so tall that I had to hold my head as far back as I could to see their faces, tall as three men staked on top of each other. We continued past them, our journey followed by the cacophony of the trumpets and drums, the stream of flower petals, and all manner of celebration, and shouts. We jolted to a stop in front of the temple. Columns depicted battles and stories from the ancient kings and queens of the past. Marble staircases were decorated with tiny tiles of lapis lazuli, and crystal quartz the size of my thumb decorated each stair with images of stalking lions, stories of sea voyages, and of flying gods of lower stature, and off course, at the top of the stairs was a statue of Ishtar, the goddess, our mother who was part bird. Women were already settling themselves upon the stairs to wait for the man who would throw coins to lay with them in honor of our great mother.

Malek hoisted me off the chariot and drew my gown over the top of my head. The sun was sinking slowly behind our beloved mountains, and its rays caught the mahogany glow of my hair. I stood nude before his admiring eyes, and the gasp of those who witnessed rippled through the crowds. I shook my hair as it cloaked my breasts and grazed my hips like a fine cloak. He held my hand in his, and placed a gold ring on my thumb, set with a purple stone engraved with two people coupling. He turned the palm of my hand, which he kissed for a long while, trailing his lips across my wrist. He led me up the stairs, and I walked with shoulders and back straight, barefoot, and stripped of all but the gentle jingle that my gold ankle bracelet made as I stepped towards the top of the steps. He turned to face me and kissed my neck and then suddenly bit my shoulder with a violence that was unlike Malek. Not deep enough to draw blood, but enough to draw tears that trembled beneath my lowered lids. When I dared look at him, he was smiling at the obvious teeth mark he had made upon my shoulder. He clapped his hands, and a slave ran to meet us, holding out a blood red cloth, which was in fact the finest weave I have ever seen of the deepest red, blood red, like the roses I grew by the south side of our terrace. He allowed it to ripple down about me, but I barely felt anything heavier than a breath.

"You are to walk to the palace when your duty has been accomplished," he whispered.

I nodded my head, remembering well the instructions the priestess had offered me these many months in preparation for this very day. From all accounts, the highest bidder would be allowed to bed me and no one else, a man of royal blood, of that I was assured. Still Malek had marked me his. I wondered if he would break with the gods and disguise himself as another. I could only hope.

Scented with rose oil, my woman-hood plucked clean, my mound shone with the finest oils that had been rubbed upon it to make it moist for the one who would enter what only Malek had known.

I sat, the red breath of air floating about me like a cloud. I stayed with my straight back and my head held high until my lower back began to ache. A crowd of men with bags of silver and gold had gathered and were bidding with the priestess for the right to touch the queen. The sun was a sharp red on the horizon and colored all that it touched with its hue. The sky was deepening and the night was gathering its courage to stain out the sun. Torches and large brass pots were being lit with fire.

Without much sound, a man wearing the headdress of a ram appeared. He held a harp of pure gold. In his other hand he held a sword of a workmanship that was both foreign and wonderful. Large and broad, with a handle that held stones of various hues glimmered. He was tall, tall as a cedar tree, and his chest was covered with fine spun gold hairs. His arms and shoulders were broad; he was the largest man I had ever seen, and I began to tremble with fear and thrill at the sight of him.

He did not address me, and with great

reverence walked to the high priestess with the harp handing her the gift.

"Will this please Ishtar?" he asked in a deep voice tinged with an accent I could not recognize.

The priestess was no fool, for had she dared refuse him, I know now, that he would have buried his sword within her without a thought to the sacrilege of the act.

A golden mask hid the content of his eyes and upper face from view. He wore amulets about his upper arms, and a strange design snaked about his left shoulder and arm, a design of smoke, and winged creatures, a design made by demons. He did not look at me but simply brought me to my feet and threw me across his back. He continued up the stairs and walked through the open gates that led right up to the altar. His sword in hand, he howled like a dog, and all who stood near, fled in fear. I was deposited upon the large altar. He tore the red sheath off, smiling with a grin that even his mask could not hide. "Who are you?" My voice trembled.

"I am your new king." He growled, taking off his mask and headdress and throwing them to the ground.

"He has marked what is now mine," he remarked coldly, trailing a fingertip across Malek's teeth marks. He lowered his head and sucked on my breast swallowing me whole in his mouth and brought me to such a trembling that I was sure to fall into darkness. He let go and his mouth trailed a tangled web of his magic down my belly, brushing lips against my mound, teasing me, inhaling my scent, and softly entering his tongue between those parts no man had ever dared possess but Malek. I threw my head back in surprised pleasure. He withdrew his mouth and kissed my upper thighs, and then without any words exchanged, he lowered his head and bit me hard within the inside of my upper thigh. I cried out in pain, and tears ran free down my cheek. He bit hard but stopped before breaking skin. Still the pain weakened my strength. He stood back staring down at me. He wiped the tears off my cheeks. I stared back at him, defiant in my gaze, contemptuous of his power over me, and yet before me stood the most magnificent man I had ever seen. Light brown hair tinged with the golden kiss of the gods, pale gray eyes that spoke of thunderstorms and heavy rains. I could smell him, his sweat, his scent, which was like no other.

"And you are to be my new queen." He untied his loin cloth and what sprang out made me cry out. He was built large and long, and before I knew what was happening, he was straddling me, pressing his softly-haired knee between my thighs, and guiding himself straight through me. I was stunned and arched against him. He rode me like a ferocious beast, and I dug nails into his heavily muscled back, digging my small heels against his buttocks, and still he rode me, capturing my mouth with his.

"Ahh... my queen, you are summer rain, you are fresh and clean like snow in my mouth." And still he rode me until I was sure to fall into a deep sleep, and still I cried with pleasure unable to contain the heat of pleasure that erupted with his every thrust. I found myself falling backwards until I saw nothing but blackness. When I awoke, the high priestess and her followers were cleaning my body with sea sponges, wiping his seed from between my thighs, tenderly administering to his teeth marks that proved to be deeper than I had first believed.

I involuntarily tightened them, and felt the pain of his mark. Still, I wanted to feel him between my legs again, and as that thought struck my mind, I felt shaken with shame. My duty had been done, and back to my king and my children I would go.

And then I remembered what that man had said, that I would be his queen and that he would be my king. My body sank into a shaking that I could not control; the priestess called for herbs to be mixed and for me to drink.

The fever of passion broke to reveal the truth of his purpose. My mind unlocked to expose what I had refused to accept until now, that he was the conqueror! The conquest had begun, and I was its symbol. What was I to do?

5

BEYOND THE PROPHECY
SEPTEMBER 18TH, 1997

Malek had messaged me when I had been away to a business meeting in downtown Los Angeles. We always met in Chinatown. I was part of a team of four account managers and out of those, I had befriended a man by the name of Ted Johnson, who, like me, dealt with many challenges on the home front. His wife had left him in Denver, Colorado, when he had lost a small fortune. He'd pursued her in LA and now they lived in a tiny house. He'd been relegated to sleep in the shed which was also his home office.

Another woman in our group was Tracy, who was married to a dumb but very wealthy man. She needed to work in order to keep her mental health balanced. Then there was a fifty-some-year old ex-swinger, Holly, who was dealing with crystal meth issues, which often exacerbated her inability to filter her inappropriate thoughts that would slither out as racist comments without warning.

This work situation was possible for me to

handle because I only saw them once a week. Had I been stuck in an office with them, I would have been unable to deal. Again, I felt lucky I got to telecommute. Anyway, I had made the mistake of rushing out of the office upon hearing Ted honking his horn, and had forgotten to log off my PC. Returning home, I was faced with a wall of rage in the form of a furious Daniel.

"Who the fuck is Malek?"

I didn't know how to answer, what to say, even how far to admit.

"I ...." My voice trailed off.

"Is that why you're so fucking busy, you're fucking sending sex messages to each other? Is he your new boyfriend?" Daniel spat.

His eyes were turning a feral light green and his whole body was getting bigger.

"I . . . look... it's not what you are thinking. He's a tech engineer, and anyway he lives in Paris with his wife."

"Who the fuck is he?" Daniel didn't want a story, he wanted a straight answer.

"Someone I knew in a past life."

Now if anyone else had heard that answer, they might have gone off. Not Daniel. He was stunned and sat down on the bright pink futon in the living room.

"What the fuck?" he said, looking up at me.

"I know, it sounds completely insane, but

it's true."

I sat next to Daniel and held his large hand in my mine; the palm of his hands were like oven mitts. Though he was six foot two, he sometimes appeared taller, and much bigger.

"How did you meet him?"

"On AOL. Believe it or not, it was completely innocent. He remembered me."

"How the hell could he do that?"

"My email, you know Bacchor? Well, in that life my name was Bakor."

"And you believed him?" he smirked.

"You know better than that Daniel."

"So what gives?" Daniel pushed on, his eyes like stones.

"I remembered and never dared tell him how I looked, and yet he described me. How could he know unless he was there, in that life?" And then I found the words and brought them forth, and I told Daniel everything, well almost everything, enough to satisfy him and to tell him that I wanted to know, that I needed to uncover this mystery to the very end.

And then he said what I had feared most.

"I want you to stop talking to this mumkin."

"Malek," I corrected him, angered by this demand.

"Whatever the fuck his name is, stop talking to him right now."

I stood up and went to the kitchen looking out the window at the avocado tree, at the squirrels running pell-mell between the large branches that lay upon the slanted roof. Alexander, our cameo Persian cat, saw my distress and meowed up at me. I petted him, trying to calm my heart from beating so fast. I was angry and afraid.

"I can't!"

Daniel stood behind me and grabbed my shoulders spinning me around to face him. I stared up at him, glaring at him. His face was inches from mine.

"If I catch you IM'ing him again, I will fucking take that PC and throw it out the window."

"Really? Really?" I said crossing my arms across my chest and stepping back from him.

Still, he moved in, crowding me with his body.

"What's next, you're going to tell me that you want to meet him in Paris?"

"It's not like that, not at all. It's more about us knowing something that is mind-blowing, and we both want to know what this life we shared was about."

Daniel was breathing hard.

"You do as I say, do you understand me?"

I pushed passed him. I was walking towards the front door; I needed air.

"I need to go on a walk," I said as I grabbed the door knob jerking it open. I couldn't wait to leave.

He slammed the door shut. "You're not going anywhere!"

"Then come with me. Please Daniel, let's take a walk and talk. It's such a beautiful night." I felt alive, and anxious. He actually agreed. I changed into my hiking boots, and he threw on his old bomber jacket with the WWII John Wayne and a depiction of the Flying Tigers design on the back. We walked out into the cool, crisp night. The moon had disappeared and what remained were stars. The streets were poorly lit, and so it was easy to hide in the shadows, talk softly, and stroll. No one walked then, and there were rarely any cars on the little streets of Pasadena. From Marengo we made our way to the little streets that hosted cozy houses bordered by exquisite gardens. We passed the plum tree that had fed us the year before last. We'd been so broke that we'd walked hoping to bury the hunger in activity. We'd found this tree filled with plums ripe and warmed by the sun. We'd glutted ourselves upon the fruit, until we returned home, happy, the pain in our gut sated, and finally we had been able to sleep.

Things had never been easy with Daniel. It seemed as if together we could not make one right move. From moving down from San Francisco to Pasadena, to taking jobs that barely paid us a living wage. When we'd first arrived, it'd been hard because we'd had no car and had to walk everywhere we went. We had no credit and paid everything with cash. This past life was a gift because it was trying to tell me something, and I wanted to hear the message before time ran out. I understood that nothing was ever static and that this was here for now, and at some point, would be gone forever.

"I haven't changed my mind," Daniel began to say." I want you to stop talking to this guy."

I walked in silence for a long time. I could feel his eyes bearing down on me. I felt the weight of his hurt.

"If I was talking to a girl like this, what would you do?" he asked me. Though it was a fair question, Daniel's personality would never allow him to enter into that kind of journey. He just would do all he could to avoid this type of soul-searching with a stranger. Trust for him was not something he easily shared while I eagerly leapt into such things like a mad woman throwing herself into a mosh pit. I was impulsive that way, unafraid, and quite often trusting of those I knew I should not trust. Yet this was not about trust, this was about a shared experience, some kind of metaphysical mumbo jumbo that had been brought to me for reasons I needed to understand.

Then I did something that utterly surprised me. I lied.

"Fine, I'll stop talking to him. If that's what's going to make you happy, that's what I'll do, okay?"

I felt a twinge of guilt but not enough to back out of this lie. From now on I would be more careful.

Daniel bent his large body towards me and hugged me tight. His light brown hair fell over his right eye, and caressed his cheekbone. I didn't know what else to do, so I kissed him tenderly on his lips. I had no choice; I had to keep going. I saw Daniel smile with relief, and I felt my heart crush with pain.

The following day, I woke up at six a.m. I didn't even bother making coffee. I logged on and saw that Malek was online. I IM'd that Daniel had found out and was angry with me and told him that he wanted me to stop contacting him.

"Do you want to stop?" he asked.

"No, I can't. I need to know what this is all about. Do you know what I mean?"

For a long while, he didn't answer.

Daniel knocked on the door.

I minimized the screen and brought up my database.

"Yea," I called out.

He walked in and stood behind me, placed his hands on my shoulders and bent down and nuzzled my neck.

"Why are you up so early?"

"I told you, I have much to do in order to make goal."

"I got a couple calls on the Datsun truck. I made two appointments. Maybe I can sell it today. If I do, how about me taking you out to Nativita for dinner?" It was one of my favorite restaurants run by the most colorful couple, the husband was Greek, and the wife Mexican, and they had married the flavors of their foods, Dolmas with tacos, and hummus with salsa. Their dish of grilled prawns and chicken with onions, mushrooms, and artichoke heart made me salivate.

"I'd love that!" I exclaimed with pleasure. "But instead, why don't you deposit a hundred dollars in my account so that check doesn't bounce?"

"If you don't sell the truck, it's okay."

"It's a date. No matter when I sell it, I'm taking you there with some of the money."

He stepped away and stood by the door.

"Coffee?" he asked, winking.

"Ahhh, yes!" I smiled at him. He was about

to leave the door ajar.

"Please, can you close it? I really have to bear down this morning." I hated lying, but he had given me no choice. Wrong or right, I could not stop.

He kissed the air and closed the door softly.

I opened the chat screen. Malek's message was still waiting.

It was long so I sent him a message before reading it.

"I'm sorry; I had to talk to Daniel. I'm back. Give me a moment to read this."

He typed. Don't hurry, take your time. I'll be here for you. I won't leave."

So I scrolled back up to read his words.

"You have been returned to me," he wrote. "Shaking, yet head held high like a queen, like the queen that you were, Bakor. And yet, I could not forgive you. Anger raged within me. I could not embrace you, but possess you I would."

How could he have known, unless he had lived that life? At that moment, I realized that whatever doubts had plagued me, this experience, that life, had been lived, and he had lived it with me.

"After you bathed you stood glowing gold and splendid. I took you and brought you down to the floor, amongst the many carpets that blanketed the large, flat marble slabs. Stacked upon each other, they cushioned your fall as my body followed you down. The slaves fled, and I parted your thighs with my hands and saw his message."

I sat reading his words, and all the air in my lungs escaped. How could he had known, and yet here it was. He knew, as he had known then.

I began to type. "Did you see the look in my eyes that he had conquered me?" And then I erased the question and all I sent was a question mark. It was all I could do.

Malek is typing, the screen said, and I waited.

"Why would you deny it now? Why, when nothing is to gain by lying? There is no shame here, only recall."

I was ashamed, so terribly ashamed that I wanted to curl up on my chair. I then realized I had already done just that, my knees pulled up beneath my chin and my right arm holding them tight against my chest.

Daniel knocked and then opened the door holding my favorite mug in his hand.

"Your coffee, my royal princess."

I minimized the screen. I turned to face Daniel, and it came to me like a lightning bolt that he had been the conqueror.

6

THE CONQUEROR'S MARK

When I returned from the temple, I was told that a bath was being prepared for me.

The Nubian's downcast eyes told me more than words would share, so I allowed myself to be bathed, massaged with oils, and then dressed in linen shot with gold threads. I asked for my children, and yet my request was ignored. I was stunned.

When the moon had reached the pinnacle of the sky, wine and bread was brought and soon after that, Malek came.

His eyes did not meet my imploring gaze. I had found refuge in my terrace, watching the sky move, and the stars shift. I was soothed by perfumes of every beauty, and from the sounds of wild birds and beasts. I'd asked my lyre player to strum as I had bathed, and he had followed me onto the terrace. His voice held such power and love, that I felt tears course down my cheeks. In a matter of moments my whole life had been transformed. I saw the images of walking up the steps, and being taken by this barbarian, of the very desperate chill of pleasure I had felt between my thighs, of my hunger to taste more of him. For this hunger, I had traded what I loved most for an unknown path. Everything I held close to my heart had changed forever. There was nothing left for me to do. I felt alone; I was alone. I felt the shame that I'd taken pleasure in my own conquest. I felt lost.

Malek stood before me. I saw his booted sandals, for I could not raise my head to look into his eyes. He took my hand and raised me to my feet.

"So you are well, my queen?"

"Yes, my beloved," I answered softly, my eyes downcast, my whole body shrunken by shame. All I could see before my eyes was the barbarian's big body, his light brown hair touched by gold, and his spear thrusting within me. I was lost, and hungered for him, like a fevered lust in my blood.

I was ill from want of him. I felt Malek's hand beneath my chin and raised my face to meet his searching gaze.

"You must be proud to have performed your duty so quickly, my love," he added without emotion.

How could I be? I fell to my knees, wrapping my arms around Malek's knees.

"Please, my lord," I begged.

"Come, come." He raised me to my feet and carried me in his arms to our bed. I knew that he would see the man's teeth marks. I hoped that somehow, within the dark night of passion, Malek would not find his message.

His eyes were dark, as they had always been, but behind their blackness raged a storm I had never seen. A wild beast that was unable to voice words but howled the jealous rage of one who's most precious possession has been stolen, for even I knew that I was no longer Malek's.

I felt it in the way he held my body against his. I saw it in the way he took me. Careless, as he had never been before, riding me as if he wanted to break something within me. He was right. My hunger for the man overtook all sense and reason. And yet still Malek rode me, crashing into me like furious waves pounding against rocks, and yet when he had released his frustration between my thighs the ache between my thighs still pounded. I wanted the barbarian's hips against mine, and I needed his strength to fill me as he had done before. Malek was spent, tears flowing from his eyes, and he began to kiss me, as tenderly as if I was a most precious and fragile possession. His lips trailed down my breasts, capturing a nipple, hardened by the memory of the barbarian's mouth upon me. His lips travelled down about my waist, nibbling so deliciously around my stomach that my body arched, and yet still I thought of the other man's mouth upon me.

Again, he was relentless exploring every nook and ravine, sending pulsing surprises of pleasure until his mouth found my mound. Holding my thighs with both hands, he opened me and then his eyes saw the barbarian's message. He sat up abruptly and pushed me away from him as if he had come across a demonic image. Alert to his distress, I sat straight up, and I reached for him. I wanted to bring him within the embrace of my arms. He pushed my hands away. He scurried away from me and stood over our bed. He stared down at me, tears threatening to spill.

"He marked you his whore!" He shook with rage.

"Malek, you knew that this day would come." I realized then that he had no idea the importance and the power this man held over me, over Malek, over our very kingdom. He thought of this man as a threat to my love for him. He had no idea that this man had walked through our gates, taken possession of me, and would soon take our people and our land as hostages. I did not have the way to tell him my heart was breaking, and so I curled up like a newborn left to die in the cold wind, and howled my pain. I shut away the present and hid within the deep ravages of my grief. I saw and heard no one for days.

***

Through the tangles of my hair, I was surprised at the sun rising and breathed in the sharp perfume of jasmine flowers blowing in their petal scent upon the wind. It was already hot and dry. My stomach had been empty for days. I wanted roasted meat and bread I wanted my children, and I wanted Malek. The barbarian's touch seemed more like a dream then a real event.

Somehow, my mind found peace, and no longer troubled itself with the thoughts of being conquered. I thought that all was well in my world. I was so innocent in the ways of men and war. I had never experienced it, never studied it, and hence, knew nothing of it.

I only knew that nothing of any major consequence had happened since my duty to Ishtar had been fulfilled. Not one missive had come to declare war. I was sure of that or else Malek would have moved the gods to wake me from my oblivion, but he had not. So I led myself to believe that all was back as it should be.

My belly cramped for food, and my body

craved a bath, but what I needed more in the entire world was to see Malek's face. I arrived to his rooms and saw him deep in conversation with his head of the guards. Men of high births stood about, and a map had been painted upon the marble floor. Small figures of houses, and of our palace, soldiers, horses, chariots and archers; all miniature replicas had been set about this map. Malek's brow was heavily furrowed, and he moved to speak to another man whose back was to me. When he turned, I realized that Malek was in deep conversation with his astrologer. My heart plummeted to my feet, and I felt the urge to retch.

7

Y2K CONVERSIONS
PASADENA SEPTEMBER 19, 1997

I was listening to Chris Isaac's "Wicked Games." I was doing what I do best, multi-tasking, sending out faxes from my PC while surfing the web and writing a proposal letter. On my end, business was flush with possibilities. The thing is no one had any choice but to launch their conversions, it was a time of do or die. If they didn't have a budget, they had better create one. My job was to offer them the most compelling quote. In the end, a deal was not made on the lowest prices but on trust.

An IT Manager had to know that no matter what happened, he had chosen the best team for the job. It was about not fucking it up, and somehow paying a little more to ensure a successful project was more important than the lowest quote. I banked my approach on that very philosophy every time I approached a new client. So far, I was closing an average three out of every five deals. Not bad, for a girl that had, up until twelve months ago, never owned a computer. Everything I knew had been self-taught in what I can only describe as a crash course. Up until now, I didn't even know what a network was, but I was well versed in the language of that business.

Most of these network engineers were either quiet as mice or brash as pirates. It was a funny world, and because I was a woman in a business dominated by men, I broke their monotonous lives by talking about their wives, their kids, and even flirting a bit, making them laugh. I wanted them to take my calls, and they always did.

So exactly what is the Y2K conversion all about? Well, besides the fact that the very infrastructures of our daily lives are managed with computers, government-led special committees were formed in 1995 to determine the glitch, or the Y2K bug, as it was called. Essentially, unless solutions were found when January 1, 2000 rolled in, whole infrastructures would collapse, unable to roll over to that number and instead would revert to the year 1900. This would cause banks to fail, governments, stock markets, utilities, in other words, whole systems to collapse. The oracles of our day spoke of a real apocalypse that could spin society into pandemonium where chaos would rule. It was simply dealing with a series of numbers that had never been coded to go beyond the 21st century.

So as you can imagine, people were scrambling. It was never a matter of were these companies going to convert, but how soon they would go online with their new system to test it, and to make sure that when that silver ball dropped in Times Square on January 1, 2000 that the numbers would transition from 1999 to 2000 without a hiccup.

Like I said before, there was a strange panic among the masses that was nurtured by the media. People were stocking food, cash, gold, water, and guns. I was knee deep in a world that saw no reason to panic; after all, the conversion would happen, no one had a choice. Having said that, it never occurred to me that it could fail, that parts of the country or the world might fail and collapse. I believed otherwise.

So to say I was immune to what may happen was true, because as far as I knew nothing cataclysmic would happen. All I knew was that Daniel had sold the truck; he'd taken me out to dinner, and that we'd made love.

Daniel had no intention of getting a job. He insisted that the car auctions would get better. Since renting this apartment we had bought a car, a gorgeous little cream-colored 1976, 560i BMW. It was mint, a real gem.

Daniel had taken the last three hundred dollars we had to our name and was at the auction this morning. It was Monday, and I was busy working my ass off when Malek came across my Instant Message. "Good Morning, my Cherie. How are you today, any dreams?"

I closed my eyes, and all that I thought was forgotten flew forward.

It was strange how easy this was becoming, how easy to bring forth all that had been buried for over 3,000 thousand years. It was too easy, and that somewhat scared me. Was I suffering from schizophrenia? Or was this really happening? I was beside myself with doubt, and yet I could not stop the course.

I typed, "Malek, my dear king, my lost love. I've remembered so much with you. Is this fiction? Is this just our minds playing tricks upon us? How can such a thing be real?"

My screen read: Malek is typing. And for a long time I waited. I imagined him writing his answers, and then erasing them, and then pausing, writing again, and then editing. Finally, when time had lost its meaning between two phone calls from a VAR, and then a colleague, his answer was received.

"My lovely Bakor, what you doubt is fear. You do not trust the ease of our shared experience, the ease to which our past lives flow makes you doubt. But how would it help if it stumbled over itself and twisted half-truths and nonsense. You and I would have long parted. The reality of this journey is that it needs to be recalled. I am not sure what the big purpose is; all I know is that once long ago in land and kingdom long forgotten by men we lived, we loved, and we dreamed. We have returned to find each other; we have remembered a glorious life filled with lessons still to be learned. Would you end this now when we are so close to revealing all that is to be revealed? We are on the greatest excavation ever! Let us continue, and taste the sweet fruits of our labor."

I read his answer over and over. I copied and pasted his message to a new Word document. I saved it under a file I had created long ago titled past lives. Only then did I answer him.

"Malek, your sweet words of wisdom soothe my timid soul. I am lost in this vortex of images, sounds, smells, and voices. I remember it all to a fault. It is too perfectly recalled and yet, I cannot stop, will not stop, until the images stop sliding into me with such ease. I agree this is the greatest excavation ever undertaken, an excavation of the soul."

"So tell me, my dearest queen, what did your dream reveal? But first allow me to reveal the images that came to me today and perhaps you can tell me how these shreds tie together."

"Malek, please tell me all that you saw," I replied, leaning forward on my chair. A call came through, and I ignored it, letting it go to voicemail. Outside a flock of wild parrots flew by, laughing and chatting like old friends. The winds were high and moved large white clouds across the deep blue sky. The six sisters, which I called the six tall palm trees, swayed deep as if in curtsy. I had such a view from the four windows that bordered the left side of my office that I always felt lucky to live in this little attic apartment.

The screen blinked: Malek is typing.

I walked barefoot to the kitchen, poured myself a large cup of coffee into a handmade mug Daniel had bought for me at a flea market last year. It was indigo blue and turquoise, with a handle the shape of a Gingko leaf. I turned to my Cadillac fridge and pulled out a small milky white and gold Limoges creamer and poured drops of half and half into my coffee, watching the cream spin mocha color which pleased me. I found myself taking pleasure in the smallest things.

When I returned to my seat, Malek's message had been sent. Alex, our Persian cat was sleeping on my desk. I tried to shoo him away. He blinked at me with large golden eyes, yawned, and turned his back to me curling into a tight ball of cream fur.

I leaned forward to read his message.

"You have slipped away from me, dear Bakor. Fallen into a deep grief from which I could not wake you. So for days, you slept and raged undisturbed. I felt a strange coldness towards you, my love and yet, my heart was breaking for you, for us. I saw no reason for your self -imposed exile. On the third day, the captain of our cavalry came urgently to our palace.

Legions were fast approaching; we'd have little time to prepare. No message had been sent, no declaration of war. When I consulted with our astrologer, he confirmed that according to the alignment of the planets, war was fated upon our doorstep and that we should prepare. The next thing I remember is that I am in a large room with men talking. A mock-up of our kingdom had been set up. I am confident that we will beat these barbarians back; I know it. Then, I look up, and I see you standing there pale as moonlight, your large eyes bright with tears. At that moment, I recall the crone's oracle, and my heart sinks to my stomach. I watch you bend your body like the supple willow tree caught by a rough wind. You are vomiting bile. I rush towards your side, but you have fallen into the black clouds of grief."

My past life memory had not been shared with him. I'd recalled all of it yesterday and had not had the time to do so. I sat shaking. I was hesitant to type. And then, I responded to his message by filling all that had been unsaid by him, placing the missing puzzle pieces so that he could see the whole picture before we moved forward. I was an explorer cutting the tangled web of our lives with a machete

8

THE ORACLE'S PROPHECY
3,500 B.C.E.

I must have left the land of sun and skies, the land of my people. I was supine upon my long chaise which was outside on my terrace overlooking the many terraced levels of my gardens. Beyond that, were the mountains that overlooked our valley, the sun was crossing the sky, signaling a late day. I called out and my Nubian appeared.

"Bring me wine, water, bread, figs," he called to a slave and repeated the order. His arms crossed over his ebony chest. He did not move, nor did he look my way. He was stoic, solid, like a statue from Egypt.

I buried my face in my hands in despair. I wish I had never woken from the world of lyre and light. I was doomed to live the oracle's prophecy and see the grief unravel. The course had been set; war was upon us. I thought of the conqueror and wondered why he had bothered to pay for the privilege to bed me when his right would be ensured when he took the kingdom.

What had been the reason? I trembled at the idea of his flesh upon mine, and not even the doom of my kingdom could make my desire disappear.

The food was brought to me swiftly; a roasted bird stuffed with dates had been added to my request. I was grateful, and tore a leg, devouring it like a starving wolf. The wine was poured in a large hammered goblet and water was added to it. I drank and drank, and then ate three figs. I sat back, the goblet of water and wine in my hand, sipping slowly trying to find a calm place in my mind in order to think things through. I found no refuge. I stood up.

"Bring my hunting garb, my boots, my bow and have my horse ready!" I ordered.

"The king forbids you to leave the palace," the Nubian said.

"Then bring me to my king, for I have much to discuss with him." He knew better than to refuse me. "And have my ladies bring me all that I need in order to prepare".

Within no time, I was readied and was astride my gray mare. I was riding fast to where the Nubian had explained was the location of Malek's campsite. My Nubian was running paces behind me. When I came to the encampment, which was an hour from the palace, I leapt off the mare and ran my kidskin boots silent on the soft earth.

I rushed to the tent where Malek was in deep conversation with his consul. His face was pale and strained. Malek was with his general and two of his most trusted captains.

He looked like sleep had evaded him for days. He glanced up and his eyes brightened and then hardened.

"Why are you here?" His voice was hoarse and heavy. "We have no need of a woman now."

The Nubian, upon hearing Malek's words, grabbed my arm to pull me back, but I threw his hand off.

"How dare you touch me, you impertinent beast!" I stepped forward managing to bring forth my ancestors who had lived for thousands of years. Long dead, long forgotten people whose blood coursed within me, I saw the black wings of Isis surround my body with her strength.

"And you, my king, how dare you speak to me as if I am nothing more than a woman. I am a descendant of Isis. My grandmother was a princess of the greatest kings the world has ever seen. My blood runs thick with the fire of great Egyptian Pharaohs. I am a warrior! I am an equal to you, and not just a woman. How dare you address me in such a manner? " My eyes narrowed as I spoke, locking eyes with every man that stood in that tent, and then I leveled my gaze to Malek. "I am your queen set forth to rule the kingdom with equal power as my king. To forget this is to forget your place in the world."

I stepped forth. Malek's eyes softened and he told me that a missive had been sent to Egypt for more soldiers. As I had said before, I had never studied war; however I had studied diplomacy, and I understood the machination of courts and of men. In that, I was confident. "Now show me your plans. We must win more than a battle, for that will not save this war. Let us do all we can to avoid bloodshed and see if we cannot bring about a peaceful agreement."

I prayed that my brother would have some kind of influence over the pharaoh, but I doubted any help for months to come, and by then it would be too late for us all.

The general spoke to me of a battle that would be launched at first light. No emissary had been sent, which surprised me.

"Send one immediately," I demanded. "Find out what these people want." I was sure we could negotiate terms, something that would send them on their way.

A young lad of fifteen who was a grandson of the general was sent. In response we received his hand in a basket holding a clay tablet that said that the king of their land wanted to talk to the queen of ours.

I was stunned. Malek was beside himself, and outright refused. But I knew that if we did not do as we were bid, blood of such magnitude would be shed, that all of worth would be lost.

***

The sun set, the moon was absent in the sky. I waited for Malek to fall asleep before I snuck out of our tent. I'd sent my Nubian to the palace to guard our children knowing that with him out of the way, I could do as planned. By torchlight I walked amongst the men, and settled upon the face of a greedy soldier playing dice with three others. I called him to me. He seemed surprised, but got up and approached. He was easy to bribe for he had lost heavily. On foot, he guided my mare to the barbarian's encampment. As soon as we saw their fires, he ran, leaving me to make my own way. The moment I approached their tents and stepped within the light of their bonfire, my horse was surrounded by men as tall as the cedars. I was frightened by their vicious smiles and rough caresses upon my thighs. The conqueror strode out of a tent of red hue. He was as I remembered him. My cloak had fallen aside, revealing the thin tissue-fine tunic of my sheath. My nipples stiffened to hard points caused by my fear and the sharp wind that blew the warm air about the camp. My hair flew about me. He approached my horse, barking orders to his men, who fell away like children beaten back by the whip of his voice. He grabbed my waist and dragged me off the horse. He held me against his chest staring into my eyes for what seemed like a full sunset. He grunted an oath, and he carried me thus to his tent. No word more was said to his men, nor me. He deposited me upon a carpet strewn with pillows and more woven rugs. He pulled my cape away and tore the thin tissue fabric until it fell about me like shreds. My breath caught in my throat. He did nothing but graze my body with the tip of his index finger, gently touching me with his eyes and then his mouth. I pushed away, beating at his chest, and he sat back. His large gray eyes staring down at me, smiling with arrogance I found hard to digest. I glared up at him, and gathered my cloak about me. "I am here to talk terms," I announced.

He nodded his head.

"What do you want from us? What can we negotiate with you so that you will leave us in peace?" I asked.

He pushed my cloak aside with a rough hand, large, long-fingered and covered with golden hair. He cupped a breast and then stared deep into my eyes, his lips inches from mine. "All that I want, I can take. I want you, and I want your kingdom."

I shivered beneath his gaze. I turned my head away, but he grabbed my chin and forced me to face him, burying the lust of his mouth upon my lips. I felt my belly leap with a flame I had never felt for Malek and that wounded me. "Please..." I whispered within his mouth, "Please, let me go and..." His tongue ravaged my mouth and I was lost in his arms, afraid that I would fall into the dark pit of his magic.

He nibbled my neck and kissed my shoulders, trailing his lips upon my skin like hot brands; I was writhing beneath his touch and had forgotten my purpose. I felt him turn me upon my belly and part my thighs with his knee entering from behind. His hand was on my neck and his other hand on my mound touching that pearl that Malek always loved to tease with his mouth. This barbarian had it between his thumb and forefinger rubbing it fast between the hard calluses of his fingertips, and I felt myself shake again and again, all sense of duty, loyalty, love, and honor lost for the touch of this man. I felt unashamed and became a she-devil beneath his touch. He threw me upon my back and rode me hard and fast, bringing my thighs around his waist, holding one leg in his arm as he thrust fast and hard. Licking and nibbling my neck, his root rubbing my pearl, until I exploded into him, moaning hard, sweat meshing our flesh sliding into each other, crying for him to stop and begging him to go faster. I felt the pinnacle of a wave catching me upon its back, rushing me to the hot shores of deliverance. I felt my body release a wave of water, running moist between my thighs and fusing his entire body to mine.

He cried out, his eyes locked with mine, softening, widening, turning a pale gray of such purity that I was amazed by their paleness. I saw his face fall apart, vulnerable, as his seed spilled within me. He looked away and breathed deep and hard against my neck. I held him in my arms, caressing his head, and then I remembered the youth's hand that had been sent to us in a basket just that morning.

9

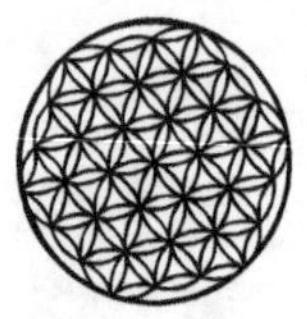

THE SILENCE
SEPTEMBER 26, 1997

For five days, I'd stopped talking to Malek. One good reason was that Daniel had found my saved IM messages from Malek, which I would often revisit whenever a new memory blasted through. As you can imagine, the scene between Daniel and me was an explosion of rage, accusations, name-calling, and all around hell, and it lasted for hours. I had been able to sneak a message to Malek letting him know that I would have to lay low for a few days. In the interim, I had created a new email, Bakor, from which he and I could chat undisturbed and from which I could save my messages on cyber space.

Finally, Daniel's sulking had come to an end. He asked me if I wanted to walk to Cliff's Bookstore, which sold used books and stayed open till midnight. It was around nine o'clock at night, and the air was cool.

It would be a long walk from Marengo and Fillmore to Colorado Boulevard and Madison, but I was looking forward to it. Again, the rent had been paid, bills paid, and we were broke. Daniel had bought a 1965 blue BMW from the last auction. It was a cute car, but when would he sell it? I was hitting my bonus which is the only reason why we had a hundred dollars to carry us over till I got paid the following week. I hate it when people say that money doesn't make you happy.

Money has always been a tool that provides the person the freedom to experience greater things. I have been blessed with both states and know what it offers. It cannot offer the intangibles of love or peace; however, when money is present it can offer clean water, food, and medicine. Anyone who says there is no need for it fails to understand the machine we live in. As for the avatars, we know all that they needed was provided to them by those with money. I do not understand the fear we hold onto that says that money is the root of all evil when in truth it is only men and their egos that make that saying true. I rant and rave like a nut! Let's face it, money means nothing if the ones you love most are ill and nothing can help them get well. Just as money is everything when there is no food to feed the ones you love.

I was tired of thinking about bills and money; it made my head hurt. So I shook myself out of my mood and followed Daniel to what we called the "little streets," the residential neighborhoods that hid the most beautiful bungalows and Craftsmans. We walked until we reached the yellow house with the large sunflowers. The streets were not well lit, and we liked that.

"So tell me about mumkin," Daniel mumbled.

I didn't dare correct him. "What do you want to know?"

Daniel stopped dead on his tracks and faced me. "Everything!"

His green eyes bore down on me, and I matched his stare without blinking.

I turned and walked ahead of him. He reached for my arm and pulled me to his chest. I breathed in his scent and leaned into his warmth, feeling safe and forgiven.

He held me like this for a long while, and it felt like all was right with him thus. It was both strange and wonderful. At last we reluctantly broke away, and began to walk. As we strolled, I told him everything, even about the day I met the conqueror at the Temple of Ishtar. He never interrupted me, but nodded his head for me to go on, and so I did, telling him about the war. But I did not share my last recall of going to the barbarian's camp and having sex with him because even now I was ashamed of it.

By the time I was done, we stood in front

of Cliff's and entered. One aisle smelled like someone had been using a corner as a urinal for months. Still, the arrays of books were too good to allow that scent to send me on my way. I seemed to hover over the poetry and philosophy section which is where I was headed while Daniel went to the classic cars and flying section, which was a step up and two aisles away.

I found an exquisite copy of Kahlil Gibran's The Prophet printed in 1966. It was the Alfred Knopf edition complete with his drawings. I held onto it hoping that they would hold it for me. After some time, Daniel and I met in the middle. He carried a book about ancient Mesopotamia, a huge tome with pictures of excavations, of statues of lion bodies with wings, and the heads of men, and of angels, images of the Goddess Ishtar, and the gates to Babylon. Everything I saw in the book, I had seen in my visions. But truth be told, there was much more that was not in this book; not one accurate image of my palace as it had been was in that book. The gardens famed for thousands of years were reproduced by various artists who had conceived ideas of what it must have looked like from what they had read from the classics written by the ancient historians. Together, we pored over the book, saw the price tag of forty five dollars, and wished to own it.

"We can't afford this at all," I said.

"We'll figure something out. I want you to have it." Daniel answered. He bent his head and a lock of hair fell over his green eyes; I pushed it back and placed both my hands around his face, searching his eyes.

"I don't need it; put it back and let's go." I kissed his forehead so tenderly that he closed his eyes to receive it.

He stood his full height and returned the book to where it came from. I asked the guy behind the counter if he might hold my copy of The Prophet until next week. He smelled of too many cigarettes and cheap after-shave. But he was kind, and had me fill out my information on a Post It note.

When we left, it was past eleven thirty, and the sky's dark color seemed to give off a velvet quality to the night. Stars blinked and shimmered and the thought came to me, that in that past life, I may have stared at the same stars as I did now. Somehow, that idea soothed and calmed my troubled mind. We held hands as we walked. We spoke of little things, of a book he'd seen about the Mitchell Hedges skull that he'd really wanted to get. That book spoke about a Crystal Skull that had been found in British Honduras in the mid 1920's. The skull dated back 4,500 years. It was the perfect shape and size of a woman in her twenties. It had a lower jaw that was separate from the upper skull.

It was being cared for by Anna Mitchell-Hedges, the adopted daughter of F.A. Mitchell. She had found the top of the skull and months later, the bottom half was excavated. Psychics from all over the world came to visit her in Canada in order to work with the skull. They claimed that it dated back to Atlantis, and that when you meditated upon it you could see holograms and images bounce off its surface, or that it drew you within its depth, depending on who was working with it, the messages it shared may be similar or entirely different. Daniel paused walking with his head down, in deep thought and far away from me.

"It sounds like such an amazing book; how did you find time to read this much information?" I mused out loud.

I dug my hands deep in my jeans, raising my scarf around my head, trying to protect myself from the chill. He shrugged his shoulders. We matched each other's pace so effortlessly; we walked as one.

"Why didn't you put it aside with my book?" I asked him.

"No, need," Daniel announced pulling it out of his jacket pocket.

"Daniel!" I cried out," That is not cool,

and what if you had been caught?" I scolded him, seriously worried and angered by this surprising news.

"Nope, not me. Not ever!" He threw me a devilish grin and was so carefree that I found myself smiling up at him.

"Besides," he added, "I couldn't wait!"

10

THE BARBARIAN'S PLAY THING

For two days, I lay with the barbarian, and from all I could tell, not one message was sent to Malek. I begged him to send a sign that I was well and unharmed, but he laughed harshly.

"Why trouble yourself with such a small man as he? Now that you have tasted the pleasures of a lion, why return to such as him?"

I was ashamed, for his words rang true. I had never been with a lion until now. I felt the need to feel his force within me, even now in spite of my shame. Still, I loved Malek.

When we had been newborns, we had been fated to be king and queen. I had been raised with him in order to create the bond I felt so strongly now. I was bound to him in ways I could not explain nor wanted to. He was my brother, my love, the father of my beloved children, my world. Yet, this man, this barbarian had become my sun, my very source of life. I was stunned by the thunderstorm of thoughts that crowded my head. Only his touch drowned my pain and my doubts. When he was away from me, my head spun with pain and howled for peace. It was thus the conqueror found me, twisted into a ball, buried into the black bear fur that lay on top of the rugs, my head upon my curled arm. I was sobbing.

His slave stood behind him, a tall, slim lad with a long red hair and deep blue eyes. He took his lord's sword and placed it against the wall of the tent. He left and quickly came back with a bowl of water which he held aloft so that the conqueror splashed it on his face, his blood spattered chest, and then cleaned his hands over and over. The boy dragged a linen piece from the bag of his thick leather belt that kept his loin cloth up and handed it to him. The conqueror looked at me, his eyes searching my face, whilst wiping the water and traces of blood from his face and chest.

He barked an order, and the lad fled.

He stood right above me and pushed me with his booted sandal.

"Rise from this darkness and stand with me in the light," he ordered.

I sat on my hands and knees for a minute feeling a whirlwind within my head. I shook it away and very deliberately rose to face him, my chin tipped back as far as it could to lock gold eyes with gray.

He drew me into his chest, and I found

myself closing my eyes. Breathing in the sweat of his scent, the earth, and blood of our people, I could not find haven in his arms. I pushed away.

"I am not one of your play things, a whore for your pleasure!" I screamed.

He stepped back, a twisted smile playing upon his lips.

"You are what I say you are." He brought his big arms across his chest and stood still, and silent, like a statue, his eyes devoid of warmth.

I rushed at him enraged beyond words, howling like a she-wolf, my teeth bared. I jumped against his body and fell back to the floor, my attack impotent to his wall of power. He laughed, shaking his head and clapped his hands. The lad appeared bearing a hammered bronze tray with a clay pot filled with wine, clay goblets, and a platter of roasted meat and flat breads.

The conqueror sat amongst the large pillows that faced our bed. I realized that I still did not know his name. I was shamed and needed to find a way to get back to Malek. I also needed to find out what had happened on the battlefield this morning. So I got up and sat opposite him. His eyes warmed over my body, and I felt a shiver ride my skin to the tips of my toes.

He handed me the roasted leg of a fowl and

poured me a cup of wine. I ate in silence for a long while staring into his eyes, as he stared back. I found his eyes grazing my mouth as I ate and his eyes locking with mine as I drank. I felt the heat rise in his eyes as our meal progressed. For a long while we sat thus, a hunger building between us that rose like a flame that hovered over the platter of meats.

"Enough!" he abruptly stood up and grabbed my arm and slammed me against his chest. He was staring down at my eyes, my mouth. Then his mouth fell upon my lips like rain. I tasted the strong, young wine of our people upon his breath. I felt ravaged. I was sure I would disappear beneath his desire. I was afraid, and yet at that moment, I was willing to have every single piece of my being melt beneath him. I could feel his intent to tame something inside of me, which made him feel soft. We were both whirling within the magic of what it was to be in each other's arms. I knew it. He knew it, and I wanted him to stop.

"Your name, my lord! What is your name?" I managed to whisper breathless.

He did as I wished and stopped suddenly. He pushed back and looked at me for a long time, his member hard and straining against his loin cloth.

"I am Kryu," he answered like a young lad.

I moved towards him, and kneeled before him. I untied the wide belt and un-wrapped him from the loin cloth, which slipped away to the floor. He was looking down at me, searching my face for answers. I held the strength of his member in my hands, and placed my mouth upon the tip of his flesh. I felt his whole body shiver. I swallowed him whole, left hand upon the root of him, whilst my right moved up and down in rhythm with my mouth. I licked the tip of him, nibbling so delicately on it that he groaned like a wounded lion.

I wanted him to trust me. I needed him to forget that he was obviously winning the war, and to tell me all that was going on. I needed him to let me go, and I could only accomplish this if he trusted me and desired me above all women. If I had been more clear about my real desires, I would say that I needed him to love me. Kryu, I thought to myself, such a name for such a demi god. I adored his heat, the velvet length of him, the perfection of silken sack. The scent of his manhood was unlike Malek's and yet I breathed him in, as I would the jasmine scent caught off the winds. I tasted his seed, spilling slightly, and still I pleasured him, faster and faster until he howled his release into my open and willing mouth.

He collapsed to his knees, like a bull whose

throat had been cut. He was shaking, his eyes closed, his member falling innocent and spent between his muscular thighs. He raised his eyes searching mine with the look of a man who had lost something and found something more precious. He looked at me with a tenderness I saw fleeting behind the gray sentinel of his eyes. I saw something rise like the sun. For the first time I saw his smile, innocent, like a child's. I felt my heart swell and tears come to my eyes.

"Come," he said, and we made our way to the bear rug, and fell upon it with arms and legs linked as one. I watched him fall asleep. In that moment, I knew that no woman had ever brought him such pleasure, that what I had given him had been foreign to him, until now. I knew that if I was careful, I could be the one to conquer him. Not since the night before the temple of Ishtar had I felt this strong and this aware of everything. I fell asleep, with peace a dream in my heart.

I awoke before the dawn and felt Kryu's big body curved against mine. His large arm across my hip, he was sleeping facing me, as he had not done before. Previous to the magic I brought with my lips, his back had always faced me. I moved his arm away, and tried to comb my long hair with my fingers. Plaiting it to a side braid, I had only the cape I had arrived in, for the tunic had been torn that first night. I sat on the bear rug watching him sleep. He awoke with a start and sat straight up and the memories flooded him like petals falling about his head and shoulders. He looked at me and shot me that childish smile. So strange, I thought, to own a man of such magnitude with such ease. I lowered my eyes, unable to smile, trembling for a way to speak and gather the words to ask him about the battle, about my kingdom, about those I loved.

He clapped his hands together and the sound was loud and high pitched. The lad appeared.

"A large container of water." The lad nodded. "And bring me wine and meat." Again the lad nodded. "Find something for the lady to wear." The lad looked puzzled. "Find something from the captains' whores. You are sure to find something there." I shot him a look of hate. He caught it, smiled, and shrugged.

"Go!" The lad ran out of the tent.

I sat furious with him. He looked at me puzzled.

"What? Anger? After your magic?" He leaned forward and touched my cheek trailing his finger tip down my neck and hovered between my breasts.

"You would have me wear a whore's

discards!"

He stood up, magnificent, a golden being, and walked to gather his loin cloth and his leather belt.

He stood before me unashamed of his nakedness and began to dress all the while he considered me with thoughtful eyes.

"Ah, the ways of woman." He shook his head.

"How could you have me wear such refuse?" I continued, my voice tight with indignation.

"Would I have you walk naked to show my men what I have enjoyed in secret? I would have them battle me to gain one taste of you. Better you wear the discard of a whore, than bed my entire army," he laughed.

"Then bring me the garments of a boy," I pleaded.

He called for the lad, and told him to do as such. A boy's garment was easier to procure and within little time, he re-appeared with a loin cloth, a long tunic, and a leather belt, simple sandals that were just a little too large, and a cape of a rough brown linen which were deposited upon the floor before my feet. The lad bowed and rushed away.

"Is this what you would prefer?" he asked, one eyebrow raised in question. I stared up at him, noticing that his eyebrows were shot with golden light. I looked away.

"Yes, yes." I gazed down at the pile and cocked my head towards him. I gave him my most enchanting smile. I saw his eyes widen, for my teeth were even and white. Rare was a woman of any rank blessed with such teeth. Most may have beauty to rival my own but few had all of their teeth. So whenever I wanted to capture full attention, I would use my smile with powerful results.

I was grateful and planned to quickly dress with my back to him. I was not going to ask him for help as I struggled with the loin cloth, the material falling out of my hands. He came around to face me and tenderly, for how else can one explain his care and patience, he dressed me. His eyes caressing every limb, leaning towards my neck as he settled the belt around me. His breath hot on my ear, his lips inches from my flesh.

When I was dressed, he stepped back and looked at me.

"There is just one thing amiss," he said.

I was puzzled and looked down at myself. I was bewildered for I even had the cape on. I could not wonder what was lacking. He disappeared into a large room that I had never explored. It was the room where he met with his generals and captains. He returned with a small blade of such magnificent work that I gasped. Upon its sword handle were many fine stones which shimmered with light. He thrust it between my belt and loin cloth. He stepped back and admired me.

"Now you are like the Amazons I once fought."

I shook my head in questions.

"Amazons?" I had never heard of such a word.

"Female warriors, taller and much larger than you...Fierce..." His voice did not continue, lost in a memory I could not follow. But the idea did not flee from my mind. Female warriors, I wondered. So it was possible? With that understanding something inside of me shifted, like the sun that catches the moon's impertinence to rise in late day, rather than waiting for the night.

11

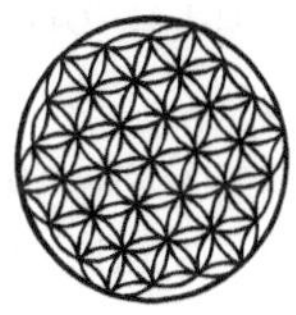

THE CRYSTAL SKULL
SEPTEMBER 28, 1997

I seriously loved Sundays. There was something about doing nothing, but believe me, there is an art to that. Most people can't stop moving, but I learned long ago the benefits of a languorous day.

I wanted to have brunch at Burger Continental, a Middle Eastern restaurant that served sausages sautéed with onions and bell pepper, chicken and lamb shish kabob, scrambled eggs, home fries, Dolmas, pita bread, hummus, Baklava, and Cook's champagne an all-you-can-eat buffet for thirteen dollars a person. It was worth every penny.

We decided to walk. It was around ten thirty in the morning. The sky was overcast, a slight chill colored the air, a perfect day to just putter around the house after a good meal.

When we arrived, we were greeted by a big bear of a man who carried a perpetual look of confusion. However, he was kind and polite and seated us. The waitress came to our table to ascertain if we wanted to order from the menu or go all out. We cut loose. After she poured champagne in the little plastic champagne glasses with bottoms that screw on, I realized they could topple over and spill champagne at any moment if either of us made any sudden moves. So I asked our waitress to bring us water glasses, so we could pour the contents of our champagne into these more secure vessels. I poured with a smile and asked her to leave the champagne bottle on the table, and charmed her by appealing to her sense of 'what's in it for me?' unsaid question. I explained to her that it would save her a trip since we planned to get toasted, and she laughed. I winked a promise of a good tip, and that guaranteed her fawning over us for the rest of the meal, making sure that we never ran out of that cheap champagne or of anything else we might need.

The coffee was the only bad thing in the place, but then again, I was a coffee snob. Daniel was more easygoing about everything. I was the one who always made special demands and quite often got them granted. We ate with an abandon that comes with camaraderie. We enjoyed the tastes of a country we hoped we would one day visit, any country. We always played this game that we were sitting in a courtyard in Greece, that we were fifty years old and retired. This was so easy to do for we sat in the inner courtyard of the restaurant, olive trees in large pots added to the ambience, as sparrows stole crumbs. The floor was cobblestone and the music was Greek. How could we not travel to that land sitting at this little table, that kept swaying back in forth? The waitress came with folded paper and placed it under one of the legs, stabilizing our meal.

We talked of small things, of the book Daniel was reading about the skull, that he had read in two days and was now rereading it. He was fascinated by the idea that the skull's purpose was to protect the world, that there were six other skulls whose purpose was similar, and that there were two missing.

"There is a story that says that it was created in Atlantis. A priestess of some power had been beheaded by a warring faction in Atlantis. This was the time of flying machines, of high technology, of human engineering. It was a time when scientists played with nature and brought about centaurs, mermaids and Cyclops. There was a rebel force that fought against the arrogance of the elite. They refused to listen to reason and so a war erupted." He stopped and took a gulp of his coffee. His face was animated, his eyes flashing green and gold with the passion that poured forth.

"And then?" I leaned forward, elbows to

table, well aware that my French mother would have frowned at such poor table manners for a well-bred person never placed their elbow on the table while eating; it was considered uncouth. I felt that my best moments were when I was uncouth because it was then that I was real.

Daniel gathered his thoughts and began to lay down all the things that struck him most.

"Well, Jesus! There's so much!" he exclaimed.

"Okay," he continued. "Apparently the priestess was heading the rebellion. She was captured and her head was sent back as a message for them to back off." He paused, drinking champagne from the water glass, and grabbed a sausage with his hand, eating in that casual way that would have driven my mother crazy. Only barbarians ate with their hands, she often said. Ah, yes, and Daniel was mine.

I stared at the sensuous curve of his mouth. I adored the dark lashes that rimmed his green eyes and found my belly leap in response to his heady magnetism. He was so freaking sexy that I often saw women stare up at him forgetting themselves, lost in a dream of their own making. The fact that I stood right next to him had no bearing on their desire. That made me furious; he never flirted back, well at least, not in front of me. He had the good sense to know better.

He caught my look, one he knew so well. He threw me a devilish grin and winked.

"Go on." I stared at him coldly, hiding the promises I had made myself to rip him to pieces when we got back home. I wanted to taste the salt of his chest and the sweat between his balls. Yea, later, much later, I was a patient pussycat when I wanted to be. I was biting into the drizzled honey sweetness of a baklava, enjoying the contrast of sweet and the salt of the sausage I tasted.

"Go on," I repeated mouth full. God, my mother would have shuddered.

"Where was I?" he asked, knowing damn well.

"They received her head."

"Ah, yes, so when they received her head, they stripped it clean of flesh. Ceremonies were performed with all the priests and priestesses, and they did some kind of ritual, where they transformed the skull of her head into the quartz crystal skull that we have today."

"Are you kidding?"

He shook his head.

"How do they know all that?"

"Well, psychics from all over the world have worked with the skull in deep meditations, and what they saw they wrote but never shared the information with each other until enough had been gathered. A team was organized and they pored over each report, and each one told a similar story."

I felt a chill run down my body and visibly shivered.

He nodded his head, "Pretty heavy, eh?"

"Holy fuck!" I swore, swinging down a glass of champagne and pouring another. I nibbled on my dolma as he continued.

"Many other skulls were created, and when placed together, they manifest a power that can create or destroy. In this case, her presence is the reason why the world has not annihilated itself. She is a guardian, but that's just my opinion; it's what I feel when I read about her."

"You know what fascinates me most?" I said.

"What?"

"That we are so bogged down by bills and the minutia of daily life that most of us, the masses, barely have any time to ponder the ancient gifts and understand how they still impact us today. There is so much to learn and yet we are pushed to the edge of reason with work and lose our real sense of purpose in the world. Surviving is just not enough!"

"Yea!" he said combing his fingers through his hair. It had gotten long, and grazed the nape of his neck and now it always fell over his eyes.

"You need a haircut," I remarked.

"I need a blowjob," he responded.

"You first!" I challenged.

"That can be arranged." he laughed. It was amazing what money in the pocket, a good meal, some bad champagne, insipid coffee, and great conversation could accomplish. I wanted him without reservation or resentment.

We walked home, and to say we were drunk was an understatement. We were schnokered, ripped, and completely spent, so the walk was long and filled with giggles, while we jostled each other. I told him we should hurry as a soft rain had begun, but he disagreed and said that it was a heavy fog.

"This is not San Francisco," I retorted.

"Trust me, it's just a fog," he countered.

We made it home in one piece. I crawled up the stairs on all fours, bellowing with laughter. Daniel was having a hard time finding the lock and was having a harder time finding the right key.

He knelt before the threshold of our apartment door and stared straight into the lock. He craned his neck and asked, "Did you, by any slim chance bring your key?"

I laughed my answer.

He groaned his disappointment.

"Give me your keys." I extended my hand in front of his face.

He dropped the keys into the palm of my hand with a sigh. I narrowed my eyes and stared down at them.

I picked one that felt familiar and within seconds we were inside.

Daniel set up the futon to lie flat, and we both fell onto it and crashed for hours. When we awoke, it was around four in the afternoon. The sky was dark gray, the winds had picked up speed, and rain fell like a solid wall of water that blew sideways.

I opened all the windows, which totaled six, and blasted the heat. Drops of rain threw themselves against our windows and still we kept them wide open.

Our cable had long ago been cut off, so TV was not really an option, since we both hated the commercials, and PBS was just not cutting it lately.

"Are you in the mood for an audio book?" I asked. "It's erotic," I added to entice him.

He shrugged with a smile. I put on the cassettes of "Lady Chatterley's Lover" read by Dame Judi Dench.

We lay side-by-side on the bright pink futon and drifted into the story of forbidden passions, love, and loss. It was so beautiful. Daniel was as mesmerized as I was, and we listened to every cassette.

When we were done, we put on a record to repeat, the "Best of Billy Holiday."

We turned to each other and slowly stripped every garment we wore. I wanted to taste his cock; I wanted it to pulse in my mouth, but he had other plans and grabbed me and threw me on my back. Straddling me, he grabbed my large breasts in each hand and devoured my large aureoles, sucking on my nipples until I arched my back from the pleasure it sent my body. We fucked and made love like mad lions. Rolling and growling at each other, we were insatiable, and for a long time, we savored every pleasure that slid out of our lips, tongues, hands, and lost ourselves in a soft haze of pleasure. He grabbed my legs, placing them roughly over his broad shoulders and his long, beautiful cock was unmerciful as it hit my G-spot over and over again.

"Stop!" I begged," I don't want to scream."

The inner light of his eyes grew bright with fire. "Scream!" he growled.

"No, no, no." I was shaking my head, biting my lip whenever he swung deep into me, tickling that soft spot, that pearl hidden deep within. I was sweating, shaking, and I found myself groaning deep, muffling the sound with my hand, biting into the palm to stifle my screams. My belly contracted with pleasure, as waves upon waves crashed into me, and yet he would not stop.

"Come with me!" I begged again.

He didn't answer but moaned low, a sound that rose from deep within his throat. He moved faster and shouted my name, his cum spilling into me, overflowing. He then buried his head between my neck and shoulder. His broad back was slick with sweat. We fell asleep in each other's arms and slept for hours.

Suddenly, we leapt out of our bodies and traveled to places that offered us such colored dreams that we awoke in the middle of the early morning to share our journey before falling into each other, feeding on each other's flesh until satiated, and then we slept.

It was the most beautiful Sunday I had ever spent with him. Later that morning, I woke realizing that Monday was upon me. I didn't hesitate and called in sick. We stayed in bed and savored each other until we were too sore and tired to do any more... It turned out to be the best Monday I had ever had.

12

THE MOON TAKES THE SUN

The night glimmered with stars and a crescent moon. Kryu was in a deep sleep, for I had given him the gift of my mouth to his member. He had drunk clay jugs of wine, so I knew that hours would pass before he awoke. I managed to dress myself in the lad's garments; loincloth, tunic, leather belt, sandals, cape, and the short staff Kryu had gifted me. I crawled out into the night. I had no plans, but hoped that I would find my mare that would bring me home without guidance in the dark of night. My heart squeezed with pain as I made my escape, yet he had given me no choice. Whenever I had asked news of the battles, of my people, he ignored me. I had to find them and secure my children's safety by any means, which included sending them to Egypt, to my brothers, where they would be safe from harm.

I covered my head with the hood and crawled past the many tents and fires, spiriting myself to the encampment of horses that stood not far from the circle of tents. I could not see and called out my mare's name. I heard her neigh; I crawled toward the trees where a round fence had been built to contain the horses. She must have caught my scent for she approached me, walking with her slow careful gait, and lowered her head. I swung upon her back. I had to take that fence in one jump or else I would die. I realized my foolishness but then understood that again, I had no choice. The gods had blessed me for we had ample room to canter and jump. She took the fence liked a winged horse and landed without a sound of any consequence upon the soft soil.

I patted her neck and leaned my face against the side of her arched neck. We rode hard and fast as she jumped over small ravines and small streams that surprised me with their presence, and still she cantered until we stood before the tall gates of our city. It was shut to any outside world, so I had to call up to the guards that stood sentinel.

They laughed at my claims of being their queen, even when I drew my cloak away from my face.

"You, Queen?" One guard taunted.

Another guffawed," You are but a dirty little peasant!"

How stupid they were. They did not even recognize my mount. I pulled aside my cloak, and with both hands tore my tunic to my waist. My bare breasts pointed to the sky.

"I am Queen Bakor!" I shouted to the winds. I will never understand why, but the large doors opened, and I was allowed in. I entered and continued past the exterior of the palace and came to the second portal guarded by the pair of stalking lions.

"The queen! The queen! Queen Bakor is amongst us!" The shouts of soldiers, and courtiers brought my Malek to greet me, the children at his heels. He could not contain his joy and though in front of his subjects, he allowed tears of joy and relief to wet his gaunt face.

I slid off my mare, and my most beloveds rushed me within a circle of their love. We stood clinging thus for a long time. I was surprised for my children would not let me move without moving, their tight little fists gripping my arms and my waist. They would not let go, so we moved together, up the stairs, and to my rooms.

We fell together upon our large bed and clung to each other until I fell into a deep sleep that lasted two sunrises.

When I awoke, Malek was lying next to me, his head in his hand. I saw that he had not eaten well in days. His cheeks were sunken deep and his eyes looked like dark pools of sorrow.

"You are returned me to, my sweet Bakor,"

he said, managing to smile. I rubbed the sleep dust out of my eyes and rose. I was nude. Ama must have removed my clothing while I slept.

"I would like a ..."

"Bath," he said, finishing my sentence and wearing a wide smile that softened the lines that had appeared overnight and suddenly creased his pale face.

"Yes," I sighed.

The calm of his gaze hovered above my eyes and trailed a journey which I followed to the bath I so desired. It had been poured. I jumped out of the bed and ran to the bronze creation, my nose wrinkling in disgust at my own stench. I stepped one leg in and felt my body melt in response. Once my body was immersed in water, I allowed my head to lie back against the wide lip of the tub and felt my whole being's breath exhale. A large bronze tray was brought to our rooms with a large jug of water and wine, an array of roasted meats, flat bread, figs, and green melons. My mouth was famished to taste and for a moment my hunger confused my choice, but chose, I did. I settled on the large leg of a fowl and ate with great pleasure whilst I savored the sweet flavors of figs and melon. When I was done, Malek poured a goblet of water and wine which I drank down fast. He refilled my goblet, and again it was gone in the time a hummingbird alights from a flower to the sky. He smiled, all the while humming a most beloved song to me:

The sun settles its golden rays upon the lands while the gods gave us lives of eternal doom.

For we are but playthings in their hands. The moon weaves her magic upon the loom. Come my sweet love, let us play in the water. Come my sweet love, let us be children again. Eternal, eternal, eternal, my love, our souls are eternal, my love Life is but an instant of love, and fear, Come my sweet love, let us disappear. Eternal, eternal, eternal, my love, our souls are eternal, my love.

I sat soothed by the truth of his song. I adored his voice; the sound of it lulled me into a place of calm. I felt wrapped within the warmth of his tone which drew me within the garden of his love.

I no longer wished to eat; I sat back. Every part of my body had become like the water I bathed in.

"News of the war?" I asked.

"Tell me what happened," he whispered.

I saw him swallow hard. I handed him my cup, but he waved it away.

"You must eat, my love," I urged him, but he waved his hand, for even I knew that he could not eat.

"The day you left our camp," he began, "we waged a battle that lasted until the sun no longer lit the sky. We waited till the sun rose, and saw his men rise from every corner of the mountains, tall as cedars, Men the like I had never seen. I knew then that Ishtar had deserted us. We lost many men; we were cornered. We fought our way out! We managed a retreat to the palace."

I gazed into the black pool of his eyes and saw despair, and something else, something I had never seem in them, fear. He continued his tale, looking out towards the open windows that opened to the large porticos.

"There must be a way," I murmured.

"If there is, we cannot find it." He stood up and paced upon the large stone slabs. "I have consulted my astrologer, my generals, my captains, but none can find the chink in that barbarian's armor." He sunk upon our bed, hands on his face, lost in the despair that swirled about him.

He, unlike myself, had been trained, not only in the ways of diplomacy, but in the art of war.

I was still for a long time. I sought to gather

some wisdom, a whispered word of guidance from Isis, or Ishtar, or whatever god could help us now. No answer came, only silence, the quiet of our breathing and the soft, whispered sounds of curtains fluttering in the soft winds that blew in from the east.

"We must get the children to Egypt," I stated.

"It is too late to get them out safely." He saw my look of disbelief. "He has every valley covered by soldiers. He must have over two hundred legions."

"I got out," I shot back.

"You got out because you came back to us; you did not try to leave the valley." His voice was devoid of feeling, and yet I knew he raged to ask what I had done with this barbarian since I had left his side.

My heart sank. I realized how trapped we were. How could we save our children? That troubled the uppermost part of my mind. I had to find a way out for them.

The day was bright with sun and soft winds. I called for my slave, Ama, to come.

She brought scented oils and herbs that would wash the dust and dirt from my hair. She led me to my long divan outside and plucked any offending hair that grew between my thighs and between the creases of my arms. Then she did my most favorite of things and rubbed my skin with scented oils of herbs and crushed rose petals, digging the tips of her fingers upon my neck, back, hips and trailing her hands upon my thighs and finally the bottoms of my feet. I was lost beneath her care and wished Malek would allow her to heal his wounded body. Ama presented me with an indigo sheath, embroidered with silver threads. I sat before the large circle of my copper reflector as she brushed my hair and plaited the length to one side. I had been deep in thought and had found a solution, but only two would be able to get out of our valley, more than two and the plan would fail.

That night, I entered the war room. Malek was alone, sitting by clay tablets reading a missive from a neighboring king. He looked up and smiled.

"This king will not aide us in this matter." He threw the tablet to the floor where it shattered into a thousand small pieces.

"Which king?" I wondered.

"Does it matter?" he responded.

I shook my head. My eyes scanned over the miniature terrain Malek's spies, engineers, and slaves had created.

I saw Kryu's soldiers spread on every peak of our beloved mountains. I wondered at a particular mountain peak that held many caves, confusing catacombs to anyone unfamiliar with our land. My Nubian slave and I knew the caves like the palms of our hands. It would take days, and they would have to travel by night, but they would be able to walk and climb the ravines and find shelter by day within and move thus until they were too far away to pursue. They would be using the stars and crescent moon for light. I knew that my Nubian would guard Damion with his life, but the journey would take two summers, and I knew that once they arrived my brothers would care for our son, and perhaps the Pharaoh would help Damion regain the land. Though I carried a quarter blood of an Egyptian Pharaoh on my mother's side two generations back, I could not rely on the goodwill of blood relations, for my grandmother had been a princess of the lower order. Still, I could hope.

For the whole of my life, time had been a place of golden light and soft moments, infused with laughter and passion. All had been done with ease and little care for the future.

Now, time had become my enemy. A foe that neither attacked me directly, nor threatened me with words, or actions, it just swung through space like a curved sword to cut down anything that stood in its path. Time had become a mad being, and there was nothing I could do to stop it from bringing more destruction upon the ones I loved.

There was no future foretold, only what we made it be. So it was that I began to realize the idea of destiny and free choice. I could allow destiny to take my whole being and do with it as it may, or I could fight and make choices as to what I did and did not accept to be my fate. In other words, I could change my destiny. If I should die, then let me decide how and when. I would not be like cattle on the day of slaughter. So I chose. I told Malek of my plan. Egypt was two summers away from our land, so the journey would be long and arduous; gold would be their messenger to safety. I trusted my Nubian to show my son the way.

When I sat at Malek's feet and began to weave the intricate detail of my plan, I could feel his eyes upon me. But as I spoke, I was gazing out the large windows that unfolded the wide expanse of a moving indigo sky, bright stars, and large black billowy clouds of the silhouette of mountains and the welcome scent of jasmine caught upon the gift of a breeze. When I was done, I locked eyes with Malek. It was then that I saw his tears. I rose and embraced his large head against my breasts, cradling him, sending soothing tones from my voice. His body shook and shook a storm of grief and shame.

"There was nothing you could have done,

my love," I whispered. Still, he trembled, the wild winds within him no longer violent but sighing out of his soul. I helped him thus, until he lay still in my arms.

He unlocked his hands from around my waist and rose. He turned his back to me, his head bowed.

"He will go," he said in a voice shredded by loss and by the weight of imminent loss to come.

"But Malek, you cannot think to…"

He turned suddenly to face me.

"Let us trust your Nubian to bring our son to safety. Perhaps he will win where I have failed."

"But, my love…" He cut me off with the raise of his hand.

"I am king, and I have failed to protect my people from this barbarian." He shook his head.

"I wish we could send Amytis and Cycrus with them," he mused.

"Cycrus could never make the journey," I said sadly. Now, more aware than ever of how sensitive my little copper-headed jewel was to all elements of life. He could not absorb the discomforts that life offered. Such a journey would have him howling with grief; the heat, the urgency, the need to be stealth, all these demands would drive him mad. As for Amytis, such a princess pampered all her life could not expect to do what had to be done to cross deserts, to travel as a warrior. Damion had been trained in the ways of a warrior since he could walk. We had to protect him. Three traveling back to Egypt would have been pushing the limits, two would be easier, and thus their journey would be successful, or so I hoped.

I could not argue with Malek, for we had both failed in our own way. Mine for succumbing to my desires, and Malek for not heeding the oracle. So my Nubian was called, as was Damion, and Ama. We sat at a short, round table upon pillows. At this moment there was no hierarchy created by roles as inconsequential as royalty or slave. There sat a mother and a father, entrusting their most beloved child to a man with the hopes that Ishtar would carry them on wings of speed and health.

"You are to go on a great journey," I announced with a forced smile.

"Where am I to go?" he asked.

"Egypt!" I said brightly.

Damion understood the whole of it immediately, for I saw the realization of what I had said settle upon his shoulders and drag him down to fall upon the pillows, his eyes filling with tears.

"There is a war, mother!" He choked back a sob. "I cannot leave you!" My heart twisted with pain as I saw his face implode with grief.

His head hug down. My eyes caressed the curve of his neck and traveled to his small shoulders which fell forward in dejection. I saw his tears fall upon his hands, long-fingered like his father's with squared palms like my hands. I noticed once again, for the millionth time since his birth, the little brown birthmark on the pinky of his right hand, which reflected my own. I could feel my throat choking with the deep anguish that rose from the very depth of my soul. I swallowed hard which brought me physical pain.

"Damion..." I managed to whisper.

He looked up his face tearstained, his eyes large green pools of fear and rage.

"There is a war! I am to stay with father and fight!" He raised his little chin with defiance.

Malek spoke, his eyes bright with restrained emotions.

"Damion, my beloved prince, your duty is to your people; that is true."

Damion nodded.

Malek paused and took a deep breath. "But you must go to Egypt to call upon the aide of the Pharaoh to raise an army!"

Damion shook his head, his eyes a torrent of sorrow.

"Come, my son." Malek's elegant hand waved in the air beckoning for Damion who crawled from his pillow and sat to find refuge upon Malek's lap.

Malek held him thus within the embrace of his love, fully aware that this would be the last time he would ever hold his child. I saw it in the way he cradled him in his arms, rocking him, and issuing hushing sounds of comfort.

Malek's eyes rose above Damion's little head and met mine. Our eyes locked. I had never seen him in such pain before this moment. I wanted to embrace them both, yet I could not. I could barely maintain myself as it was. We both knew that Damion would not return for many seasons. He would be a man, if he returned, and we would be long gone – nothing more than dust.

This realization hit me so profoundly that I had to lower my eyes to contain the dam that threatened to burst wide open. Damion's thin arms circled around his father's neck, his body shaking with sobs.

"Damion, no more of this!" I called out to him. I felt the sharpness of my words. But this sadness would not help Damion prepare for the inevitable. He turned to me, and Malek released him from the circle of his arms. Damion rose wiping the tears from his eyes, and yet they still flowed like an endless fountain.

He stood before me declaring, "Dear mother, I cannot leave you!"

I wanted to hold him. I needed to feel the warmth of his body one last time. I knew that my desire was a selfish act, yet I held my arms out to him. He scampered upon my lap and found comfort. I felt his body sink into mine with complete abandon. I held him thus rocking him to and fro while I buried my nose within the crook of his neck, and I inhaled his scent which transported me to the day I first held him, the day of his birth. The veils of the past parted, and I was there pushing him into the world. I saw myself sitting in a large birthing chair. Ama was upon her knees, her arms outstretched to catch the baby as it came. I was sweat-drenched and water gushed from between my legs.

I smiled at the memory of Ama's cry, "The baby has crowned, my queen!" I recall reaching down and with outstretched fingertips, feeling the crown of his head and the smile that broke wide open from touching him. I caressed his wet hair, and I sent out a silent prayer of thanks and welcomed him home. I gulped all the air I could muster and gathered the strength to push him into the world ...and push I did, with all my might. The sun pierced through the darkness and began to rise as Damion slipped from the shadowy lands of my womb into Ama's waiting hands.

"A boy! My queen, a boy!" She cried tears

that streamed down her face.

I felt my heart explode with such deep emotions that I felt dizzy. She was about to cut the cord that bound us when I halted her hand. "Hand me the blade," I commanded. She did so, and I held the cord in my hand, wistful in that moment, pausing with a hesitance that surprised me, I cut the cord with a savagery born from that moment, that first moment when a mother first lets go of her child. I would find that this would be one of many to come. Released thus, my ladies helped me rise upon shaky legs and led me to my couch. The blood was wiped from my thighs. My body was cleaned with sea sponges perfumed with rose oil and then wrapped in a fine linen. More linen was placed between my thighs to staunch the flow of blood. I sat upon my elbows waiting for them to bring him to me. They laid him upon my breast; he did not cry, not once. He had been quickly cleaned, and I recall how well he fit in my arms. He stared up at me with serious blue eyes and then as if recognition dawned, his face broke into a wide toothless smile which left me speechless and swelled my heart with the kind of love that can never be matched in power, for it was the kind of love one only feels for one's child. Infinite as the sky, that would expand with a life of its own; it would be timeless, the most pure love that can never be matched by any other love.

I would never love Malek or any man as I love Damion. It was a power that I did not question; rather, I plunged head first into it. I marveled at his tiny feet, his perfect fat toes, the beauty of his form, the dark hair that was thick and shiny black. I recall falling in love with him, and knew that feeling would never leave me.

The sun was making progress across the sky, throwing rays of gold, orange, and the purple lights of the gods.

I called for slaves to carry my couch to the terrace. I wanted my son's eyes to see the welcoming sun. We sat thus for a very long time. I recall burying my nose within the crook of his tiny neck and inhaling the sweet innocence of his skin, the scent that only babies carry for too short of a time.

The vision fell away, and I was present within this moment holding my son of nine summers, my nose breathing in his scent, the scent of his boyhood. I took his little chin in my hand and raised his eyes to mine. I stared at his beauty for a long time, savoring every line of his face, the green of his large eyes, tinged with the flashes of gold, his straight little nose, and his mouth, full and pink. My heart was choking with the tears of this farewell and it was unable to beat smoothly. It was filled with grief too heavy to shed.

I felt my eyes burn. I buried my nose within the soft locks of his light brown hair and again inhaled his scent, trying to commit to memory every nuance of his being. I held him thus waiting for the storm to calm. I held onto the silence that allowed me to engrave this moment within my soul to carry forth until the end of eternity. I sighed, and the pain leaked out of me like blood coursing from my soul—unending, fleeing from the very depth of my solar plexus to twist like tendrils of smoke that rose to the heavens with an anguished prayer.

Given the chance, he would grow into a magnificent man, and in time, if Fate was kind and favored him, she would return him to our land as a man, a king with an army to reclaim his rightful place. And though I found some comfort in this possibility, I could not disengage myself from the quicksand that pulled me deep within the well of grief.

I wondered if in another life, in another time, I would see him again. Would I recognize him? In that moment, I wished I had the oracle to ask. I needed someone to give me the hope that there was another world where lost souls meet once again to share love and perhaps even share the memories of lives long past. I wanted to find sense in all of this. What was the reason for it all? What was the grand design?

Yet, in spite of my philosophical musings, I knew that if I allowed the claws to tangle themselves within the insanity that wanted to rise and howl, I would go mad, and so I choked back all that threatened to erupt from me. I feared it, for this grief had never visited me until now, and I feared its madness. If I allowed it to possess me as it threatened to do, I would become a shadow, howling to the sky for this to stop, for I could not find refuge in the thought of an afterlife, not now, not yet... perhaps later, much, much later. For now, I only felt pain, a pain that was threatening to paralyze me.

All that crossed my mind with any certainty was that my time on earth would not last another summer, and somehow this made it bearable, this new pain of mine. It was a voice that did not speak in my head, but flashed the knowing of it. By next summer, I would be gone. I felt my throat tighten, tears threatened to mark my cheeks, but I could not allow my child to view my distress. So I raised my eyes to the sky watching the white clouds billow above us like long arms that stretched and shifted shape upon a sea of perfect blue. I felt the arms of Isis lift me from the depth of despair and settle me upon the solid soil of sanity. I lowered my head placed my chin upon his little head. I squeezed him tight against my body, feeling his warmth envelop me. I placed my hand between his little shoulders, rubbing him softly as I had done when he was a babe after breast feeding. I breathed in his scent one last time, and I lifted my head. I turned his body to face me, and I lifted his chin, tilting it so that our eyes met. I hoped that my gaze would offer him the strength and the love that I bore him; these would be my parting gifts to him as he journeyed to Egypt.

I found the power to possess my voice, keeping it from shaking with emotions. I kept it still as a calm pond. "When you are ready to come back, I shall be here waiting for you, and so will your father." I was able to smile brightly at him. "We shall be so proud to see you again soon, for by then you will be a man of the world."

We locked eyes for a long time, staring into each other's souls. We both knew the lies I told, but he did not choose to dishonor me by refuting my words. Instead, I saw a strength rise from behind the green gold of his gaze. He wiped the tears from his face with an impatient hand, and it was he that broke away from my embrace, rising to his feet to meet the day.

"I will honor you, for the blood of Ishtar and Isis runs in my blood."

I nodded my head, my heart swelling with pride.

"Tell me about Egypt." He was sober. Duty had settled its hand upon his shoulder. He felt it. I saw it in his eyes.

"Well, I have never been there, but from what my brothers say, it is a land of great buildings, and gods, a land of sun and sand, and of rich soil and water."

"So I am Egyptian?" he murmured.

"You are part Egyptian, and long ago your grandmother came here and married your grandfather. We have blood ties to Egypt and now that your uncles are there..." My voice trailed off.

"Why did they leave us for Egypt?" His brow furrowed with a concern I could not gauge.

"One uncle is a mathematician and works in a great library, and your other uncle is an architect, and they found that they loved being in a land that understands their thirst for learning."

"But I don't like mathematics or building." He was troubled that he would not fit in with their schemes.

"You will be taught what you do best. You will not be forced to break with your gifts. The Pharaoh, I am certain, will raise you in the royal household as a future king to our land, and your training as a warrior will continue, have no fear."

"Will you visit me?" He asked.

"As often as I can," I whispered, again repeating what we both knew was this lie. For some reason he preferred this pretense over swallowing the whole truth. Later, I would learn that we are souls who only take as much as we can digest. He was wise in accepting this pretense.

"Now go my love, prepare." The Nubian rose and took our boy by the hand. I looked over at Malek who was stoic, holding back the storm within a tight reign. I lowered my eyes, and I noticed that his hand that lay upon his knee was trembling.

"Gather what you deem is the most important; gold and provisions will be given to you. A messenger has gone ahead of you to announce your coming to my brothers and the Pharaoh. Make sure that you guard his life with yours." I lied about the messenger, but I wanted to place a fear in him in case he decided to kill our son and keep the gold. I made my voice clear and saw in his eyes only loyalty and then tenderness cross his face as he looked down upon our son's head. He would be safe; my heart knew that he would arrive to meet his uncles, that all would be well.

"My life is his, my queen." I knew he spoke the truth. Malek was silent, and sat like stone.

"Return to me before you leave, and we

will discuss the safest route," I added before he turned on his heels and walked out with Damion and Ama a few steps behind.

"Ama," I called. She turned abruptly. I saw her tear-stained face, as I knew I would. I wiped my hand across my eyes. "Do not..." I ordered. She nodded, and wiped the tears from her face. I saw them, silhouettes in the doorway. The giant Nubian was holding the hand of my little boy who stopped and turned to gaze upon us, but I could not see his face, for it was hidden by casting shadows. He stood there for what seemed like an eternity, and then he turned and squared his little shoulders and disappeared from our sight.

My breathing grew labored; my heart shook within my chest, and still I drew in breath trying to calm the shuddering that rippled in waves and was threatening to paralyze me from my duty. I turned to Malek hoping to find solace in his eyes, some sort of comfort, but what I faced was emptiness. Something inside of him was closing down. I saw that my king, my Malek, was disappearing; he was giving up. I could not take the time to reach for him. I left his side, calling for our treasurer. Much had to be done before Damion left, too much. My son's very survival depended on it.

13

SUDDENLY, ALL THINGS CHANGE
OCTOBER 8, 1997

Life is never static; this is not only a good thing, it's a sure thing. What was the benefit of remembering things that occurred over three millennia ago? What was the point? I'd been wondering about that. Daniel was re-reading the book on the Crystal skull for the third time and had gone to the Pasadena library for any additional information on it. Although I appreciated his fascination, I just wasn't feeling as obsessed about it as he was. I believed that Atlantis had once been a formidable society. I believed it had sunk from a cataclysm created by its people's own arrogance. I knew the story of the flood was told again and again by various peoples from different continents. How could one explain that? The truth was we didn't know anything about the ancient world, and what we did know was based on a handful of scrolls that had traveled through the ages surviving the destructions of conquering nations, burnings by the churches, and just plain loss. Guys like

Plato wrote about Atlantis and that is the only reason why we know of its existence. Homer's "Iliad" was the only reason why we knew of a city called Troy, and for many centuries we believed that it was a myth until some German millionaire by name of Heinrich Schliemann, uneducated in the ways of archeology, began to illegally excavate a site, and that's how Troy was discovered in addition to gold artifacts that would decades later be authenticated from the Bronze period.

So my point is this: we only know what is recorded, and even then we're not sure it's true until we find proof of its existence. The fact that my past life in Mesopotamia seemed impossible in terms of historical data made me doubt the veracity of my visions and of my waking and sleeping dreams. The only thing that kept me on this course was the fact that I was walking parallel to Malek in these recalls. We logged on and daily exchanged notes. I always held back just enough detail, and boom! There he was plugging all the holes that I'd purposely left out. These private chats never failed to amaze me; in fact they always blew me away. I felt extremely fortunate riding this fast wave to a life that poured its story into my conscious mind. It was both surreal and exhilarating.

So knowing that Daniel was the conqueror

who loved me in spite of himself, who sometimes dominated me, whose passion for me knew no bounds, all these things that made him tick in that life over 3,000 years ago, is what made him who he was today, and that knowledge made me understand him that much better. This discovery excited me, and I wanted to share it with Daniel so badly, but to tell him would mean that I would have to admit that I had been lying all along about ceasing all contact with Malek, and I didn't want to do that until we had explored this life to the very end. I now understood our power struggle, I now understood the great sex, but what I didn't understand was why we struggled to make ends meet. Was this our karma for past misdeeds or was it our lack of self-worth, a shame that we carried deep within that made us believe we did not deserve better? It made me wonder.

***

Daniel bought a 1972 Fiat 500 last week. It had a roll-back top. It looked like a car two men could carry down the street. I was shocked. Why the hell he had bought such a Coke can for three hundred dollars was beyond me. I mean, what was he thinking? Was he even thinking?

I was going crazy, and before I knew it, I

said what was on my mind which wasn't pretty. Two weeks later, I ate my words. For Daniel had taken this diminutive car to a friend who shot it with a coat of red paint. Then he had another buddy of his help him work on reupholstering the seats in a cute red-and-white vinyl. He detailed the hell out of it, and placed in it in the "Auto Trader", and then placed a 'for sale' sign on the front windshield, parking it on the front of our house on Marengo Avenue. Within a week, it sold for two thousand dollars to a woman in her forties who wanted something fun to drive. With that money we paid some bills.

He made a profit of fourteen hundred dollars, not bad at all, and I had to re-think everything I understood as sensible. Here Daniel had not limited his thoughts. He bought the car and had a solid idea from day one that a woman would buy it. He restored it with the idea a woman would buy it, and he made it as cute as a bug so that the purchase would be an emotional one and not a sensible one. She loved that car and was thrilled beyond words when she drove off, pink slip in hand (which Daniel had received in the mail the day she bought it. Talk about kismet.)

So life was easier, and yes, a little bit better then.

That Thursday, Ted picked me up for our

weekly meeting. Instead of Chinatown, we went to dine at a Mexican restaurant. I ordered chicken chimichangas and Bob ordered two pitchers of margueritas. Everyone got drunk fast, and that means we all got stupid. Soon, it was decided that we all knew what goals we needed to hit for next month and could move on to beers with chasers of our choice. I just wanted a beer, so I could burp off the tequila while most of my compadres wanted to drop shots of tequila in their beer. I didn't even want to keep up. I was worried about Ted though, as he was my ride home and his sobriety meant the difference between my getting home in one piece or landing in the E.R.

"Ted," I said, leaning close to his ear, "I'm not here to judge but going home drunk from a business meeting will not get your wife back into your bed." I paused shrugging my shoulders, just in case he doubted the purity of my words.

"I'm just saying," I added with a wry smile. He nodded his head, shooed away the shot and drank the beer to clear his head from the marguerita fog. I sighed with relief. We each got our hundred-dollar bonus in cash for hitting our numbers that week, except for Holly, who looked crushed. I felt sorry for her, even though her finding out about my black father had given her a look of twisted shock, like biting into chocolate and finding it tasted like lemon, a real shock. I saw her eyes fall to the table, as if staring into another reality.

It was kind of good thing that they always waited until after dinner rather than before.

We all parted from each other admits hugs and goodbyes and off we went. Ted always talked shit about these meetings.

"So they want us to close ten deals a week and lower our pay by ten percent so we can stay open?"

So, okay, I did fail to mention that our meeting spoke of less money and higher goals, or the business would close. Why mention it? In all the years I have been in sales, such ridiculous demands have always been placed upon us by various managers and were always due to poor management. Couldn't they see they had a crackhead milking them for money, and couldn't they see that they had a bored rich housewife unmotivated by money, but who needed outside distractions? Ted and I were the only two motivated by real money; we had two leeches on our team and they needed to cut them loose. That alone would allow us to keep our salaries while we got their leads. I bet that we could turn their dead leads into viable business given the chance. But that's not what happened. They kept the dead wood with the viable wood and floated the whole of it with bullshit. It was business as usual.

Ted kept ranting and raving as he got on the 110 Freeway to Pasadena, but I had long blocked him out. He was like an old fish wife, a real pain in the ass. I could see why his wife had kicked him to the curb. Instead of listening to his high-pitched voice, my mind was traveling, watching the freeway run its course, trees and houses, and more trees, and the long curving stretch of freeway. We ducked beneath the bridge which led some to Highland Park and others to South Pasadena into Pasadena. It was dark now, no excuse for delusion or fantasy, and yet I was lost in my own private world that was Mesopotamia. I was reliving all that had been and then when all had been re-lived. My eyes focused back to the present, and I realized how crazy Ted's driving was. I wasn't scared, but I was anxious. In all honesty, I hoped to get home and log on as soon as possible. I wanted to know if Malek had sent me a message, for I sensed that he had, and all my cells were pulsing in high time to the octave of his call. It was driving me crazy.

Ted wanted to stop at Trader Joe's for a bottle of his favorite, Vodka of the Gods, can you imagine? Who would think to name such a drink something like that? I thought it close to a lethal poison. Anyway, I decided to get Daniel and me a six-pack of German beers. I was steps from home, so I walked. I was in no hurry, lost in the images that teased my eyes as I strolled beneath the dim yellow street light. Nothing mattered now for my vision was hampered by the images of my life as Queen Bakor. They came before my mind's eyes and then scattered into dust and reformed into new images.

Up until now, I had been able to control the memories from flooding my mind, but most often, they came unheeded during the night. I wasn't even safe to drive as they might flood my vision with a past that would blur all else. Truly, had I told any clinical psychologist, I would have been placed on seventy-two-hour hold. Fortunately, I knew no one who could commit such an act. So I was safe living these moments of insanity, at least, that's what I called them. Most often, I just wanted to know when it would all end.

I came home, eager to log on. Instead, as I reached for my key, Daniel opened the door and stood before me with a wide grin.

"Come in, come in," he murmured. "I have a very special night planned for you." To say I was surprised was a two-fold truth. My plan to check my messages was thwarted and the love nest Daniel had created floored me.

"Take a shower my love, and make sure to

shave between your..." He smiled as his gaze caressed the V between my thighs. I giggled and shed my clothes like autumn leaves falling from a stiff wind.

I entered a candlelit bathroom and wrapped my long mass of wild curly red curls in a self-contained knot. I turned on the shower and tested the water before venturing in. I stepped in, letting the water massage its magic upon my tight shoulders and back. I stood there, a silent vessel to the healing powers of a simple shower; it was as good as it could get. I got out and I rubbed jojoba oil all over my wet skin, drying the furred V between my thighs, which made me remember that I had forgotten to shave it. So back in the shower I went. I reached for Daniel's razor, soaping down that part until it foamed white and fluffy. I took a good long look at my V shape and shaved in as close as I could to my inner thigh. A bikini shave that would be close cut and soft to the touch. I cropped all excess hair so that it curled close to my labias. I grabbed Daniel's shaving mirror to check my work and looked down upon my lips with great care. I was satisfied to note that all that shouldn't be there was gone and that my vulva looked clean, moist, and strong. I actually liked the way I looked. I slipped two fingers between my ripe lips and brought them to my nose. My scent was clean and smelled of woman and soap. Had I been a man, I would have liked this scent. I smiled, satisfied with my labor and stepped for the last time out of the shower. I set aside Daniel's mirror and rinsed it. I stepped back on the bath mat and dried all that made sense and oiled all that needed to be oiled. By the time I was done, I shone and was scented with a soft perfume, Miss Dior, spraying it behind my knees, upon my V, beneath my breasts and on either side of my neck. I turned to look at my reflection, and I was surprised to see a woman of uncommon beauty stare back.

I saw a voluptuous creature with eyes large and almond shaped, their color shifting from brown to the palest amber, high cheekbones, an aquiline nose, and a small chin, all in all beauty set upon an exquisite heart-shaped face. The face perched upon a neck that was long and elegant and supported by shoulders that were broad yet delicate, that swept upon large breast that hung low but held no less beauty with their dark plum aureoles the size of espresso saucers and nipples the size of a man's pinky nail. The waist was small and swept into hips that sprang lush to reveal that dark red triangle and accentuated long strong thighs and big strong calves and thick ankles, I added ruefully. But yes, in spite of all that I disliked, even I had to admit that there was beauty here, and that made me smile with gratitude. I grabbed a tube of lipstick from the linen closet where I stored all my skin care supplies and makeup. It was a tube of Russian Red by Mac.

It brought out my eyes and made my lips sexy as all hell. I loved it. Daniel loved it. Red hair, red lips, he would murmur. I stepped out of the bathroom naked. Daniel stared with appreciative eyes and shot me a reverent smile. He nodded his head to the bedroom. I winked at him and followed his gaze. What caught my eyes were three boxes stacked upon each other like a tiered wedding cake nestled upon our small full bed. He was grinning from ear to ear. I turned my head and saw that he had transformed our small cocktail table and turned it into a romantic setting with two Moroccan bronze candle holders bearing red candles and a red rose in a small vase.

"Don't you want to see what's in the boxes?" he whispered. I threw him a broad smile and sat on our bed, soft from the featherbed I had bought from QVC just three months ago. I couldn't wait to slip in between the four-hundred thread count sheets my mother had gifted me for my birthday.

I loved our bedroom, and I felt good in my skin. I ripped open the first box to unveil an indigo silk chemise which had a thousand pleats; the way to preserve the pleats was to swirl it into a twist and tie it into itself with knots. I slipped it over my head and shook the coil from my hair allowing it to fall around my shoulders and waist. I saw his eyes widen and then darken with a passion I had not seen in a while.

"I'll be right back!" He brought scissors to cut off the tag and lifted my hair off the nape of my neck depositing a kiss that sent shivers up my spine. I felt a warm blush heat my cheeks. He breathed in my scent. "God, you smell good," he murmured. He waved his hand to the remaining boxes. I looked up at him, my eyes clouded with concern.

"What?" He sat next to me, his arms around my shoulders. I pulled away, capturing his eyes.

"Are you sure we can afford this?" I bit my lower lip feeling guilt wash over me.

"What do you mean, can we afford this? I can't afford not to treat my baby." He grabbed my chin and tilted my lips towards his. We kissed for a long time, savoring the soft feathery feel of each other's mouths, tongues dancing so softly that my belly shook with tiny tremors. I wanted him so badly. He swept the boxes off the bed. He lowered himself to his knees and placed both hands on my thighs, lifting the indigo chemise up to my waist. His mouth caressed my vulva with soft petal kisses that made me shake. His tongue began to explore, his fingers playing with my clit first gently and then rubbing it fast, the callus of his large thumbs felt excruciatingly good. I was getting near to the edge, and still his mouth tortured me enclosing my clit and sucking it hard and then soft until I trembled into him. My hips thrashing as he scooted me into bed, straddling me. He quickly unbuttoned his 501 jeans, letting his cock spring out. He was rock hard against my thighs.

"I want you inside me," I groaned.

"What do you want?" he whispered against my ear, licking the inside of it and then blowing warm air. I shivered.

"I need you, please Danny, please." He touched my outer lips teasing me. My belly howled to be filled by him, my hips thrashing. I lowered my hand to grab him and guide him within me, but he pinned my hands above my head and slid into me with a hard thrust. He lifted my thighs high against the side of his hip and thrust even deeper.

"Is this what you want?" he growled against my mouth. He lowered his head to capture a nipple between his teeth, and then sucked it hard until it ached. But such a good ache. He let go of my hands, and grabbed my thighs over his waist. I buried my fingers within his wild hair. His lips on my neck, his cock spiraling me to such a state that I searched his eyes for an answer to this sudden wave of passion. I was not staring into green eyes, but gray eyes. I blinked and looked again; I must have imagined it. Because now, it was Daniel's deep green eyes staring back with a heat that made me want to lick his cock.

"I want you to come," Daniel murmured against my ear.

"Not yet," I answered, pushing him off me; the heat of him slid out, and I felt my insides protest. "What are you doing?" he asked petulantly.

"I have a surprise."

I ran to the kitchenette, pulled down two champagne glasses and grabbed the bottle of Moet Chandon from the fridge. I grabbed ice cubes out of the tray and threw them in our old champagne bucket which we had brought from San Francisco. Then I grabbed our big Euro pillows from the bedroom and threw them on the queen-size futon. Our bed no matter how nice was a full, not big enough. I took Daniel by the hand and walked him to the futon. His cock was softer; I kneeled before Daniel, slid his jeans down around his hips, and slid them down his thighs. I tossed a look to the champagne bottle.

"Do you mind opening that?" He smiled, taking off one pant leg at a time, and pulling the gray T-shirt over his head. He stood nude, so stunningly nude. He was tanned, his big, shoulders broad, his muscled arms rippled beneath his skin as he uncorked the bottle without a sound, or a mess.

He poured us each half a glass. I had lowered the futon so that it lay flat, and now sat on the edge admiring him. He brought the glass bubbling golden, and I took a large swallow of champagne and held it within my mouth. I put the glass down next to me and slid his beauty into my mouth. Holding it, letting my tongue slide across his head, the champagne bubbles and the coolness a contrast to my warm mouth he threw his head back and moaned. I swallowed the champagne and took another swig, sliding him back and forth, until he fell to his knees, the champagne spilling on my chin and chest. He swayed against me.

"It feels too good," He murmured his eyes heavy lidded.

"Lay down on your back," I instructed. He moved his big body, his flat stomach with just the right amount of beer gut to make him sexy. I always thought six packs were over-rated. He was all hunky male. I nuzzled the soft sack between his muscular thighs. I took another swallow of champagne and brought one, then the other testicle into my mouth holding them in my mouth like precious jewels until they slid out of my mouth. I took the length of him within the warmth of my mouth and with my hands and tongue I released all he had within the content of my mouth.

I took another swallow of champagne drank the rest of him down. This time when I took another gulp of champagne, I held it in my mouth and brought his vulnerable cock into the cool bubbly of my mouth, and a groan erupted from his throat. His body shook and shivered. I held him cradled in my mouth until he was spent and soft.

I crawled next to him and laid my head on his chest, hearing the thundering heart of his release and kissed his chest. He drew me tightly into the power of his embrace.

"How do you do that?" He smiled with such sweetness that I felt tears prick my eyelids. I lowered my gaze, afraid to look silly, afraid to show him how much pleasure it gave me to make him feel this good.

"Do you know how much I love you, Kat?" He lifted my chin to meet the soft green sweep of his gaze.

"I love you," I whispered. "You must know how much I love you, don't you?" I added.

"Sometimes, sometimes I do, and sometimes I wonder. I'm not wondering now, but you know when we're fighting about ..." he shook his head unable to finish.

"Let's not worry about that now. Let's just be here together now, okay?" I pleaded, afraid that going any further might dispel the magic and bring chaos. We fell asleep.

***

That morning, I woke up before the dawn and went straight to our small bedroom which doubled as my office. I logged on, hoping to find Malek. He was there.

New Instant Message popped up.

"Why are we remembering this?" I typed.

I knew he was online and waited until I saw the light blinking, Malek is typing.

"Because what happened was something that we have carried into many lifetimes. The pain, the loss, the love that was there and gone—Bakor, I have carried you in my heart for lifetimes, and my soul needed to know that you were fine. That you are loved."

I sat back trying to digest what he was saying. Still, that didn't answer my question.

I typed, "Do you know that ..." I paused and then hit send. Perhaps I shouldn't tell him about

Daniel.

Malek is typing.

"That the man you are with was the conqueror?" I'm pretty sure the color in my face must have drained, a chill shot across my left arm.

"How do you know?" I responded.

For a good five minutes I waited for Malek to respond. Was this it, was it finally going to end? Had we come to the end of the road?

I saw Malek is typing and felt a sigh run out of me. I must have held my breath.

"I know because I have always known. He needed to possess you, and you will one day marry him, even though saying that pains me. I would love to be with you my dear Bakor, but it is not to be, not in this life. This is about you and that man clearing the pain brought about by that life which spilled into other lives. You must forgive him and accept the whole of him, and he must forgive himself for what he knows he's done."

I instantly typed.

"But how can he forgive himself? He doesn't even know about this? He doesn't know he was the conqueror, and if he knew I was still talking to you he would go crazy."

Malek is typing.

Daniel called out. I jumped out of my skin,

shaking like a leaf.

"What?"

"Come to bed; what are doing up? Come to bed right now!" he ordered.

"In a minute," I called back.

"Now!" I looked back at my screen and read just two words.

"He knows."

I hurriedly messaged him. "Have to go. Talk later, okay?"

I shut down.

"What in the hell were you doing?" Daniel was scowling. "Just checking the news," I answered him. I was pretty annoyed that he could not let me breathe.

"At fucking five a.m. in the morning?"

"It's five-thirty. Look, I don't want to fight." I was hoping to hide the anger I felt rising. So he knows he's the conqueror? My eyes narrowed.

"Come here, woman!" he reached out for me, and caught my arm dragging me on top of him. My hair dangled over us like a curtain. He drew his hands on either side of my face, pulling my hair back.

"You've stopped talking to that mumklin dude, right?" His eyes bore holes through me; it seemed like he knew I was lying. I shook my head afraid to lie out loud. Maybe, I was just being paranoid. I mean, Daniel had always been possessive, and over protective. During the early part of our relationship in our twenties, it worked. I mean, it didn't bother me then, but now. . . now, it felt stifling. I pushed against his chest trying to rise. He smacked me so hard on the butt that I cried out.

"How dare you!" I raged at him, trying to fight him off. He laughed throwing me on my back pinning me down with his body.

"Answer me," he demanded.

"No, I'm not talking to Malek." It served him right. He didn't deserve an honest response, the hell with him.

"You're mad at me?" He looked perplexed.

"Imagine that," I spat? I was in no mood for him to mess with me like this.

He began to nuzzle my neck, kissing my shoulder and whispered.

"You know you belong to me; you always have and always will." His voice was warm honey that drizzled down my ear.

I wanted to love him right then, but I just couldn't. Something inside of me was rebelling.

14

The Rays of the Sun

The sun rose and spread its mantle of gold across our land with a soft glow. I was watching its progression across the sky. I saw Malek. He was in battle armor, but I did not go down to wish him well. I stood on the highest terrace and could see the procession of charioteers, archers, and foot soldiers march towards their death to the sounds of trumpets and drums. I knew as surely as I took my next breath that this was a doomed day for them all. I wished Malek would simply surrender, but I knew better than to tell him to. The end was near, and perhaps a valiant death on the field of battle would be better than surrendering to the chains of shame.

I was waiting for the inevitable to come. Cycrus knew nothing of what was happening. I had Ama busy him with activities of catching insects in our garden facing west, away from our entrance which faced towards the east. As for Amytis, she was with me now, laying her head on my lap. We lay thus upon the long divan. We did not speak, for what could I say to her? So the comfort came from this little intimacy between mother and daughter, and it was good.

The noontime meal passed and the early moon showed its face. Amytis had fallen asleep, so I waved a slave to carry her to my chambers, as I wanted her close. I rose from my couch and requested wine, water, green melon, figs, and roasted meat.

Once the food was brought forth, and though the scent brought me great pleasure, I found that I could not eat, and so reached for a goblet of wine and water to calm the storm that raged within me. When would this end?

Amytis rose and joined me. Her eyes fell upon the meal with ravenous delight; at least she could eat. The sounds of shrill trumpets resounded a call of triumph; they did not come from our people. The sounds of armors and weapons, the sounds of many men, of many horses, and torch lights approached fast. I stood and gazed down from my terrace to see my Malek walking like a slave, ropes around his throat, around his waist, and circling his wrists. I did not know that I had been crying until my daughter reached across my cheek to wipe tears away. I held her in my arms, and together we stood thus, watching the conqueror cross our gates.

***

There was nothing else to do but prepare my children, and if possible, make them as inconspicuous as possible. I called Ama and gave her my directions. I wanted my children to be hidden in the underground cellar where we stored our grain and amongst the large jars of wines and oils. I could not think of any better idea. I should have planned for this ahead of time. I could not stop accusing myself of failure. Now I realized what Malek carried in his heart, shame, the sting of it every day, this inevitability a constant rock upon his very soul. Now I understood his loss of appetite for everything, for life. I asked Ama to search for a slave who knew the mountains and caves as well as my Nubian, and when she found that person to bring them to me if she could, for I had no idea what Kryu would do once I was brought before him. I did not have to wait long. I heard him shouting my name through the halls as he walked purposely to find my rooms. I stood as still as I could, feeling a trembling rip through my body. And there, led by one of the slaves, he stood staring at me with steely eyes that glittered like swords. Blood covered his face, muscular arms, and armor.

The slave ran, and we stood for a very long

time, like two adversaries on a battle field. His gaze traveled to my mouth and I watched him lick his lips. My belly tingled in response.

"My queen," he spoke softly, as if to a wild mare worth taming gently. I shook my head and my hair swung around my waist to capture his attention.

"Please. . ." I could not continue.

"Yes?"

I lowered my gaze, and then finding the strength, I met his eyes and said:

"Do not kill my king." I hoped that he would find a place within his heart to give us mercy.

"I am your king!" he shouted, moving swiftly to stand before me. I smelled his scent mingled with the stench of death upon him. I stood back.

"Do not kill Malek," I implored.

He responded with a snarl that turned into a cruel smile. "What will I have in return?"

"What do you want?" I could not stop wanting him, my eyes riveted by the darkening gray of his desires.

"Many things and I will demand them all from you tonight." He stood legs apart, his sword held loosely, as if he were holding a shepherd's staff and not a killing tool.

"Call your slaves; have them bring water and all manner of scented stuff to drown the death that clings to me. I can see by the look in your eyes that I will not win you over with my stench."

I stared at him shocked. I was sure that he would take me willing or not.

"No, my lady, not by force, for I have enjoyed the pleasures of your gifts when you are willing and would not lose them now."

I clapped my hands sharply and Ama appeared.

"Prepare the bath, bring oils, and do not forget to bring us meat, wine, and fruit."

She was gone. I turned to him; he smiled a genuine smile and walked about my rooms with admiring eyes.

"What will you do with Malek?" I asked. He turned as if surprised by my question.

The moon reached its zenith and he ventured through the large windows, passing through the billowy curtains. I followed him out. He was standing in the exact spot I had stood when he crossed our threshold. He turned to me and then allowed his eyes to roam the riotous wonder of plants and tiny waterfalls that created this oasis of magic, my gardens.

"I had heard of these wonders but thought them lies." His full attention was upon me.

I could not speak, spellbound by the beauty of his form, and my anger rising within me for even thinking that he was magnificent. I hated him, but mostly I hated my body and my mind for twisting and turning its hunger for him against my will. He must have seen the war from behind my eyes, for he threw his head back and laughed a deep laugh that was genuine and without malice. I realized suddenly that it was the laugh of a man enjoying his victory. I shuddered.

I sat upon the divan, all power flown out of my body. I felt timid and lost and still I knew my duty to my king.

"What will you do with Malek?"

He crossed the distance between us with few steps. He brought his large fingers beneath my chin and raised it towards his inscrutable gaze.

"That, Queen Bakor, is fully reliant upon you." He flung the last words like a challenge.

I drew a breath in. "I do not understand?" I managed to whisper.

He placed both hands beneath my arms and lifted me straight up to face his eyes directly.

I faced a lion, a beast whose every desire was more precious to him than how they destroyed others.

His lips inches from mine, he growled. "Every act you bring onto me will affect your Malek. Abandon your false allegiance to him. Become my queen in heart and body, and you will not have to fear. He will not come to harm.

Betray me and . . ." He lowered me back to the ground.

The slaves had brought large pots of hot water and were filling my bronze tub. His attention was now upon the prospect of taking a bath, something I doubt he had ever experienced. His bathing must have consisted of rivers and streams. He was no more than a barbarian, I thought to myself.

He stripped off every inch of armor; one by one the pieces fell to the ground with the sound of metal echoing in my large rooms. Everything was discarded until he stood bare. He stepped within the tub and sunk beneath the water and rose shaking his head like a wild beast, droplets of water flying everywhere. He laughed with delight.

"Come," he waved me forward.

I shook my head.

"Woman!" he roared.

I approached him tentatively.

"Administer me with oils and your cleaning potions; do with me what you will." He sat back and closed his eyes. If I could but grab a short blade, I could easily cut his throat and all would be over. But there was something in me that could not and would not do it. It was not fear; it was something else that kept my hands from destroying him, and instead I administered him with a gentleness I had only shown Malek. A groan rose from Kryu's throat but erupted from deep within him. for he may have never known such a moment, a time spent not for fighting, or eating, or taking a woman, but a moment spent just for being and enjoying the motionlessness of the inner world reflecting an outer world that showed no chaos and offered only stillness. I could cut his throat, I kept thinking, but instead I found my hands caressing his broad shoulders, his broad beautiful chest soft with golden hair.

My fingertips explored a large scar across his right breast and traveled on to his flat stomach, to the dark gold hair that rose from between his thighs. I felt his breath catch as I circled my hands around his manhood which rose to meet me. Kryu grabbed me and brought me into the bath. My tunic now wet, clung to my form in a way that was more captivating than had I stood nude. I saw the glow of his eyes as they traveled over me with a hunger that made me shiver with ... I could not say, but I could not deny that I wanted him in a way that was both desperate and foolish. My nipples hardened from the heat of his eyes, and I lowered them to his waiting mouth. I shuddered as his lips circled one and then the other. He was as starved as I was. I almost fell, but I was thankful that he held me in his arms, hoisting me over his member and lowering me into the pleasure of his thrusts. I arched against him, water splashing over the bronze vessel that contained us. He held me tight, riding me thus until we both exploded the release which we had held back these many days. I did not think of Malek, or my children. I only saw him and nothing else; no one else entered my thoughts. He carried me as one would a child to my bed, and there lay beside me, the tunic clinging to me like second skin, his eyes warm and soft, all the savagery gone, and then one of his generals came upon us.

"My lord!"

Kryu sat up as if he had been caught doing something he should not have done. Love me? Was that it? Was he loving me, for how else could I describe this tenderness?

"Tanis!" Kryu raised his eyes to his man.

"So, my lord I see that you enjoy the spoils of war!" he grinned at his king.

Yet Kryu frowned and stood up, nude in all of his splendor, and seemed as powerful now as if he wore his armor. I was baffled. I sat up and the general's eyes grazed my form with an impudent and appreciative look that brought a shiver of fear upon my person.

"Spoils of war," Kryu grunted.

"Is she well worth it, my lord?" The general spoke as if I was nothing, no more than cattle or a jug of wine.

"Well worth it? I must join my kingdom to this and marry the bitch!" he answered.

I was stunned for he had never spoken to me thus or about me. I felt my heart shatter. I felt shamed and all my duties rushed forth. I gathered the white fur around me for protection.

"May I?" The general asked Kryu approaching me.

Kryu stood before him.

"No one is to have her. She must bear my son and then we will see…"

The general nodded.

"The men?" Kryu grabbed a jug of wine and drank deep.

"Enjoying the fruits of these gardens, my lord." It was then I heard the cries of women, the sobs of children, and the shouts of men, all the sounds of despair when one loses a war.

I hoped that Ama was keeping my children hidden in the cellars that kept our grain dry during the winter months and stored our wines, as I had instructed her. I hoped then when this madness of pillage passed, I could summon them forth to some sense of safety.

Kryu nodded his head.

"And the king?" he paused. "Shall we kill him?"

I cried out.

"No! Hold him, feed him, and make sure he is unharmed."

"Yes, my lord."

Kryu waved him away. The man nodded and left. I got up from the bed, and took the wet tunic off. With no slave to help me, I managed to find a clean tunic, which was a dark purple and twisted into knots when I undid it, and slipped it over my head. It fell in tiny little pleats about my form.

I walked to my terrace and could not escape the cries of horror lifted to the heavens for help. I sat on my divan and wept for my people and wept for my children and wept for Malek who should have died on that field rather than to be captured, for I knew how broken he was and how these sounds shattered his very soul. Kryu stood above me, dressed in loincloth tied with belt; his sword was sheathed. I saw his booted sandals through blurred eyes as I looked up through my tears.

"What are they doing to my people?" I asked.

"Taming them, for how else will they know that they have been conquered?"

"Make them stop, please, make them stop." I covered my ears from the sounds.

"I cannot. I will not!" He lifted me up to face him.

"My lady, these are the ways of war, the ways of lions. This is their day to celebrate as they will."

He sneered at my weakness, his eyes steel.

I looked away.

"And I am but a bitch to breed upon?" I muttered.

"Yes," he answered, his face like stone. "Never forget that! No matter what you may think you see. You are nothing to me, nothing but a way for my kingdom to join with this one. When you are heavy with child, I will not think of you again until it is time to breed another." His voice was cold and cruel. I felt for the first time since I had known his touch the weight of deep shame, the shame of being violated. Though he had not taken me by force, it made the shame that much heavier to bear.

I sunk my head. Yet I could not forget the tenderness in his eyes, the warm glow when he looked upon me. What was that? Who was he then? He deposited me on the divan, turned on his heels, and left me thus. I was alone until the moon began its descent. The feasting was still pulsing its sounds through the night. I felt the hands of love deposit a fur blanket across me; when I looked up it was Ama.

"The children?" I asked her grabbing her hand.

"Well hidden my Queen, safe." A small smiled appeared behind her tears.

"How did you. . .?"

"I was able to sneak by. . . no one wants an old woman like me," she laughed ruefully.

"Have you found someone that could lead my children to the mountains and begin the journey to Egypt?"

She shook her head. "Later in time when the chaos has quieted, we will find a way out for them."

I was reassured by her words. In time, if time permitted, I would secret my children out. I was afraid of time, for it had become my enemy. I prayed to Ishtar and Isis to take time by the hand and demand its compliance to my needs. I worried about Cycrus. Would he be able to make such a journey? My heart squeezed in pain, my tears spent. Ama placed a goblet of wine laced with the resin of poppies into my hands. I drank it down and spiraled into a place of veils and voices.

15

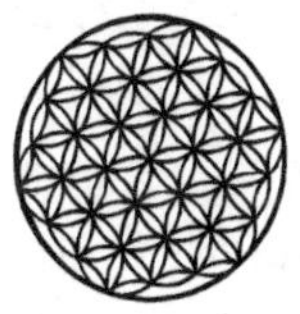

There is Nothing More Important than Love
October 9, 1997

Daniel knew the pressures I was facing with my job. The management was blowing money left and right. Out of the thirteen techs left that were contracted with us to compete for quotes only three actually bothered to show up on time at client sites or even send quotes that were clear. Most of the others simply forgot to show up at appointments we had set up for a walk-through in order to set up a proposal. It was amazing how these guys were still in business.

Unfortunately, this lack of integrity from our techs reflected on all of us. It's true what they say that people judge you by the company you keep. They thought of us as idiots and very quickly our reputation went downhill. I mean, we were really pissing off our clients who began to stop taking our calls. That was the first death knell; the second was that our bosses came from privileged backgrounds, which meant they just weren't hungry or excited enough to make this pig fly. Bob was just floating by; John was the son of a wealthy entrepreneur; and Rick was a self-made multi-millionaire who showed up once in a blue moon since he was too busy building a large estate in Marin County. Frankly, I often wondered if they had just started this company as a hobby.

Because rich people never use their own money, they had investors, and so they had a board. They were accountable, and yet, there was no urgency to win. So at the end of the day the monies were mismanaged, and we knew that it was just a matter of time before the other shoe dropped.

Ted was on the phone with me, ranting and raving about his wife's fat ass, and the fact that she refused to let him sleep with her. He was still the dog kicked to the shed. He hated her for hating him for failing. She was a concert pianist, and from what he said, she wasn't that good, hence why she now taught master classes at UCLA.

None of that mattered. There was too much hate for him not to try to get back together with her. Then, when she gave in and trusted him again, he would fuck a girl twenty years her junior just to get back at her. I saw it all in my mind's eye. Ted's relationship made me realize how lucky I was to have Daniel in my corner. No matter what we went through, he was always loyal and would protect me with his life.

"So can you believe their stupidity? Why won't they just get some new techs and get this boat to water? What the hell is wrong with them?" he shouted into the phone. I had the phone away from my ear, every once in a while giving him an empathetic, "I know, I know, I know." It's not that I didn't care about his strife; it's just that I had all heard it before. He just couldn't seem to let go and move forward. Anyway, I realized that he just needed to have a good rant and rave, and who would I be to deny him?

I was surfing the web looking at Bibliophile for two books, one I had sold a couple years back, one I was planning to give Daniel; it was called "Atlantis: The Antediluvian World" by Ignatius Donnelly written in the mid 1800's. I was nineteen when I first read it; it was perhaps one of the most fascinating books on the subject I had ever read. I knew Daniel would adore it. I was able to find it, pay for it with my credit card, and get back to the business of downloading my database for the fresh leads Bob had promised to send me last night.

"So what do you think?" Ted asked me.

I was in deep shit because I hadn't expected that question.

"Well, how do you sleep?" I was really grabbing at straws.

"What does that have to do with me looking for another job?"

"Plenty," I answered without missing a beat. "Without sleep you are going to double your stress level which will totally mess you up when confronted with the prospects of interviewing for a new gig." I was amazed by my ability to recover and move the conversation without a hiccup.

"You got a point." No longer brash and enraged, Ted was taking it in.

"So how do you sleep?" I insisted.

"Not well at all," he admitted.

"Well, what seems to be the problem?"

"I suffer from neck pain. Look, this might sound strange." He paused.

How strange can this be? I thought to myself. "Go on."

"When I sleep with a pillow, I get panic attacks," he admitted sheepishly.

WFT? How do you help someone with that?

I was speechless for longer than I should have been.

"Told you it was weird," he laughed, obviously embarrassed.

"No, no, hang on there." It came to me like gong. He needed to go see my hypnotherapist who I had not seen in five years but who had helped eight of my friends get through trauma using her services. She was amazing.

"Did something happen to you as a child? You know some kind of trauma?"

"Nope, nothing, I actually had an amazing childhood; living in Colorado was a great gift for a kid. Growing up, I spent my summers in the great outdoors; we had horses. No, seriously, that's not it." His voice was perplexed.

"Well, then perhaps you might want to consider checking out my hypnotherapist Lucy. She is petite, quiet, sweet; she makes you feel so safe." I was completely expecting him to either laugh or back away like I was some religious fanatic trying to sell him that hell was coming. But instead he asked me to tell him more.

"Do you lose control? Because if you lose control I won't, I can't..." He sounded genuinely worried about barking like a seal, or reverting to being a baby in diapers and sucking on his thumb. I understood those fears, as they were normal.

"No, Ted, listen to me. You are in complete control of your mind. What happens is that your subconscious mind is opened into your conscious mind and they work in tandem, and so because of it, you can tap into things you can never do when you are not under hypnosis." I didn't have the time nor the willingness to tell him that quite often even without going under you could open both channels of the brain and remember, as I was doing with Malek. What I was suggesting to him sounded nutty enough.

"Well, give me her number, and I'll set up a time," he said, surprising me.

"I have to warn you though," I added cautiously.

'What?" He seemed wary. "Well, the whole session will take place on a recliner in her..." I paused, "bedroom."

"Ok, so?" He was so desperate to find some way to get some sleep without taking horse pills that he was nonchalant to the methods I offered him.

"I just thought you'd like to know," I added, a little miffed that this detail seemed more relevant to me than it was to him.

"Look, if she takes advantage of me, I'll be sure to let you know."

I laughed with my head thrown back, surprised at his cheekiness.

"Deal?" he added.

"Deal"

"Here's the thing though..." he hesitated.

"What?"

"I need to know I can go somewhere safe to talk about this when I'm done."

I felt his vulnerable request to find a safe harbor to lay down any and all that came from this session. "Do you want to come here?" I asked hesitantly.

"I was hoping you would say that," he sighed with a long breath.

"Sure, let me know what day and around what time you'd want to come by, okay?"

"Yeah, I will."

Lucy always prepped her clients before she met them, so she interviewed Ted for an hour to get some background. They decided to meet at around twelve-thirty the next Saturday. The session might last between an hour to as long as three hours. Having been paid my bonus, I was prepared for collateral damages. One can never under estimate the power of a past life regression, and though alcohol was not the most beneficial choice, it's what has served humans for centuries, and who was I to break with traditions? So I bought a bottle of white wine, a good little bottle of VSOP French brandy, just in case he needed a little more of a boost.

That Saturday came, and Ted called me to tell me that he was on his way to his hypnotherapy session. I wondered what he would discover.

16

THE SUN IS IN THE LION'S JAWS

I was watching Kryu talking to a handful of my slaves with a care and respect that seemed foreign to him. It appeared as if the rape and pillage that my people had seen through his men's hands were forgotten. I saw the way their eyes followed his magnificent form, they respected him. I even saw some of the female slaves' eyes caress his limbs with desire. I decided not to trouble myself with such trivial concerns and stepped off the last stone unto the large courtyard to my waiting mare. She stood pawing the ground impatient and eager to run the wide expanse of our lands. I saw him spin upon his heels and stare long and hard at my state of dress.

Ama had prepared my hair and braided the mass to one side which fell to my right hip. The soft suede boots were pale sand, and my tunic and cape seemed spun in yellow butter. I did not bother to look at him. He crossed the courtyard and stood before me, his eyes boring holes upon the top of my head, and so I looked up at him. I gasped at the obvious desire in his eyes, and I felt a shiver snake down my spine.

"Where are you going?"

Should I tell him the truth? That I was hoping to explore a route to assist in my scheme to secret my children out once I found the right slave to trust? No, I'd better lie, for he deserved nothing better than lies.

"I was riding to the pools," I answered, my chin raised as high as the sky in order to look into his eyes. I was defiant and arrogant.

He smiled wide, for he knew that I lied, and yet, he was amused, or seemed to be.

He turned to a nearby slave, a boy.

"Tell the cook that I will need a jug," he said, and then paused. "No, two jugs of wine, roasted foul, and my lady would want her flat bread and dates. Hurry! The sun is soon to arc the end of the day."

He turned to a soldier who stood guard at the entrance of our palace.

"Prepare a chariot, two horses. Now!" he shouted.

The soldier leapt at attention and ran to the stone rooms that protected our horses from heat, rain, and dust. Within a surprising short time, the boy rushed forth holding a large basket with what I assumed was filled with all that had been requested, and a chariot harnessed with two grays were brought forth.

He held out his hand like a man who suddenly had been taught the intricate ways one treats a queen, but his smile was filled with mirth and I bristled at his superiority. Still, I placed my hand in his, which he kissed very deliberately while looking into my eyes like a wolf staring at a prey soon to be devoured; I lowered my eyes before I could stop them. I was so angry at myself for allowing him to place this trembling in my heart. I hated his power over me and that I hungered for his thrusts like a she-wolf howling at the moon for her mate. He drove me mad with desire and he knew it and reveled in my weakness. I doubt he felt anything for me, for hadn't he made his purpose quite clear. I was but a bitch to breed upon, isn't that what he had said? Yes, and I hated him for it. Hated him for I loved him with a fever that quite often made me too ill to eat. Ama was fearful that I would fall ill from lack of food; she chided me that no seed would hold unless I ate.

A part of me wanted to hold the golden child that would spring from his seed. I was a whirlwind of turmoil and within all these thoughts. Malek was under guard, roped to a wall that prevented his escape; I had not been allowed to visit him since the fall of our land. So my news of his wellbeing came from Ama. He was lucky to live, or would death have been a greater gift? Or perhaps it was I who wished him dead, for then my lust for Kryu would have been easier to bear. As it stood, I could not lose myself completely within Kryu's arms, for at some point, at the least planned moments of sensuous bliss, Malek's eyes flashed before me. It was the shame that erupted out of nowhere and stole my appetite. It was the shame of knowing that if Malek had been killed on the battlefield my surrender to Kryu would have been complete. If he knew this, should I ever allow these thoughts to escape from my mouth, Kryu would misunderstand my meaning and kill him. What kept Malek alive was my compliance to Kryu's every whim. If I was honest about my own feelings, I would have faced the idea that I used Malek's life as an excuse in order to lose myself in Kryu's arms. For in truth, I loved Kryu.

Kryu lifted me upon the chariot as if I was but a leaf. The basket had been placed in front of my legs, and he settled behind me, his legs wide apart. His arms reaching around me, he held the reins, my head pressed against his formidable chest. He drove the team with ease, and instructed me to give him directions. We got to the pools within a short time. Before us was a place of heaven, a small cave from which erupted a waterfall of clear water that fell upon a pool of clear turquoise. Surrounding parts of the pool were tall reeds, and floating upon its calm surface floated water lilies of white blooms. I craned my neck and saw his eyes break into a genuine smile.

He carried me off the chariot as if I was a small child too young to walk and settled me upon a rocky moss that overlooked the pool. He returned with the basket and spread his cape upon the whole, creating a table for us to dine on. I had never expected such tenderness from such a barbarian.

He drew a jug of wine and poured two clay goblets. I drank the first with a swiftness that left me a little dizzy. He simply laughed and poured another goblet full.

"Take your ease, Lady, for we are free to do as we wish here." Surprised by his words, I turned to him and leveled my full gaze into his eyes and what I saw made my heart tremble with hope. For love was present; there was no mistake love shone from his eyes. But what brought the cool clouds of doubt across the sun of my hope was a simple truth. Did he even know that he loved me or had the life of battle brought him to grab moments he did not even recognize for what they were?

He mesmerized me as I did him; there was no doubt of it, for he could not keep his eyes from straying too long from my face or limbs. He wanted me as desperately as I wanted him.

"Tell me of your news, my Queen." He wanted to play the silly game of simple talk experienced by any farmer and his wife. As if our lives were clean from blood and fear.

I could not play. I rose and drank the goblet to the dregs, and threw it across a rock; the sound of crashing clay made me feel a little better. I shed my cape and tunic upon the ground and walked free of cloth into the waiting arms of the pool and sank beneath the crystal clear calm, hiding for an instant from the reality of what this life and the gods planned for me and for those I loved.

When I rose from its surface, Kryu was facing me, his visage a tender mask of desire and confusion. He drew me to him and lowered his lips upon my mouth like drops of rain.

I was unable to feel anything of any honor when he touched me. All I felt was the pearl within me shaking and begging for his thrusts. My breasts hardened to points pressed against the soft gold hairs that mapped the landscape of his chest. There was nothing I wanted more than to feel and smell every inch of him. I lost all sense of duty to my family for in this moment, their very existence was lost to me. All that mattered was his eyes turning a warm gray, and his hands touching me as if I was the most precious possession he owned.

I wanted him to own me, to possess me, to dominate me. He hoisted me up with his arms, using them like a cradle for my thighs as he thrust his hunger into me. My arms wrapped around his neck, and broad shoulders, my head thrown back by the joy of his body within me. I cried out his name from within a deep groan that rose and leapt out of my heart colliding with the soft wind that rippled its gentle caresses upon our skin. His lips were merciless, upon my neck, my shoulders, nibbling my earlobes and wrapping their hot warmth around my nipples, suckling on me with a hunger that erupted into a sliver of heat that coursed down between my thighs, and still he rode me tirelessly. I tightened my legs around his lean hips. He walked to the edge of the pond and spun me around. He laid me upon the soft green grass mingled with moss. He raised my hips to his, my buttocks to his mouth and ate from me, licking parts of me Malek had never explored. Pushing his large rough fingers inside me, he whispered words I did not understand, but his voice was soft and imploring.

Then he lay his hand flat on my back and pressed my belly to the ground and entered me into that place many said was never to be entered, and his fingers separated the lips of my vulva and plundered deep within. I shook against him as he rode me thus; I felt my body explode and forgave him everything. His lips against my ear whispering again and again words I would never understand but hoped spoke of love. His hand on my breast pulling hard on the nipple, and his fingers within my most tender place, he roared his pleasure and spilled his seed within me. He sunk his body against mine. I felt the soreness of his assault upon my person and wished with a shiver that it would have never ended.

Fourteen sunrises came to prepare us for our daily journeys to the pools. Our chariot rides were the time of ease when we spoke and laughed. I loved making him laugh, for he always threw his head back, his teeth white, and his eyes warm and crinkling at the corners, his hair had grown to his shoulders and swung back with golden waves that caught the sun and made my eyes widen with desire. I found myself wishing I had met him when I was a girl of fifteen. But these were the musings of a silly woman. For here we stood, conqueror and conquered. I chided myself for forgetting the truth of this life. I knew that when we left the palace, I escaped all other thoughts but him. I was no longer Queen Bakor, mother, wife; I was his woman. I knew that he felt the same. Away from his men, he was but a man allowed the simple pursuits of pleasure.

I fell back unafraid to travel this moonlit path of passion even though I could not see more than ten steps ahead of me and could not devise the future for us. The only certainty was the truth of his eyes, which showed me the love he caressed upon me. I wasn't sure if he understood that we were falling into the wild winds of love, and I wondered if he would have fought his way out if he had. I wouldn't have to wonder long. Still for now, I wanted to trust him and to trust that this was Ishtar's plan. Why else would he have tasted me upon her altar? This must be the fates that the oracle would have shared with me had she lived. I no longer felt the sting of guilt for Malek.

Perhaps, I could plead to Kryu's sense of honor and have him send Malek to Egypt. Perhaps, Kryu would agree. But I was innocent in the ways of men and how they wielded power. I was too naïve to understand that he would never free Malek, for if given the chance Malek could raise an army to claim back his kingdom. In fact, it was Malek's presence that his men puzzled over. Why keep alive the king of a captured land? Had I known that such questionings were a danger to his hold over his men, I would have understood that he risked everything by keeping Malek alive to please me. I would have known why he took me to the pools away from questioning eyes. But those understandings would come later.

For now, we rested from a morning spent in sport, my head buried beneath the crook of his shoulder. I breathed in the scent of his skin and licked the hairs beneath his arm, trailing my tongue down the lengths of his ribs and up again circling the small nipple, he gasped. I straddled him and placed the palms of my hands flat against his large chest. I leaned forward locking eyes with him. I wanted to ask him if he felt love. His hand draped across my hip, he flipped his hip over and threw me flat on my back. He was on top of me; I gazed into gray clouds overtaken by the black moons that swelled full within his eyes. He rose and dragged me from the ground and carried me to a flat rock the length of two men. It was covered with moss that pillowed my body. He lay down next to me, his fingers trailing every corner of my face, my eyebrows, my lips, my throat where the blood of my people pulsed the beat of my heart, and explored the hard points of my breasts, my ribs, my flat stomach, and my thighs, and then he circled my foot, and looked up at me giving me the most tender smile I had ever seen. He kissed my toes and the arch of my foot; he explored every inch of me with gentle finger tips lips and tongue. He was free to show me a part of himself that was true and real, and I felt for a moment that for the first time in forever, he loved me. Was I wrong to even think such a thing? Would the gods punish me for loving the man who had conquered my kingdom? I shuddered.

The heat of his desire rose hard and straight. My mouth circled him and fulfilled every wish I saw rise from behind the glow of his eyes. He stared at my magic, spellbound by the way I conjured such pleasures that brought a storm to rise from deep within his belly and spill into my throat. I loved his taste. He kissed me full on the mouth and smiled.

"I taste myself on your lips."

"As I when you feed yourself upon my..." I paused. "Do you enjoy my taste?" I wanted him to find pleasure in all that I offered.

"More than you will ever know. At times you fill my mouth so well that I am distracted to listen to my councils. I must beat you the next time your magic taints my mind from the tasks at hand." He patted my bare behind.

"Would you beat me?" Suddenly he frightened me, for I realized that he was many men, and wore many masks. Again, the question came forth, who was he now?

"I would enjoy beating your rounded rump," he chuckled. "There are many things I would enjoy doing to you, but first, we must plant my seed."

Our hunger abated for a time, it was our eyes that simmered the promises of pleasures to come. We ate like old friends. We spoke of nonsense and sat supine upon our backs watching the clouds move across the sky. I wondered if the gods watched us now, if they somehow had engineered this moment. I wanted to love, wanted to trust, and yet I knew that nothing here was real, and then I wondered were our interactions at the palace real, or was this who he really was, was this moment real? I wanted to ask him, but could not find my voice.

He saw my eyes clouded by the many thoughts that crossed them and turned to me, his head propped by his hand.

"What thoughts travel through your eyes, my golden-eyed gazelle?" My belly lurched with a tingling upon hearing his words. I gazed at him for a long time, marking his face as it stood now soft and devoid of rage, and hate, the ease of this day erasing the lines across his forehead. I wanted to memorize his face as it was now, pure and perfect.

He nudged me with a callused fingertip that was as large as two of my fingers.

"I cannot say, for you will. . ." I paused.

"You cannot say that you love me?" he said with a vulnerability that surprised me.

"Do you understand what it is to love?" I asked tears rushing to my eyes.

"Not until you." But as soon as he released the words, he frowned and rose. He shook his head, as if shaking the last vestiges of too much wine and too much heat. I followed him and stood before him; like two columns we were, side by side, face to face but unable to touch again.

The chariot ride back was silent. My heart skipped like birds beating their wings to escape.

We arrived to the main courtyard, the gardens hanging their bounty in long tendrils of leaves, flowers, and fruit. Two of his generals were squatted upon their haunches playing dice with three men. They looked up, sending Kryu a quizzical look, and then shrugs and laughter followed their perusal of their king's face and form, for they saw what I had seen, his softness.

Kryu's body froze, for he knew what they jeered at. I saw his mind working through his confusion, and his resolve not to allow me to distract him from what was to be done. I recalled his words that I was nothing more than a tool to be used to hold onto this land, and that once I bore him a son; the people would accept him as their true king. Two slaves ran to grab the reins he threw towards them. He jumped off the chariot and joined his men in a dice game. He called for more jugs of wine. His back squarely faced me. His men patted him on his shoulders welcoming him. I heard the sharp voices of his men speak of money lost, of crooked dice, and willing women. I heard Kryu laugh, his head thrown back.

That night, Kryu joined my bed but did not touch me. I felt the heat of my hate rise. His back to me, he slept the heavy sleep of wine and of woman. For Ama told me that he had taken one of the female slaves during a banquet, throwing her upon the long table and entering her from behind like a stallion with a captured mare. The roar of his men's approval shook the very walls of our palace. Had I understood that the very hold and loyalty of his men came from his power to master their respect and their fear of him, had I realized that for him to love a woman was not to be borne, not by his men and not by him, I would have understood the cause of his desire to destroy all such links, and why he would pursue it with a ferocity that would leave me shaken.

17

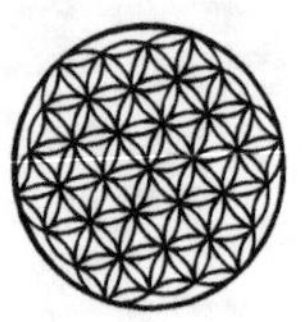

RECALLS
OCTOBER 11, 1997

By three o'clock sharp Ted stood on my doorstep. Daniel knew he was coming and made himself scarce by leaving our little apartment, claiming business across town. Alone with me and feeling safe and un-judged, Ted melted upon the pink futon. I asked if he wanted wine or brandy. Opting for the brandy, I handed him a generous glass. He nestled it within the palms of his hands, leaning his elbows upon his knee.

"Take your time, or maybe you don't want to talk about this," I shrugged, my eyes wide and questioning his feelings and his needs.

He took a deep swig of the brandy. He seemed out of his body. I sat opposite him, I watched him gather his thoughts.

"It was really a strange experience." He paused," It's like what you said that I was completely in control but then something opened up and images came like a movie reel."

He took a deep breath, and what he experienced began to unravel out of his mouth.

"It was amazing. I didn't know what to expect. You're right, by the way," He looked at me a shy smile crossing his face. "She made me feel safe."

"I was a child in bed, and it must have been during the Middle Ages. I was an aristocrat, my father had died and I was to inherit. I was murdered; a pillow was placed over my face while I slept, and I was stifled to death."

"Oh, my god!" I cried, a hand to my mouth. "Apparently, it turns out it was my uncle who killed me. If I died he would be next to inherit." "Wow. That would explain the pillow issues," I mumbled.

"Yeah, yeah," he said, nodding as if in another world. "So Lucy made gave me an exercise and asked me what I would tell my uncle if he faced me."

I remembered this exercise; it was a way to create closure; it was about talking it out to the person who had hurt you in this life or a past life and facing them; it was about forgiveness, and most importantly, it was about moving on.

I nodded for him to go on.

"So I faced my uncle and told him that I was just a child, just a little boy who was afraid, and that he had terrified me until I could not sleep on pillows anymore."

He paused, taking a sip of the brandy and

swirling it in his mouth.

"Lucy asked me to ask him why he did it. So I asked him."

"Did you see him as he was then?" I leaned forward on my chair. I took a sip of white wine. I felt the coolness travel down my throat. My mouth filled with the taste of fermented grapes, peaches, and honey. This was a damn good Entres-Deux-Mer.

"Yes, it was you know, shadowy. He was a tall man, and he seemed regretful, so I asked him, Why did you kill me? And you know what happened?"

"What?"

"He told me that he had no choice, that if I was not out of the way he would never have inherited what was rightfully his. I felt his hand on my shoulder, and he asked for my forgiveness which I gave him."

"What happened next?"

"Well Lucy asked me if that was enough, and I realized that it was. She brought me back slowly, and when I opened my eyes I felt as if a weight had been lifted off my chest."

"Well, we'll see if you can sleep better tonight."

"I've got you to thank. I just have this feeling that I'm going to sleep like a baby." His eyes were filled with gratitude and calm.

"If you feel that you will sleep well, then you will," I answered back.

"So what are you doing with the rest of your day?" I was glad I was a conduit in helping Ted, but my Saturdays were for the most part sacrosanct, and I wanted to spend it with Daniel.

"I don't know." Ted shook his head bewildered by the whole experience. The thing you have to know about Ted is that he didn't believe in reincarnation, but he knew that there was something more out there that couldn't be explained. He was open-minded, a seeker who didn't trust but wanted to know.

"May I suggest something?" I asked placing my hand on his forearms. I saw a look of confusion cross his eyes. Jesus! Does he think I'm coming on to him? I withdrew my touch.

"Go home and take a nap. These sorts of experiences are very draining and will kick the shit out of you if you're not careful."

"That sounds so good," he whispered, grazing his fingers through his thinning hair. He drained his glass of brandy and handed it to me.

"Do you mind? I could use another shot." I took his glass and walked to the kitchen wondering how long this was going to last. I poured him a stiff one.

I was getting a major headache. I undid the topknot I had hurriedly twisted and my hair fell like a tangled mass around my hips and that's when I heard a sharp knock on the door. I handed Ted his brandy and opened the door. Eric was at the door.

"I'm sorry to disturb, but my toilet's plugged." He was a tall delicious dish of a man, the kind of guy that makes you travel down the dark corridors of your mind, the kind of guy whose grin moistens your panties.

"Your hair's grown." He nodded his approval.

"Come in, Daniel's gone," I said, grabbing my mass of hair and throwing it to the side of my shoulder. It cascaded over my left breast and hovered above my hip.

"Eric, Ted, Ted, Eric." I said, as I introduced them. The men shook hands politely and both turned their attention full on me, one with a neediness I found disconcerting and one with desire I found distracting. "Care for a drink while I try to figure out which plumber our landlord is now using?" I asked Eric.

"What are you having?" he asked Ted.

"Brandy," he answered, caught in his own musings.

"Ahhhh," Eric said.

"It's a French V.S.O.P," I added.

"I'd love one!" Eric answered, throwing his head back on the futon like he lived here. I poured a generous shot and handed it to him.

He caught my eyes with his blue gaze and for a second too long we had a moment. Ted looked at us quizzically, and I blushed.

I sauntered to the bedroom/office and found Daniel's address book. I called the latest plumber and was able to confirm that the account was still open. Our landlord was in Italy visiting family and we were on our own, which was fine.

I called out to Eric, "They can come out today between five and nine. Does that work?" I held the mouthpiece against my chest.

"I'm going to be at work." He had risen and was in my bedroom standing behind me. I was so uncomfortable. I turned and craned my neck to look at him. "Would it be okay if I let them in?"

He was holding his glass of brandy and considered me with a long appraising look and finally nodded his head.

"Yes! It's okay."

I was back on the phone talking to the scheduler. "Have them call my number. Do you still have it on file? Yeah, that's the one, and ask for Kat. Great." I hung up.

I abruptly stood up and turned when Eric's hand settled on my shoulder. I had no choice but to meet his blue eyes. "Thanks for handling this." I nodded my head, afraid that whatever I said might sound shaky and garbled. He took another swig of his brandy.

"This is good, who is it?"

I shrugged. "Some Trader Joe's Brand, nothing special but it's French."

I walked ahead and then turned back to see Eric appraising my ass like it was some kind of bonbon; he saw me stare at him in stupefaction and threw me a wicked grin. My heart missed a beat. This guy was such a player.

I sat next to Ted, which made Eric the orphan, and he had to take my seat. There was no way Ted was going to talk about his hypnotherapy session in front of this stranger. I could pretty much count on the fact that they would have to go within the next ten minutes. Ted got up abruptly and said "Kat, it's been a long day." He bowed to me, which seemed so awkward. "I'd better go; besides you seem to have a full plate."

I was about to give Ted a hug and decided to give him an encouraging pat on the back instead.

"It's going to be great now," I promised. "You'll see, and let me know if you need to talk." He nodded his head and left. When I turned Eric had made his way to the futon. He patted the seat next to him," So here we are," he said, smiling.

Thankfully, I heard the key in the lock. Must be Daniel, I thought, relief flooding me.

The door swung wide, and I rushed to hug

him. He was shocked, as I never did that. Then he saw Eric. Daniel raised a questioning brow, and to say he didn't look too happy would have been an understatement. "What's up Eric?" he asked, as he walked in and closed the door behind him.

"He's having a plumbing problem with the toilet again," I rushed in. Daniel shrugged.

"Want a glass of wine?" Daniel smiled in response. He sat next to Eric, and I could see that the tension was getting tight. I handed Daniel his glass of wine. No one spoke.

"So Eric, how's the restaurant?" I had to break the silence because the room felt like the coming of a second Ice Age.

"Yeah, fine. Fine. Can't complain," Eric grinned. He was holding his brandy glass with a casualness that left me to wonder how long he planned to stay here and fuck with Daniel.

"How's the brandy?" I asked, sending Daniel a sharp stare; fuck, talk to him, I thought to myself.

But Daniel would have none of it. He hated games. He got up and began to pace the floor. I was dazed. What the hell did he think he was doing? But then what was I thinking? Daniel knew me like the back of his hand.

Eric drank the rest down and got up and handed me the glass.

"Thanks, that hit the spot." He was heading

towards the door. "Hey, later man," Eric called out, but Daniel never turned around and grunted a reply. Eric turned and looked down at me giving me his most devilish grin. I answered in kind and saw his eyes widen. Fuck, this arrogant ass.

When the door closed, Daniel turned on his heels. "So what's going on?" he barked.

"I called the plumbers and they'll be here in the late afternoon. Eric will be out so we'll have to let them in."

"That's not what I meant." He was pissed off.

"What?"

"You know damn well, what!"

"Uh, no, I really don't."

He crossed the room and stared down at me hard.

"That guy wants to fuck you and you know it! And the worst part is that you like him," he spat the last words with disgust.

"I don't have a clue..." I started to speak but broke off. "He's just a player." I realized that I had better be honest because if I wasn't, Daniel was going to blow.

"Ok, fine, he's cute. But I would never fuck him, I mean come on..." I twisted my index finger around the length of my hair.

"I'm not worried about you. I'm worried

about him," he said, pointing to the door, as if Eric still stood there.

I stepped within Daniel's body and snuggled myself against him. I knew that this would be the only way for me to get him to calm down and breathe. Right now he was like a pawing bull about to charge. He lowered his cheek against the top of my head and inhaled and exhaled very deliberately. His big arms enfolded me and that's how we stood for a long time. Alex, our Persian, meowed his approval.

"How's Ted?" Daniel whispered against my forehead.

"He's ok; he's really tired. But you wouldn't know; you've never done it." I flung these last words like accusations. What was wrong with me? Why was I turning on him like that? All I knew was that I couldn't help myself. I just couldn't understand why Daniel refused to visit Lucy for a past life regression. But he would not be pushed, and told me everything he needed to know, he already knew, and what he didn't know, he preferred it to remain so. He could be so infuriating. I mean with all our relationship challenges, you'd think he'd want to know why. It seemed as if he had no interest. I had no idea how wrong I was.

***

October 13, 1997

"You won't believe this!" I threw the phone down on its cradle, and it almost tipped over from the force. I walked into the kitchen and found Daniel making a second pot of coffee. He turned on his heels.

"I just spoke to Bob. He basically said that things look dour." I was fuming.

"What does he mean by dour?" Daniel raised a questioning brow.

"If we don't get our numbers up we are out!" I couldn't believe such mismanagement.

"So they're not trying to get some new techs?" Daniel poured us each a cup of coffee, our Braun coffee maker sputtering the last drops of water through the filter, a little steam rose.

"No! No new techs, it's too late for that. We have to work with what we have." I stared into Daniel's eyes feeling my heart skip a beat in panic. I might get laid off right before Christmas and then where would we be? I wanted to cry and scream. I had absolutely no control over my fate—or did I?

"Come on," he said, leading me by the hand to the futon. We sat together nursing our coffee in silence, the only witness to our moment. Alex was asleep on the kitchen counter without a care in the world. Tears welled up and began to pour down my face.

"Sshhhh, it's going to be all right." Daniel pulled me to him and rocked me against his chest. We swayed back in forth. I'd begged Daniel to get a 'real' job just in case mine caved in.

A week before, I'd set up a job interview with one of the three techs who actually took the business seriously. They said they were looking at other account managers and would get back to me in two or three weeks. When I'd left the interview, a strange twist slithered within my stomach and weighed me down with doubts. Now here it was; we had until December 15 to get things turned around or the board would pull the plug.

As soon as the other account managers heard the news they fell into a flurry of activities. Instead of bearing down and hitting the phones to make the thing float, they bailed and were busy sending out their resumes and going to interviews. No one wanted to be in the unemployment lines two week before Christmas. Frankly, I couldn't blame them. We all had bills to pay and none of our creditors gave a shit what our sob story was; late notices and cut-off notices would be sent regardless.

Yeah, tell me again how money doesn't bring you happiness. I had my health I had my love, and the stress in our relationship was caused by lack of money. Money may not buy happiness, but it sure as hell would make my life easier and sweeter sharing it with Daniel instead of fucking dealing with these major episodes constantly.

Right now, I could have used a mini-vacation to the Bahamas or somewhere just as exotic, but I didn't have a pot to piss in, much less the funds to buy a plane ticket to anywhere. Bitter? Maybe, and mad as hell! Yes, right now in that moment, I was both of those.

I felt a temper fill my lungs against Daniel. Why the hell wasn't he out looking for a fucking job? I wanted to howl but was terrified that if I opened my mouth all hell would fly out and destroy everything that stood in its wake. Anger issues? You're damn straight. I had them in spades, a rage that shock against the cage of limitation caused by lack of choices which are caused by a lack of cash.

I got up and took a strong swig of my coffee. When I turned to look at him, Daniel was grinning from ear to ear. "Guess what?" he asked like a mischievous little boy who had a secret to share. I just wasn't in the mood. He pushed off the sofa and stood in front of the kitchen entrance.

"Do I look like I'm in the mood to play games?" I muttered, pushing past him to the kitchen.

"What the hell is up with you?" he asked surprised.

"I don't know." I opened the fridge and reached for the little Limoges creamer. "I'm about to lose my job," I said as I poured a little more cream in my coffee. The interview last week sucked! Do you need any more reasons?" I slammed the fridge door and turned so abruptly that I hit my head on the slanted ceiling above me. "Fuck!" It hurt like hell. I rubbed my forehead.

"Karma!" Daniel called out.

I stuck my tongue out. Daniel came to my side and wrapped an arm around my shoulder and led me back to the futon. "Come on, Baby. It's gonna be all right." We sat together, my head on his chest. He placed the palm of his hand against my forehead. I knew he was sending healing energy; I closed my eyes to receive it. We sat still for a while until the pain diminished from a high throbbing pulse, until it finally disappeared altogether. I sat up. "I'm sorry Daniel, what's your news?"

"I got a job!" he announced joyfully.

"Oh, my god! Are you kidding? That's awesome!" Whatever deep weight I'd carried lifted like birds freed from their cage.

"Where? What?" I realized that my heart was lighter. I wanted him to know how much this meant to me.

"At a car dealership, in Duarte; it's not much, but it should help." I placed my fingertips over his lips and whispered, "You have no idea how much better I feel." Our lips met as we spoke promises and exchanged thank yous, and prayers for better times, all in between feathered kisses. I had work to do and pulled away. Daniel wasn't going to start until first thing tomorrow morning and wanted to make love. I held the choice between my hands, and then my inner voice shrugged and said, fuck it! I followed suit. We fell into each other's arms feeding on each other's passions and a thirst for life's gifts. It was the balm my soul needed and my body cried with joy at every touch of his hand, and every kiss of his lips. I felt alive. I felt free.

18

THE LION DEVOURS THE SUN

Two full moons had marked the sky before Ama confirmed what I already knew; Kryu's seed had been planted. I would bear his son. I felt it, as I had known that my first born was a girl. I knew. I begged Ama not to say a word. How foolish of me to ask, for Kryu never spoke to her.

I should have known what type of man Kryu was, for he was aware of all that went on around him. I was deep in thought taking my bath when he appeared. He waved the slaves away; Ama stood her ground, but I nodded that she too was to leave us. He pulled a short carved chair, which was strong enough to bear his weight, and he sat near the tub and watched me for a long time. I felt as if a thousand birds were trapped within my heart and fought for release.

I sat up in the tub, my hands covering my bare breasts. He reached towards me and pulled my hands away. He held one breast and then the other in his hand, his thumb stroking my hard nipple. A flash of lightening travelled from his touch to my belly. I hungered for him; my eyes lowered afraid to meet his gaze. He was without mercy, and pulled my chin up and leaned forward so that I would meet his searching eyes. I stared and recoiled by what I saw. A coldness cloaked Kryu. He frightened me.

"What little secret do you keep from me, my dear Queen?" He challenged me to lie.

"I have no secrets from you," I answered.

"My King," he said.

I shook my head in confusion.

"I am your king, address me as such."

"My King," I answered dutifully.

He threw me a cool smile that never reached his eyes. What was this anger he carried. What had I done to displease him so?

I rose, red rose petals clung to my skin gleaming with oil, rivulets of water slid down my limbs, my breasts, my belly, and down my buttocks and thighs. I stepped one foot out and then the other. I stood before him defiant and took out the long stick of horn that held my hair up; it fell in a wild mass about my body. He stood up, his hand grazing the curve of my jaw line and trailed down my neck to my collarbone. He grabbed me within the embrace of his arms and carried me to my bed, a bed he had not shared with me these last seven nights. Where he had been, I was not told, for Ama knew nothing and none of the slaves dare address me.

He lay me down among the white furs and his body followed mine. He buried his face between my neck and shoulder. I felt him shudder. I tentatively touched his broad back, and wrapped my fingers around the base of his neck. His hair fell over my hand. He was so beautiful. I inhaled his scent of sweat and leather; he felt so good to me that I moaned. He broke free and propped himself on his elbow, his face upon his hand to stare down at me. His hair fell over his brow, both of which were touched with gold. I brushed the tendrils aside and smiled at him with a tenderness that mirrored the very depth of my heart. My eyes spoke to him with words I could not utter.

The cool gray of his eyes was warmed by the sun of my love. I raised my head to tenderly place a kiss upon his lips, dry from the extreme heat we had felt over the past days. He devoured my mouth like a wolf feeding on its prey. I wanted him to desire me, but I wanted him to open his heart. I cried out for him to stop. I pushed against his chest. He was relentless in his hunger and would not stop the trail of his mouth from burning me with a yearning for more. His armor dug against my bare breasts and pricked my skin, and I cried out. He rose without a word and stripped his armor off, his belt, and his loin cloth. His large heat released thus was long and hard with want. He sank between my open thighs. The tip of his manhood caressed my mound, and he suddenly swung sharp and strong within me. I cried out with joy. All my doubts, all thoughts disappeared like leaves ripped from a sudden gust of wind falling from a tree. I was free to be his woman now. His lips circled my nipple, and I arched within the curve of his arm. He held me high against his chest, kissing my breasts, my high ribs, his hand caressing my belly and hips. He swung positions so that he fell upon his back and I was astride him. He held on to my buttocks as I rode him across lands we had not yet discovered. I saw his eyes melt beneath the sway of my golden hips; I saw him spiral as I savaged his seed from his body. I threw my head back, and closed my eyes, moving fast as the sweat of our mating dewed our skin. He bellowed his release and shook into me as I fell across his chest, my long hair a dark curtain across us. I felt the words escape my lips before I could gain sense. "I love you," I whispered against his jaw.

"I know," he groaned against my ear, nibbling on the lobe. I shivered.

"I am to bear your son," I whispered. I gazed up at him expectantly. His large hand covered my belly; his eyes were gray clouds moving across a sky of emotions I could not fully understand.

"Is this the secret you thought I kept from you?" I continued hoping for some reaction to this long-desired news.

He did not answer, but held me close in his arms as if he was afraid I would float away.

"Please speak to me . . ." I felt an overwhelming need to feel the closeness I had felt with Malek. I wanted Kryu above all else. He was all that I wanted, even knowing how he was, silent and unwilling to give me his heart, or share his thoughts.

"A son from your body will be a great gift to my people," he finally answered.

"Can you find a place in your heart for me?" I begged him, tears running down my cheeks.

He stared at me for a long time, never once wiping the tears from my face as Malek would have done. He was hard stone, and yet something in his eyes glimmered, a light that was directed at me, or did I imagine even that? Was there nothing in him that he could give me besides his sex, his hands, his lips, and his body?

He brought me to lie on top of his broad chest. I placed my hands on top of each other and cradled my chin thus staring into his face. His hands caressed my lower back and buttocks. We stayed in that position for some time, regarding each other more like adversaries than lovers.

I was the one to break the silence.

"Can you find any one area of your heart for me?" I pleaded again.

"My heart is not your realm. Take care of my desires and you will have my protection and my gratitude."

I was shaken by the cold words he offered me. I rose abruptly and called for Ama to help me dress. I knew that all words of any value had long past. She appeared swiftly, which surprised me.

He lay on his side, nude and unashamed to cover his body from her view. He watched me dress. Then I sat in front of my polished copper mirror and saw him watch me as she brought some order to my disheveled hair, which she oiled and combed into a long braid which she placed over my left shoulder; it swung down to my hip.

"Call the lyre player and have him follow me to the terrace. I will take my late super there," I ordered Ama. The sun's light had journeyed three quarters of the sky and would soon be devoured by the moon's desire to take her rightful place amongst the stars.

Kryu spoke. "How long has my queen not bled?" I was shocked for he had never addressed Ama until now. Ama's face turned white as the linen tunic I wore. I nodded for her to answer him.

"She's not bled for two full moons, my king."

He rose from the bed and stood next to me, his hand on my shoulder.

"I will have my physician examine her tomorrow at first light."

"Yes, my king." Ama bowed and was about to turn to fetch my meal when Kryu stopped her.

"I am not done." Ama turned all flushed and trembling.

"I will have my meal with my queen. Bring jugs of wine, roasted meat, and whatever else will please my lady." He smiled down at me. "I will be spending my days with her."

He held my hand and had me rise. We walked to the terrace where my favorite divan was strewn with pillows.

"You will please me with your mouth . . ." I swallowed hard and gazed into his gray eyes hot with hunger. "No woman pleases me as you do. Does that answer your question?" He glanced down at his rising member, hard with anticipation for the taste of my mouth. I found myself eager to bury my face between his tanned thighs. I wanted to lick the silken sacks filled with his seed. I wanted to know once again the power my mouth had upon his being. I wanted to watch him collapse and look into my golden eyes and know that he loved me in spite of his battling the truth of it. I wanted him beneath the sun's dark rays. I took him again to that whirlwind of pleasure he had sought to replicate with other women but had not found. I was the one who traveled his mind. He may not have told me he loved me, but I was beginning to see it rise like the sun that breaks through thunderous clouds. My mouth closed over his heat, and he groaned deep as if in pain. He buried his hands in my hair and moved his hips in motion. I allowed him his way and then pulled my mouth away and trailed my tongue around his orbs scented by the maleness of him. My tongue explored the region between his sack and his anus, right there soft to the touch. He growled.

"Please..." He swallowed hard staring down at me holding his length in his hand.

"Your mouth," he whispered. I smiled up at him and surrounded his heat and pulled on him, lips and tongue with a swiftness that made him shout as he pulsed his seed into my mouth. I was famished to taste the salt of him. It was at that moment that Kryu collapsed upon the large divan and Ama appeared carrying two jugs of wine, the lyre player close behind, and two slaves in tow carrying our meals upon large bronze trays.

Kryu laid his forearm over his eyes, his member spent across the left of his muscular thigh. He was like a god fallen from the skies, fallen to be with a woman like me. I reveled in that knowledge, that I could bring him to lands he had never explored, and this knowing make me feel light and powerful.

*****

At first light, Kryu's physician came to examine me. This was to be the third man to ever touch my person. Kryu stood watching while the physician touched my breasts and ascertained swelling and pressed upon my flat stomach. I lay on my back, and he instructed me to raise my knees as far as I could. He placed two fingers within me, pushing deep which brought me discomfort so that I squirmed my hips away from the depth of his prodding.

He glanced up at Kryu. "Your son lies sleeping in her belly."

Kryu's face broke into a wide smile. I found myself mirroring his joy. I'd already known but this somehow this made it official.

"When?" Kryu asked, his large forearms folded across his broad chest.

"When the snows cover the mountains peaks she will push him into the world."

Moons would rise and fall before I would hold this child in my arms. Then a dark cloud scattered its web of confusion within my thoughts. Would I live long enough to see him born? A chill gathered from my neck and ran down my spine. The answer was clear.

The physician left my side. I rose from my state and pulled my tunic down. A slight soreness troubled my walking. Kryu called for his men to be brought to our apartments. They came, all twelve of his most trusted. They filled the room with their presence, each of them tall creatures from a land I did not know, and speaking in a tongue I did not understand. How did Kryu come to speak our words? I had wondered often enough, but he had refused to answer my questions. The general, who first caught us in the tender moment that launched Kryu's guarded demeanor, what was his name? Ah, yes, Tanis. It was he who approached me. He lowered his gaze to my belly and leveled me with green eyes of such a light color that I gasped by their transparency. He was so close that I could smell the heat of his desire.

"Now that you bear his son, I will endeavor to know your talents," he said.

I swung my head up to his eyes dark with unfettered passions. I searched for Kryu who was encircled within the heated congratulations of his men. Tanis grabbed my upper arm and pulled me close; he lowered his mouth to my ear and whispered, "I have heard of the magic of your mouth. I've seen you ride my king to the ends of the world. I will have you before you give birth to his cub."

"He would never share me with you!" Be still, my inner voice counseled, be still and learn who these men are. So I listened to my voice and changed from rage to seduction. I glanced up at him and smiled. His eyes blinked as if clearing his vision to see if I was real. I nestled close to him; he lowered his head. "I doubt he would share me, but I would not mind tasting the secrets you hide." I was a whore in that moment and felt a slight shiver of shame but pressed on.

"You speak so well. Where did you learn our language," I cajoled. Unlike Kryu, perhaps he would share what our king had withheld.

He smiled, a good smile with teeth still intact.

"Kryu's mother was a priestess from your land. She fled to be with his father and taught us the language of her land."

His hand circled the orb of my buttock, out of sight of Kryu. He massaged it and whispered, "I would want nothing more than to have you to myself, but Kryu will not have you out of his sight," he sighed. "But I am assured of tasting you for one night." I shuddered and turned to him, my eyes wide with question.

He sneered. "My dearest queen, I will taste you; it is our way."

I knew that he lied; I wanted to know that he lied. I pushed his hand away. He laughed and licked the inner part of my ear and blew warm air, I shivered. "And our king," Kryu glanced up and stared at me from across the room as Tanis continued, "will watch as I conquer your body and tame it to my will." Tanis nodded his head and Kryu answered in kind. O' dearest Ishtar would this be my fate to be taken? Was Kryu so fearful of love that he would do all in his power to destroy it within himself and within me? I wanted to run, but Tanis held me within the hard grip of his hand, and I stood about to fall to my knees when Kryu approached me. He must have noticed my distress.

"My queen, your face is devoid of color?" He spoke and glanced at Tanis unaware of words exchanged.

"I cannot…" I felt myself bend over and all that was in my belly came up.

When I was done, Kryu lifted me in his arms and called out to his men to leave, that his queen was to bed.

Amid laughter and shouts they shouted, "Your son is impatient to walk out of her belly. Your son kicks her belly and demands to be born!" Many salutations were thrown his way as they left his company. Tanis stood silent waiting for his lord and master to command him. "She is young and strong my lord." Tanis announced. "When will I taste her?"

Kryu cradled me in his arms and glanced over his shoulder at Tanis. So it was true; I would be his soon enough. Kryu looked down at me, and watched my eyes fill with tears. I saw something soft, something. . . a confusion cross his eyes, and then he coldly called out:

"Soon, once she is able to control the sickness." Tanis laughed roughly. Kryu deposited me upon the bed, tore the linen tunic off my person and said, "Look upon her and know that soon you will taste everything she is." Tanis's green eyes lit up and grazed every curve exposed to him.

I saw his loincloth pull. His eyes met mine and threw me a silent promise.

"We will share her, perhaps, until she gives birth to my son," Kryu shrugged and then waved for him to go. Tanis saluted, "My king," turned and walked out of the room. A howl lifted out of my heart and spilled upon the open air. "Why, why would you destroy what we have?" I cried. He stood above staring down at me with the most impassive look. I was terrified.

19

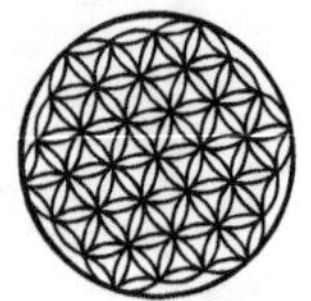

NOTHING IN LIFE REMAINS STATIC
OCTOBER 15, 1997

Thank God it was freaking Wednesday; the week was coming to an end. That's the thing about life, it always moves forward. Nothing ever remains the same; it was my mantra, my hope, one of the things that made life bearable when things got too tough. The knowledge that all things changed and that in time what swung down would swing back up.

I'd gotten a call from the Value Added Reseller who had interviewed me. The VAR said the job was mine if I wanted it. I would still work from home, and they would provide me with a decent salary plus commission with the promise of promotion. I was combustible; I was so happy. Daniel was working at the dealership and was scheduled to work until midnight every night until Monday. They were having some kind of Midnight Madness Sale. It was fucking insane. Who the hell would buy a car at midnight? But apparently I was wrong; they did buy and sit at the dealership sometimes until as late as three in the morning. I was shocked!

The masses never failed to amaze me, from getting up at two in the morning to get ready and show up at a store to stand in line and wait for the store to open at four a.m. so that they would save fifty to hundred bucks, perhaps even four hundred. Save! What were they really saving? The ads were bold in their promise that the more you spend the more you saved. That just killed me! It made me laugh out loud. What a hustle. I mean who believed such malarkey? The answer: a huge majority did and fell upon these Black Friday deals like locusts. Even I, an avid shopper, found this alarming. Imagine what they could do with this type of energy to change the politics of this country. No, too simple; these were the kinds of people who would prefer to buy a generator on sale in preparation for the apocalypse rather than take this type of focus and launch it to make some radical changes that could transform the world. Strange, I wondered at the politics of consumership.

Things were looking up for us. I had a job, which was good, but since Daniel had started his job, he was never home except to sleep. I felt abandoned. When he wasn't working, he was always underfoot, and now that he worked I never saw him. The writing was on the wall; as long as he had that job, this would go on indefinitely and on a guarantee of minimum wage or commission, whatever was greater. He'd started a week ago, and already I wanted him to quit.

Malek and I were talking every day, drawing back the veils to unearth the most amazing details. All sense memories more than anything, the recollections as I said before, came in my sleeping dreams, in my open-eyed meditations with Malek, and during the most mundane moments. Say, like doing the laundry I would zone out for a moment and see the images roll before my eyes like what Ted had called movie reels. It was on such a very occasion while doing my laundry that Eric surprised me in the laundry room in the basement of the old Victorian house. I'd forgotten to wear my bra and had thrown on an old white sweatshirt with a gold design on the front, which I hoped disguised my nipples standing straight out and hard from the cold. Though there was a frosty chill to the air, walking up and down the stairs with baskets of laundry made for sweaty work.

"Hello, neighbor," he called out. I jumped out of my reverie and laughed nervously when I saw his face peeking around the door. I climbed the three stone steps up to meet him. He lived right above this make-shift laundry room and storage area.

"I'm just starting to start the laundry." I sounded apologetic and rather stupid. Starting to start the laundry? What the hell was wrong with me? I laughed nervously.

"No worries, I can wait." He shrugged and his eyes scanned my bare shoulders peeking from my large sweatshirt, the neck of which I had cut so that it always fell off my shoulders. It made me feel sexy when I did the laundry. I was wearing black leggings and little gold mules. My hair was twirled onto a top knot and long tendrils fell over my brows and temples and the length of my neck. I was hyper aware of all that I describe to you because I saw his eyes scan every inch of me, and as he did I was doing my own mental inventory. He's just a player, I told myself. Do not believe this thing; it's just lust.

"I can knock on your door when I'm done, if you like."

"What are you doing right now?" he asked.

"Right now?" I was truly puzzled.

"Yes, I mean when you're done with putting all your stuff in the machine?"

"I'll just go back upstairs and wait."

"Do you like red wine?" He tossed me a wink.

Ahhh shit! I thought, of course I love red wine. "Well, it depends on the wine. I have to warn you, I only drink French wines." I stood on the stoop of the doorway and faced him squarely. He gave me a long slow smile.

"Help me try this one." He grabbed my hand and dragged me into his kitchen; then he brought me to his living room which doubled as his bedroom. It was clean, the wood floors swept. There were two large impressionist paintings on his wall and his bed stood by the window, right below our pink futon. The thought flashed before me that he may have heard Daniel and I have sex. The idea made me blush. I checked my Swiss Army watch, which I wore loosely on my right wrist. It was 3:15 p.m.; I had a half hour before I would need to unload the washer and load the dryer and do the whole thing all over again with two loads of color.

"Sit here." He pointed to a large dark brown leather chair crackled with age, the kind you'd see in an old English gentleman's club. I had to give this guy credit, he had style. I saw a bagpipe leaning against the wall next to his bed.

"You play?"

He was in the kitchen, and popped his head around the door.

"Eh, yea, I do. . . I'm... you know, teaching myself." I heard him uncorked the bottle and within seconds he was carrying two large balloon glasses of red wine.

"Is it French?" I asked expectantly.

"I'm not telling until you try this." He sat across from me, in a plantation style chair.

We clicked glasses. "What shall we toast to?" he asked provocatively.

"Clean laundry," I answered.   We both laughed.

"I'll drink to that." I sniffed my glass and swirled it just so and caught the scent of black cherry and then the flavor changed into a meatiness that took over all senses. This was not a wine one drank mindlessly; this was something one had to think and savor, a perfect wine to share while chatting with a friend. It was good and bold, and quite frankly took my socks off. Which I imagine is what he had intended. I hadn't eaten, so it hit me right away.

"What do you think?" He was staring at me.

I held the glass aloft, "It's good, but it's not French is it?" I smiled. I was doing a little victory dance in my head.

"No, it's not." He went into the kitchen and brought the bottle back. It was a 1996 Thomas Coyne.

"Do you like it?" I nodded my head and took another mouthful letting it travel through my palate. It was heady.

"What do you think?" I asked Eric. He stood above me and said, "I'm damned impressed."

"You like it that much?" I was puzzled.

"No, I meant you. You just impressed me." He kneeled across from me. He was getting too close. Why had I been playing Russian roulette with my libido? What was wrong with me? What did I think was going to happen? I needed an escape I would beg off to handle my laundry. So without thinking, I tilted my hand to glance at my watch, and when I did my hand that held the glass of wine poured out like a stream and splashed his jeans, and leather driving moccasins. I was mortified. "I'm so sorry!"

He laughed so hard that I began to laugh and before I knew it my stomach hurt; we laughed, and the ice had broken. Had he reached for me at that moment, I'm not sure I would have pushed him away. I heard a knock on his door. I was wondering if I'd be facing one of his girlfriends. Instead, it was Daniel holding a bag of Pollo Loco, his face a mask of anger and confusion.

20

TANIS

Kryu rose before the dawn and left without a word. I was no longer allowed to ride, or hawk, nor had I been allowed to see Malek or my children. All that I loved had been removed. It was no wonder my new king was becoming my world.

Unable to sleep and restless, I called Ama to prepare a bath which at least would distract me for a time. It was from her that I gathered news of those exiled from my presence. I stood nude before my copper reflection and saw that my belly barely rose to show that a child was coming. My breasts were fuller, and my hips perhaps rounder. Ama came followed by five slaves each bearing large bronze pots containing water warmed for this purpose. Ama swept my hair up securing it with a large carved bone in the shape of a thunderbolt. They poured the water containers into the large bronze tub, and walked out as Tanis walked through the large open doors.

I shielded my breasts from his burning

gaze. He could not possibly take me now? Had Kryu told him he could? My mind ran rampant, rushing to find answers to his unwelcome presence.

Ama stepped before him, "My queen is to bathe, my lord." He raised his hand and signaled for me to step into the tub, which I did, finding solace in the water, perfumed with oils and floating rose petals.

"What do you want?" I asked, my chin held high.

"I am here to keep you company, my queen." He smiled, his eyes alight with admiration.

"Bring me a chair." Ama pointed to one beneath the arch of a large window that led out to my gardened terrace. He walked to it and carried it to my tub, placing it right by me so that now we could speak face to face.

He breathed in the air around me and nodded his approval. "You will be sweet to taste, good to smell."

I bristled with anger.

"I am not your woman to bait as you will. I am Kryu's. I belong to him! I demand that you leave my presence."

His hand dipped in the water, his fingers circled a breast and then pulled on the nipple; it was hard and pointy. I shuddered and pushed his hand away. He laughed and placed his hand beneath the water to trail fingers down my breastbone to my belly and between my thighs holding my sex within his grasp. He leaned forth to deliver these words, his lips pressed against my ear: "Cry out and I will call the woman who attends you to slit her throat. Allow me my way, and I will not hurt one of your children. Tell Kryu, and I will let Malek die." I drew back and locked eyes with his.

"Do you understand me?"

I swallowed hard and nodded my head.

"Now stand," he snarled. I rose and stood with my shoulders thrown back. His hands were all over my body, touching me in ways that frightened me. His long golden hair fell about his brow and swung about his broad shoulders. He was tall, not as tall as Kryu, but as with all these men, he was big. He lifted me from the tub. The sounds of booted sandals resounded upon the large stone slabs and alerted me that Kryu was back. I felt a sigh escape my lungs and relief flooded my being.

Tanis dropped me to my feet and stood back. I twirled upon my heels and faced Kryu, who saw Tanis first, and then me. He raised a questioning brow.

"Bakor, what is this?"

I glanced at Tanis and was about to answer when he answered for me.

"Your son has brought about a hunger for the heat of a man's sword. I was summoned to her side." I whirled to argue his lies and then my thoughts fell upon my children, and what he would do to them should I speak out. Kryu must know this is a lie. Hadn't I begged him not to allow this man in our bed? And yet Kryu did not counter Tanis; instead, he shook his head and muttered that the ways of women always surprised him. I felt the tears of shame fall from my eyes.

"I am weary from riding far to the outskirts of the mountains securing our hold upon these lands."

"Rebels my King?"

Kryu shook his head.

"How goes it then?" Tanis asked.

Kryu was undoing his chest armor and ignored Tanis's question.

"A bath! Ama is the water still warm?" Ama nodded her head.

"Shall I bring you wine, my king?" Kryu was stripping off his loincloth and stepped into the large tub.

"Shall I leave you, my King?" Tanis approached the tub.

Kryu looked up, his large forearms resting on either side of the tub, his head thrown back on the rim.

"You must try this, Tanis, it is a wonder." He grinned, and then his brow furrowed. He was like the weather in winter, ever changing.

"So you say she summoned you?"

I wanted to shake my head and scream denials; instead, I stood still and meek.

"Then take her Tanis, bring her to heel. Pleasure her now!" Tanis grabbed me around the waist and threw me on the bed that stood steps from Kryu and his bath.

Tanis removed his loin cloth and what rose from between the gold hairs was a member long and thick. I wanted to scream. He climbed beside me and kissed my lips with a gentleness that surprised me. His hand was between my mound, and he separated my thighs, venturing a large finger over the pearl that peeked out. A shot of pleasure rushed through me, and I arched in surprise. "She is hungry for a man," Kryu called out chuckling.

Tanis lowered his head and trailed his tongue down from my aching nipples to my trembling belly until he met my mound and there slipped his tongue within me and circled my pearl until I moaned deep from within my throat. Still, he would not allow me to breathe and tugged hard with his mouth until I exploded into his waiting mouth. He rose laughing. "She is easy to cajole into submission, my King."

Kryu nodded his approval. Tanis continued his assault and lowered his head between my thighs to wage his unmerciful attack and would not stop his siege upon my body. I thrashed my head back and forth; a riot was forming at the base of my belly. My breathing was fast, and I looked down to see his gold head buried between my thighs again, eating from me as if I was a date dripping with honey. My hips arched into the cradle of his hands as he raised my hips to meet his open mouth, and still I cried in pleasure. I gathered a trick in my head and closed my eyes and imagined that it was Kryu's mouth and not Tanis that brought me such pleasure. When Tanis settled himself between my thighs, I was wet and warm for him. His member pushed hard; my mound would not allow him entry and still he pushed breaking down my gates until I swung them open, and he rode me until I could no longer hold back. My arms embraced his shoulders and my legs held up by his powerful arms, so that he pressed deeper within me touching that pearl within, stroking it with every thrust and deeper still he rode. I felt all sense of honor fall away. I locked gaze with his green eyes; I saw that he too was lost in the swirling mist that now surrounded us, shielded us, from Kryu's amused gaze. Together we shouted our release, falling from the sky and landed upon trembling legs. When I came to my senses, I saw Tanis looking down at me; he raised one gold brow in mock question. I began to feel hate for him that grew from my belly and spread to my heart.

"She was well worth the wait, my King." He rose from between my legs and pushed my thighs away from him as if I was now more of an encumbrance than a need. His manhood was still hard and dripping with seed. He, like Kryu, was nothing more than a barbarian, yet what was I? What had I become? A whore who responded to any man's touch? Yet my heart knew the truth of it; I loved Kryu, and though my body responded to Tanis I could never love him as I loved Kryu.

Kryu waved for me to come to face him. I glanced around looking for a cloth or something to cover my person. "Do not cover yourself my Queen, come to me. Join me now." I stepped into the tub that was now cold and settled between his large thighs, his member long and hard and pressing upon my buttocks.

Water splashed over the tub as he settled and turned to Tanis.

"Come, Tanis join us. There is room." To my horror and surprise Tanis settled to face me. His hands found my mound and he fingered my pearl again. I lurched with surprised pleasure. I turned my head to my king.

"Could we not?" I whispered, but Kryu silenced my question by laying a fingertip over my lips. "Lean forward, on your hands and knees," he growled. I did as he commanded.

As Kryu rose the water level fell so that it reached my chin. He settled his heat between my buttocks and pushed himself as if I were a she-goat and he a ram.

Tanis's manhood rose in response to Kryu's dominion over me, who held a handful of my hair in his fist as he savagely thrusted within me. I cried out every time his entry brought about a flush of pleasure to ride its shiver down my body.

"Take him within your mouth and show him the exotic worlds you have shown me," Kryu demanded of me, as he relentlessly drove his fury within my shivering vulva. I felt nothing but the want to gain power over Tanis. I stared up at him; all the while I lowered my head and circled his member with my mouth. He gasped and closed his eyes, his hand tangling themselves within my hair, his hips rising to plunge his manhood deeper within the velvet warmth of my mouth. Kryu took me hard which threw me forward swallowing Tanis's manhood even further. I reveled in licking his length and feeling Kryu's spear plunge into me, again and again, water flying over the tub. Tanis threw his head back groaning. I saw his mouth open and the howl of his release spill all the arrogance he held between his legs. I was like a greedy beggar swallowing every drop until he shook all that was left. I wanted my revenge and licked the silken sack between his thighs which brought him to fall beneath the power of my mouth. He disappeared from the world and slept but not before he let out a long sigh. Kryu was relentless and after a time bellowed his release like a bull. I shuddered with a pleasure I had never felt before this day. My body was warm and my nipples hard. Kryu's head was thrown back upon the rim of the tub resting. I sat up and stepped out of the tub. I saw them together; two conquerors lay to waste by my mouth and body.

I smiled and called for Ama. I dressed and had my mare readied. I had Ama secret me to Malek. He was held in a stone room far from the cellars that kept our grains and wines. She handed me a dark brown cloak, torn to shreds, but the hood hid my face well. Ama told the guards that I was a healer summoned by the king to tend to his needs. Ama had hidden wine and fine foods deep within the basket I held that was also heavy with herbs and potions. When I stepped into the room, the cold of the stones shivered my body and the stench was unbearable. Malek was sitting with his back against the wall, staring up at nothing. It was as if he was waiting for death to end his sorrows.

"Malek," I whispered low for fear a guard overheard me. Malek blinked, and I threw the hood of my cape exposing my face to his blurred gaze.

"I am here my love." I came forth and held my hands out to him. He would not stand, and so I knelt to face him. His face carried confusion and then he broke into a wide smile. Tears began to fall down his gaunt face. His beard was matted with dirt, and his hair disheveled into a tangled mass of knots. His body was so thin that I saw every bone as he moved. He held my face in his hand. "You are my love, my most beloved Queen." I had just lain with two men and the shame I felt buried itself deep within my heart. I lowered my gaze unable to meet his trust.

"I've missed you," he whispered through a beard so long that it hid the shape of his mouth.

I brought his hands to my face, tears falling from my eyes, and kissed his long elegant fingers. How could this have happened? Why had the gods abandoned us and destroyed everything that had been beautiful and fine and good? His body shook with dry sobs. I embraced him, and rocked him as if he was a child. His head was pressed against my breasts, his arms encircling my waist. I felt the bone of his shoulders cut through the thin wool tunic, as my fingers travelled to cradled the nape of his neck, so thin. My mind traveled back to what we had been. Malek riding his stallion fast and hard over our lands and I pursuing him—Malek looking back at me and laughing wildly, his large black eyes shining with the passion of the moment, the joy of living, and I, catching up to his mount and throwing him a kiss with my hand and rushing ahead of him calling out that I had won the race. That is how I saw us. I closed my eyes, rocking him thus, and saw us as we had been, making love, embracing our three children, always laughter following our days. Now, all that was left of those days were images in our minds. Malek sheltered himself within this moment between us now, and I reached for him. I needed him to step out of the ravages of his shame and into the light of hope.

"Please my love," I whispered. "Hold tight to your courage; do not allow it to slip now. I will find a way for you and the children to escape." My words brought him back from the grief, and he stared at me.

"Will you come with us?"

I shook my head. "I cannot, for if I join you they will hunt us down, and that will mean your death." Malek's face fell apart at the realization that if my plan worked, he would never see me again. For me to leave with them would mean that Kryu would pursue me to the ends of the world, and now that his seed was planted, there was much, too much for Kryu to lose.

"My queen, please..." Ama said.

I gently disengaged Malek's fingers from my hands and rose. I stood above him. Malek, my love, my gentle king. Here is a basket for you, eat, drink, become strong. I will come again, when I can." I stepped away.

"My lady, your hood!" Ama cried out. I hurriedly covered my head and shielded my face within the folds.

A guard entered. "Has the healer healed?" The guard laughed harshly and kicked the basket. Ama grabbed it away from any further attacks and placed it near Malek's hip.

The guard grabbed my arm," Come here and let's take a look at your face. . ." Ama sprang between me and the guard. "She has the evil eye, and if you look upon her she will bring you disease and destruction." His hand fell away.

"Be gone then; your business is done here." He prodded me with his foot. I moved forward very slowly so as not to raise his alarm. This annoyed him and again he raged. "Be gone!" We left.

We moved through the windy catacombs, torch lights swaying their feeble light breaking through the dark corners. We came upon double doors that opened from the ground into the open light of the sky above us. I stepped up the little stairs and breathed in the fresh air. I pulled the cloak off me and handed it to Ama who took it over her hand. I leaned forward and gave her a hand up.

"When will I see him again?"

Ama looked away and muttered, "It will be some time."

My heart shivered,

"Why? Ama, I must see him again." She nodded her head, "I cannot say when, but I have found a man who is willing to take them out." My heart leapt with joy and wondered why she hadn't she told me this sooner.

"I will arrange a meeting with him." Ama stared into my eyes with a guarded look.

"He is a slave and with the right persuasion might not betray us." she added.

"Gold? I will give him all the gold that he desires."

"Yes, my queen, but he would want his freedom," she added.

Of course, why hadn't I thought of that? Freedom. Now I understood what it meant to be free, for now I no longer was free.

My mare had been readied and was waiting in the courtyard with my indigo cloak, and thin linen tunic spun of blood red and gold there was no mistake that I was a queen. I rode to the pools to bathe the sweat of their passions off my skin, to wash away the image of Malek buried deep in the earth, thin and dirty, alone and ravaged by loss and grief. I wondered if his death would have been a better way. I discarded my clothes and slid into the cool waters, my mind troubled by rage and fear, and desire.

I was feeling the healing powers of the waters, for swimming always cleared my mind and settled me into a place that brought me a sense of calm even during the most troubled times. Swimming beneath the waters cleaned me and made me new. I broke the surface of the water and heard the sound of approaching hoof beats. I was sure that it was Kryu. He swung off his mount enraged and ready to punish my disregard to his demands.

He tore through the water despite his full armor. I decided to ignore him and was floating on my back, my hair spread out like a wide fan. As he grew near, I stood up, my heart beating fast. He grabbed my arm and pulled me to shore. Again it was my body, the glow of it, the high golden breasts, and the secret portal between my thighs that brought him to heel. His eyes turned from thunder to soft gray clouds. He buried his face between my neck and shoulder.

"I thought you had gone," he whispered savagely, his arms crushing me against his body.

"Are you angered that Tanis brought me pleasure?" I asked against his chest.

He shook his head.

"You do not care that another man possessed me?" My mind wanted him to rage at what had happened.

"I am pleased. Tanis is a good and loyal friend. "He stepped back and gazed down at me.

"So you do not love me?" I muttered, my head bowed to his will. "Shall any man then have the right to possess me? What next?" I stepped away from him. "What man will you chose to take me next?" He moved towards me, his eyes alive with emotions that I could not place.

"Tanis is not any man, Bakor. He is as close as any brother. Please him, and you please me." I wanted to fall to my knees; instead I bowed my head to his will.

"Allow your body to enjoy his touch," he continued. "I will not desire you less for it. For we have and will always share our pleasures." He gently brought my chin up to gaze into his eyes. So this is how he had always kept love at bay? I thought. I lowered my gaze, and inhaled deeply the scent of the pools, of green plants, of the sweat from his body, the leathers he wore, and I opened my eyes to look at him. Tall, his light brown hair touched by gold, with a broad and beautiful face like a lion's, and with those eyes so filled with secrets, so unwilling to share thoughts that would help me understand him. I stood to face him and I now realized that what I gazed upon was a man where love had failed to ever set camp upon the field of his heart. How could he love? His heart was riddled with caves and the catacombs of his own deceptions. He must be a god, a man from another world, for how else could I explain the desire that howled mad against the constraints of my mind? How else could I explain his passions mired within the ice of his eyes? I would have done anything to win his heart. I would have allowed his very army to take me if I could but hear the words I longed for, words of love, the kind of love that held me above all the creatures of the world. I closed my eyes, my shoulders drawn forward; my arms embraced my body in protection against the truth of his heart. I felt him cover me with my cloak, rough linen dyed in the deepest indigo. He lifted me gently into his arms and carried me to my mare. Once upon her, I rode beside him. He brought his stallion next to my mount and took my hand in his, kissing it so tenderly, his eyes upraised to mine that I felt my breath catch. Our horses broke away, and so we rode the rest of the way in silence.

21

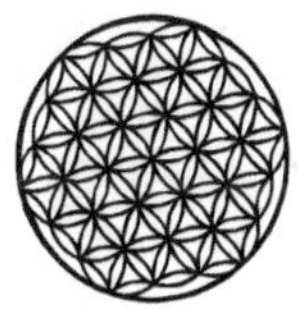

TRUST COMES IN MANY FORMS
OCTOBER 18, 1997

"Kat, what are you doing here?" Daniel mumbled, his eyes ablaze. Eric stood behind me.

"I wanted her to try a new wine the restaurant is thinking of adding to our wine list."

I wanted to sink. This moment would only have needed ten more minutes before it went from an innocent drink to a sexual encounter. I wanted to sink beneath the floorboards. I stepped out of Eric's apartment and sunk within the bewildered embrace of Daniel's arms.

I knew Daniel would never make a scene unless pushed to his limits, and we were still skating within the periphery of the safe zone, meaning he was not going to kick Eric's ass and given the choices if push-came-to-shove, I wasn't sure who would have come out the loser.

I thanked Eric for the wine, and though I had sampled just two sips, I was dizzy. Daniel and I walked silently up the stairs. He pulled out his key and found the lock and kicked the door open with his foot. He walked in leaving me behind to follow.

He dropped the bag of Pollo Loco on the kitchen counter and made his way to the bedroom.

He was undoing his tie, sliding it off his collar, and then began to undo the buttons of his shirt.

I walked to the kitchen, washed my hands and brought two plates down from the dish rack. He stood watching me, and then turned his back to me and paced the room. He abruptly swirled on his heels sent me a scowl. "What the fuck was that?" he whispered fiercely.

"I was doing laundry and . . ."

He crossed the room in two steps and grabbed my face in his hand and raised it to his burning green eyes. "Did I interrupt something?"

I managed to shake my head.

"If I ever see you with him like that again, I will kick the living shit out of him, do you get me?"

I'd never seen Daniel so angry. "Do you understand?" I nodded my head. I was concerned; why was he home early? What happened to the Midnight Madness Sale? Why in the fuck had he caught me doing nothing more than sharing a glass of wine with a man, and yes, possibly a screw. Oh, Christ! Why couldn't I break this link with Daniel? What fates bound us so tightly? I had forgotten that previous to his interruption I'd been planning to bail from Eric's not so subtle seduction, and yet had I really? I was utterly confused. I wanted nothing more than to feel Daniel's cock within me and yet, I didn't know what to say to Daniel. We ate in between silent accusations and vicious glares, and after a while we went to sleep. As tired as I was, I rose in the middle of the night to pee, and as I returned to the futon, I saw that Daniel was up.

"Can't sleep?" I muttered climbing in between the sheets shivering from the bitter cold that rose right through the floors and snuck in between the cracks of these old windows. I gathered the down comforter over us, and I felt Daniel's hand settled over my breast and cup it with determination. "He can never hold your big tits in his hands, do you know why?"

"Because, I won't let him?" I mumbled still drugged by exhaustion.

He shook his head, "No, he won't ever touch these beauties," his thumb rubbed my nipple possessively and it sprung hard, and ready, "because you belong to me." He pushed me down flat on my back and straddled me. I pushed him away.

"I 'm too tired Daniel, not tonight." He gave

up and rolled on his back, exhaling a long sigh. "Do you love me?" he whispered.

"What?" I played dumb. Did I love him? I thought I did; I knew I did. But I wanted something more, something he couldn't give me. I wasn't even sure what it was that I wanted. All I knew is that whenever I was faced with a choice to take another man as a lover, either circumstance or my own reluctance ended all opportunities. The bond we shared was strong, stronger then lust, stronger then hate. It was a shared connection, a trust based on acceptance of who we were as individuals, and behind all that stood the burning flame of love. So when I answered Daniel, I knew that I was telling him the truth, "Yes, I love you."

It was then that we fell asleep.

The first thing I did when I woke up was message Malek. I had been having the strangest dreams, wild sexual dreams that left me drenched in sweat.

"Malek, I have a question."

"Malek is typing."

"You are up early, my sweet Bakor. What troubles you?" I shook my head, even now in this life, without even seeing my face he knew me.

"Did I tell you about my neighbor that lives

below us?" I messaged to him.

Malek is typing--I could hear Daniel snoring loud and deep. I didn't have to worry about him at all. The answer came within minutes. "When messages come to me without thought I trust them. Your neighbor was known to you in that past life, my sweet Bakor."

"How?" was all I managed to type. Minutes passed before his message revealed his knowing. "He was a high ranking warrior, wasn't he?" How the hell did he know?

Then a thunderbolt shuddered through my body; Eric was Tanis. I sat back in the chair and all the air exhaled out of my lungs. Was I going crazy? How could it be so simple? How the hell had we all gathered from different parts of the world to meet here? What was the grand plan? I couldn't even tell Malek about Tanis; I had been too ashamed and had shied away from anything so personal.

The pieces began to fit into place. I was both horrified and awed because to see the big picture one had to admire life and all the marvels it offered. I was so damn lucky to experience this. If people could only understand the simple brilliance that reincarnation offered us. Yes, Buddha called life Dharma, and yet I called it magic, all of it, even suffering brought about a deeper empathy to others' plight. I did not follow any one religion for they all sought to judge me either sinful or misled. I have no need for such teachings, and when the time was right I would learn more. The main thing for me was to be kind to others and love without ego or care for my own pleasure and to hold onto such beliefs as often as I could. How could such a philosophy be wrong?

I'd been up for two hours. My new boss, Michelle, was a sweetheart. She had just sent me some leads and wanted me to concentrate on some network conversions. They had a new system which they hoped would be a perfect fit for banks, hospitals, and government agents. It was called Slim Client technology, a series of Windows-based PCs, say fifteen or fifty, acting like dumb terminals sharing one server. The positive was that it made file-sharing easy; the downside was that if the server went down the whole system went down with it. As far as I was concerned, there was a second negative, supervisors would be able to log on to users' PCs and see if they were working and what they were doing. It would cut down on surfing and supposedly increase productivity. That's how Michelle wanted to pitch it. Frankly, I hated it. The thing you have to understand about my selling technique is that if I don't believe in it, I can't stand behind it. I had bills to pay, and I needed this job. She had been pushing me to start coming in to the office. That's not what I had negotiated with her and her husband, but they were trying to change the agreement we had made in mid stride which really pissed me off. They knew they had me by the cojones.

"So what do you think?" Michelle was relentless.

"I can come in once a week and help you set up a seminar. I'm sure we can increase your enrollment by fifty percent," I answered with confidence. I could make such a statement because none of the people at New Line Tech could sell water to a thirsty man. They were brilliant techs and that was their only power.

"Are you kidding? That would be great!"

"So what is the new hot certificate that everyone is dying to get?" I asked.

"Well, John just got back from Cisco and we're now certified to teach CCNA." She sounded over the moon.

"CCNA?" I asked.

"Cisco Certified Network Associate; no one else in L.A. is teaching it."

I was getting excited. This was hot.

"That's amazing! Are you setting up some

advertising?"

"Well, we always use Micro Now, but we haven't created an ad yet." Micro Now was a free technology mag that seemed to reach a good-sized population. "We were hoping you could help us with that," she added.

"Sure, sure. . . How's your website going?"

"Well, we were hoping you'd help us with that too." She sounded soft and imploring. I could see that once a week was not going to happen. These people were dragging me in. Fuck!

Though Burbank wasn't too far by car, it was hell by public transit which quite frankly sucked in L. A. I had to get a car. I could hear the next nail in my coffin rolling out of her mouth. "Can you come in tomorrow?" Pow! Right between the eyes! When I hung up, I realized that Daniel hadn't awakened yet. I checked on him; he was fine.

By noon, I'd made a second pot of coffee. I sat and watched as Daniel slept something off.

When he awoke, I asked him point blank, "What did you drink last night?"

"Brandy," he muttered, rubbing the sleep from his eyes.

"And work?" I asked fearing he'd lost his job, my anxiety coming in spite of the fact that I had wanted him to quit. Now that he was right there in front of me, I wanted him back at work. My desires were a strange sort of confusion which I often felt were more trouble than they were worth the time to dissect.

"Ahhhhh, shit!" He jumped from the bed and ran to the office and slammed the door. I went back to the kitchen to pour myself another cup of coffee. I heard the door open and he stepped out, looking sheepish." I called in sick," he said, and I bristled at the news.

I walked straight to the office, "That's all well and good, but I have work to do. You forget, this is a new job and I have to perform." With that I shut the door, locked it, and settled into the large office chair. I logged back in to type a message to Malek.

"Do you know what will happen to us?"

Malek is typing. I waited. I heard the front door slam. I guess Daniel was getting the message that I wanted nothing to do with him today.

"What will happen to us, my sweet Bakor, is that one day in our next life you and I will be reunited as husband and wife. It will be a time of peace and love. We will have children, and we will see them grow up. We will have a simple life, but we will be happy." I couldn't help but smile. Right now I hated Daniel. I hated his overbearing bullying, his arrogance, and his belief that no man could have me. Yet, one day in another life, I would not be his but Malek's again and that made me feel light and hopeful. I typed, "I love your words. They fill me with hope with such a deep longing for that future. I wish I could leave my boyfriend. I wish I could just break away. My heart is heavy with love for him, and yet, I do hate him so much! What should I do?" I hit send.

Malek is typing. "What you must do, is realize that you are together to clear the negative veils from the past that cling to you in this life. Love has brought you together. Perhaps as you sink into the healing waters of love, you will both heal." A shiver ran down my left arm. Healing waters, why did that sound so familiar, like a déjà vu? I closed my eyes and saw myself as Queen Bakor swimming nude in a cool pool of calm waters, large white lilies floating. I was alone, and I felt at peace. My eyes flew open and settled on the screen.

Malek is typing. I waited for his words to appear. "Do not live for the future, my love. Live now, life fully. Do not place yourself on a shelf and wait for death before you live this life. This is the life you were born to live, so live it, savor every day, and adore the one that holds you against his body at night. Make children, create a future." I felt tears roll down my cheeks.

"I long for you. I long for what we had. I am homesick. Does that even make sense to feel homesick for something I can barely remember?" I hit send.

Please, please something in me has got to stop all desires. All this wanting is making me hurt and yet, this was life, my life now. I re-read his last message to me. Yes, he was right. I needed to learn to forgive here and now or else I may very well have to relive this life with Daniel again and again until I got it. Oh, my God! Perhaps that's why I was here now; perhaps I had failed many times before. I was trapped in a cycle and here we were to get this right again. So this life was all about forgiveness.

"You long for a life that has become a dream; you long for a place that has long ago been buried by dust. No one will ever find our kingdom for it is buried beneath kingdoms that have come after us. We are not remembered; we are not even dust. We are air and our souls and our memories are all that is left of what we once were. The only proof of our existence lies in the Akashic Library, and these images come from those records. Do not weep for what can never be. You are homesick because you regret something. Once you realize what you regret, you will no longer feel that desperate yearning that is your homesickness. All such longings will vanish."

I realized that this journey to uncover my past life as Queen Bakor was leading me to discover my regret. "And when my regret has been unearthed, then I will be free to join you as your wife in the next life?"

"Or perhaps I will be your wife?" he typed. We messaged each other for a long time; I shared with him all that I recalled, keeping back the details that dealt with the warrior who had joined me and Kryu. I couldn't recall his name, but I saw him. Tall and powerful in his build with blond hair and green eyes. The fact that Kryu willingly shared me with another man surprised me. Weren't these warriors territorial or something? But the images were strong, and so I knew that this was something that had been done willingly by all parties involved, and that included me in that life. I didn't think I had sought this arrangement; it felt more like I was manipulated into it to shame me, and that I fell into the pleasure of it, that I had used sex to turn the tables on these conquerors. I shuddered. If Daniel ever approached me to have a threesome, I would run. It just wasn't my thing, at least not in this life.

We spoke of Malek's job and of his wife. She wanted to get pregnant, and so they had been trying. It didn't make me angry or jealous or envious. I was happy for him. I wanted him to be happy. I was just signing off when the phone rang. I picked it up thinking it might be a client. It was Daniel.

"Hey, it's me," he whispered in the phone.

"Hi, me." I was a little cold to him.

"Can you meet me in Old Town? I have something very important I need to tell you." His voice was soft, low, and almost contrite.

I glanced at the clock; it was three. I hadn't realized, but I had been talking to Malek for hours. "Can't you just tell me now?" I hadn't gotten any work done today.

He cleared his throat loudly and then said, "No, this is not the kind of thing you say on the phone." I was on full alert.

"Do you want me to pick you up?" He had the only car we owned. I thought for a moment, and then decided that I would walk. That would give me about forty minutes to think. I needed that time to digest all that Malek had told me. It was a lot to take in. Maybe Daniel was going to tell me that our relationship was over. What else would make him act so serious? Maybe this was it. I arrived at the Argentinean restaurant, stepped in, and immediately saw Daniel sitting at a little table. The place was empty. He stood up and smiled at me. "It's been a thousand years since I've seen you. I had forgotten how much I've missed you." he whispered. I felt the wide gulf of emotions dislodge from my throat and fly out like hundreds of birds released from their cage and from that moment another door opened to release the kind of emotions I could not articulate but riddled through me to travel my blood stream.

I sat across from him.

His eyes were a warm spring green. "Do you think we will meet in the next life?" he asked.

I laughed with surprise. I saw his body shiver at the sound. I sat silent for a time, waiting for the answer to come. It would be a long, long time before I would see Daniel again. I looked at him with a sadness I could not hide. He nodded his head in quiet understanding.

He clasped his hands together and lowered his gaze. I always marveled at the size of his hands. He raised his eyes to mine, leveling me with a focused stare that made me very nervous, and my stomach was so twisted that I wanted to jump out of my own skin.

"So here I am," I said, taking a deep breath that rushed out trembling. "Tell me."

The waiter interrupted us just at that moment. He set down a carafe of white wine and a plate of fried calamari. He poured us wine into short little water glasses.

Daniel took his glass and cradled it between his hands.

I held my glass, afraid to say anything more. "What shall we toast to?" Daniel asked nonchalantly.

I shrugged.

"Let's toast to past lives and past loves." He smiled brightly.

I didn't want to even question this one, so I raised my glass.

"To past lives and past loves," Daniel announced.

"To past lives and past loves," I repeated. We clicked glasses and each took a sip.

Daniel squeezed a wedge of lemon over our calamari.

The suspense was really killing me.

I was about to interrupt this little ceremony when he cleared his throat rather harshly.

"Are you okay?" I was worried that perhaps this was even worse than a breakup. Maybe he was going to tell me that he was diagnosed with something. Oh, Christ! My mind was really traveling here.

He leaned forward stared straight into my eyes for a long, long time.

He cleared his throat again. "Kat, I've been trying to figure out how to tell you this." Oh, my God, has he been cheating?

He sat back in his chair and leveled me with his green eyes. I ...Well," he paused again. Oh, fucking bloody Mary get on with this. It is a break up; he's going to tell me that he fell in love with his soul mate, and that he's going to be moving in with her, and that he's very sorry .

My heart was beating fast. I took another sip of wine.

"Kat, there is no other way to say this." He took another deep breath. "I was the conqueror."

Oh, shit! I felt relief flood me like a hot shower after coming in from a freezing downpour when you're shivering and soaking wet. Those are always the best showers. I felt that relieved, that good. I could even say I felt mellow.

"Oh, my god, I thought you were breaking up with me!" I exploded.

"Is that why you wanted to walk?" He was laughing.

Tears threatened to spill from my eyes.

"How long have you known you were him?" I asked.

He pushed his fingers through his hair, and sighed. "Since the first time you told me about Malek." So he did know how to pronounce his name. "I was afraid you would want to leave me once you got in too deep and found out everything."

He was looking down at his wine.

"What do you mean?" I leaned forward and placed my hand over his. He looked up and saw the love that poured out of my eyes. He seemed relieved.

Gray and gold eyes locked in a gaze.

"Kat, I've been having dreams, a lot of dreams, and I remember. I remember it all."

I felt a flash of heat rush down my spine.

22

THE LION'S HONOR

The sun rose and set, and yet Kryu did not allow Tanis to touch me again. I could not see what may have changed his mind. Hadn't he told me that he shared everything with Tanis and that he would share me again without remorse? Kryu was gentler to me, more protective.

His physician was brought to ensure that all was well with the child that grew. I was healthy, ate better than ever. Ama spent hours massaging my shoulders, back, and belly with aromatic oils. I thought of Malek and decided that it was time to venture another visit. A full moon had risen and my belly was now showing. Unlike Malek's seed, Kryu's was growing large much faster. I hoped that the birthing would not tear me apart. But then the thought slithered that I would not be alive long enough to see its birth. I wondered where this feeling came from. I saw no signs that death would come my way, and I knew that Kryu would do all he could to guard me from any who dared threaten my person.

I called for Ama and asked her to help me

see Malek. She shook her head.

"I demand that you take me to Malek!" I shouted, my mind whirling with fear. Was he hurt; is that why she refused me? "What has happened to my king?" I hurled the words with a rage that came from one who has lost their power to command.

She fell to the floor imploring my forgiveness.

"Please tell me that our king lives."

I heard Kryu's voice answer, "He lives!"

Ama and I swung our eyes to see that Kryu had stood for some time watching us. I fell to my knees, shaking with fear.

"If you wish to see your king, I am here." He strode in with a casual air that betrayed the rage that he held at bay.

"But if you mean to ask about the man that was once called king," he said as he shrugged and stood before me, "then he has been kept alive." He took my hand and raised me to my feet

I flung my head back and stared at him with defiant eyes, "How can you say that you keep him alive? He clings to life by a breath." I could see was how Malek looked when I had last set eyes upon him.

Kryu walked past me, his back to mine. "He is well treated and lives with all the abundance available."

Malek's face blurred all sense of caution, and I swung on my heels ran towards Kryu attacking him with my fists. "You lie! You lie! He lives like a common thief waiting for execution." Kryu grabbed my wrists and pushed me back until my knees pushed across the large bed. He lay me down and then straddled over me.

"How come you know so much for one who hasn't seen him since this land was taken?"

I shook my head, screaming for him to let me go. "You will not upset my son with your madness." I was trying to push him off me, my legs trapped beneath his, and yet I struggled against his hold.

"Calm yourself!" he shouted into my face, his eyes the palest gray that shone with an anger that stilled my struggle.

I lay still, my breathing labored.

"I will arrange a meeting between you and Malek. Will that suit you?" I nodded my head, tears rolling down my cheek.

He unleashed my wrists from his grasp and rose.

"Give your queen wine and something for sleep." He nodded to Ama. He did not leave my side until she returned with a wine jug, clay goblets, and a little vial. Kryu took the vial and poured a small amount on his index finger and asked what it was. Ama swallowed hard. I lay on my side, propped up by my elbow watching them.

"A tonic of roots and herbs, my king."

He held the vial out which she took from his large hand. She mixed the cup of wine with its content. "Taste it." Kryu ordered. She did so. He nodded his approval and gestured for her to give me the cup. I drank it down, and I was grateful for I did not have to wait long before the mists lifted me out of this world into the welcome arms of sleep.

***

Kryu had ridden out to oversee the land that he had amassed. The moon was hidden from the sky when he left. Tanis was left to secure my protection.

I was sitting on my divan; Amytis and Cycrus were with me. In his absence I had been allowed to see them. I felt light and hopeful. My meeting with the slave had gone rather well. He was willing to take Malek and the children out of this land and escort them to Egypt in exchange for gold on my end and gold when he brought them to safety. His freedom was immediately granted, so that his collar was removed.

I was stroking Amytis's hair; Cycrus curled against my back sleeping while I spoke in low tones to my daughter, telling her of the plan. She nodded her head. Suddenly, Tanis appeared.

"Why did you offer freedom to a slave that is not yours to command?"

I waved Ama over. "Please take the children back with you."

I kissed Cycrus gently, ruffling his hair. He yawned, and Ama had a slave pick him up and carry him, as my daughter followed them, but not before shooting me a fearful glance. I sent her a broad smile.

I considered Tanis. Had I gone too far in securing the slave's freedom now? Perhaps I should have waited until the day of their departure. But I could not take the chance that the slave would have changed his heart. The love of gold and silver was one thing, but freedom was the most precious.

"He was born in our household as a slave, and he has proven to be loyal." I saw how weak my explanation was.

"A slave is a slave, my queen." He strolled casually. His hair was shorn and shone like dark wheat when it dries in the sun.

"Why not free Ama? Is she not a loyal slave? Has she not served you all of your life?"

He stood before me, his loincloth too close to my visage, so that I made it rise. But he settled his hand upon my shoulder and pushed me down.

"He seems like a young tall man. Does he please you in some way?"

His eyes twinkled with mirth.

"I do not understand your meaning?" I shook my head, confused. Then the realization of his words broke over me like warm oil and slithered down my back. Was he accusing me of taking this man for my pleasure?

He sat beside me. He grabbed my face in his hand guiding it back to lock eyes with his.

"I would fear that you know exactly what I mean. Have you forgotten that I am here, at your service?" He leaned forward embracing me. I pushed him away.

"I am Kryu's . . ." I hurled at him. How dare he treat me like a camp whore? He took my hand and rubbed it over his loins. He was hard, and his eyes closed with a deep sigh that escaped his lips. I tried to pull my hand away but his grip was unrelenting.

"Tanis, I cannot!" I pleaded.

"I have very little patience, my queen." He was loosening his loincloth.

"Kryu cannot give you love. Can he?" His green eyes softened.

"But, I, my queen, can give you that and much more." He nuzzled my neck.

I began to tremble, for surely if Kryu heard

of this he would kill us both.

"Are you mad?" I whispered fiercely, afraid that someone in Kryu's service would hear this and run to tell him all that he saw upon his return.

Tanis pulled back and allowed his gaze to travel freely from my face, to my breasts, to my belly and back. "I am mad, for you. Mad for your touch, your mouth, and your loins. Kryu will not allow me to touch you again." He seemed bewildered by his own words.

"Then be gone before someone reports what they see," I lashed out. He chuckled ruefully.

"They fear me as well. No one will say a word unless I allow it to be said." He buried his face within my neck and whispered, "I want you."

He had slipped out of his loincloth and his hunger rose from between his thighs.

Could he be as powerful as Kryu? He was his most trusted of the twelve. Could I make him love me and use him to my will? I searched his eyes to see if what I saw was love. What looked back was lust, a fever that was just as powerful as love. For if he desired me to a fever pitch, then his thoughts belonged to me to be used at will.

I circled his manhood with my hand and lowered my head, kissing the tip of his manhood, and licking it. He groaned loudly and placed his hand on my head, pushing me to swallow the whole of him, which I did. I savored his heat and saw before me a warrior whose green eyes reflected the look of a man taken to heights by the resin of poppies. I knew that he was mine to do what I willed and that power filled me with a strange euphoria, for I too was drugged by this power.

He howled, spilling his seed into my open mouth.

We lay upon the divan. I looked at the stars wondering what they had in store for my future.

Tanis held me tightly against the length of his body. When the stars grew brighter, and Tanis found his footing, he took me from behind. His thrusts were unlike Kryu's, who preferred to lie between my thighs and move to a slow rhythm that hastened in pace and gradually built a tension within me and brought me a rush of pleasure that came in surprising waves. He kissed my naked breasts which he had exposed by savagely ripping my tunic from neck to ankle. He held me against his chest and inhaled the scent of my hair.

"Kryu does not return tonight?" I whispered against his beating heart.

"He will return when the moon reveals the first crescent." He threw his long leg over mine.

"You cannot stay with me tonight," I

answered, pushing him away.

"I cannot my queen, but I will visit you until he returns." He raised a mocking brow.

"What if I tell him of your pillage upon my person?" I sat up looking at him with wonder at his arrogance and his rather misplaced fearlessness.

"You cannot and you will not, for you have freed a slave for no good reason. I think you are scheming something," he paused, then mockingly added, "my queen,"

"Perhaps I plot to murder Kryu?" I taunted.

"Not you, no, for you could have cut his throat in his sleep," he said, shaking his head smiling. "No, what you are planning is not a murder." He wrapped his arm around my waist and pulled me to him. Our lips were close, so close that I swallowed his breath as he spoke.

"Then take the slave and question him?" I challenged. I was so foolish; I should have known that something was underfoot.

"No, my queen," All I need to know will surface on its own." He captured my mouth and plundered it with his tongue, drawing out a moan as his fingers played with my mound. His desire was upon my thigh, strong and hard. He wanted to ride me, but this time he demanded that I stand by the balcony. He wanted me thus as he took me from behind, his hand tangled in my hair and the other grasping my hip as he slammed his power into me. He would use me in various ways until the day Kryu rode into the courtyard. I was still wet with his seed when Kryu's mouth touched my lips.

I called for Ama to prepare Kryu's bath. The sky was bright with stars. He ordered me to join him in a bath. We did not speak, but his hands were all over my heavy breasts, the aureoles now dark plums, and my belly visible to any who looked upon me.

Tanis appeared, and a shiver of apprehension shook me. Kryu smiled at my discomfort.

"My king." He was in full armor and stood tall and powerful, his legs slightly apart. His eyes caressed my limbs with an intimacy only I could see.

"Bring the man they call Malek."

Tanis's eyebrow rose in question.

"I have promised my queen." Kryu nuzzled my jaw as he spoke.

Tanis flashed a wide smile that never reached his eyes and swirled on his heels, his long cape swinging behind his heels as he walked with a quick step to fulfill his king's command.

I rose from the tub. "I must dress." Kryu drew me back down to settle upon his lap, his manhood hard with desires that had yet been fed. "There is no need." I shivered. What did he mean?

It did not take long before Malek appeared, hands and feet bound, his neck roped like a slave. Tanis led him into what had been our bed chamber. Kryu rose from the tub and lifted me nude, water slithering down my pointed breasts and growing belly. He settled me to the ground and turned to Malek.

"Look at what now belongs to me," Kryu roared, as his arms rose to all that stood before us.

Malek was a shadow, his eyes so large that they dominated his face. He stared at me, and his eyes skimmed over my form and settled on my rounded belly.

Kryu grabbed my arm and brought me to stand before him. He circled his fingers around the back of my neck and pushed me forward for Malek to see all that had changed.

Malek lowered his eyes.

"Look at your queen, she carries my son. All that you once thought was yours is now mine." I realized that my cheeks were stained with tears.

"Look at her!" he shouted. Tanis placed the tip of his sword beneath Malek's chin and raised his eyes to mine. These giants stood around us like devils from another world. I wanted to show Malek that I had not abandoned him that I was still his Bakor. My eyes spoke of a thousand regrets and promises, and yet none did he see, for he would not look at me. Tanis pressed the sword right below his throat. "Look at her and look at your king, or I will take your daughter and cut her throat!"

Malek's eyes met mine. I could not see through the blur of my tears.

"Is this what you wanted?" Kryu shook me. "To see your Malek? Did you think I would allow him the pleasure of your embrace? Did you ever think that all would be as it was?" He hurled each question like arrows that pierced my heart. I was shaken.

"What will you have me do?" I pleaded.

"Accept this new life with me as your king. Honor me, please me, and only think of me." He pointed to Malek. "He is your past." Kryu pulled me to him, his hand on my belly, the other caressing a nipple that stood out hard and ready for pleasure. "I am your future." He kissed my neck, my jaw, and turned my face to meet his lips. My mind wanted to run, but my body trembled in response. I wanted him, and my mound was wet for him.

"Your queen hungers for my every touch," he whispered as he raised his head to watch Malek. I saw my love weeping tears that fell like a sky raining a storm. My Malek watched as Kryu buried two fingers between my mound.

He brought his fingers to his nose and breathed in my scent and then licked them, as if he was savoring the ripe juice of a fruit. I shuddered with shame.

Kryu picked me up and carried me to the bed.

"Tanis, have him watch how a conqueror possesses a queen." Tanis pulled on the cord around Malek's neck and led him to stand by the bed.

Kryu was unmerciful as he lowered his head to my mound. Raising my hips up to his mouth, he drove his tongue between my thighs. His mouth circled my pearl which sent shudders of pleasure course through my body, and then did his tongue pulse around my pearl and then tugging on it hard and again circling it with his tongue. I shut my eyes tightly against Malek and saw my body destroy any shred of self-possession. Kryu's mouth circled my nipples and pulled on them which made me cry out, a sliver of fire ran down to my belly. I hungered for his thrusts. I thrashed my hips.

"Look at me," Kryu commanded.

I opened my eyes as he pushed my face sideways to face Malek and entered me thus as I locked eyes with Malek. A cry of pleasure flew out of my mouth; I tried to turn my head away, but Kryu held me thus as he swung in and out of me with a passion that brought my body to the heights of pleasure. I shut my eyes tight. Even Tanis could not make me feel this wild.

"Look at him," Kryu whispered in my ear, "or I will have Tanis end his suffering now." My eyes flew open. Malek's eyes stared but did not see me, for he had escaped this moment. Where he had gone I could not say. I buried my face in Kryu's shoulder. He did not force me to look upon Malek again. His hand cupped over a breast that he suckled upon as he rode me. He groaned his release which rose like a warrior's cry after a battle is won.

Kryu propped himself upon his elbow and nodded to Tanis. "Take him back."

Malek was led away, and I moved from Kryu and curled my legs into my breasts and rocked myself to a sense of quiet, for the storm in my head raged. I could not rid myself of the images of Malek watching me with Kryu; the shame choked me. I wanted to rid myself of all that whirled within me. I was afraid that I would lose touch with the world. I was afraid that all was lost now.

Kryu grabbed me by the ankle and dragged me down to him. His face hovered over mine. "Did you think I did not know that you visited him?" My eyes grew wide with fear. I could not speak. "I am no fool!" Kryu said between clenched teeth. "Take care my Queen, for I know all that needs to be known at all times." I trembled. But my mind could not let go of my plan to secret Malek and our children out. It would have to happen now, for I feared for Malek's life. Either Kryu would order his death, or Malek would allow himself to starve. I had no choice. Kryu had given me no other way. I could never accept him as my king. If the gods had brought about different times, perhaps ... I could not say. I carried his son, but that did not impose a hold over me. Nor would it prevent me from doing what I would have to do in order to protect those I loved.

Kryu left my side. I called for Ama and told her to arrange a meeting with the freed slave. They would have to leave immediately. I hoped Tanis would not deliver my secrets. Though he did not know my plan, he knew I had one. We had very little time left.

23

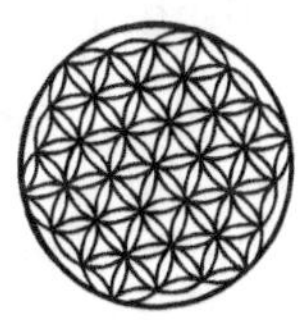

OCTOBER 25, 1997

"But it's Saturday. Why in the hell have they got you coming in on a fucking Saturday?" Daniel blustered.

It was eight o'clock, and I had been up for a couple hours gathering my notes for New Line Tech's website and some ideas about setting up a process to promote the new CCNA certificate.

I was on my third cup of coffee, which explained why I was a little jittery. I had to eat something.

"Look, it's not like you'll be home anyway," I said. Daniel was lying in bed his forearm shielding his eyes. "Well, that's the thing," he mumbled.

I was in the kitchen getting some bacon out of the fridge and was pulling down a vintage Le Creuset cast iron skillet I'd picked it up at a garage sale. It was pre-owned, but it worked perfect. "That's the thing?" I called out. "Wanna' join me in some bacon and eggs?"

"That sounds awesome," he called. I stuck my head out the kitchen and watched him roll on his stomach, cradling his chin on his hands. "That's the thing, what?" I repeated. I laid six strips of bacon on the pan and placed a couple of slices of bread in the broiler oven.

"Ahhh, shit!" Daniel groaned. "What's wrong?" I called out.

"Look, when I called in sick yesterday, I called in sick for the whole week end. I just thought..."

He was out of bed and stood behind me in all his nude glory. He grabbed my waist and pulled me against him, my head cradled within the breath of his wide chest. I turned my head around and looked up at him. "Daniel, we need the money. Why did you call in sick anyway?" I wasn't angry at him, just disappointed. We were late on so many bills. He kissed my forehead and turned around to grab a mug from the dish rack and poured himself a cup of coffee. He walked to the futon and settled back in bed. "I thought that with all that we discussed yesterday. Well, l called them back and told them I was too sick to come in. We have so much to talk about."

Of course, he was right; there was a lot to talk about. But the fact is, we live in this world, and in this world bills don't wait. Fat was sizzling and popping out of the frying pan. I pushed Daniel out of the way. "Nudity and bacon, not a good combo. "He covered his family jewels with both hands and crossed his legs and threw me a wounded puppy look that made me laugh. "Come on; get out of here before you lose the use of that fabulous cock!" He left. I turned my attention back to the bacon. I flipped it over and grabbed the bread out of the oven, buttering the pieces and cutting them in triangles. I popped my head out of the kitchen. Daniel was sitting on the edge of the futon, the blankets over his legs.

"I know I shouldn't have, but I just wanted to be with you. I mean, I feel like I live at the dealership," he yelled over the sound of frying bacon.

"I know, I know, but Daniel, I made the commitment to come in before I spoke to you. I'll just go in for a couple hours and get out, okay?" I yelled back.

"Fine!" He was petulant. "I'll drive you," he added.

I knew he'd get over it. I took out the bacon and placed the strips on a paper bag I had torn for the purpose and placed it over a plate. I cracked four eggs into the bacon fat, sprinkled some pepper flakes and flipped them over, so that the egg white would be completely cooked but the yellow nice and runny. Now, this was not heart healthy, but I rarely ever made such a fattening breakfast. We deserved it; last night proved to be a long night. Daniel and I had sat up sharing all that we remembered. I kept going over his words that brought forth images floating between us. "I had such a hard time letting go. I wanted to love you," Daniel confessed over that past life. "I just couldn't let go. I had to be untouched by any deep feelings... especially for a woman."

He'd given me a shy smile and reached for me, cradling me within the crook of his arm, my head on his chest as I heard him bring back moments buried so long ago that they seemed more like dreams then lives once lived. I had to remind myself that this was real, that this had happened, and it had happened to us.

"So you were my Queen Bakor, my great love, the woman I could not love but did. You were so small and dark." He laughed, his eyes far away looking through the mist and seeing us as we once had been. "God, but you were so feisty! Exactly, as you are now. "He chuckled and bent his head to deposit a kiss upon the tip of my nose. I growled like a fierce cat.

"Same temper too," he laughed. I joined him.

Daniel's voice suddenly turned from sunlight to a low thundering storm. I could smell the rain of his grief. "And then, it all changed. I did something, something so wrong that you never forgave me. No one could forgive such an act." Shaking his head, he ran his fingers through his hair. I felt tears prick my eyes. I knew my soul remembered, but I did not! I wondered about that. About soul memory, how to bring it forth and why, and to what to end? Quite often there was a reason why we came through never remembering our past lives. It was a safety block so that we could move forward with as little baggage as possible. Yet, the truth was that for some of us, just being in the presence of something or someone could launch soul memories or total recollection that either came in dribbles or full on a day-by-day awakening of that past life.

It was strange, and not everyone experienced such a gift, for that's how I saw it; it was a gift.

Actual soul memories were ones that could be tapped in the Akashic records, which were the great library of souls, where every thought, every word, every deed was stored for every single soul that existed. This concept of a great library was not a new one and came from the cultures of the ancient world: From Egypt, to India, to Greece and Persia, the oracles were able to tap into the Akashic library. It's how they could see the past and the future; it's how Nostradamus claimed to have seen the world's future. But there was the argument of fate and free will. In my mind, both worked together. If my fate was to give birth to a son, my free will would choose the man who would father it. I saw that Fate and Free Will walked together hands linked.

The Vedas were a religion before either Buddha or Jesus had ever walked the earth. It believed that we had reincarnated as animals, even as gods and goddesses.

For many these would be strange ideas, and yet in some respects we believed in the core of one singular truth; the Akashic library was for us, a fact. It spoke to me and Daniel. It said that we were the only ones responsible for our actions. It's what they said Jesus had originally preached.

Daniel and I share the idea that Buddha showed a way, as did Jesus, that we could all master, the concept of reincarnation, which is to learn, to grow, to understand, and to gain enlightenment.

It was that singular understanding that linked us together. We could not follow any one religion. Our spirits had lived in the ancient worlds for so many lifetimes that we could not follow any religion, for all had been created by men and stained by blood and egos. I'd propped myself on his chest, my chin on my hand staring up at him. "Tell me."

He shook his head," I can't, not yet." He'd

taken my hands in his and kissed my fingertips and removed them from his to roll over. His broad back faced me like an insurmountable wall.

"Get some sleep; it must be one in the morning," he yawned.

"Please tell me," I pleaded.

"Goodnight," he paused and exhaled heavily, "I love you."

All that had taken place had been filled with pathos and longings to discover more.

I wished I could just call Michelle and tell her I had an emergency, but I was too new on the job, and we'd be in dire straits if I lost this job.

The next morning, I set up two plates and arranged the toast, the eggs and bacon. I placed the plates on our old teak tray and carried it to the living room and sat on the edge of the futon and placed the tray over Daniel's legs, his large muscular torso exposed to my admiring gaze. He smiled and took a bite of his bacon.

"Do you think we could talk about what happens next?" I asked dipping my toast in my egg yolk.

He took a long swig of his coffee and took a moment before answering. " I think the memory has got to come from you," he said. I was perplexed. Why from me? Why not get on with it and get this thing wrapped up so that we could discover why this was even happening.

"Look, I don't need to have this past life memory drag on. Just tell me." I was impatient and didn't understand what I was asking of him. Later, I would realize that it had to be organic; it had to bubble up from my subconscious, or else I would not experience what I had lived through. I just didn't understand that yet. "I'll tell you what, let's meditate tonight. Whatever comes through will come through, okay?" he murmured gently. That sounded good to me, so I agreed.

"What time do you have to be at the office?" He was devouring the eggs, and washing it all down with coffee, the toast barely touched. I grabbed a slice from his plate and got up, heading to the bathroom. "Around ten." I nibbled on the toast and then thought better than to finish it and placed it on the bathroom sink, stripped down, and jumped into the shower. I had to get my act together.

I was wondering if Daniel might want to go to the auction and look around for a car. I had about three hundred and twenty five dollars in the savings; maybe he could turn that around for a quick profit. When I got out of the shower, I gave him my credit card with my pin code. The smile he gave me was brighter than the sun, and

I felt my heart skip.

We drove to Burbank talking about the most mundane things, skirting around the issues of Malek, of our lives in Mesopotamia. It was too raw to be exposed in the light of day. There was something more to come. Daniel knew what it was but was afraid to tell me.

I had made my peace with the process of recalling and had decided not to push him.

We got to the office in no time. He dropped me off and promised to be back at around two o'clock. I just hoped that I would be done by then. Michelle and John were waiting for me; they were both very excited. John and I toured the two floors they had rented. The top floor was set up for our offices; the bottom floor was all labs. One lab was for hardware training, the other was for the basic Microsoft certified network engineer training, and then they had the Cisco lab all set up. It was small but pretty impressive. They had a couple of potential students scheduled to tour and asked me if I wouldn't mind taking over. I think it was a test, but I was okay with that.

The first guy I escorted worked for Nestle and wanted to get into the CCNA program. He enrolled on the spot. I asked for a deposit to hold his seat. He gave me his credit card. When I approached Michelle and handed her the credit card asking her to put a hundred dollars through as a deposit, she was shocked. They'd never done that before; students paid the first day of class. This again proved my point that techies were not salesmen. They averaged a fifty percent show rate for every class they launched. I walked away shaking my head.

The next guy was a janitor. He wanted to change his life. He didn't have a clue about computers; he just knew that it was the next big thing. He was eager and wanted to learn all about them. He was so hungry to change his career. I asked him if he was married. He said that he was. I told him that I would not enroll him unless he brought his wife to our next meeting. He was surprised, but I explained that for him to change his career he would need her full support and understanding because without it he would sink.

I laid down the reality of what he was facing. He would be working full time and taking our night classes. On the weekends, he'd be studying. If she was one-hundred percent behind this and his absences, then he would be a success. If she fought and nagged him to spend more time with her, he would lose. I think he appreciated my honesty and threw me a grateful look. We set up to meet that Monday at around five o'clock with him and his wife. Lunch swung around and though I was hungry, I wanted to get things wrapped up so that I could get home by two. John and I brainstormed over the website. I asked them if they had any testimonials, but none had been captured, so it was agreed that John would email me a list of satisfied students and that I would create a release form giving us permission to use the testimonials I gathered, both on the website and in print. By two o'clock I was done and Daniel was there waiting in our little cream BMW. I loved that car.

"So did you find anything worth buying?"

"Yeah, we are the proud owners of a Fiat Spider. It's a convertible." He was excited.

"How much?" I smiled up at him.

"You won't believe it, but I got it for two hundred bucks!" He placed his hand on my knee.

"Wow! What's wrong with it?"

"Well," he paused, "it needs an engine." He breathed out the words.

Fuck! Fuckety fuck! This is what I was afraid of, a fucking car with no engine. I wanted to start screaming. I took two deep breaths.

"What the fuck were you thinking?" Believe me I tried not to explode. Where the hell are we going to find an engine? I threw his hand off my knee.

His hand was loosely curved around the steering wheel; he placed his hand on my knee again. I pushed him off. "Answer me and stop touching my knee. You have no right to touch me right now."

He turned and gave me a wolfish grin, "Come on, baby. You know I have a plan."

I settled my head on the head rest. I was seeing red and was having a hard time calming down.

"Okay, lay it on me," I muttered, crossing my arms over my chest.

Daniel got on the 134 going east.

"Right now the car is being towed home. I called one of my buddies who said that he can shoot two coats of red for a six pack of beer and the money to pay for the paint. The interior is good, just needs some detailing. I can get some used tires for about forty bucks, so we'll be in the car for a total of five hundred."

"And the engine?" I hadn't forgotten. Where was he going to find a fucking engine?

"I got it covered."

"So you're talking $500 dollars and that doesn't include cost of engine, right? Fuck! Is it even worth five hundred dollars?" I shrugged disgustingly.

"Kat, that includes the engine. Like I said, it's covered. When I'm done it's going to be worth well over two grand!"

I turned to him and then it hit me: He had

the job to pay for this, but when would he have the time?

"The dealership has been working you to death. How are you going to get the time to get things done?"

"Whatever I've got to do, I'll do" he shrugged. He placed his hand back on my knee. I covered his hand with mine, giving it a little squeeze. We drove the rest of the way home in silence. Daniel dropped me off and went to Trader Joe's to pick up some things for dinner.

When he came back he had a bag filled with two boxes of angel hair pasta, olive oil, grated Parmesan, canned Roma tomatoes from Italy, a packet of white mushrooms, an eggplant, a good bottle of red Côtes du Rhône, and unsalted butter from Ireland.

"Guess what's on TV tonight?" he said excitedly... I didn't have a clue.

"The Godfather!" he cried out, and we both did a little dance out of the kitchen, around the living room, and made our way back to the kitchen.

"You know how I love my pasta when I watch that movie," I smiled up at him.

"I sure in the hell do, sweet little pea." He kissed the tip of my nose.

We were interrupted by a knock on the door; it was the tow truck driver. Daniel ran downstairs to accept delivery of his Fiat.

Meanwhile, I washed my hands, took the apron off the hook, and tied it around my waist. I pulled down the nine-inch frying pan and peeled about five garlic cloves. I then poured a little olive oil in the pan. I'd stuffed the olive oil bottle with sprigs of rosemary, so that the oil was infused with its wonderful perfume. I peeled the mushrooms, preferring that method over washing them, and then thinly sliced them and tossed them in the frying pan. I sliced the eggplants and added salt to them to sweat them, while I took a small container of Kalamata olives from the fridge and chopped them up and added those to the frying pan. I tossed this around until it was nicely cooked and placed them in a bowl to set aside. The eggplant was cut into cubes, and I added those to the pan and sprinkled them with garlic powder to draw out the sweetness of the eggplant. When those were soft and golden, I added the contents of the bowl. I heard Daniel running up the stairs. He threw open the door.

"Wow, it smells incredible." He dropped a kiss on my neck and held me against his chest. I exhaled and fell back into him, holding my wooden spoon in the air.

"I'm so glad. Can you do me a favor and open that can?" I asked him.

"Yeah, sure." He washed his hands and

pulled open the drawer looking for the can opener.

"Do you want me to pour these tomatoes in a bowl?"

"No, let's just add them to the pan." Daniel poured the contents of the tin into the pan. I took a fork and crushed them roughly, leaving large chunks of tomatoes. I took my wooden spoon and tasted my creation and decided that a couple drops of soy sauce would add a depth that plain salt could not bring to the dish. It was around four o'clock and The Godfather was showing at five. I lowered the flame and placed a lid over the sauce. I grabbed my big red Le Creuset pot, and filled it with tap water, a pinch of salt, and a sprig of rosemary. I set the egg timer for ten minutes. I took a stick of unsalted butter and placed in a small bowl to which I added crushed garlic cloves and parmesan cheese; I mixed this all together. Daniel had cut the baguette in half and we slathered the bread with this mixture and sprinkled a little more parmesan on top. Those we placed in the broiler oven.

Daniel opened the red wine. I sunk on our pink futon, tired from the long day. He handed me a glass. I was grateful and breathed in the fine scent of grapes and sun and took a sip. A sigh of bliss released from my lungs' life was good.

Daniel sat cross-legged across from me on the floor.

"I want to tell you something." His voice was tender and filled with pathos.

"Yes," I said, unable to suppress my yawn. I hoped I wasn't going to fall asleep during the movie.

"I can't imagine being with anyone else but you. I know how hard things get. I want to give you the best and one day, I promise you –it's all going to fall into place." He placed his hand on my knee. I leaned forward and kissed his forehead. At this moment, I wanted to believe him. Besides having a passion for cars, he had a passion for aviation and had wanted to be a pilot since I had met him. Money had been the trap that had kept him from ever getting any sort of flight training. He'd discovered the magic of hot-air ballooning in the mid '80s while we still lived in San Francisco when there had only been two pages of advertising for ballooning in the yellow pages. By the time we had moved to Pasadena, the business had grown with over fifteen pages. He had been right about the business all along. But once again, things had prevented him from pursuing his lessons. It would have changed his life, our life, in so many ways, had he been able to go after his private pilot's license and then graduate to commercial. He would have had a job skill that would have brought him a good living. He was excited about banner advertising and had talked for hours about the simple beauty of the hot-air balloon business, how eco-friendly it was since it burned clean fuel, and how gentle it was to the environment since it was a balloon floating on air. He'd approached his mother for a loan to get his lessons started and to buy a small three-passenger balloon, but she had refused him, preferring to refinance her house and build her dream kitchen to the tune of twenty-thousand dollars.

So he had taken a job as a title searcher in Oakland, holding on for dear life until he had worked there six months. Then he'd approached a loan company that approved him for the loan, but there was a caveat. In order for them to disburse the funds, they wanted a letter from his boss stating that his work was solid and secure. The boss, jealous of him for too many reasons to mention, kept playing games and stalling him. In the end, he never wrote the one letter that could have launched our lives. The boss just kept fucking with Daniel, making him come in on the weekends to do all sorts of jobs like moving files from one office to another, to even picking up his dry cleaning, but it was all bullshit. But in the '80s none of us had much recourse. So when he realized that his boss would never give him that letter, he quit.

He moved to another title job, hoping to try that loan company all over again. But fate intervened. His mother had been letting him use the garage for the buying and selling of his auction cars and now wanted him to stop doing that. She wanted the garage to be used to park her car, which was fine, except you could easily park two cars in that garage and still she refused even though she knew it meant that would end his car buying.

He looked around for a garage to rent but hit a dead end. Finally, a friend of his told him that jobs and opportunity abounded in Los Angeles. So Daniel applied for a job at a title company in Burbank. He got the job, but we had to pay for our own move. We sold our car in San Francisco to finance our life change and hadn't realized how hard things would be in L.A. without a car. We packed two suitcases, put everything we owned in storage, and brought Alex, our beloved cream-colored Persian cat with us.

We found an apartment in Pasadena even though we would have preferred moving into a place in Venice Beach, but at the time it was just too expensive. The title job fell through, and we were both stuck looking for work. For months we walked and bused it everywhere. I found a job at a Godiva store, which paid minimum wage at the tune of four dollars and some cents per hour. At the time, what I earned paid for food and what he earned paid the rent and other bills. That was two years ago.

So I felt my heart constrict for all that we had been through, and I knew that Daniel wanted to make things great for us; that was all he had ever wanted. But he couldn't seem to find a way to make the life changes we so desperately needed. What I earned now gave us the type of breathing room we hadn't enjoyed in a long time. It still wasn't enough to take a vacation, as we lived paycheck to paycheck, but it was a hell of an improvement from what we had gone through.

Daniel sat next to me and we hugged for a long time. I heard the timer go off. I didn't want to let him go. "I love you," I whispered against his throat and got up. He watched me from the futon as I prepared the final touches to our meal. The angel hair pasta was dropped in the boiling water; I added olive oil to the water to prevent the pasta from sticking together. In no time we had a feast. We pushed our TV tables together and sat side-by-side, drinking red wine and eating pasta to the theme music of The Godfather, as the opening credits rolled.

I didn't think about Malek or my past life. I was here in the present enjoying the love of my life. A simple moment of just being. I understood what Malek had been saying. Don't wait for your next life to happen, don't put yourself on a shelf, just be present with the one you love. For the first time in years, I wasn't troubled; I wasn't scared of our unchartered future. I was here in the moment with Daniel and wanted to feel that all was well.

24

THE HARVEST MOON

Ama returned with the freed slave, a tall kindly youth. He was slim and his long black hair was tied in a long braid that fell down his broad back. He was without beard, and his eyes were a clear blue and devoid of greed or cruelty.

I questioned his desire to lead my family out of this land into Mesopotamia, why would he want to leave now that he was free.

He knelt before my feet." I am your servant, and am grateful to you for my freedom but without gold I cannot start a new life." I smiled to myself, "What would you do with so much gold?"

I wondered if he would even know how to live without being a slave.

"I would like to buy sheep and make a profit and take a woman to bear my sons." His name was Ilus, a good and noble name for a free man. I trusted the passion in his eyes. He had every intention of making it to Egypt and once there, my brothers would make sure that he was well rewarded. I know that Malek would keep my word sacrosanct by this man. I just hoped that Malek would be able to make the journey with Cycrus; our daughter would muster the strength to do it, but there would be a desert to cross. We had no choice; I felt it in my bones to delay any more seasons would be their doom.

We discussed the many trails that could lead them out, and we both agreed that they would travel at night and sleep in the many caves by day, avoiding Kryu's scouts that bordered the edge of our land and patrolled it for rebels.

The fall harvest celebrations would begin tomorrow. For eight sunrises the kingdom would be deep in the festivities for Ishtar had blessed us with an unusual bountiful year. Yet, she had abandoned us, the royal family. What offense had we given? The thought shivered between my shoulders that the killing of our Oracle was the cause. But then, the whispered voice that was barely heard slithered within my mind and delivered the words, this is your fate.

We decided that the journey would be set seven nights from this one, the day before the last harvest festivities when the moon would rise full and bright to light their way out of danger into their freedom. I did not want to think of what Kryu would do to me when he found them gone, for he would know full well that I was the instrument of the plan. However, I carried his heir and I was sure, as I took my next breath, that no harm would befall me.

What worried me most were the steps that we would have to take to secure Malek's freedom. When Ilus left my heart felt strong and powerful, for I was sure that our plans would be fruitful. Night was falling fast; I called to Ama. I took my cape for the chill in the air sent shivers through my body.

"Let us go to the temple and ask Ishtar for her guidance."

Ama nodded as she wrapped herself in a black linen cloak. Together we walked, our heads covered by our hoods and bowed from inquisitive eyes for I did not want to be waylaid. Slaves scattered about lighting oil lamps, torches and big bronze bowls with fire. We made good time walking down the many stone steps, and we avoided the courtyard; instead, she led me through the kitchens. I had never seen such large stone fireplaces on which large meats were roasted on a spit turned by little boys. Heavy wooden tables straddled over a dirt floor and women were gathered working on the bread dough, pounding the bread into flat wheels which they threw against the side walls of the stone fireplaces where they stuck until done. Large earthen bowls held melons, jars of honey, large containers of wine and mead, and large men stripped to the waist were slaughtering a cow, others butchering meat, and the sounds of fire, and of popping fat, the heat, the smells and the sounds of people shouting orders, and one head man cuffing a boy over the head because he had fallen asleep while turning the spit of a whole calf being roasted for the first day of the harvest celebration.

It was a cacophony of sights and sounds that left me dizzy, and the smoke of the fires made my stomach turn. I walked ahead of Ama who took my hand in hers and led me into the cool night. I inhaled deeply of the sweet cool night air and exhaled with a sigh of relief. A sudden calm enveloped me. We walked to the temple of Ishtar; it was small compared to the one where I had met my conqueror, but it had served us well these many summers.

We arrived to an empty hall, long and lined with quivering torch lights that valiantly fought the rough winds that blew through the large doors. Slaves that stood on either side of it pushed it shut, and the noises of a dissonant world were silenced. We were bathed in scents of burning incense, and the sounds of our own footsteps upon the large stones echoed. The many columns stood like priestesses dressed in the blue mosaic tiles that Malek and I so favored. A gold statue of Ishtar stood at the far end of the hall, and right before it was a marble table in which sacrifices of small animals were performed. I walked fast, my cloak flying behind me, my feet wrapped within the soft ties of kid leather sandals. My tunic was so long that it impeded my long strides, so I hitched it over my knees and ran. I threw myself across the floor before Ishtar. I begged her to release my family and to send them away from this place that we could no longer call home and bring them to safer shores. I begged her with such a ferocity my hands formed into fists burying themselves upon my eyes. I did not want to see what was before me. I wanted to feel her answer. I wanted to know that she would be just and protective. My heart felt no answer and that frightened me. I began to weep. Ama was beside me, holding me within the embrace of her soft rocking and shushing my fears away. But her soothing touch was no longer a balm that I could count on, for I was no longer a child. The world was no longer a simple place of laughter and peace. The world had become a dark place that was no longer black or white but threw off deep gray shadows across the landscape of my heart and my confusion over all the emotions that collided within me created the kind of suffering I had never experienced until now.

"My queen, my queen," she whispered

against my hair.

"How will we secret our king out of this madness?" I wailed.

She pushed the hair off my face and tipped my chin to face her.

"I have thought of this and there is only one way." I sat up and broke her hold over me, facing her, my tears drying, and my heart hardening for the tasks to come.

"I will bring wine and mead to the guards. These will be heavy with opium and sleeping herbs. Honey will hide any taste. When they are well done with drink, we will spirit him away. It will be of such ease, my queen. Have no fear."

I trusted her plan because I trusted the greed of Kryu's men. They would drink without question and this would allow Malek's release. Now it was time to wait.

Ama called for slaves to bring my large bath to the open air upon the terrace. The sun was high in the sky. Kryu was out hunting with Tanis, so I was left to my own amusements. My lyre player sang. Tonight was to be the second day of the feasting.

I bathed and allowed my mind to slip away to the time when I first met Malek. I had been betrothed to him at birth, and though we shared the same grandmother, we were far enough apart for our bloodline not to taint our future children. Unlike my Egyptian ancestors, we did not believe that bloodlines should intermarry, for we of the Fertile Crescent feared the breeding of fools and of illness in the blood. When I had turned fourteen winters, we were joined as one. Soon after, I brought forth our beautiful daughter.

I recall his tenderness towards me, his every care to honor me as the most precious being in his heart. He had never brought another to our bed, nor had he ever taken another woman. Now, I wished that he had. Perhaps a greater alliance with another king outside our lands may have prevented this disaster. Yet, I could not bring myself to regret one day spent with Malek sharing his pleasures and his plans to build. How he had laughed when I had suggested we build our grand gardens. At the time, my brother, who was a great architect and understood mathematics in ways that made my head spin, still lived amongst us. He worked with our builders and gardeners, and he had devised a plan to pump water into our palace which would irrigate the plants and bring our water fountains to life. When the whole of my dream came to pass, I recall my brother leading me up to this very terrace on which I now bathed, how he had covered my eyes with his hands. I recall laughter, and teasing, and Malek standing before me as my brother unveiled the whole of it. A slave had released wild parrots at the precise moment my brother's hand fell away to reveal the most beautiful scene my eyes had ever beheld. A world that only dreams can conjure. The sounds of my most favorite water fountain woke me from my reverie and brought me back to this moment. It was at that moment that my eyes settled upon Tanis.

He strolled upon my terrace with a casualness that had me sit upright.

"Ah, my lovely, scheming, conniving queen, how fare you this fine day?" My heart dropped to my belly. Did he know? Had he somehow found me out? I could not play such games. I placed a bright smile upon my face which I knew full well never reached my eyes.

"I prepare for the feast. Tonight my son is hungry for meat and bread." I patted my belly hidden from his searching eyes. He settled upon my bare breasts now heavy and round, the aureoles dark red plums. He licked his lips and approached me like a fox that has found a wounded rabbit within its lair.

"I thought you were with our king, hunting. Is all well?"

I could not see how Kryu did not know of this man's hunger to possess me any moment that Kryu was away. Since I was plotting, I could not fling my outrage at his feet and demand that Tanis be beaten until he fell into the dark arms of death. But no, hadn't Kryu told me that Tanis was to him as close and dear as any brother. So what would be his reaction to Tanis's visits to my bed? Would he beat him, or would he slap him on the back and laugh? I wondered.

Tanis's eyes caught my gaze. "You often bite your nail when you are thinking, did you know that?" He strode to my side and caressed the top of my head absent mindedly. His fingers trailed down the back of my neck and caught a wayward lock of hair trailing between my shoulder blades. He deposited a kiss upon my shoulder.

"Ah, to be with other women and to hunger for you, even now as heavy as you are with child. I still dream of you." He breathed the words within the mass of hair that had been swept up by copper pins. "No one knows how to make me feel as you do, sweet queen." I turned to look at him. His eyes were warm with something I could not place. I waved a slave over to bring me my linen wrap. I stood up. "Please allow my slave to attend to me." He abruptly stood up and made his way to my divan. He sat one leg crossed over the other, lying back on the many pillows waiting, his eyes touching every inch of me.

"Your mouth has become legendary my

queen. My praises and your king's have made men of every corner wonder of the magic that you carry. Unlike the many women I have had, you know what to do when a staff is pointed at your mouth!"

I shook my head, wrapping the linen thrice below my waist. Ama appeared with a basket of various oils and scents. I lay upon my side, my nudity something that no longer concerned me. Tanis's eyes were alight. Ama handed me one little vial after another, unstopping them so that I could smell. I choose a little vial of rose oil, and I placed a small amount upon my wrists and breathed in the wonderful scent. I relaxed and sighed into her working wonders as she massaged the rest of the vial into the small of my back and shoulders.

I saw Tanis's loincloth pull; he always desired me, and I knew how to push him to the edge.

"You have not answered me, my lord. Where is Kryu since you have not gone hunting?"

Tanis laughed heartily. He stood up and approached me as I knew that he would. He cupped one heavy breast into his hands and weighed the fate of his words before answering.

"I have never risked so much for the taste of a woman." I waved for a slave to begin buffing the heels of my feet with a flat black rock that smelled of the sea.

"I cannot allow you to risk so much for this woman. Who is she?"

He released his hold on my breast and spun on his heels and walked to the balustrade. He leaned upon it looking down at the courtyard below and exhaled a heavy weight. He was troubled by his desire for me, yet he confused lust for love. My power was to allow him to sink deeper into that confusion. It was the only way I could control him. During the many banquets I had enjoyed at Kryu's side, I savored watching Tanis's eyes follow me. His desire for me was a fever that grew with every day that he looked upon me. I adored seeing his eyes darken with passions that I knew he would not be able to release upon me. I would watch him sink into his cup, and drink mead and wine with an abandon to forget, and then I would watch him pick a woman or two to bury his frustrations within their soft flesh. His body howled for my mouth, my body, and for what I could do to him. He turned.

"To answer you, the king allowed me to return when I told him that I must have eaten tainted meat." He shook his head. What else was he holding back?

"And?" I prodded gently.

"I want your mouth to take me . . ." Tanis

froze. I turned to see that Kryu had entered.

"Come, come, my dear brother. You speak so well. Continue." Kryu moved in a deliberate way that had me pull the linen blanket around me.

I swung my legs around, shooed the slaves away, including Ama, and sat up.

Tanis threw him a smile. "I am caught by the passions I carry for your woman." He shrugged too casually for it not to be feigned.

Did Kryu grow in height and size before my eyes, or was I dazed by the moment? He moved across the space that separated them and grabbed Tanis by the throat. His eyes were steel blades digging out questions with his unmerciful gaze.

"I thought. . ." Tanis began to say.

"You thought nothing!" Kryu muttered between clenched teeth. He pushed him away and Tanis stumbled backwards before he regained his footing.

Kryu never once looked at me. "Do you find me to be the fool? The husband who has lost his wit for want of love?" He pointed towards me, and yet he never once glanced my way.

"She bears my son. She is not yours to desire. I shared her once but never again, and if I find that you have taken her when I was not..." He broke off. He shook off the rage that was threatening to turn him into a wolf about to tear to pieces one of the pack that has gone too far.

"Do not test me again, Tanis."

"My lord!" Tanis shouted.

Kryu roared, his eyes glowing hot with rage. He turned his back to Tanis and breathed deeply. When he swung around to face him, his eyes were calm soft seas of grayish blue. "Do not test me Tanis. You cannot imagine what I hold back." He approached Tanis and patted him on the back. "Go to the temple of Ishtar and pick any temple maidens you chose. Take what you will, but do not ever touch what is mine." He swung his attention to me.

He waved for Tanis to go. I watched as he left, his head straight, his shoulders thrown back, but he did not dare look at me. When he was gone, Kryu exhaled and let out an explosive laugh; he ran his fingers through his hair. He turned to me.

"Has he ever touched you?" I swallowed hard, as a man like Kryu would only ask such a question if he already knew the answer to it. I turned and walked back to our rooms. He followed me.

I sat at my table before the large round copper reflector.

"Have care with your words," he whispered. I understood his warning for me not to lie. So I would tangle this question with veils of deceit, for what else could I do?

"What would you have me say?" I shook my hair out, combing it through with my fingers.

He moved like a thunder snap and grabbed my shoulder spinning me around to face him. I gasped and gazed up at him. Tears bordered my eyes and threatened to fall.

"Tell me the truth." He was angered but in such control that I trembled.

I shook my head.

"My dearest queen, do you fear that I will kill your lover?" He seemed taken aback, as if this was a thought that had not occurred to him until now. How could he even think such a thing? Did all men forget what they heard? Did they only react to what they saw, what they thought they saw?

"For to call him so, implies that I love him." I was now as angry as he. I knew that I misspoke; in truth I did not consider what I had done with Tanis, love. It was brutish and though it had given me pleasure, had never meant anything.

I rose and moved against him, pushing my finger against his hard chest. My neck stretched as far back as I could, so that I could look into his face.

"Do you love him?" he raged as if fierce winds hid within his being. I stood back.

I felt turmoil of loss, of fear, of confusion, and before I could stop the words, I allowed my tongue to take over my mind.

"I love you, my king! Are you so blind not to see it?" and when the words flew out of me, I felt a strange sadness, for in telling him that I loved him I knew that I had distracted from answering his question. Had Tanis taken me? For I knew that to tell him that Tanis had taken me again and again and that I had not raised a cry to have it stop, that in my own way, I had encouraged Tanis's pursuit in hopes to twist his feverish obsession to my own ends to deliver my children.

I knew that somehow, some way, the love that I carried in my heart for Kryu would be ravaged by the twisted fates that had so far conspired to destroy all that I had ever held dear.

I felt no freedom in the release of my declaration of love and yet Kryu grabbed me in his arms and twirled me about the room as if I was no more than a child. He was laughing, laughing madly with a joy I had never heard in his voice. "Why are you such a child? Have I not told you before that I loved you?" I sullenly asked.

Kryu's eyes were molten silver. "Not with a tone to your voice that carries its music. No, not as you did today," he answered and settled me upon my feet.

"Tonight, we dine alone," he laughed.

I clapped my hands and Ama appeared.

"We shall dine on the terrace tonight." She nodded and left.

But I could not shake the thoughts that plagued me. I watched Kryu strip all that he wore. And the thoughts came to me in a torrent of questions. How had I failed to show him in the past what I had always carried within my heart? How could he now hear my love? Was he ready for it now? Why had he been cruel in rejecting what he now held so highly? Was he reaching the shimmering joy with fingertips? Did he now understand the love that can bring a man and a woman untold bliss? Was he able to see its life pulsing between us? Did he simply love me now and had he made peace with the idea of it?

25

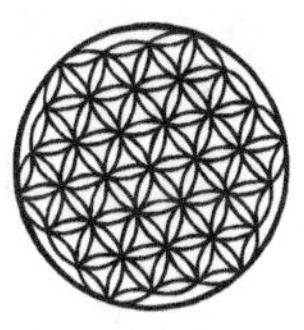

OCTOBER 31, 1997

Daniel had been working like mad. Between the dealership and getting that Fiat Spider together he was barely, if ever, home. Or if he was home, he was busy working on the car. He had it parked on the street; the cops knew him and left him alone. He'd bought an engine from Pik Your Part and had installed the engine within the spare hours he had in the very early mornings. It was seven-thirty in the morning and I needed to get to work. I had dressed up for Halloween as a pirate bordering on the slut aspect. I had no money to buy a new costume and had put something together with what I had in the closet.

I had settled on a white ruffled blouse from Betsey Johnson that I had bought in the mid '80s. It was very sheer. I had a black cotton training corset, black leggings, and thigh-high suede boots with flat heels to complete the whole look. My makeup was simple; black liquid liner, some gold shimmer on the lids, and my favorite Russian red lipstick was the tour de force. With that, I had an old Hermes scarf I had received from my mother from one of her trips to Paris, which I tied around my head. Some large gold hoop earrings, and voila, I was the pirate slut. I stood in front of the bathroom mirror and slipped my hand inside my demi-bra to adjust my breasts. I was all cleavage pushed up by the bra and further accentuated by the rise of my corset. I gave myself a nod of satisfaction; I was having a really good hair day. It swirled around my waist and grazed my hips. I glanced at my Swiss army watch and noticed that I was pushing eight o'clock. I needed to jam out of there to get to New Line Tech on time. I was about to leave when I remembered that I had not sprayed myself with any Miss Dior perfume. I spritzed behind my ears, between my breasts and at my wrists, only then did I feel complete. I grabbed my black leather purse and slammed the door behind me. Daniel was already on his way to work, and I was getting a ride from Ted who was meeting with Michelle for a job interview. I skipped down the stairs and ran straight into Eric.

"What the..." I exclaimed.

I looked up to see Eric smiling down at me his eyebrow quizzically raised. He wrapped his arms around my waist and pulled me against his chest.

"Whoa, there pretty Mademoiselle."

I pushed my hands against his chest, and he broke his hold. I was so flustered and could barely meet his gaze. I now knew why I wanted him and that made me stop to think upon the nuances of desire and love. It wasn't just a matter of pheromones in this life; such lusts, such chemistry, harked back to other lives that impacted our choices now. That very idea shook the very foundation of my being. How could I trust desire when it stood on the very pinnacle of all that had come before it? But here was what puzzled me the most: I trusted my love for Daniel and that love superseded what had transpired in Mesopotamia, of that I had no doubt.

Eric's lust was no different than it had been in that life so long ago, and I felt both an attraction for him and revulsion. It was really just plain weird.

He bowed with great flourish, "Stand and deliver, my dear Mademoiselle."

"What?" I was a flipping idiot unable to formulate sense into words. What the fuck was fucking wrong with me? I was determined to beat this and stared straight into his big blue luminous eyes, and I felt myself turn red. Oh, fuck me!

He was pressing something into my hand. It was a white envelope.

He bent near my ear and whispered, "November rent." His warm breath made me shiver from that ridiculous erogenous zone in that absurd place called my ear and plummeted straight down between my legs. That son of a bitch! That fuck! How dare he try this shit with me again in this fucking life time! That fuck!

Where was I? I shook the shock out of me and gathered what little sense remained in my head. The thing was, I remembered him as that tall blond warrior, and I knew how good his cock had felt then. I could only wonder what... what am I saying? No, he was no one, nothing and not for me in this life. I narrowed my eyes and stared at the place between his left shoulder and his jaw line, that delicious and very sexy five o'clock shadow he so purposely fostered with such tenderness it made me wonder how scratchy he would feel if I got on my tip toes and planted a kiss on his cheek. He knew he was hot; what a bloody manipulator. I stood my ground.

"Rent isn't due until the first," I managed to push out into the air that stood between me and his mouth.

"So sue me," he shrugged insolently.

I tugged on the envelope, and he slipped

out waving it over his shoulder. I wasn't going to play this game. I crossed my arms over my breasts, pushing them up and then glancing up at him.

"Let me know when you're done."

He gulped, his eyes glued on my tits. It never failed, not with him, not with most anyone and that includes girls. He handed me the envelope, and I took it.

"Thank you." I swallowed so hard it hurt my throat. I didn't look back at him as I walked back up the stairs to put it in my deposit envelope which I or Daniel would take to the bank this week. When I came back down the stairs Eric was nowhere, which flooded me with relief. Within minutes I heard Ted honk his horn, and I was out of the house eager to start my day.

"Wow! You look stunning!" Ted exclaimed as I climbed into the front seat of his 1983 Volvo wagon. It was periwinkle blue, which suited his conservative demeanor.

"So, are you ready?" I asked him. I saw his jaw tighten. He answered stiffly, like a duck with a lemon stuck up his ass, granted that would make anyone cranky. I wished he would get laid. If he'd just get some, he'd be much happier and easier to hang with. He turned to look at me, his eyes warm and his mouth tight and thin. "I do, I mean, I am ... ready."

"Okay, let's go. Oh, but before we hit the 134 do you mind a quick detour? I need a coffee so bad that if I don't get a good cup I may go postal," I pleaded, giving him my best moue.

"Don't they have coffee at the office?" He was a little pissed, but then he was not out of his comfort zone as he was always straddling that paradox between pissed and mad. We made a quick stop at Starbucks and I grabbed a freaking large, what do they call it? Grande. I asked the girl rigging me up if they could set me up on an IV. I was so tired and out of it.

She laughed like she was serving a mad homeless person and not the pirate slut I insisted that I was.

Naturally I was against all dress codes. The fact that New Line Tech didn't even have one was beside the point. I was outrageous, and I knew it, but I also knew that I was going to kick some ass today. I just knew that my enrollments were going to go through the roof.

I had ten appointments set up, and I had doubled them, so in truth I was interviewing and touring five pairs. If I did my job right, I was pretty sure if I signed up one guy the other would follow suit. Even just out of high school, peer pressure was a gold mine one could always count on.

We crossed the Colorado Bridge, hit the 134, and made it in no time. It was as if we had hit some type of time warp. Ted parked the car and ran up the stairs with me to the second floor.

Michelle's husband John laughed nervously and could not keep his eyes off of my cleavage, and Michelle threw me that Miss America smile that looks pasted on. Look, the truth was that even though I worked for these people, I wanted to make this work my way. I knew they wouldn't talk to me because ever since I had started working for them I was making them money and closing Y2K conversion deals like crazy. They were due to cut my first commission check the following Monday. I was excited by the prospect of actually earning more than I needed. What a novel idea. I introduced Ted to John and Michelle and off they went to her office to interview my nervous little friend. I hoped they would hire him as he was perfect foil to my wild and brash humor. Between us we could really wrap up this town. We were like Frick and Frack, so different that our techs would call just because we were interesting and fun. However, what was nice about Ted is that he would make the tight-asses that dominated some of the business sectors, such as city and government, feel at ease.

Meanwhile, I walked into my private office, which was the size of a small walk-in and shut the door. I threw my legs on the table and casually logged into my PC and signed into to my AOL account. There he was, as I knew he would be. Malek was waiting.

26

THE CROWN KING

The fourth sunrise propelled our harvest celebration day to begin. My eyes were shut tight. I felt the rays of the sun cajole me with warmth, and I buried deeper beneath the furs. I yawned, rubbed my eyes, and opened them to gaze into Kryu's searching gray gaze. He was smiling down at me with a tenderness that made my heart scatter like leaves blown by a rogue wind. I wanted him. In this very moment, I felt only love for him. My eyes must have glowed this truth for he lowered his head and possessed my mouth. I allowed my senses to whirl beneath the heat of his passion.

I felt his desire push hard against my thigh. He turned me upon my side and entered me thus. His large hand holding my thigh aloft with a tight grip as he thrust his hunger into me, I felt a joy rush through my body as he buried himself ever deeper and faster until a chill cascaded over my shoulders and rushed down to my pearl, which his rough thumb had claimed and was stroking. I fell into a mad pulse of pleasure. I cried out his name and quickly he followed his lips against my neck, his breathing raged and warm. At that moment, it came to me that I always felt whole when we coupled. Tears sprung to my eyes; he held my rounded belly within the gentle cup of his hand, and thus we fell asleep until the sun had reached its zenith.

When I awoke, Kryu was gone. I stretched like a cat and rose. Ama was beside me to help me comb out my hair and braid it into two long braids which she then twisted, attaching the coils with copper pins low upon the nape of my neck. I dressed in a long white tunic of spun linen of a heavy weave. I wrapped the gold girdle with the purple stones and completed the outfit with a long black stole of a fine weave of wool bordered with gold embroidery of simple design. I walked down to the common room and found Kryu in deep conversation with Tanis. When I approached them, they hastened a glance at me, each with an expression upon their faces that seemed dark and secretive. I felt the leap of my heart catch in my throat. Something was amiss.

I doubt Kryu would tell me. I reached his side and slipped my arm within his.

"Will you walk with me? Your son kicks, and I fear I need the distraction."

I held my rounded belly. He placed his hand over mine and nodded. Tanis's eyes scanned my face for anything that would tell him if he was still welcome in my bed. I looked away.

Kryu and I walked together towards the east side of the gardens. Kryu had to bend his head as he strolled beneath an arbor of red and white roses. His words were silenced by some emotion that held them back. I could not say what kept him silent. And though I would not look upon his face, I felt that something had changed. His large brown hand, gripped the handle of his sword. I noticed the large ring that encircled his thumb. It had a red stone that had been carved with a design of a Ram's head. I had never seen it before this day, and I wondered about it. Something held my tongue. We came upon a small garden, which was my private sanctuary and had been kept so ever since Kryu had taken my land.

"Is ..." I began to ask but Kryu abruptly cut me off.

"Malek is fine; he is healthy and eats well," he paused. "I have kept my promise. Will you keep yours?" He stopped and turned to face me.

"Have I done something to displease you since you left my side?" I was unsure of what he meant.

"Do you not know what I ask of you?" He seemed ferocious to me, like a wolf restrained by chains and foaming with rage and gnashing teeth. His eyes were other-worldly, possessed by the fury that he contained. Why this anger? I shook my head.

"Do you hold me above all those you love?"

I stood back shaken by what he asked of me. How could he ask such a thing? My children, no matter how much love I carried for Kryu, my children ranked above him in all things.

I struggled to find the words to explain to him without offending him, but I knew that no matter what I said, he would never understand until one day he too would hold his child in his arms. I realized that until he did, he would never know how the heart worked its magic to ensure the love and protection of one's child.

I stood back and stared up at him searching his face, the depth of his eyes for the opening of his heart to understand selflessness.

"My king, you are the very center of my passions; you are my great love. You, my king, have replaced Malek as the center of my passion. I will never be able to honor you enough to thank you for Malek's well-being, for he is the father of my children." I approached Kryu and caressed his unshaven cheek. My index finger trailing the shape of his mouth, he took my hand in his, gazing deeply within my eyes, and he opened my hand to kiss my open palm.

"Malek understood that," I took a deep

breath and found the strength to continue. "He understood that our children were our most precious responsibilities. That they would forevermore inhabit the very pinnacle of our hearts."

He scowled while I continued.

"When your son is born, I will love him more than I love you my King. This truth should please you." He turned his back to me. His pale red linen cape, which nearly touched to the ground, moved and swayed with his every step. I approached him, reaching for the nape of his neck to caress it. He flung me away.

"You spirited your eldest son out of this land, did you not?" He swung around to face me.

What was this anger from? What had caused the sudden turn?

"I have!" I approached him, my eyes full of fire, "You would have done the same. What would you have done to my prince had I not?" I did not wait for an answer. What would any conqueror do to the one next in line?

"You would have killed the prince!" I shouted.

He shook his head no.

I laughed, my head thrown back and turned away from him. My laughter turned into a wild cry of rage. I spun on my heels and moved towards him with a menace I would have never dared otherwise. For he who threatened a hair of one of my children's head would face my wrath.

"How dare you lie to me?" I snarled like a cornered lioness. "How can you not face the truth?" I hurled at his feet.

His eyes widened, surprised by this sudden change, for he had never seen me in a true rage.

"I have not killed Malek," he rebutted. His lips tightened into a straight line, and his arms crossed over his broad chest.

"Ha!" I spat. I was so infuriated by his inability to just tell me truth.

"You will in time kill him, will you not?" I flung the words at his feet like a challenge that he must pick up. But he did not. He stood staring at my face and whispered, "I would never kill any child unless there was something greater than my own whims that pushed me."

I felt a shiver rush through my skin, like a wheat field moved by a sudden gust. What did he mean? What was he saying?

Was he thinking of Cycrus? He would not dare; he would never do anything to harm Cycrus for he had lived only seven winters; he was all innocence and sweetness. I knew, as did all the people who spent time with him, I knew that he would never be able to rule. No, it was my eldest son who would one day reclaim the kingdom, or so I hoped.

"Do you fear my daughter and her claim to the throne?" I was shaking.

"I am not from a land that would allow a woman to rule," he laughed. "Her purpose is to breed, my queen, not to rule." At that moment I hated him, and yet a sigh of relief escaped my lungs. My children were safe. So what was this change?

"Then why were you talking to Tanis so...." I could not find the word. "You looked as if you were plotting something." I shrugged. He smiled. "An oracle has come to offer services. She heralds from a long and respected line. She claims visions which I will discover soon enough."

"Has she spoken of you losing your kingdom?" His eyes widened and then narrowed. He shook his head. "My hold on what I have taken is strong; I know it," he said, hitting his fist into the open palm of his hand.

"Then tell her that her services are not needed." I feared that she would expose my plans before the deed was done. I had no need of an oracle now.

He stood legs apart and examined me for a long time.

"Will you send her on her way?" I continued.

He gave me a long cool smile.

"I hunger for your mouth, take me now—here, and show me how much passion fills your heart."

I would not be so manipulated.

"Will you send her off?"

"I cannot say, my sweet adoring queen. Your mouth holds that very power to sway me at your whim."

I approached him. He sat upon the stones that circled a beautiful water fountain. Ishtar spewed a fountain of water from her mouth. He laid both of his palms upon the stones that lay on either side of his hips.

"Take me now, and if this moment pleases me, I will do your bidding." He was no fool, and yet perhaps if I did please him… I was about to kneel before him when I hurled my rage into his face. Demons possessed my soul at this moment, for how else could I explain it.

"What makes you different than your men is only that you hold the Crown! But you are no better; you are led by your hunger to plunder all that you feel you are owed. I will not beg you for anything. Take your oracle; bed her if you like. Stay away from me with your games."

I began to run, hiking my tunic to my thighs. I could hear the pursuit of his footfall. I would not seize, and then a hand grabbed me from behind and hoisted me around the waist and lifted me off the ground. He held me thus against his chest; my feet did not reach the ground, and so I swung my legs trying to kick him.

"Take a care for what you wish, my queen, for your wish may be granted," he whispered in my ear. He allowed his mouth to trail down my neck, sending shivers of hunger down to my belly. I was filled with his seed, and yet I wanted more of him; I wanted all of him. I took deep breaths to calm myself. He set me down upon my feet and turned me to face him. He grabbed my face with both hands and stared into my eyes to say with his gaze what he could not say with words. His lips fell upon mine like raindrops, for with him it was always so. I was drenched in the healing wave of his desire, of his love, and I fell backwards within the crook of his arms to receive all he had to offer me. The garden blurred, and my vision was nothing but lights and colors. He swung me into his arms and carried me out of the garden, up the long stone staircase past slaves, some of his men, and passed Tanis's searching gaze, and into our chambers. He laid me upon my bed as if I was the most precious possession he owned. The heat of his eyes traveled down my body as he loosened his leather belt and peeled his loincloth from around his hips. His long thick spear sprang from between his muscular thighs.

The pearl that sought pleasure within me shook with joy at the sight. I was shaking from hunger for him to plunge his length into me. I wanted all of him. He leaned into the bed on one knee and ripped the gown off my body, caressing me with the intensity of his gray gaze. I could not fight my desire and fell into the wonderful feeling of letting go as he leaned against his elbow and began to trail his tongue against my skin. He lit me like a torch with the flame of his tongue, and there was nothing I wanted to hold onto except the power of his shoulders as he rode me. I did not want to grasp control from him, nor did I desire to tame this fever that howled within. The madness in his body made mine respond, for he held a power over my body. I hated him for it and wanted nothing more than to feel his plundering heat between my thighs. I was goddess, queen, and whore, and I reveled in the riot within my mind.

He swung between my thighs without care for our child, but I knew I was safe. I grabbed his shoulders with fingertips that dug into his skin and my thighs wrapped around his lean hips as he rode me faster, and faster. I moaned loud against his mouth and did not cry out. He grasped a fat nipple in his mouth and tugged on it hard. I moaned low. I locked eyes with his; we were in combat as to who would let go first.

"Do you like this sport, my queen?" He was merciless, riding me hard and then slowing to a pace making his hips twist and turn, digging deeper within me. I wrapped my legs tighter around his hips and moved my hips to his rhythm. We rode each other for a long while, our breaths ragged from the hunt we had launched long before this day; it had started on the day he had claimed me upon the steps of the Temple of Ishtar.

Perhaps, before the world had a name, perhaps we had stood on a battlefield, swords in hand and in full combat, yes, perhaps long ago we had been... but for now we were linked by an unnamed tie that bound us like chains to a wall. I cannot say how, but I was able to flip him upon his back, and it was my turn to conquer his pleasure. I rode him as I had ridden my mount across the plains of my beloved lands, for he was now my beloved land. He shuddered against me. He cupped his hands over my breasts, holding them thus, and his breath was coming fast. His eyes had the look of a man when he is about to cross the river of death, vulnerable, lost and all trusting to come out the other side alive and well. My heart was crushed by the fist of my love for him, and I rode him safely into the harbor of my hope that perhaps all would end well. My chest tightened, and my tears fell shamelessly down my cheeks. How could I not hate him?

He caressed the tears off my cheeks and smiled like a child into my eyes, and I was lost to him and fell across his chest, my face pressed against the curve of his neck. We were covered in a dew of sweat, and it felt good to feel so alive and to have life kick its existence within my belly. And then the thought ripped through the perfection that I had experienced. I wondered what I would have to do to get rid of this oracle, for I was sure she brought doom and despair.

27

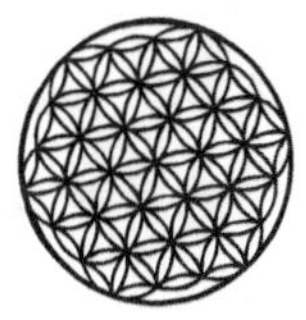

OCTOBER 31, 1997

What have you recalled my sweet Bakor?" It was early morning, and I knew that Ted would be wrapped up in this interview for a good hour, so I was free to talk. But here's the thing, I didn't want to share any more with Malek. I was ashamed, and there wasn't anything I could do about that shame. I had fallen in love with the conqueror who had fucked me in front of him, (which I had never admitted to him) whose friend I had shared, and all the while Malek had been kept in a dark dungeon which I barely visited. How in the hell could I tell him all that shit, when in that life, he had loved me so perfectly? I just couldn't, and so my conversation was at best, stilted.

"Everything, nothing of any importance," I typed, knowing damn well he would see right through me.

Malek is typing, "You carry shame," he wrote, "Why?"

I was shocked by his question. Why oh why couldn't I be home? This was not a one-hour chat.

I took a deep breath and typed the truth. "Because I didn't do enough to protect you." I hit send with a half self-disgusted punch on the enter key. I was still mad at myself after three thousand years. That shit called karma is really a bitch! I could feel Malek gathering his words to share something I had needed to hear for a long, long time.

"Bakor, my heart, my most precious love, it was never your job to protect me. There were many things in place, fate and free will. I chose to allow my capture. The fate of the kingdom was in place, but I had free will and could have taken my life or fought to the bloody end. I did not; I allowed my capture and I allowed you, my sweet gazelle, to become a hawk."

I shook my head. My legs were planted on the ground and my hands on the table as I typed quickly on the keyboard." What do you mean I was a gazelle that became a hawk?"

Didn't he know I had fallen in love with the man who had ripped his life apart?

Malek is typing. "Come my love, you know what I mean. Close your eyes and ponder on the full meaning of my words."

I did as he said, and leaned back in my chair. He was still such an elegant soul, nothing like Kryu, Daniel, Tanis or Eric; they were such rough beings. But he was like a polished diamond, and the thing is, he had been polished over three thousand years ago where as I had gotten rougher, edgier. I was no longer a gazelle but a hawk that could see from different vantage points. I had learned to see what others could not or would not see. I understood what he meant.

I typed, "I get it!" I hit send and something within me felt light.

"I knew you would," he wrote back and added a smiley face. I smiled deep within my heart, for the journey had changed me, transformed me into a warrior and in this life. I was learning all that I had gained from that past. My office had a window that looked out upon the hallway. I saw Michelle approach my office and knock on my door. I minimized my screen and flipped up my database.

"Do you have a moment?" She was all smiles, genuine this time.

It was at that moment I knew that Ted had gotten the job. I got up and joined her. We walked together to her office where Ted and John were both talking like comrades. They both sat up and watched me with guilt pasted on their face. Strange? But okay. I stepped in.

John stood up. "Ted has agreed to take the position as..." he paused, as if gathering the right words.

"As Director of Sales." Michelle said.

I felt like I had been kicked in the stomach. I know that I must have turned either white as snow or as red as blood because the look in their eyes announced quite well my reaction. I stuck out my hand to Ted. "Congratulations, Ted I had no idea the position was open." No shit, I had been told that after six months of employment that I would be up for the position, but they had given it to him, and they had never worked with him before. To say I was stunned, hurt, mad, didn't even describe it. I was dealing with a cacophony of expletives such as son of a bitch, cocksucker, fuck and mother fucker, and yet I managed to give them my brightest smile. Ted wanted to believe it, and hence he reflected my smile with his own.

"I am so looking forward to working with you; we are going to make a great team." He patted me on the back like I was some buddy he had met for a beer and had beaten at pool.

He was no better than a Borgia; Machiavelli would have been fucking proud. I was angry at my own stupidity. I wanted to take myself out and beat the crap out of myself for being so naïve, so stupid, so bloody female. I kept it cool, and was the essence of excited for the new projects for New Line Tech. Internally, I felt like a third-class male crew member on the Titanic.

"When do you start?" I was like a yapping Yorkie on crack. I was just so excited to bat for the home team. The truth is, had I been a dog, I would have raised my leg and pissed all over his pants. He'd tread on and stolen my territory, and I was raging mad.

As soon as I could, I ran back to my office and shut the door. I was crying. I logged back on to my AOL account which, thank God, had timed out.

"Malek," I typed, tears pouring down my face, "I am so sorry."

I waited for a while. Malek is typing. I glanced at the time. It was around ten o'clock in the morning that meant that in Paris it was seven o'clock in the evening. I wondered if he had just finished dinner; perhaps his wife was washing the dishes.

"Guess what happened?" I wrote.

"?" he typed, a response which was no surprise.

I rubbed my eyes not caring that I was smearing my makeup and plunged forward with my story of being stabbed in the back by the ones who smiled in my face. He understood, and then when I was done he typed this simple question. "What do you think you owe Ted that would have brought about this situation?" I sat still, and thought for a moment.

"You mean what I owe him in a past life?" I asked Malek.

"Precisely, ma cherie." I breathed in and out. My tears dried, and I thought long and hard.

Malek is typing, "Take your time; do not over-think it. Feel it, Bakor; let your mind feel the truth of your karmic debt to Ted."

I sat back. Michelle buzzed me, "Can you come to my office?"

"Sure, can you give me a couple minutes?"

"Yes, of course." I was shaking with rage.

What did I owe Ted? What in the hell did I owe Ted? Then like a seam ripping apart I saw myself as a man holding a pillow in my hand approaching the bed of a sleeping child.

That could not have been me; I must be taking that on because I know all about it.

"Do not deny what you know," Malek wrote. How did he know so much about me?

I typed back, "He told me about that past life. It's not possible that I was a man who killed him when he was a child. I mean come on, that's just too simple." I hit send.

Malek is typing. I was watching the screen with anticipation.

The phone buzzed, it was Michelle again. God, she could be a real pain in the ass.

"I'm really sorry Michelle, I have a brutal

headache just give me a couple minutes and I will be right over." I hung up abruptly not allowing her to speak.

Malek's message appeared, and I leaned forward to read every word. I felt like I was lost in the desert thirsty for water, and he was like an oasis in the middle of nowhere.

I drank in his words. "Bakor, why do you think life is as complicated as you make it? The image came to you, and your soul recognized it as such. Close your eyes now and ask your soul if that was you?" I did as he asked and my soul was quiet for a while. I asked out loud, "Was I that man who murdered Ted when he was a child in that past life?" Very softly, ever so softly, the voice whispered, "yes." Above that voice were my cries of denial, but it was that voice that spoke the truth.

"It says, yes. What shall I do with that information?" I asked him.

"Do what you will with it. But the most important thing now is to allow yourself to forgive yourself. You are not that person any longer and to hold on to that tie will only hurt you. Let go of everything. Your ego will step away if you allow your soul to come forth and heal."

I wanted to ask him so many more questions. Why did I remember so many lives with so many people right now? What was this all about?

"You have come in this life with one purpose, Bakor." Malek is typing. "And that is to make amends with as many people as you can so that when we meet again in the flesh, you will be free from all that binds you now. Do you understand what I am saying to you?"

Michelle was buzzing me again.

"I have to go…I think I understand. I will talk to you tomorrow, okay?"

"Ciao, bella Bakor." Malek is no longer logged in.

I got up and walked to Michelle's office more concerned with these past lives than the shit Michelle had in store for me.

28

THE SUN IS BLOOD RED

The night was loud with the rhythm of drums and the strident sounds of trumpets rose towards the gods thanking them for a plentiful harvest.

Ama was helping me dress. I had chosen a long linen tunic of deepest purple which suited my coloring. I wore golden earrings that cuffed over my ears. Ama combed my hair out and added precious rose oil. She twined my hair in long strands and clipped them with long golden cylinder, that when squeezed clung to my hair strands and glimmered in the light of the oil lamps that lit the room. When she was done, she massaged rose oil from my shoulders down to my fingertips. I breathed in the perfume and smiled. Golden sandals wrapped my feet and ankles.

I was ready to join Kryu and the lord and ladies of his new kingdom. For I knew that at least for now this was a new age. I thought of Malek, for I had not been able to see him. I feared that I would never say goodbye to him.

I exhaled heavily. I reached for a fan delicately carved from ivory. I did not wish to be caught in the stench of unwashed flesh, mead and wine, roasted meat and strident laughter at the great hall. I wanted to meet my children one last time before farewells were to be made. I wanted to hold them close to me, but I could not do so until I first made my appearance. For to do anything out of the ordinary would alert Kryu that something was amiss. I held back all my desires and my motherly instincts for the purpose of keeping the plan safe. Later, much later, I would hold them in my arms and capture the feel of their bodies against my breasts to breathe in the scent of their skin. I doubted that I would ever see them again.

I needed strength and reached for Ama and held her within the embrace of my arms.

"I am so lost," I whispered against her ear. She nodded her head and rubbed the length of my back in comfort. I broke away from her and looked down at her upturned face, her eyes wrinkled by joy and time. She gave me a smile and said, "Have faith, be strong, for you are a queen of Mesopotamia." I wanted to weep but instead tightened my mouth and blinked my eyes from spilling tears.

I walked towards the open doors that led down the long wide stairs that would take me into the bowels of lies and dark secrets. I was surprised when an arm grabbed me from behind and pulled me within the arch of a doorway hidden by a curtain.

I cried out, but a hand muffled any further sounds. Hot breath grazed my right ear.

"Be still!" The voice barked. I was spun around and stood before Tanis.

I stepped back, but he grabbed my arm and pulled me towards him. "How is it that I still want you even now as you are?" He glanced down meaningfully at my large belly.

His hand traveled up my tunic between my thighs. I was about to raise an alarm. His fingers plundered my vulva and played with my pearl making my body shudder in surprised pleasure. He swung me against the wall and was unloosening his loincloth; he was hard and ready for me. He lifted my leg and pushed the heat of his hunger within me. I pushed against him, and yet my body wanted him.

"Stop! Please, stop, he will kill you," I whispered urgently. He would not stop and pushed himself within my womb, and my body arched against him. I wrapped my fingers around his neck as he lifted me off the ground, pushing my back against the wall of the archway, the curtain a thin wall between us and anyone who might pass. I trailed my hands down his powerful shoulders and my fingers dug into them. He crushed me against his length. He pulled away to lock eyes with mine, moving his hips fast and hard until I felt the wave of shudder ripple through me like a rough wind against a wheat field. Still, he would not relent. His mouth captured a nipple and sucked hard, which made it spring impudently, bringing me more pleasure. His mouth trailed my neck kissing it, and still he rode me fast and hard. I felt a sharp stab of guilt that was replaced by the shiver of pleasure that rushed through me with a rise that made me gasp for him to stop. Still, he rode me, until he cried out against my throat, spilling his seed within me. He was breathing heavily, his head bowed but for a moment before he captured my mouth.

I pushed him away, and he let me slide down the wall to find my footing. I felt a whirlwind of confusion lash out at me. I wanted to shout my rage to the world, rage for the pain I carried within, rage for the guilt of having left my Malek to meet his fate, rage at my desires for Tanis and my love for Kryu, but most of all, what kept my mind from finding an oasis of peace was the guilt that I had failed my children. I would not know for many summers if my eldest son, Damion had made it safely to Egypt. It was possible that I would never survive long enough to hear the news. I knew not what the fates had in store. I moaned in pain. He steadied me.

"This was foolish," I muttered.

"I would risk everything for your touch," he growled, his green eyes twinkling with a fire of such intensity that I wondered at the true cause. He leaned his face towards me and inhaled my scent. He laid his lips against the corner of my mouth and savored me before whispering, "One day. . ."

I wondered if he was plotting against Kryu. The thirst for power never failed to corrupt. He turned, pulled the curtain back, saw that it was clear and left my side.

I walked back up the stairs to my chambers, to make right what he had disheveled. Ama did not question me and fixed my hair, pulled the dress off of my body, and cleaned Tanis's seed from between my thighs. She brought me a long tunic of the finest cobweb weave of blood-red linen.

I finally appeared at the banquet. Kryu looked up at me and sent me a broad smile of pleasure. Tanis rose, as did all the lords and ladies upon my appearance.

Women were brought forth to dance, strange, sinewy movements I had never seen before. Their skin shone like fine oiled cedar wood polished to a fine glow. They were bare of any cloth or jewels and there was a beauty to their limbs and large limpid eyes. Kryu was in deep conversation with Tanis and a general of his who was older than him by at least ten seasons. I was left to my own amusement, for I had refused long ago to eat with ladies who did not meet my rank. They were set off far from me to another table away from the men. I never spoke to them. What would be the point? I was a Mesopotamian queen; the blood of gods ran through my veins. Besides, what of any meaning could I possibly share with them? I had little time to speak of women talk.

Ilus, my freed slave, approached me with a clay jug of wine.

"More wine my queen?" I nodded my head for him to pour. He leaned close and whispered against my right side while he poured. "Tomorrow night is the planned day. Is all as you wish it, my queen?" I nodded my head.

"Your will is done," he whispered and moved to pour wine for another high-ranking warrior who had waved him over.

Tanis shot me a conspiratorial grin. I lowered my gaze and stared hard into my cup of wine and thought that by tomorrow everyone I loved would be gone forever from my side. Except for Ama, I would be alone. I felt a tear about to pierce through my resolve. I took a deep breath and held it back. Tears would come soon enough, but for now, I needed to gather my power like a warrior's shield.

I rose from the table, at that moment all rose and bowed. The large room was silent. Kryu's eyes were scrutinizing me. "I am tired my king, and beg rest."

He nodded his head. He returned to his conversation without so much as a word of kindness or concern. Tanis watched me while he listened to Kryu. All sat back down as I walked slowly out of the great hall.

Ama appeared by my side.

"I feel as though I have held my breath for a thousand years," I whispered to Ama. "I am so tired." I brushed my hand across my forehead. My heart was a whirlwind of fears. Exhaustion bent my body. I wanted to feel light and free again, and I didn't know if I would ever feel this way ever again. I shuddered. "It is the babe, my Queen. All will be well." She placed her arm around me. I held her hand, for she was a comfort to me. I cherished her as much as if she were my own blood. With her there was no royalty or slave, there was only a woman who loved me as well as my own mother had. I valued her as a child frightened by the dark adores the flame that light their way to calm rest.

I gazed into her eyes and saw the sincerity

of her words, and yet I did not feel healed. I felt utterly alone. We walked in silence to my chambers where guards stood at either side of my doors, and we walked through. I made my way to my terrace and stood beneath the expensive umbrella of a potted palm tree; the moon was full and bright. I wanted to sit beneath the night sky and pray to the Ishtar, to the gods, to any who would listen and hear a voice that would tell me that all would be well. My stomach was shaken from the fear that snaked its poison through my body. I did not know what I could do to release this hold. Suddenly, all I wanted to do was see my children. I spun on my heels and faced Ama, "Let us go say farewell to them." I turned once more to look up at the moon and sent her a silent prayer to guide my children safely to Egypt.

"When I return, have a fire lit and my couch prepared. I will sleep beneath the stars," I instructed Ama. She nodded. For the past two nightfalls Kryu had not joined me in my chambers. Where he had been was beyond me. Perhaps that is why I had responded to Tanis's touch? I could not say.

I walked to Ama's quarters where I found my children finishing their meal. I did not allow my children to dine in the great hall with Kryu's people. I distrusted their very being. My daughter, Amytis, had shared rooms with Ama ever since Kryu had taken the kingdom, and Cycrus stayed with them as he was so young. I was quietly watching them in the doorway as they ate the last remains of their meals. They were sitting on large pillows before a small table that bore their meal. It was good to see them thus. Amytis was tearing the last bits of meat for Cycrus and rolling it within the flat bread handing it to him thus. He ravished the taste. He was so pleased that he was humming as he ate. I felt tears prick my eyelids. I was warmed by them. Amytis was finishing off a slice of green melon. She was rubbing Cycrus's back. When they were done eating, a young slave boy gathered the empty gold plates and left.

His footsteps were silent upon the large colorful carpets strewed upon the stone floor. The children glanced up and saw me simultaneously. Amytis came to me first; she was taller than I. My head titled up to gaze into her large eyes, and I smiled, my heart full in their presence. She was so strong and unafraid of what was to come, or perhaps she was learning what it was to show the world what they wished to see? I held her tight in my embrace breathing the perfume of her jasmine-scented hair. Her arms surrounded my waist and her head was bowed upon the curve of my neck and shoulder.

We stood thus for a very long time.

"I want Mama now!" announced Cycrus, pushing in between us.

"Let us hold each other all together like this," I said, enclosing my children within the glow of my love. We had not told Cycrus that he would be journeying to Egypt for we feared that he would utter the plan without thinking of the consequence. He knew nothing of what was to come.

Finally, he looked up at me complaining of his tutor teaching him the history of the harvest festival; he would much prefer it if I allowed him to take a dead bird and cut it open so that he could determine what made it fly. I wanted him to learn the history of our people. I knew that if any misfortune were to befall my eldest son, Cycrus would never be next in line; rather the crown would fall upon my daughter's sensible shoulders. Cycrus had a brilliance that did not work for the daily running of a kingdom. He would never have the ability to hold it and rule it well. He had other gifts; his was the genius that would create new explorations of mathematics, discover the mysteries of the stars or uncover new healing methods. He wasn't born to rule. He was born to better the world we lived in.

I grabbed his little shoulders and pulled him ever so tightly against me. I wanted this moment to last until the stars no longer shone their light upon us. I stepped away and felt the sigh of their disappointment rush out of their bodies.

Ama stood before me and shooed them to ready for bed, for time had sought the sand of forgetfulness. Cycrus ran to get ready, whilst Amytis could not cut the tie that bound us within her gaze. It was I who had to turn my back on her and walk away. I could not have her view my visage stained with tears.

Ama was afraid to leave me to myself and so had decided to sleep not far from my couch. She slept and I followed to find solace in the silence of the empty world of veils and mists. I awoke with a start, and for a long while I sat supine staring up at the sky. I was sure morning was to deposit its stain of light upon the dark sky. I rose, unable to find peace in this place.

I found a long black cloak of linen and threw it about my shoulders, sheltering my face from prying eyes with the hood. I needed to find refuge at the small temple of Ishtar. I passed by the guards who did not stop me, and yet I was sure they knew who I was. I descended through a palace that was heavy with a somber quiet drowned by too much mead, wine, and sport.

I walked barefoot upon the packed red dirt cooled by the icy glow of the moon and the harvest winds. As I approached the temple, the torch light's soft glow welcomed me. I was sure the temple would be empty, but as I slipped through the heavy door that was cracked ajar I heard the chant of male voices -- powerful male voices, but I could not understand the words.

I flattened myself against the wall, crawling along the side to gain a closer look at what I realized was some kind of ceremony. I saw a priest wearing the head dress of a ram, the curly mane falling over his broad shoulders and down his back, the horns hocked in a curve that circled over his ears. I saw him in a simple loincloth, and then I realized that this was Kryu in some foreign ceremony. Tanis and all of his twelve most favorite men wore their helmets, which shielded their face from view, and they surrounded him. He was standing over the long sacrificial table, and upon it was someone that I could not see clearly.

Tanis held a beautiful crystal skull aloft presenting it to the men who bowed, and Tanis uttered foreign words in a strong voice. He presented it to Kryu who took it reverently and stood holding it above his head. It glimmered with fires that were both frightening and marvelous in mystical beauty. He turned to the east, to the west, to the north, and then faced me in the south. Tanis took it from his hand, disengaged the bottom jaw from the main and handed that piece to Kryu's third in command. Then he knelt before the table to lay it upon the floor right below the head of the table. My eyes rose to see that someone of red hair was lying still upon the table. I wondered if this was Kryu's servant boy I had only seen a few times during the war, for he had the same red hair as... would he actually sacrifice a young boy?

My eyes tried to focus hard on who was on that table, yet the torches flickered and swayed preventing a clear view. Kryu pulled out a short blade which shimmered. He uttered more words; he seemed unaware of all else. I found myself in a trance walking against the side of a set of pillars. I moved towards them, unaware that I was no longer hiding myself from view, yet they did not notice me, so intent were they on the task at hand.

Kryu placed the blade upon the throat of the victim and slowly pulled it away as if wiping it clean. Tanis knelt below holding the bottom of the shimmering skull which he used as a vessel to capture the blood as it flowed like wine from a goatskin bag. I saw the victim's feet shake, and the body convulse, but I never heard a sound or a cry of fear or pain. I lifted my tunic and began to run.

So much blood flowed so freely into that

skull and then began to spill over and fall upon Tanis's hands and redden the marble floor. I ran, and ran, and yet I never felt as if I neared the site to get a better view of the person who lay upon the table. When I stood before the table, I looked down to see that this was not Kryu's slave, but my own son, my most precious Cycrus, in the last of his death throes. I grabbed his body against mine and we fell together upon the cold marble floor slippery from his blood. My hand was cupped below Cycrus's shoulders, and my hand circled his throat trying to staunch the blood from escaping his body, his skin turning as white as the pillars of this very temple. Kryu and the men did not approach me, for I was a wolf, a hawk, a lioness defending her cub, and I howled from the very deepest recess of my soul, from the very depth of Ishtar's womb did my voice gain sound and resound across the temple, with a pain that left me suspended upon the hocks of my grief: For as he bled, his soul spilling out into the air to leave this world, my own soul was bleeding. My very being was sinking into a place of such hellish state that a small voice told me that I would never return to what I had once been. I held him against me. The blood was a never ending flow that pulsed out of his throat, his eyes fading from life, wide open, and then whatever had made him my son, whatever had housed this body vanished, and what I held in my arms was still. I took a breath and howled to the sky, to all the gods that had turned their backs on my most innocent prince. I was rocking him against me with a ferocity that shook me and held me paralyzed. I was raised by the invisible hands of my own madness, stone upon stone, building a tower that enclosed me within. I did not care, for I saw it within my mind, an unscalable wall, a narrow tower, and when I looked up to release the howl of my grief, my very heart flew from my mouth and escaped out into the ethers never to return. I could no longer see ceiling, sky, or anything that surrounded me. I was blinded by what I would not accept. I was buried alive within this small tower that locked me in a place of such anguish that nothing, no one, would ever enter me again. My hands were slippery from my son's blood, and I breathed in the scent of it, for I did not want to forget him, not any part of him, not even this.

"Take her!" I heard a voice cry out. "Take her from him!" I heard a voice shout before I fell across my jeweled red-headed boy who deserved more than to be sacrificed like a lamb of no consequence. I shouted to Ishtar, cursing her to die as he had died. Hands pried my fingers off of his body and pulled him from my loving embrace. He slipped out of my grasp like a wet fish caught but already dead.

Tears streamed down my face, and I pulled at my hair, shrieking, covering my face with his blood, tasting it in my mouth, tearing at my tunic hearing the shredding sounds of it. I was nude. My hands attacked my own flesh, using my nails to scratch at my face, my belly, and my arms. I begged them to cut my throat to take me now. I felt a hand descend upon the back of my head and hit me so hard that I fell into a spiral of colors that whirled me into the thankful silence of nothingness.

29

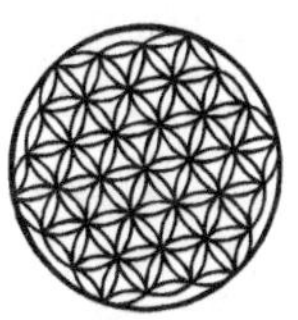

November 8, 1997
3:30 A.M.

I was running and blood was everywhere. I was holding a child in my arms, but whenever I looked down to see its face, it was blank. I saw torches and men. Kryu had cut his throat. I had tried to run to stop him, but the more I ran, the more he ran. The long, high ceiling temple hall was never ending. He had cut his throat! He had cut my son's throat! I kept running and fell into the slippery pool of blood and that threw me into a spiral and swung me out, sliding off the side of a blood red mountain. I was falling, spiraling trying to hold on to the child who fell away from me and disappeared from view. I woke up screaming. I was screaming for someone to stop this. I was sweating, and I was shuddering with a fear and horror that I could not control.

Daniel grabbed me within the soothing embrace of his arms, calming me with words of comfort. If I had dreamed anything else, his gentle voice would have helped. But he was the enemy, for he had been Kryu.

"It's just a nightmare; it's not real," he whispered against me, rocking me against his chest. "You're safe," he whispered. "It's over. You're back home; it's over." I was shaking, my body suspended between this world and the world I had just come from. I shook my head.

"It wasn't a dream."

"Yes, baby. Yes, that's all it was. Just a dream. You're back now, and it's going to be all right."

I pushed against him. "It wasn't a fucking dream!" I shouted. "You killed my son!" Tears ran down my face as if it had just happened now instead of three thousand years ago. "You killed my son." Daniel's arms fell away. He sat back and whispered, "Now you know almost all of it."

I sat across from him staring at him with fear, disgust, and rage. So there was more to come? My God! How bad could this get?

***

November 8, 1997
9 a.m.

I was lying on my back, my arm shielding my eyes from the sun's rays. Daniel had turned on the heat and the room was cozy. I didn't want to get out of bed.

"Come on sleepy head, get up." Daniel called

from the kitchen. He was acting so nonchalant, as if nothing mattered, as if nothing of any major significance had gone down. I turned on my stomach and buried my face in the pillow. What would Malek say about this? My mind could not see my son's face in that life. It was just a series of images and feelings that attacked my waking mind.

I got up. Daniel was approaching me with a cup of coffee and a broad smile.

I took the coffee and mumbled, "I can't talk right now." He seemed disappointed.

"Come on, Kat. It's a past life; it's over," he said, running an impatient hand through his tousled hair. He had bags under his eyes, and they were bloodshot. It had been a rough night all around. I shook my head. I wanted to throw the hot coffee in his face. Was I wrong to hate him? Was I being crazy over this whole past life thing? I couldn't say, for there was a lot to take in. I turned on my heels, went into the bedroom that doubled as my office, shut the door, and locked it. He heard the lock click because he came to the door and knocked on it.

"Come on, don't do this. Please, baby don't do this." I heard the pain in his voice and yet my heart was like ice to him.

"Daniel," I called out. "Please leave me alone. I just need some time alone." I took a long swig of my coffee and sat down at my desk and switched on the PC.

"You're going to talk to Malek, aren't you?" he called out.

"Daniel, please just leave me alone!" I screamed. "Fuck you! Leave me alone now."

"I Love you Kat," he shouted back. "Goddamnit, I fucking love you!"

"I need some fucking time to myself right now, you asshole!" I fired back. I heard him move away from the door. I sat on the floor cross-legged and placed my face in my hands, covering my eyes. I didn't want to talk to Malek. I didn't want to talk to anyone. I had to think. What did this whole fucking mess mean? What was I supposed to learn from this?

Would Bakor forgive Daniel? I waited for my mind to answer, but the rage that whirled within me drowned out the voice and I could not hear it. Please, I thought to myself, please someone out there give me an answer. I rocked back and forth shielding my eyes. I waited.

Daniel hit the door hard. "Jesus! Kat stop doing this!"

"Leave me the fuck alone, right now!" My voice was vicious and cold. I began to weep. Can't you see that you love him? A voice drove through the mists, tearing away at the madness of my anger and made itself heard. Can't you see? It's all right there for you to see. I wiped the tears from my eyes. I wanted to see, and stared hard at the wall, and then my eyes rose to look out the window. The short white curtain billowed away and exposed the sight of a blue sky and a tall palm tree. It's all right there, it whispered. I saw Bakor standing before me, her eyes sad. I was staring at myself as I had once been, small, dark, and so beautiful then. Chance, take the chance. Second chance. I rose to my feet.

My god, this was a second chance. God knows what evils I had done in my past lives. I realized that I was hanging onto a rage that no longer served me, an energy that was alive at this moment because I chose to make it so. I could either grieve over something that had happened lifetimes ago, or I could love. Daniel loved me. Whatever Kryu had been, that ego was no longer in Daniel. I was different, a million times different than I had been as Bakor, and so was Daniel. I felt a shudder release my body from the hold of past stains and with a calmness that I hadn't felt since the nightmare. I walked to the door with every intention of opening it, when I heard Daniel shout, "Fuck this! I am not going to lose you over this shit!"

He kicked the door open and broke the lock. I was shocked and scared. Daniel's eyes were a feral green.

"What in the hell are you doing?" I cried out. I'd already run to stand against the windows.

Daniel reached for me. I was beating his hands away, but he pulled me to him, cradling my head against his chest. I began sobbing. "Kat, I'm not that guy. That's not me. I don't..." he paused and began to shake with sobs. I pulled away and gazed up at him. His face was ravaged by grief and something else. Oh, my god! It was fear. I snuggled into the warmth of his embrace and listened with my heart to his words.

"I just can't lose you. We've gone through so much, and I can't bear the thought of losing you." His tears wet his face and it was I who began to soothe him.

As the words emerged from my mouth, I knew that I was telling him the truth when I said, "You won't lose me. I ..." I paused afraid to say the words that had slipped from my lips so effortlessly and for so many years. I forced them out. "I love you, Danny." And then everything within me tumbled out. "I love you so much." I held him against me, and we stood there weeping for a long time until the phone rang.

"Let the machine pick it up," Daniel muttered.

I wiped the tears off of his face. His hand caressed my hair, my face. He leaned forward and then fell back. I knew that he wanted to kiss me but felt it was too soon.

We walked back to the futon bed and lay next to each other, staring up at the ceiling. My head on his shoulder his right arm beneath me and wrapped around my right shoulder. We lay like this for some time, quiet. Alex jumped up on the bed and snuggled between us, his cream fur glowed pink beneath the light that fell across us. It felt easy and good to be in his arms. The rage I had felt hours earlier was slipping out of me like a sigh, that long held-in breath finally exhaling out. I turned my head to look at Daniel's profile.

"Tell me," I whispered.

"Tell you what?" He turned his face and gazed down into my eyes.

"Tell you that I love you? That I'm crazy about you and that everything that happened in that past life was wrong!"

"Why do you love me?" I felt like a little girl. That made me feel foolish.

"I don't know Kat," he sighed heavily. "There's so many things about you that make me love you."

"Why do you love me?" he asked. I shook my head, feeling that his answer was perfectly said for how I felt for him.

"It's not easy, is it?" he muttered.

"What's not easy?" I wrapped my arm

around his neck and snuggled even deeper against his body.

"To love, to live, to remember beyond this life." He pulled me closer; his hand caressed the length of my back and settled on my hip.

"Yes, it's hard. What I don't understand is why this has all come back. I mean for what?"

I had been trying to figure out why some people walked through life feeling that their life was the only one they were going to have and to make the best of it. For me and for those like me, like Daniel, there is this never-ending stream of understanding that goes beyond this moment and circles us within time that has no beginning and no end. What I mean to say, is that if time is infinite, then how can one believe we only live one life? And if time is a circle, then there is no beginning and no end, it just loops and we're souls that fly down to take on new DNA, new cultures, new bodies, new everything!

The question that I cannot answer is why we were remembering some lives and not others. Why not remember every single life we had lived? Why this one as a Mesopotamian queen and conqueror and not the ones when I was a slave, or a poor farmer, or a foot soldier. Why this one and not the rest?

It all seemed so far-fetched, and yet it wasn't. It was as real as my life now.

Then it hit me. I had murdered Ted in a past life when he had been a child, so how could I judge Daniel in his past life for murdering mine? Was my child more valuable than another? I knew the answer to that, and suddenly I felt a deep shame sweep over me. This recall had not been given to me to hate Daniel, rather it had been given to me to get a deeper understanding of what was the Samskāra that marked our lives together now.

Samskāra is a term that goes a little deeper than Karma. It reflects all the deep impressions from our present lives and our past lives. Karma is the actions we have taken good or bad.

So for me to understand the gift of remembering past lives, I realized I would have to learn to detach myself from a past that no longer reflected my present life. What had been done was done. I could, however, control what I chose to do from now on. It became obvious. Daniel and I had been given a second chance to make it right. Then I remembered something he had said to me when I had met him at the Argentinean restaurant, that it had been a thousand years since he had last seen me. Suddenly, my heart overflowed with love for him. If you had asked me if I trusted Daniel with my life, I would not hesitate to say yes. I trusted him in a way that I could never trust another man. What I felt bound our relationship for these past twelve years. What had riddled it with difficulties and strife were the impressions from those past lives, the Samskāra that still reverberated now. So our past lives as brothers and the one in Mesopotamia had been recalled in order for us to heal and move on. Suddenly, I felt the sun rise within my heart. All was light and free again, fresh air filled my lungs and cleared itself from the stains of grief.

"Oh, my God!" I cried out jumping out of his arms and straddling him. My thighs wrapped around his hips. I bent over him, my hair dangling like a curtain, shielding us from the world. "What is it?" His eyes were bright with hope.

"We've been given a second chance. Daniel! Oh, my God!" I jumped off him pacing the floor. Alex had leapt off the futon and was staring up at me with his big golden eyes.

Daniel sat up, his face breaking into a wide grin. "Yes, we have."

I twirled on my toes and turned to him. "I love you, Daniel McCabe!" He jumped off the bed and twirled me in his arms and shouted, "I love you Katherine Mona!" He cradled my face in between the palms of his big hands and lowered his head, nuzzling my nose with his.

He claimed my mouth and we savored each

other. All that had been fell away from us like winter leaves scattering about us in a whirlwind and then blew clear away from us. When we broke away, all that had been was gone and what remained was the purity of love and regard for each other. We had been given a second chance, and we had decided to take it.

"There is just one more thing," Daniel whispered.

"What is it?" My hand was on his cheek rough with stumbles. I loved him best when he was unshaven.

"You have to get to the very end." He took my hand in his and kissed the palm.

Suddenly, I knew that there was more. But now I could handle it. I was sure that we had traversed the worst of it.

"Do you want to help me remember?" I pleaded with him.

He shook his head. "It's coming, don't worry. And when it does, I'll be here."

I nodded my head.

"Do you want some breakfast?" He grabbed me within the heat of his embrace, his chin resting on the top of my head. I felt my stomach grumble in approval. I felt so young, so new, so free.

"Yeah, what shall we have?" And then reality set in, this reality riddled with jobs, and bills.

"Don't you have to go to work?"

"Nope," he muttered.

"Why not?"

"There was a mutual separation of the ways." I shook my head in absolute confusion.

"What?" I whispered feeling that we could never get ahead.

"I quit!" he smiled broadly.

"And you're happy about that because . . ."

"I got a new job as a title searcher in Glendale, and I start Monday," he announced proudly.

"You're kidding!" I cried, laughing madly.

"Come on," he raised his brows in a mockery. "You know me; things happen for me... for us." I flung myself against him almost knocking him down and circled my hands around his neck. I threw my legs around his waist, and he grabbed my legs supporting me and walked to the kitchen where he sat me on the narrow kitchen counter. My legs dangled above the floor and he nestled his hips between my thighs. "Do you know something else?" His voice was very serious.

"What?" I just could not stop smiling. This job would mean that he would be off on the weekends and that we would finally be able to spend time together. It meant a whole lot of just enjoying each other. With two jobs, two paychecks, we could make things happen, finally!

"I've never fucked you on this kitchen counter." He threw me a wink.

"See now, that's a bloody crime," I answered, and we laughed and held each other tightly. Alex meowed at us like we had lost our minds. And in a way we had. We had lost everything and gained even more.

I glanced up at the clock; it was eleven in the morning. We hadn't done anything, and yet we had changed our entire inner world. It was a hell of a feeling. We stood in the kitchen drinking coffee, looking out the window, watching the squirrels play their own version of capture the flag. It was a really beautiful, cold and crisp morning.

We took a shower together, caressing each other's bodies with the liquid soap that bubbled into large, creamy foam that was soft and slippery. I knelt before his long, beautiful cock and savored the feel of the head, sucking on it so softly that Daniel gasped, his head thrown back. I wrapped my hands around the root of him and stroked him back and forth as my mouth slid him in and out of my mouth. I could taste the pearls of his cum. Still, I stroked him with a firmer grasp and increased the pressure and speed of my mouth. My tongue was relentless, twirling and teasing the head of his cock and then swallowing him whole. I was loving the very feel of such a gorgeous cock in my mouth. He cried out, "I'm going to come!"

I felt his hips jerk away from me. My right hand gripped his hip and brought him back towards me. My mouth devoured him, my hands, lips and tongue savaging him until he groaned as if in pain jerking his cum into my mouth as I sucked every drop he had. He cried out a shudder that ran down the length of his body. He fell against the shower wall, his head back, taking in deep breaths. He opened one eye and then the other. "You are one hell of a woman!" he whispered. I grinned.

He grabbed me towards him, the shower now growing cold. He kissed me with a passion that left me breathless. I knew that he would taste himself and that turned me on.

"You have a very beautiful cock," I said matter-of-factly.

"Now see, those are the kind of words that will get me to marry you." He kissed my forehead, and then pulled me against his chest.

"What do you think? Do you think we can finally talk about getting married?" My heart leapt. Then I realized that I was ready.

"Are you sure?" I looked up into Daniel's eyes which were like new green leaves, filled with a love and a vulnerability I had never seen before.

"Daniel, do you think we should?" I was biting my thumbnail considering this new idea that seemed so right.

"The shower is freezing my ass off. Let's get out before my dick falls off," he announced, pushing me out of the shower.

I stepped out and grabbed the peach-colored towel off the hook behind the door. He followed wrapped in a blue and white striped towel around his waist.

"Then I could carry your cock in my purse."

"What?" He grabbed a gray towel off the shelf behind the mirror door and began rubbing his hair dry. "What are you talking about?" His head was cocked sideways waiting for me to clarify. "If your cock fell off, I would carry it in my purse."

He patted his groin. "No need for that. It's safe here."

I pulled the towel off him and grabbed his cock pulling him towards me with it.

"Who does it belong to?" I whispered.

He kissed my nose, "You." I laughed and twirled out of the bathroom into the living room.

"That's right, and don't you forget it."

He followed me, ripped the towel off me, and pulled me against his chest. His index finger traced the shape of my lips. "With a mouth like this, I can't ever forget." We kissed, our tongues dancing the ancient rhythms of love. He was my perfection, and I was his.

We dressed and slung down more coffee. Daniel was upstairs making breakfast, and I ran downstairs to see if we might have gotten early mail. I went outside to the porch where the mailboxes were lined up, nailed into the side of the building. Eric was sitting on one of the large chairs he had placed outside when he had moved in. He was alone, having a coffee, reading the Los Angeles Times. His eyes rose to mine and traveled to my wet hair, hanging down around my hips, to the gray Henley short- sleeve T-shirt and white 501 jeans I had thrown on. I was barefoot, and my nipples were hard as little rocks from the cool wind that was swaying the palms to and fro. His eyes met mine after he realized that he had been staring at my tits a wee' bit too long.

"Morning," he said, raising his mug of coffee to me as if in a toast.

"Good morning." I was feeling very chipper.

"Ah, good! The mail's here," I muttered to myself. Suddenly it occurred to me. Eric had just given me the long hot look of desire, and I didn't feel anything for him. I mean, he was still hot, but he didn't make me feel flustered or shy as he had before.

"Care to join me for a cup of coffee?" Was he kidding?

I held the mail in my hand and turned to him.

"Uh, no, Daniel's making breakfast. So I gotta' run."

Eric raised a questioning brow. "He's home?"

"Yeah, listen—have a good Saturday." I turned and quickly walked away. I didn't even want to talk to him. I wanted nothing he was offering.

I ran up the stairs and opened the door to the wonderful smell of freshly made hash browns cooking and the smell of herbs.

"Any mail?" Daniel called from the kitchen.

The futon was still unmade, which was good because I wanted to just hang out and just spend the day puttering around the house. Maybe, even make love. I realized that I hadn't thought of Malek since early this morning. Everything was beginning to shift and settle.

I was holding a Victoria's Secret catalogue and three envelopes.

I sat on the futon, the sheets wrinkled and twisted and the down comforter falling to the floor. I grabbed a mass of it and pulled it back on the bed.

"Bill, bill," I announced as I looked at one envelope after another not even bothering to tear them open. That could wait until tomorrow. Today was not a day for bills but for love. The next envelope was white and very plain. It felt a little stiff. I tore it open and a black Discover card fell on my lap.

"Oh, my God!" I said loudly.

Daniel rushed to the living room and stood over me. "What happened?"

I held the black card up to him, as if offering him the most precious jewel.

"Holy shit." He grabbed it out of my hand.

"When did you apply?" I shrugged.

"I don't know, a month ago? We have to activate it," he said. "Read the letter."

"Okay, hang on." I opened the letter properly and began to read it.

I looked up at Daniel, and I think my mouth dropped open before I closed it and said, "We have a five thousand dollar limit."

"Are you fucking kidding me?" It was now his turn to pick his mouth off the floor.

I begin to erupt into peals of laughter. I was rolling on the futon and laughing until tears ran down my face. I jumped off the bed.

"I'm taking us out for breakfast."

Daniel raised a mischievous brow. "But I made breakfast."

"Awww, come on. Come on, Daniel, let's just live!" He laughed running a hand through his hair.

"I'll activate the card. You put the food away."

Within ten minutes we were heading out the door. We walked past the red Fiat 500 Daniel had for sale.

"You know what? Hang on." He turned and ran back to our apartment.

When he came back, he held the keys to the Fiat 500.

"I don't know where you're taking me, but we're going in style." We laughed.

He pulled down the top. We settled into the black leatherette seats, sat there for a couple minutes digesting all that had happened during the past twelve hours, looked at each other, and laughed our asses off.

Daniel placed the key in the ignition, popped the clutch and we were gone.

***

Sunday, November 9, 1997

I bounded out of bed ready to greet the day. The fact that Michelle had removed my ability to work from home but once a week no longer pissed me off. Daniel was out getting the L.A. Times; I was looking for a new job. No way in hell was I was going to continue working for her. She had basically told me that she did not feel that I was as productive from home as I would be at the office. Productive? What was I, a cow stuck on a milking machine?

The fact that she and Ted had decided to micro-manage me was the last straw. Hell, I had trained Ted when his numbers tanked. But hey, Malek had been clear; I owed a karmic debt to Ted and now I was done. Fucking done!

I wrote a note on the bathroom mirror using my red lipstick.

At the gym. Love You Madly, Kat XO

I had prepared myself as if preparing for combat with leggings, tank top, and my cross trainers. I had filled my large water bottle. It had been weeks since I had been to the gym, partly due to laziness the other to a funk courtesy of my boss Michelle. But now I was ready for a workout that would push my muscles to the brink. I needed to feel that good pain that comes from a grueling workout. I stuck my Walkman on the waistband of my leggings and placed the headphones over my ears. The gym was three blocks down the street on Arroyo Parkway. The walk would be a great warm up. So I power walked to the gym listening to "Dead Can Dance".

The gym was empty. I ran up the stairs and got on the Stairmaster, making sure to place my water in the bottle holder. I hit Level 5 and decided on sixty minutes. What was cool was that the machines overlooked the studio below where a yoga class was in session. I turned up on the volume on my Walkman and heard the beginning strains of Dead Can Dance's "Fortune Presents Gifts Not According to the Book", from their "A Passage in Time" album. It was a perfect track that would get me ready to really pump. I think thirty minutes must have passed. I had flipped the cassette over, was getting into a sort of blissful trance, when images began to appear before my mind's eye. I closed my eyes, and I realized that the images were no less strong when I opened them. I was in a surreal space between the now and the past. The Akashic was offering me the last piece of the puzzle before the portal would forever shut down access to the book that had been my past life. I knew it.

I was ready.

30

The Sun is Gone & Yet it Rises

Ama's face hovered above me. My eyes blinked, I rubbed them, and focused them upon her eyes. I felt frozen within. I was feeling as if I had been trapped in a deep sleep filled with blood and darkness, and then I realized that Cycrus was dead. It had not been a dream. I began to shake, and I curled my legs up to my chest.

"My Queen." She paused. What could she offer me, comfort? What words would heal this wound that bled even now. Breathing was too much of an effort. I wanted to fall into water and disappear beneath the surface. I felt as if I was floating above my body. I felt out of being. I wanted to cry but no tears spilled. My grief had crystallized.

"Malek and Amytis must not know what happened to Cycrus," I said, sitting up and swinging my legs around until they settled on the cool marble floor. I glanced out the large windows to look at the perfection of a blue sky; white clouds billowed and moved across the sky in silence. My son was dead, and yet the world continued as if nothing of any consequeice had occurred. I could not allow myself to fall into the grips of rage and grief again. I had to make sure that Ama and Ilus understood that the plan would go on.

"My Queen," Ama whispered, "what shall I tell Amytis or the king?"

I shook my head and turned to her. My baby kicked, and I instinctively placed my hand over my belly. I wondered at its fate. "Tell them the truth, that Cycrus could never make the journey and that he will stay with me."

"You will not see them, my queen?" her hands twisted into themselves.

I approached her and placed my hand over her shoulder, giving it a reassuring squeeze.

"Do exactly as we discussed, and all will go well." I could not smile.

"But your farewell? You will never see them again and Amytis has asked for you."

"Do not under any circumstance allow her to my chambers. She will see the lies in my eyes."

To my surprise hot tears ran down my cheeks. "I cannot do what must be done for their sake if I see them. Don't you understand? I cannot lie to them. You know that Malek would never leave if he knew of his son's death."

I wiped the tears off my face with a savage swipe of my hand.

At that moment Kryu entered.

"A bath Ama, prepare a bath." Ama left my side. I ignored his presence. I could not look at him without hate blinding me from the purpose at hand.

"Come, come, my queen, all is not lost." Was he mocking me? Did he not understand that he had torn my heart out of my chest? I turned to face him. I imagined that my eyes were swollen and red. I could not utter a word without the fear of vomiting. My hate frightened me. It was becoming a beast, like the fallen snake god who had tempted our people out of Eden to eat from the fruit of knowledge. It was from that point that we had built cities and worshiped our gods from afar. This demon of rage slithered within my heart and was waiting coiled within the pit of my belly. I no longer felt my unborn child kick with life. I only felt the snake's presence whispering words of revenge, blood, and death. All that I had once been was now dead. Kryu could not even see me for the creature that stood before him. For he only saw me as a woman who carried his heir. Had he only stepped away from his own arrogance, had his spirit met mine, he would have seen the havoc he had brought to my being.

"Why?" I whispered from between parched lips.

He strolled into the large room and paused before my round copper reflector. "Why?" he repeated.

He picked up my hair comb and brought it to his nose breathing in my scent caught from strands of my hair trapped within its teeth.

"The oracle came to me with the vision that one day, your son would return to claim the kingdom back." A shiver of joy, like a sliver of light, shot through my blackened heart. He would live! So Damion would survive the journey to Egypt and conquer our land. I looked down upon my hand and saw Cycrus's blood upon them. I wiped them off on my tunic. Yet, there was no blood to wipe, for it disappeared as fast as it had appeared.

"Cycrus would have never challenged your right to rule." I exhaled the words for it took all my efforts to stand silent and strong when all I wanted to do was crawl upon the floor and claw at the stones until my fingernails broke off and bled. Until the dark wings of death took me.

He shrugged and approached me. My eyes stared down at his booted sandals, his very scent made my stomach heave. I wanted nothing to do with this world. I was waiting.

"Bathe, rest, and be ready, for tomorrow we celebrate the coming birth of my son!" He stepped away from me and walked out of my presence without another word.

I collapsed to the floor and lay on my side, my arm flung out to support my head. I was unable to do anything but wait for the bath to be brought. When Ama arrived, the slaves in tow carried the large vessel; others poured large containers of hot water. Ama added my favorite rose oil, the scent of which floated like a lilting trail from the steam.

She had the slaves lift me and tenderly remove my tunic. They placed me in the bath as if I was but a babe. I found some small solace. I sunk my head beneath its surface and imagined myself in the pond diving below to examine fish, as I had done with Cycrus. I saw his face, his red hair floating about his little face, his eyes wide with amazement at the creatures that lived below water. I stayed beneath the waters for as long as I could. I was unable to tear my gaze away from his wondrous face. My lungs burned like fire, and I broke through to the surface gasping for air. I sat in the bath, until the water was cold. Ama had the slaves administer to me, dressing me and placing me in bed. Tonight, Malek and our daughter would join our eldest son, Damion. All would be as it should be.

Night fell, and the moon rose full. Ama came to my side. "It is done," she said, and I felt my heart shake with fear and hope. I wanted to pray to Ishtar, but I could not find the words, for she had already forsaken me once. Isis had turned her back to me as well. I could not think of one god or goddess I could beseech, and so I stayed silent, listening to the whisperings of the snake

****

Morning brought a dark storm, and a rough rain fell across the valley. The chill was abated by the fire Ama had prepared in the large bronze fire pit.

I lay curled up, my knees to my chin, my arms surrounding my legs. I was lying thus on my side upon the white furs. Ama brought another fur to cover me, for I could not stop shivering.

I had not eaten or taken drink since that night. My body was weaker, and yet the snake never left my side. I no longer needed to be strong for Ama, for I was abandoning all that I knew. Malek and Amytis must be out of the valley by now. I was safe to let go.

I cannot say how long the day had progressed before I heard shouts and the barking of dogs. I realized that Kryu knew of their escape. I wondered how long it had taken before he had been alerted to their absence.

Ama ran to the terrace and came back drenched from the rain and pale as white marble.

I leaned upon my elbow.

"O' my queen!" Ama 's eyes filled with tears." O' my queen..."

I felt the quickening flame of fear rip through my being. I rose and ran to the balustrade, leaned over, and saw a vision that felled me to my knees. Malek's and llus's head on spikes. Malek's large beauteous eyes were dead to the world, dead to my love. His blood ran down the spike and mingled with the rain that streamed upon the dirt in tiny tracks and disappeared in the mud. I realized in that instant that for his blood to weep, the blade of death had taken him soon after his capture.

Amytis was nowhere to be found. The rain was falling hard upon my head and shoulders. I was on my hands and knees. A grief spiraled out of my being. The density of its pain was so great that I raised my head and opened my mouth for it to take flight, but it did not. My throat was possessed by the hands of grief, for they bound around my neck so tightly that no sounds came from me. I was made mute by the wide expanse of my suffering. I was choking, for no matter how I raised my lips to the heavens no sounds released themselves; instead the anguish catapulted back and riddled me with swords that pierced my heart over and over again. Relentless in their attack, I lay bereft and blinded for I could not feel myself. I had lost my voice for no sound of any meaning could express the effects of loss.

Kryu never came to see me. Ama returned with the news that Amytis was under full guard sequestered in the rooms that had once been Damion's. She was not allowed to see me, nor I her.

I was afraid for her life. I could not clear a path of thought for my mind was cluttered by veils that I could not pierce through to see a way out for her. I was lost in a labyrinth.

Ama had been ordered to prepare me. I was to sit at Kryu's side, and he would declare our unborn child his heir. I sat quietly as Ama combed out my hair and allowed it to hang loose about my hips. She had chosen a simple linen shift of white, the golden girdle with the purple stones sat very low upon my hips. She was about to place earrings when I waved her away.

I stared into the depth of my eyes and asked for the strength to do what I must do. I saw no response emerge from my gaze. I rose, ready to meet the night.

I sat beside Kryu. I saw him take a cup filled with mead and toast his men for battles well fought. I was struck by the cacophonous laughter, the stench of bodies, and the scent of roasted meat and wine. I was so tired. Tanis' eyes were a relentless assault that I could not extricate myself from.

Kryu grabbed my upper arm and pulled me to my feet.

"Here is your queen!"

He placed his hand over my belly, "Your future king lies here sleeping, and one day he will rule this land!"

The great hall was mad with the joy of the stamping of feet, shouts and cries. They riddled my head for it ached for peace. Stuck in Kryu's leather belt was a short blade. I gathered all my strength and slipped the blade from his side and plunged it between my breasts. Blood spewed from my breast, and I felt the first moment of relief.

The great hall hushed. "I would rather die than bear your son!" I cried, my voice strong with rage. I fell to the ground, the death throes taking me home. I could not see Kryu's eyes; his voice was strong and mocking as he said "Then be assured of this... your daughter will bear my son." These words flew into my soul in an agony of spiraled lights and a choir of mellifluous voices.

It was finally over.

31

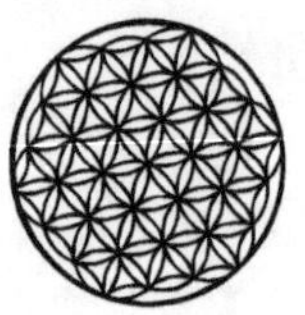

NOVEMBER 9, 1997
10 A.M.

I was shaken by the images I had just seen. I got off the machine and sat crossed-legged upon the floor, unable, to get up just yet. I wanted to talk to Malek. What good would that do? He had been dead when all I had just seen had transpired. I'm not sure how long I sat like this, but soon people were claiming the three Stairmasters that faced the studio below. I got up and walked home. When I opened the door to our apartment, I heard the loud quiet of an empty space which meant that Daniel was still out. Alex was sleeping on the futon. I was relieved, I wasn't angry at him, but I needed to say goodbye to Malek.

I went to the office and logged on to the PC. I typed "Are you around?"

Malek is typing. "I am here."

"It's over isn't it?" I typed back. I wanted to cry, but I couldn't.

"Yes," he answered.

"Will I ever meet you?" I asked.

There was a long pause and then I exhaled. Malek is typing.

"We have met, my dear Bakor, and one day we will be married to each other, and we will enjoy a wonderful life undisturbed by war, death, and loss. Have faith."

"Then how shall we say goodbye?" I asked.

"What is your most favorite place in the world?"

I thought for a long time before the image of the Isle St. Louis came to me. I saw myself crossing the Pont Louis-Philippe. The light was a buttery gold, and the clouds were white and billowy. As I crossed to reach the Quai, I opened my eyes and typed.

"The Isle Saint Louis, by the Quais."

Malek is typing. "Close your eyes my sweet Bakor. I will meet you there now. We will walk together until the vision ends." And that is what we did.

My eyes closed. I met him on the cobbled streets of the Isle. If you asked me to describe him, I could not say. I felt the presence of his spirit hold my hand as we walked and spoke of the future we would live one day, of the love I bore for him. No words were exchanged, just the energy of thoughts. I felt such a peace with him, such a feeling of bien être. We strolled like this for what seemed like a long time, and then like smoke we dissipated into thin air. The book of that life was closed. I opened my eyes and exhaled the sweet air. My eyes settled upon the screen.

Malek has signed off. I did not know it then, but we would never speak to each other again.

I heard the sound of a key turning the lock of our front door. "I'm home," Daniel cried out.

I felt my heart call out, yes, yes you are.

I rose from my desk and rushed to him, wrapping my arms around his waist.

"It's done," I cried. He smiled down at me, his hands on either side of my face.

"Do you still love me?" he whispered against my lips, for he knew exactly what I meant.

This was Daniel McCabe, and he was all that I wanted in the world. Why would I forgive a man who had murdered my child in a past life? Why? I see you ask. Because that's the whole point. These past lives show us all that we're no angels. We've done monstrous things; the vilest of things, and it is this truth that makes a majority of us reincarnate with no memory of past lives. It's our safety valve, our Soma. That life as Bakor is no more. I am not that woman, just as Daniel is not Kryu. So why the memory, why recall this life and not another? I wish I knew the answer to that question; you have no idea how I wish I knew. Perhaps, as I realized before, forgiveness is the very key to love. Why hadn't Kryu loved me as Daniel does now? Perhaps I will never know.

It took us a thousand lifetimes to share our hearts with each other, imagine that, a thousand lifetimes. And in a thousand lifetimes from now where will we be? Perhaps then I will be with Malek. Does that surprise you that I believe that one day I will be with Malek? It shouldn't, because if you understand reincarnation you'll know that Daniel may come back as my son or daughter and that Malek may be his father. Love is love. We do this again and again to get it right. To make amends, to heal, to forgive, and to love. So yes, I am with Daniel, and Daniel is my mate in this life, and I forgive him, as I forgive myself.

I am alive now! I am living my life with this man, whose heart speaks to me. For we have traveled time and space and have been transformed into who we are today. It's strange, isn't it? But there it is. And so when I looked up to gaze into Daniel's magnificent face, I saw the sun, and I was moved by him, so moved that tears pricked my eyes. It just felt so right being here with him. And so I answered him truthfully and with an open heart.

"Yes! Yes! I am crazy about you" I said like a little girl. Daniel twirled me in his arms.

I looked down to see two grocery bags.

"Sorry, I was gone so long, but guess what happened?" His green eyes twinkled with joy.

I could not help but feel glad standing close to him.

"What?"

"I sold the car for $2,700 dollars this morning; that's why I was gone so long."

"Oh, my God! That's awesome!!"

"I bought some goodies for tonight. Come into the kitchen check out what I got."

He had been to Cost Plus.

"Check this out." He pulled out two bottles of Veuve Clicquot champagne, the orange label.

"Oh my, but that's too expensive," I exclaimed.

He kissed the tip of my nose. "Nothing is too good for my baby," he whispered.

We pulled out the treasures he had bought for us--duck pate with bits of black truffle, a large piece of Gruyere cheese, a jar of cornichons, a can of dolmas, a pound of large sea scallops, a pound of large prawns, some shiitake mushrooms, a good bottle of a white Cote du Rhone (for cooking, he said with a wink) a head of butter-leaf lettuce, one large tomato, two long red candles, and a large crusty baguette.

"This is amazing," I sighed with pleasure.

"I am making you a very romantic dinner, and then I intend to make very slow and passionate love to you."

I grabbed his waist again and buried my face on his chest. He kissed the top of my head and said, "Now go take a shower! You smell." I laughed.

That night, after enjoying a romantic dinner, I went to the bedroom. I pulled out my arsenal of black garter belts, seamed stockings, and a black demi-cup bra. I perfumed myself with Miss Dior, spraying between my thighs, behind my ears, between my breasts and behind my knees. I was ready. I stepped into my high-heel Maud Frizon leather pumps. When I stepped out of the room to face him, the look in his eyes was magnificent. I felt so beautiful, so sexy, because of the way his eyes roamed my body like a warm caress.

I walked very slowly. He took my hand in his walked me to the kitchen and hoisted me upon the counter top. "I'm too heavy," I protested.

He nuzzled my neck and inhaled my scent, "No you're not." His hand caressed my thighs and he settled his hips between them. He unbuttoned his 501 jeans and his cock sprang out in all its beauty. "You didn't wear panties," he whispered.

"Did you want me to?" I felt his fingers play with my clit and then two fingers slip within me. His hand caressed my shoulder and slipped my bra strap down. He pulled one breast out and captured my nipple in his mouth. My body arched against him.

"I want you so badly," he groaned.

"Please, fuck me!" I moaned against his mouth. I wrapped my arms around his neck and pulled him to me.

"Who do you belong to?" he growled against my ear, before plunging his tongue within the soft flesh. I shivered with pleasure.

"I belong to you." I stared into the wide expense of his green eyes hot with hunger. I grabbed his cock and pulled him towards my pussy howling for him.

"Do you want me?" he teased the soft lips wet with desire. I was so ready for him.

"Yes!" I was breathless," Please... now!"

Still he teased me with the head of his cock. I grabbed his ass and pulled him to me, my legs wrapped around his hips. He cupped my breasts in his big hands and lowered his head, savaging the nipples with his mouth. My G-spot was ringing like a cathedral bell at Sunday Mass. For sex coupled with love was a holy act between two people. At that moment, I felt like I had it all.

"Tell me," he pleaded against my neck, nipping my flesh with his lips.

"I want your cock now," I begged.

"Not before I set things up," he said with a wink.

He led me by the hand and lay me down upon the futon. He turned on Dead Can Dance's "A Passage in Time". The first track, "Saltarello", broke through the quiet and held me spellbound with the sounds of drums. It seemed so ancient that it filled my soul with pathos. Daniel disappeared into the kitchen; I heard the satisfying sound of a cork popping. He was back and knelt between my legs. He set the champagne bottle on the floor, and lifted my legs over his broad shoulders. He reached down grabbed the bottle by its neck and held it aloft in his hand.

"What are you doing?" I bit my lower lip worried.

"Relax," he whispered as he poured the cool golden liquid between my thighs. My pussy had become the cup that runneth over. His mouth captured my tender parts, tasting me in ways I had never thought possible. He drank and tasted from me until I shuddered within the pull of his very talented and relentless mouth. A loud moan escaped from between my tightly-clenched lips, and I closed my eyes, sighing out. He lowered my legs and lay next to me. I turned to stare up at him. I smiled. "You know something?" I whispered.

He raised a brown eyebrow, and then he lowered his head, his lips trailing their feathered kisses across my neck and shoulders. His lips hovered above me and I reached up, caressing his beautiful mouth with mine. "When you're bad, you're great!" I breathed into his mouth. He devoured my mouth, depositing the mingled taste of me and great French champagne. He shifted and settled on top of me and pushed my thighs apart with his knee.

"I want some champagne," I whispered against his lips.

"Later," he growled.

With one hard plunge he slipped home, and I cried out with pleasure. We were built so right, for the tip of his cock banged against my G-spot with every stroke. I threw my head back, moaning loudly. I was coming and shaking with a force that left me so euphoric that when he came we merged completely as one spirit, a flash of light, so quickly that for a moment I felt that it was all in my head. We lay together, my head on his chest listening to the comforting sound of his pounding heart. Tears wet my cheeks.

"Why are you crying?" he asked, wiping them from my face.

My nose was stuffy, and I sounded congested. "Because I am moved by us. I saw a light flash when we both came."

He turned abruptly to me, "So did I."

He held me tighter against the length of his

body. "Do you think we're soul mates?" I asked.

"No," he said without hesitation. "No, I 'm sorry to say that we're not." I felt disappointed by his answer.

"Why not?"

He shrugged. "I don't know. I just know we're not. We've had so many lives together, Kat. So many..." He sighed. His hand caressed the side of my hip, my leg thrown across his legs.

"I love you, Kat. I don't want anyone else." He stared into my eyes, searching his face for something I could not say.

"What if you find your soul mate, will you leave me for her?"

He sighed and took my face and stared into my eyes for a long time before answering.

"Kat, I will never leave you no matter what. If I should meet my soul mate I will walk away because in this life we are meant to be together."

"You would walk away from your soul mate?" I was shocked.

"Didn't you do that when you told me that you would never leave me for Malek?" A cool breeze ruffled my heart so gently that I felt a calm realization settle upon me.

We stared at each other in complete unity to that link that bound us and would bind us for the rest of our lives.

32

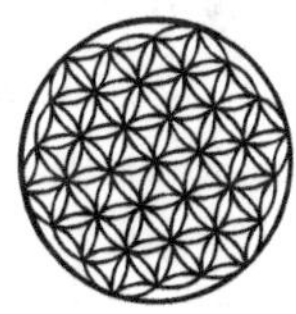

JULY 30, 1998

Daniel and I had taken the day off and driven to Malibu. We'd ordered some fish and chips at Malibu Seafood restaurant and took it to go. We wanted to sit alone, undisturbed by other people's energy. We crossed Pacific Coast Highway and scrambled down the rocks and found a mound of sand to sit upon. It was perfect. It was noon and the beach was relatively empty which is why we had taken this Thursday off. We sat admiring the waves crashing and gazed into a horizon that was endless and disappeared, merging sky and sea as one.

We opened our little white boxes containing our bounty and began to eat. "I've been reading this book about the myth of Lilith," Daniel mumbled in between bites of fish which he dipped into the tartar sauce.

"Yeah? What about her?" I swigged down a little of the rose lemonade to wash down the large steak fries I had just devoured. I had my bare feet touching each other; my skirt hiked above my thighs, and had placed the glass container between my toes. This was one of my favorite positions because it stretched my hips and loosened the muscles in my thighs.

"Well, you know how I was forced to study the Bible at that all boys Christian school and well..." he paused in between bites.

I nodded.

"You've heard about her right?"

"You mean Adam's first wife?" I grimaced, "Yeah, I know about her. Why?"

"Do you know the story?"

"Yeah, I know it!" I spat. I turned to him. "I can't get past how the church was able to malign Eve for tasting from the fruit of knowledge," I mumbled looking out at the sea. "I mean, think about it. If a sentient being came to you handing you a fruit and said, If you eat from it, you will know all that the secrets of the world. You will know as much as God knows. I mean, what in the hell would you do?"

He grinned wickedly. "I'd eat!"

"I know, and that's what I love about you." I smiled up into his green eyes. Damn, he was a delicious hunk of a man.

"Well, anyway, I'd always wondered about Adam's first wife."

"What about her?"

He had been staring at the waves rising and curling to crash into white foam that sprayed our faces, his eyes traveling to another time and place. He turned to me. "You've always reminded me of her."

"Do I? Why?" I was perplexed. "I always heard she was a real bitch," I mumbled.

Daniel shook his head, "No, that woman had fire. She was irreverent. You know that they say that God formed Adam and Lilith simultaneously from the earth."

I wanted to know where he was going with this.

"You are my equal, you match me, challenge me, fuck me, make love to me, you fight me, and yet without you in my life it wouldn't make any fucking sense!" He smiled and stared into my eyes and dropped a kiss on my lips. I pulled on his lower lip and he took my lead. We lingered savoring the moment with our mouths.

I breathed in his scent, a perfect coupling of his sweat mingled with his cologne, Monsieur de Givenchy. It helped make him so delicious I wondered if he had splashed his balls with his cologne and was suddenly distracted by the need to bury my nose between his thighs, to lick and suckle that wonderful silk sac and watch his cock rise, my nipples brushing against the light brown golden hairs that tangled in between as I took the long length of his heat into my mouth. I was getting wet. I loved every cell of his being, and my body wanted more than food. I wanted to toss the box aside and fuck him right here, right now!

We broke away. "Go on!"

His eyes flared, recognizing the hunger in my eyes.

"Do you remember how we met?" he murmured. My thighs were splayed open and Daniel stroked the inside of my upper thigh and as smooth as you please he began to finger my heat, stroking me as if I were a pet to cajole into a state of calmness. It was working. I had placed my box of food to the left side of my hip. I'd forgotten the rose lemonade, which had tipped over and spilled its content upon the sand.

"Yeah, I remember." I'd never forget every detail of that day.

"Lilith was a rebel. She was all that a real man could want, wild and impossibly beautiful."

"How do you know?" I laughed teasing him.

He looked at me with luminescent eyes. "Oh, I know."

And then Daniel did the most surprising thing. He laughed. His head thrown back, I noticed the corded muscles of his neck strong and his skin tanned from the sun and beads of sweat gathering at that little spot at the base of his throat. I was having a hard time concentrating at what he was trying to share with me. So I looked back at the sea but not before I noticed his light brown hair falling in glossy waves about his neck and shoulders. I felt my pussy pulse at the sight. He was all that and a bag of chips. He moved his hand down and settled it upon my knee.

"Do you really remember the first time we ever met?" He asked his eyes twinkling with a secret he was about to divulge. I knew that look too well.

"Off course I do. I just told you I did."

He crossed his arms across his chest.

"Okay, smart ass. What was I doing?"

"You were playing pool with some guys and I was sitting at the backgammon table sipping a rum and Coke." I glared at him, "See! I remember! Smart ass!" I tossed.

He nodded. He was smiling down at me. I could feel he was about to share something big.

"I knew about you. I'd asked the bartender about you. He told me you pole-danced at the O'Farrel."

I nodded my head, a bit ashamed of that past.

He saw that look. "Don't do that to yourself," he whispered. He pushed my tousled hair back and kissed me on the forehead as if I was a precious child who needed comforting.

"You were like a priestess to me with your wild red hair and those peacock earrings you always wore. And that mouth, that fucking amazing mouth, red and pouting that promised so many.... I couldn't stop thinking about you. I knew I had to meet you. So that night when you walked in all powerful, with that knowing look in your eyes..."

"What look?"

"You know the one," he laughed," The, I can fuck any man here look. I decided to take the challenge of making you mine, of making you want me. I've never wanted a woman as much as I wanted you."

"I'd never noticed you before." I shook my head in puzzlement, wondering how I could have missed Daniel until the day I met him.

"How?" I asked.

"I'll never forget the first time I saw you. You pushed the door open and the light from outside blinded me for a second. It was bright, the sun throwing like a stream of white light. You stood for a moment, a silhouette. My eyes adjusted, and I saw you walk to the bar and order your drink. Every man in that bar had eyes only for you, but you never looked around. Fuck! But you were beautiful! You knew your power! You had us all by the balls."

"And?" I whispered looking up at him.

"When you left I made sure to find out all I could about you. I even went to see you dance."

I'd never known that; he'd never told me.

"And?" I asked, biting my lower lip. Up to this very moment, I had thought that fate had played the hand to our meeting, but here Daniel was telling me that he had pursued me without my knowing. And then it hit me!

"You've waited over a decade to tell me this. Why?" I couldn't believe it.

He shrugged. "I didn't want you to know how much power you had over me." He was looking out admiring the ribbon of a wave cresting and slowly foaming to sweep a hand across its glimmering surface. The sound of it crashing and the sea spray flung upon our faces by a rogue breeze invigorated me. I felt whole and so alive.

He turned to me, green eyes searching mine for answers I could never keep from him. Why was it now that he trusted me with all of his truths?

"I wanted you so badly," he whispered, tears welling up, and yet he kept them at bay. I felt my heart squeezed by the painful honesty of his love for me. He took a deep breath. "I couldn't think straight for days. That's when I walked into the bar knowing that no matter what, I would talk to you. I was playing pool, waiting and fucking waiting, for you to show up, when you walked in and you ordered your drink. When I saw you sit at the backgammon table, I knew that I had to challenge you to a game. I figured that would be the only way to get your attention. Do you remember what I said?"

"Yea, I remember what you said? It was ridiculous." I shook my head at him.

He looked at me a quizzical expression on his face.

"You don't remember do you?" I prodded the side of his rib with my index finger.

"Try me," he challenged, and then it dawned on him. "Ah, yes. I remember. I told you that you reminded me of Sade."

"You have that sexy, exotic thing going on. What a line," I sputtered.

He raked his fingers through his hair. "Maybe, but it was true. So I decided to set up the backgammon board. I couldn't look at you. I'd just caught a whiff of your perfume and then everything hit me all at once. I wanted to know what you would taste like. I saw your red mouth—I got a hard-on wondering about your mouth wrapped around my cock. Then there were your big tits, those fat hard nipples. I could barely get the pieces on the board."

He smiled. "Do you know that for a full minute I thought you were going to leave? I looked up at you waiting."

"Yeah, I remember."

He laughed, "I knew that if you stayed and played even just one game my life would never be the same ever again."

"And you said…" I was leaning into him.

"And I said, 'Shall we?' "

"Then I promised to kick your ass!" I countered with a laugh.

"So I winked a challenge to you… but I never said a word after that. Do you remember?" He whispered as if he'd travelled back in time to relive that moment.

I nodded.

"Do you know why?"

I stared up at him and shook my head.

"I was afraid to talk to you—I didn't think I would be able to—I was so fucking nervous." The wind had picked up speed and was tangling his hair. I wanted to grab him right there and kiss him hard on the mouth.

He stared at me for a long time. "You were all that I ever really wanted in life, and I knew that if I said anything stupid you'd bolt. You were feral and so fucking sexy." He captured my eyes with his green gaze, and I saw my naked desire reflected back.

I threw him a broad smile. "We played for hours, didn't we?"

"Yeah, we sure did. I didn't want you to go." He grinned at me, his teeth white.

"Did we ever speak?"

"Did we need to?" he whispered.

I shook my head. "I was wet for you."

"That was one hell of a night!" he murmured.

"You saved me, didn't you Danny?"

"I saved you from hating, baby, and I knew that I would be the only man to do it. No man would ever love you like I did... like, I do now, right now."

He broke eye contact.

"So you remind me of Lilith, because you didn't give a damn about the conventions of society. You wanted more. You reminded me of Lilith because you weren't afraid to venture beyond your comfort point. You are my Lilith because you are all that is wild, real, powerful and sexy in a woman." He paused and pushed me down on the sand. I looked up at him. He was framed by the bluest of skies and his eyes reflected that blue within the depth of his green eyes.

At that moment my heart filled with love for Daniel, for he had recognized me before I had ever laid my eyes upon him and somehow that made me love him that much more.

"I have to confess something to you." I whispered, pushing him away.

"What baby?"

"I'm not sure why I carried this hate. I was so afraid of being hurt, of falling in love, of being owned by a man."

I noticed a seagull approach us, and I threw a fry that had fallen on the sand, and it caught it in midair and flew away with it in its beak.

"I was always such a cock tease."

Daniel pulled me into the crock of his arm. My head pressed against the comforting thump of his heart. We were alive right now, and that was more than enough.

"No matter how much my father loved me, I never felt really loved by him, valued by him."

"Why?" he whispered against my hair.

"He figured I'd marry, so what was the point of sending me to college. Anyway..." I shrugged.

"I know he didn't mean to make me feel less than my brother, but he did. I felt like nothing," I mumbled.

Daniel laughed ruefully at the whole absurdity of a sex subjugated by what men believed was a woman's place. We talked of beliefs that were further obscured by countless religions fostered by a society that leveled women to a state of powerlessness to think that this system had lasted millennia's with the occasional exceptions like Cleopatra, Eleanor of Aquitaine, Joan of Arc, or Bakor, and look at how these women had all ended up. In the end, we had all been destroyed by men. In the end, all women had been as powerless as any common women.

That's why I loved Daniel so much it hurt. We could speak of these things together. He understood too well the truth of our journeys as souls; he knew that he had lived the lives of warriors with the same ease as he had lived the lives of women. He embraced the Anima within his being, as I embraced the Animus within myself.

I raised his hand and admired the shimmering golden hairs that grew on the back of his hand. I loved the warmth of his palm against my palm, our fingers intertwined. It was so easy being with him.

"Do you know that my past life as Bakor still haunts me?"

"No kidding!" he chuckled, "How could it not? I still think about my life as the conqueror."

He turned to me and cradled my face within the palm of his hands. We savored each other for a second.

"These lives, Kat, these lives travel with their pain... the bitch is to get rid of the baggage. It's about letting go. You know what I mean?"

How could I not know what he meant?

I sighed. "You're the only man that has ever made me feel grounded." I didn't want to tell him, but I know that if I hadn't met him, if fates had prevented our meeting, I would have sunk into drugs and sex just to forget all that howled within me. So when I tell you that Daniel saved me from hating, I mean that he literally saved me from dying. For the path I'd been on before my meeting him ensured that my soul would have imploded.

I finally understood the tie that bound us so completely now, and I felt such gratitude that our journey had brought us to this point. Daniel was my home and I was his.

***

October 2, 1999

We'd been married for about a month. It was nothing big, just a small ceremony by the Bacchus Fountain at the City Hall in Pasadena, nothing grand. I wore a black linen dress; I carried blood red roses and a gay minister hooked us up with words I can't remember. Our witnesses were people we pulled from their lunch break at city hall. I'd always dreamed of a beach wedding, wearing a gorgeous dress made of white silk sari with a gold border. I'd always thought we would marry on a beach in some exotic place, wearing white feathers floating wild in my red hair, the sun setting, and Daniel looking down at me with the sun and the moon in his eyes. I was always a bit of a crazy romantic. This wedding was fine; its simplicity guaranteed longevity.

When we got home, Daniel put on Dead Can Dance, "The Serpent's Egg", on repeat. We made love. Long and slow.

***

March 21, 2000

I'm working this gig for a new software company. Michelle, Ted and me...let's face it, it was never going to work. And as you've surmised, Y2K came and went like another New Year celebration. Now, the next apocalypse that was supposed to hit the streets was in 2012. It never ends, does it? I'm back working from my home office which is a relief because I'm pregnant!

So here we are; Daniel and I are sitting in the waiting room of my OBGYN. He's completely absorbed by an article in a "Parenting" magazine. I feel really serene, really good.

We're next. Daniel is at my side like a shot making sure I'm okay. I turn to him and stare up as his adoring gaze. He's been pampering me like crazy with foot massages and great slow sex.

Pasadena has decided to unleash a heat wave, so I'm wearing the smallest linen shift I own, a bra, and no panties. I can't wear panties; I just can't. I'm not sure why, but they drive me crazy right now.

I slip my sandals off and change into a blue paper robe. The doctor enters; she's all smiles, her long black hair grazes her hips. She looks like a priestess from the ancient world. It's why I picked her; she seems so familiar to me, so easy to talk to. Not to mention, she won't perform a C-section which I want to avoid at all costs.

She helps me up on the table, takes my blood pressure, which is normal. Like I said, I am calm as a still pond. I lay down on the table and Daniel is sitting rather uncomfortably on a chair next to me. She dims the lights and moves the sonogram as close as she can to my table. Adjusting this and that, she squirts a copious amount of cool gel over my extended belly.

She places the wand over my stomach and turns on the screen. Suddenly we see our child floating within my body like an astronaut in space tied by the umbilical cord that binds us as one.

"See," she says cheerfully, "there's the baby's heart." We see it pulsing with life.

Daniel's face breaks into a wide grin.

"This is a very big baby!" My OBGYN exclaims.

Daniel takes my hand in his and is mesmerized by the screen. She clicks some buttons and captures the image.

"There is the baby's head." We see the brain. I'm stunned and awed.

"Do you want to know the sex of the baby?" she asks.

"Yes!" We say as one voice.

"Let's see if the baby's going to let us discover that little secret."

"Ah, there it is, do you see that?" Her wand hovers over our baby's small penis.

"Congratulations, you are having a boy!"

Daniel's eyes fills with tears. I match him with tears and am choked by the fullness of my heart. We are having a boy!

The OBGYN captures more images and prints them and hands them to Daniel who stares down at them with a look of amazement that makes me giggle.

He looks up at me, his eyes a storm of emotions.

"I love you Kat; I love you so much." I can't find words for him.

He leans forward and whispers in my ear. "Thank you for giving me a son."

THE END

EPILOGUE
MESOPOTAMIA, 585 B.C.E.

King Nebuchadnezzar II had been married to his great queen, Amytis for very little time. She missed her green lands. His tutors had taught him the tales of the ancient kings and queens of his land. In particular was the story of Queen Bakor and her hanging gardens. He had sent his learned men to seek the place many said rose to the sky. For many months they searched and had finally found the palace.

Upon the news of its discovery, King Nebuchadnezzar II rode for three days. Now, his eyes were filled with a sight that caught his breath. Even now, as destroyed as it was, it stood stoic, beautiful, magnificent! He dismounted and walked to the site, his chief architect at his heel.

Plants of many species ran riot and wild. The palace was built upon many levels which seemed to rise, breaking through the clouds above. It seemed like a place of magic.

He turned to his architect, whose eyes

spoke volumes of what he beheld.

"I have never seen anything of like," he whispered to his king.

His king nodded his head and was silenced by what he had thought until now was legend. The architect felt a familiarity to this site; there was something known of this place. As his eyes traveled the length of columns and gazed up towards the porticos, a small voice whispered within him that he had been here before. He shrugged, perhaps he had dreamt of it as a child.

A pair of wild parrots emerged from one of the many porticos and flew, cawing. Their plumage red, blue and green glimmered like precious jewels.

"Can you make it as it once was?" the king asked.

"I will make it better than it once was, my king!" The architect was fervent with passion and eager to begin the work.

The king nodded with satisfaction. "Good, for it will please my queen."

"Do what you must. Do it quickly, for she pines for her homeland and this will soothe her eyes with beauty."

The architect bowed.

"It will be done." The architect's mind spun with ideas. He knew that this palace would be sung for eons to come; perhaps men would remember his name, of that he hoped.

YOU
By Toni Barca

You have brought your face back from the
million life times you have breathed.

Like a fine crafted sword wrought from the fire,
forged into what you are today.

I see it in the square of your jaw,
the proud tilt of your head.
I see the memories in the fire within your eyes.

You walk with purpose.
Power trails like the ancient cloaks you wore as
a Roman, a Celt, an African.
There is charisma here, but such alchemy was
mixed with blood, born time after time after
time.

If I could but graze my fingertip across your
lips would you speak in ancient tongues, dead
languages studied now by only the most elite
scholars?

Would my longing to recall flood us in
melancholy or would we laugh together at the
absurdity of it all?

I wonder?

I have so many homes, none are permanent,
and yet, all are dear to me.

When do we know to what purpose we walk to?
What makes us wake and part the veils of the
subconscious truth?

Do you know where your destiny lies?
Or is this life, a place of rest?
Is this time, a life to be lived with simplicity;
the love of a woman, the birth of children, and
the death of the body and then to go on again?

I remember.
I remembered you when I first saw You, the air
cracked between us.

We were uncomfortable, and circled each other
like dogs and
then we spoke, and understood the core of
each other's hearts,

and then
all
eased.

So what now?

RECALL
THE ANIMA & ANIMUS SERIES
BOOK CLUB QUESTIONS

What is reincarnation and what does that mean to you?

Do you think that Malek and Bakor were soul mates or you do think Kryu and Bakor were soul mates?

Can a person experience love with one or more soul mates in one lifetime?

What drives Daniel from telling Kat his belief that he was the conqueror?

What would you feel is an unforgivable act when discussing past lives and redemption?

Would you have left Daniel even though his acts were from a past life or would you have stayed with him?

What is the purpose of remembering past lives and how can improve your current life?

What is the nature of soul mates? What is the difference between soul mates and twin flames?

Do you feel that our lives are pre-destined and at what point does free will come into play?

Toni is a certified hypnotherapist, specializing in past life regression. She is trained under the Newton Institute method founded my Micheal Newton, PHD author of Journey of Souls and Destiny of Souls. Toni focus is on past life regressions. She currently work with clients all over the world helping them gain clarity via hypnotherapy sessions and psychic readings using Tarot.

Want Toni Barca to join your Book Club meeting via Zoom? Email her at Recall@ToniBarca.com.